Waking the Wildflower

Celeste Montague

Published by Celeste Montague, 2024.

This is a work of fiction. Similarities to real people, places, or events are entirely coincidental.

WAKING THE WILDFLOWER

First edition. October 8, 2024.

Copyright © 2024 Celeste Montague.

ISBN: 979-8224403899

Written by Celeste Montague.

Chapter 1: Whispers of Autumn

I stood at the edge of Central Park, the crisp autumn air filled with the scent of falling leaves and adventure. This was my sanctuary, where I escaped the whirlwind of life in Manhattan. As a dog walker, I often felt more connected to the canines than to the humans around me. With my trusty sidekick, Rufus, a golden retriever with a penchant for chasing squirrels, I navigated the maze of paths that snaked through the park, the rustling leaves beneath our feet echoing the secrets of the season. The world felt alive, bursting with vibrant colors and the whispers of change.

That particular morning, while untangling Rufus's leash from a nearby bench—an act he deemed a personal challenge—I spotted him. A tall figure with dark, tousled hair and an easy smile that lit up his face stood across the path. Max was his name, the new neighbor who had recently moved into the building next to mine. He was leaning against a tree, casually tossing a tennis ball for his own dog, a sprightly beagle named Daisy, who darted in and out of the fallen leaves like a miniature whirlwind. My heart did a little flip. There was something magnetic about him, a warmth that radiated even from a distance.

Rufus, ever the social butterfly, had other ideas. With a sudden burst of energy, he lunged forward, pulling me along with him. "Whoa, buddy!" I called out, stumbling slightly but managing to regain my balance. I arrived at the scene just as Rufus collided with Daisy, a furry explosion of wagging tails and excited barks. The two dogs began a spirited game of chase, while Max chuckled, a sound that stirred something in me, something I had almost forgotten existed.

"Your dog's got quite the enthusiasm," he remarked, his voice rich and smooth, like a warm cup of cocoa on a chilly day.

I brushed a strand of hair from my face, the autumn breeze tugging at the loose strands. "He thinks he's a professional athlete. I'm just his personal coach," I replied, feigning seriousness, though my smile betrayed me.

Max grinned, the kind of grin that felt like an invitation. "Well, I think Daisy's about to give him a run for his money."

"Good luck with that! She's adorable but ferocious!" I laughed, leaning down to give Rufus a quick pat as he sprinted past, barking joyfully.

We exchanged a few pleasantries as our dogs frolicked in a swirling dance of fur and leaves. There was an ease in our conversation, as if we had known each other far longer than the mere minutes that had passed. I learned he was an artist, a sculptor to be exact, who had moved to the city for inspiration and a change of pace. His eyes sparkled as he spoke about his work, his passion spilling over with every word. "You know," he said, brushing a hand through his hair, "it's amazing how art can transform a space. I want to capture the chaos of city life, the beauty in the madness."

His words resonated with me. In many ways, my life felt like a canvas of swirling emotions and vibrant experiences. "I totally get that," I said, shifting on my feet, still half-focused on Rufus, who was now trying to dig up a particularly stubborn acorn. "I walk dogs, but I feel more like a part-time psychologist sometimes. Each dog has its own story, its own quirks. It's like being an interpreter for the heart."

Max's laughter rang out again, deep and genuine, causing my heart to flutter like a leaf caught in a gust of wind. "So, you're like a dog whisperer? That's impressive! I need one of those. Maybe you could help me understand Daisy's obsession with the mailman."

"Only if you promise to share some of your artistic secrets," I replied, unable to resist the playful banter that flowed so naturally between us.

Just then, as if fate had a sense of humor, Rufus chose that moment to charge after a squirrel, dragging me along with him. I barely managed to regain my footing, stumbling toward Max, who caught me with a surprisingly gentle grip on my elbow. "Careful there!" he said, his brow furrowing in concern, but there was a glint of amusement in his eyes.

"Thanks! Rufus has a mind of his own. I'm just here for the ride," I said, the blush creeping up my cheeks betraying my attempt at coolness.

"You should probably consider a leash that doesn't have a mind of its own," he joked, his expression a blend of concern and delight.

"Or a dog that doesn't think he's a superhero," I shot back, earning another chuckle from him.

As we continued our easy conversation, time slipped away. The park began to fill with the vibrant bustle of city life; joggers, families, and fellow dog walkers became the backdrop to our impromptu meeting. Yet, amidst the chaos, it felt like we were in our own little world, surrounded by the golden hues of autumn and the laughter of our dogs.

Max shared stories of his art and the inspiration he found in the city—the juxtaposition of noise and silence, the dance of light and shadow. He spoke of his dreams, his hopes for exhibitions, and the unending quest for a deeper connection with his craft. I found myself captivated, not just by his words, but by the way he spoke, with a fervor that made the ordinary feel extraordinary.

And just when I thought the moment couldn't get any better, I noticed a shadow cross his face, a flicker of something unspoken lingering in his eyes. It was brief, almost imperceptible, but it caught my attention, leaving me with a sense of curiosity. The vibrant energy of our encounter shifted subtly, and I couldn't help but wonder what stories were hidden beneath the surface of his charming demeanor. What was the weight behind that smile?

Before I could delve deeper into my thoughts, Daisy decided it was time to chase after Rufus, breaking the moment like a gentle splash in a still pond. As they darted off again, I felt a pull of longing for more time with Max, a strange but familiar tug at my heartstrings. We exchanged numbers with promises of future dog walks, and as I turned to leave, I couldn't shake the feeling that this was just the beginning. Little did I know, the intertwining of our lives would bring unexpected adventures, whispers of secrets yet to unfold, and the possibility of something beautifully chaotic.

The following days took on a new hue. Autumn draped itself over the city like a well-loved blanket, every leaf a whisper of change and every gust of wind a promise of something unexpected. My mornings transformed into a delightful mix of dog walks and daydreams of Max, whose laughter echoed in my mind long after our paths had parted. We exchanged texts filled with playful banter and shared our favorite spots in the park. With each message, it felt like we were building a secret world, one that held the tantalizing possibility of friendship—or perhaps something more.

Rufus, oblivious to my growing infatuation, continued to revel in his canine escapades. On one particular morning, the park was alive with the golden light of dawn, the air crisp and sharp as if the world itself was freshly unwrapped. I watched Rufus bound through the leaves, his exuberance infectious, making me laugh despite the cold nipping at my cheeks. Just as I was considering a steaming cup of coffee from the little cart at the park entrance, my phone buzzed in my pocket.

Max's name flashed across the screen, and my heart did a little dance. "Meet me at our favorite bench in ten?" read the message. I couldn't help but grin, the world around me blurring slightly as I focused solely on the thrill of seeing him again. I felt like a teenager, the flutter of excitement sending butterflies careening through my stomach.

I hurried to the designated bench, its worn wood nestled beneath the branches of a magnificent oak tree. As I approached, I spotted him leaning back casually, arms draped over the backrest, a hot cup of coffee in hand. The sunlight caught the tousled strands of his hair, casting an almost ethereal glow around him. He looked like he had just stepped out of a magazine, the kind where impossibly perfect people lounged in idyllic settings, all while looking utterly relaxed.

"Hey, superstar," I said, my voice light, feigning nonchalance even as my heart raced.

"Ah, the dog whisperer graces us with her presence!" he replied, his eyes twinkling with mischief. "I was beginning to think I'd have to send out a search party."

"Or maybe you just wanted an excuse to drink coffee alone," I shot back, plopping down beside him. The warmth of his presence enveloped me, and for a moment, everything else faded into the background.

We spent the next hour in easy conversation, swapping stories about our lives, our quirks, and our dreams. I shared my recent attempt at baking, a disastrous chocolate cake that had turned into a sticky puddle of regret, while Max recounted a humorous tale of getting lost in the subway system on his first day in the city. "I ended up in a place I think only exists in horror movies," he laughed, his eyes wide with mock horror. "The station was empty except for a guy wearing a clown suit. I thought I was going to be the punchline in a very dark joke."

"Sounds like a typical Tuesday in Manhattan," I quipped, shaking my head. "You just need to learn the unwritten rules. First rule: avoid clowns. Second rule: always have snacks."

"Snacks can save you from almost anything," he agreed, his tone serious but his grin betraying him. "I'll remember that. Next time I face an existential subway crisis, I'll be well-prepared."

The conversation flowed seamlessly, each joke and revelation weaving a tapestry of connection between us. I felt a spark of something deeper, something that stirred beneath the surface of our friendly banter. Just when I thought I had the moment perfectly captured, Max's expression shifted.

He gazed into the distance, the lively park fading away as a shadow crossed his features. "You know," he began slowly, as if weighing each word, "I moved here to escape... to find myself again, I guess. Things got a little messy back home."

The lightheartedness between us dimmed momentarily, and I found myself leaning closer, intrigued by this glimpse into his world. "Messy how?" I asked gently, wanting to know without prying.

Max took a deep breath, his fingers tracing the rim of his coffee cup. "Life just... happened. Relationships that fell apart, dreams that felt out of reach. It's like I'm piecing together a puzzle where half the pieces are missing."

"Sounds like you're still searching for that last piece," I replied, my voice soft.

"Something like that." He turned to look at me, his eyes searching mine. "But enough about me. You're the one who makes it look so easy with all these dogs. How do you do it?"

I chuckled, grateful for the shift in conversation. "It's really just about staying one step ahead of them. And plenty of treats. Like I said, snacks can save you from almost anything."

"Ah, so it's all about bribery?" he teased, his smile returning. "Maybe I should apply those techniques to my artistic process. If only my clay would behave as well as these dogs do."

Our laughter echoed through the park, the tension easing like a cool breeze sweeping through a summer haze. As we parted that morning, exchanging playful jabs and tentative plans for our next dog walking rendezvous, I felt an exhilarating sense of possibility stirring within me. Max had become more than just a neighbor; he was a companion in this unpredictable dance of life, and I couldn't help but wonder where this newfound friendship might lead.

The days turned into a blur of golden afternoons and crisp evenings. Each morning brought with it a small ritual of excitement, a thread of connection weaving through my life. With each dog walk, I noticed the world transforming around me—the leaves were brighter, the air sweeter, and even the chaotic energy of Manhattan seemed more manageable with Max by my side.

But as the days grew shorter and the chill of winter began to creep in, so did an unsettling thought. I had yet to see Max's studio, the creative space where he breathed life into his art. My curiosity was piqued; I wanted to see where he found his inspiration, to understand the world through his eyes. I could almost feel the weight of his hidden stories, waiting to be uncovered.

As I pushed the thought aside, determined to embrace the joy of our easy camaraderie, I resolved to focus on the moment. I knew I had to take the plunge and invite him to my little world. After all, in a city filled with noise and chaos, sometimes the best adventures start with a simple question.

As autumn deepened, the city transformed into a canvas of fiery reds and muted golds. Each day felt like an intricate brushstroke, the world shifting into a masterpiece of fleeting beauty. My dog walking routine took on a rhythm, punctuated by the joy of sharing laughter and stories with Max. We spent nearly every morning together, two wanderers navigating life's chaos with our dogs as guides. Rufus and Daisy became inseparable, darting between the trees and leaping through piles of leaves, while Max and I explored the intricacies of our lives, weaving in and out of each other's narratives like the branches overhead.

One particularly brisk morning, as we strolled through a sun-dappled path, I couldn't shake the feeling that our friendship was poised on the edge of something new. Max had just shared an anecdote about a rather disastrous first date involving a cake mishap and a runaway cat, and I was laughing so hard I nearly lost my grip on Rufus's leash. "You really need to write a book about these misadventures," I said, my cheeks flushed from laughter.

"I could call it How Not to Impress a Date," he shot back, his smile bright against the crisp air. "The cover would be a picture of me looking horrified next to a ruined cake. What do you think?"

"Best seller for sure," I replied, nudging him playfully with my shoulder. The camaraderie felt effortless, a dance we both knew well.

"Speaking of impressions," he said, his tone shifting slightly, "I've been meaning to show you my studio. You might get a kick out of my latest project."

I felt a rush of excitement, the kind that tickled the edges of anticipation. "I'd love that! When can I come by?"

"How about tomorrow? I'll even throw in coffee and pastries to sweeten the deal," he said, winking.

"Wow, such a generous offer! You're pulling out all the stops," I teased. "I might just take you up on that."

The thought of stepping into his creative space thrilled me. It felt like crossing a threshold into his world, where ideas took form and inspiration lived. As we finished our walk, a playful warmth bloomed in my chest, and I couldn't help but wonder what surprises awaited me in that studio.

The next day dawned with a clear sky and the crispness of autumn still lingering. My heart raced as I approached his building, nerves fluttering in my stomach like a swarm of butterflies. I had envisioned this moment a dozen times—what if it was everything I imagined, or worse, what if it wasn't?

I knocked, the sound echoing in the quiet hallway. Moments later, the door swung open, revealing Max standing in the threshold, the light from behind him casting a halo around his tousled hair.

"Welcome to my humble abode," he said, gesturing grandly as though we were entering a royal palace.

Stepping inside felt like stepping into a dream. The studio was a wonderland of creativity. Large canvases leaned against the walls, their surfaces splattered with paint in a riot of colors. Sculptures—some half-finished, others magnificent in their completion—dotted the space, each one whispering its own story. The faint smell of paint mixed with fresh coffee hung in the air, inviting and warm.

"Wow," I breathed, genuinely awed. "This is incredible. It feels like a treasure trove of ideas."

Max beamed, pride illuminating his features. "Thanks! I've been working on this one," he said, motioning toward a particularly striking sculpture that resembled an abstract wave, its curves flowing with an almost liquid grace. "It's about the ebb and flow of life. Still a work in progress, but I'm getting there."

"It's stunning," I said, stepping closer to examine the piece. "You really capture movement. It's like it's alive."

"Much like the dogs you walk," he quipped, a mischievous glint in his eye. "You should see the way they move; it's pure art in motion."

We spent the next hour weaving through discussions of art, life, and our mutual love for dogs, with Max sharing insights about his inspirations and the journey behind each piece. As I sipped my coffee, I felt the walls of my own guardedness begin to crumble. This wasn't just a studio; it was a sanctuary where Max let his dreams flow freely, and in turn, it felt like he was inviting me to share in that world.

Just as I thought I had seen it all, he turned to me, a playful expression on his face. "Okay, now for the pièce de résistance." He led me to a corner of the room where a large, covered canvas stood.

"I've been waiting for the right moment to reveal this one. It's not finished, but I think it captures a part of me I haven't shared yet."

He pulled the cover away, revealing a chaotic swirl of colors, shapes, and textures that seemed to pulse with energy. It was both chaotic and beautiful, a raw expression of emotion that resonated deep within me. "Wow, Max. It's incredible. It's like a glimpse into your soul," I said, the words spilling out before I could reign them in.

A flicker of something passed over his face—vulnerability, perhaps. "I'm not sure if that's a compliment or a warning," he said, a nervous laugh escaping his lips.

"Definitely a compliment. I can see the struggle and the beauty. It's... real," I replied, surprised by the earnestness of my own words.

His expression shifted, a storm cloud gathering in his eyes. "That's the thing about real, isn't it? It's beautiful but messy, and sometimes it feels overwhelming."

Before I could respond, a sudden crash echoed from the back of the studio, cutting through the intimate moment like a knife. We both turned, startled. "What was that?" I asked, a knot forming in my stomach.

Max's brow furrowed, his playful demeanor fading into something more serious. "I... I'm not sure. Let me check." He moved toward the sound, and I followed closely behind, curiosity mingled with a creeping sense of dread.

As we rounded the corner, I spotted a large canvas that had toppled over, the vibrant colors smearing across the floor like spilled emotions. But that wasn't all. Scattered around the canvas were pieces of broken glass, remnants of a frame that had clearly shattered. And then, amidst the chaos, something glimmered—a small, ornate key lying in the midst of the glass shards.

"What is this?" I murmured, reaching down to pick it up, feeling the cool metal against my palm.

Max's eyes widened, his voice suddenly strained. "That... that doesn't belong here."

The air thickened between us, a charged silence stretching as we stood there, the key glinting ominously in the light. I could sense the weight of unspoken secrets hanging in the air, thick enough to cut through. The moment felt pivotal, a crossroads between what had been light and laughter and what was about to unfold.

"What does it mean?" I whispered, my heart racing as I turned to look at him, searching his expression for answers.

He hesitated, his eyes dark with an emotion I couldn't quite place. "I don't know," he said, his voice barely above a whisper. "But I have a feeling it's about to change everything."

And just like that, the world tilted on its axis, the promise of the unknown looming large in the space between us.

Chapter 2: Unexpected Encounters

The sun hung low in the sky, casting a golden hue over the park as I juggled leashes like a circus performer on a tightrope. My trio of dogs, a rambunctious golden retriever named Charlie, a sassy dachshund named Bella, and a mischievous beagle named Duke, had transformed our morning stroll into a chaotic adventure. Their excitement was palpable, tails wagging like flags in a whirlwind. Just as I thought I had managed to untangle the leashes and regain a semblance of control, I caught sight of Max.

He was leaning against a nearby tree, arms crossed, a teasing grin spreading across his face. His tousled hair caught the light just right, and the sun reflected off his charmingly crooked smile. I felt a flutter in my stomach, a confusing mix of exhilaration and wariness. He was like the first sip of champagne—effervescent and intoxicating, but too much too soon could leave me reeling.

"Need a hand there?" he called out, his voice smooth as butter, laced with the kind of humor that made even my dogs perk up and listen.

"More like a miracle," I shot back, trying to keep my tone light despite the fact that I was seriously considering a career in leash management. "You'd think I'd learn to keep one on a leash at a time."

He pushed himself off the tree and strolled over, the confidence in his step making my heart race like a racehorse bursting from the gate. "Maybe I could give you some pointers. I've been known to wrangle a few beasts in my day."

"Is that so?" I laughed, trying to keep my focus on the pups. Bella had taken a keen interest in a passing squirrel, yanking me toward the bushes while Duke attempted to disentangle himself from Charlie. "What's your secret?"

"Patience and snacks," he replied, kneeling down to charm Bella, who seemed to have momentarily forgotten her pursuit of the squirrel. "You've got to show them who's boss. But the snacks are crucial. You catch more flies with honey, right?"

"Or dogs with treats," I quipped, and as he laughed, the sound felt like a soft blanket wrapping around us. It was easy, this banter, a rhythm that made the world outside our bubble fade into the background.

"Tell me about it," he said, producing a dog biscuit from his pocket and offering it to Charlie, who inhaled it like it was a gourmet meal. "They have it all figured out. It's us humans who need to catch up."

His presence made everything brighter, a stark contrast to the nagging thoughts that had been swirling in my head for weeks. But just as quickly as the moment ignited, the familiar shadows of my past crept in, reminding me of the heartbreak that had left its mark. My heart had been a fragile thing, stitched together with hope but marred by loss.

"Do you come here often?" Max asked, his curiosity pulling me back to the present.

"Every morning," I replied, trying to ignore the way my pulse quickened when he leaned in just a little closer. "It's my sanity check. The dogs demand their exercise, and honestly, it's the only time I get to breathe without deadlines suffocating me."

"Deadlines?" He raised an eyebrow, the teasing glint in his eyes encouraging me to share more. "You sound like a busy woman. What do you do when you're not wrestling with leashes?"

"I'm a graphic designer," I confessed, the words flowing more easily than I anticipated. "I love creating visual stories. But sometimes it feels like I'm drowning in revisions. The dogs are my only escape from the screen."

"Ah, a fellow creative," he mused, nodding appreciatively. "Designing for the masses can be a drag, right? What's the point of all those pixels if they don't tell a story?"

I felt a spark ignite, the kind of connection that felt rare and refreshing. "Exactly! There's something so fulfilling about crafting an image that resonates. It's like capturing a moment, freezing it in time. But I can't tell you how many times I've wanted to toss my laptop into the nearest pond."

Max laughed, the sound rich and genuine. "I think a dramatic laptop toss would make a great graphic novel cover. 'The Designer's Dilemma.'"

"Now that's a bestseller in the making," I replied, unable to suppress my smile. There was something about him, a charm that unraveled the knots in my heart. Yet, the ghosts of my past lingered, whispering doubts that tugged at my resolve.

As we chatted, the dogs momentarily distracted by an encounter with a fellow canine, I could feel the air crackle with possibility. Max was charismatic and engaging, a force of nature in his own right. But could I risk my heart again?

Just as I was beginning to let my guard down, a sudden bark jolted me from my thoughts. Duke had managed to free himself from his leash, dashing toward a nearby picnic area, where a couple of teenagers were tossing a frisbee.

"Duke!" I shouted, my heart racing as I took off after him. Max followed suit, determination etched on his face. As we sprinted across the grass, the world around us faded away, leaving only the chaos of the chase.

In that moment of unfiltered chaos, I found myself laughing. It was infectious, the kind of joy that bubbled up and spilled over. And as Max caught up to me, both of us panting from the effort, something shifted. The playful banter faded into a comfortable silence, one charged with unspoken potential, the air thick with anticipation.

Duke, proud of his little adventure, trotted back, his tongue lolling and tail wagging. He didn't care that we'd run like fools; he was simply happy to be alive in the moment. Max and I exchanged glances, a silent acknowledgment of our shared ridiculousness.

"Next time, I'll bring a net," he said, grinning.

"Or a lasso," I shot back, trying to stifle my laughter.

For just a heartbeat, the weight of my past felt a little lighter, as if the air had shifted, and for the first time in a long while, the future seemed a little brighter.

As the weeks rolled on, the park transformed into my personal sanctuary, where the laughter of children mingled with the joyous barks of dogs. Every morning was a fresh page, waiting to be filled with the antics of Charlie, Bella, and Duke. Yet, the most captivating chapters of my day were the ones where Max drifted into view. Our paths crossed with delightful regularity, a predictable unpredictability that felt both comforting and exhilarating.

One particularly crisp morning, I found myself wrestling with Duke, who had taken it upon himself to chase after a flock of pigeons. The chaos erupted around us as he dashed, barking excitedly, while Charlie, forever the peacemaker, tried to intervene. Bella, of course, decided that this was the perfect moment to dig her tiny paws into the earth, investigating a particularly intriguing scent. I was utterly entangled in a mess of leashes, fur, and frustration, my breath coming in quick bursts.

"Looks like you've got your hands full!" Max called, jogging over with that devil-may-care charm that made my heart do a little flip. He was wearing a snug blue hoodie that accentuated his lean physique, and his dark jeans fit him just right.

"Full is an understatement," I replied, shooting him a half-hearted glare while simultaneously trying to disentangle Duke from Charlie. "I should have known better than to take them out without an army."

"Or a referee," he quipped, effortlessly crouching down to Bella's level, who had apparently decided that the earth was far more interesting than any of us. "You know, I used to think dogs were easy to manage. But it seems they might just be better at chaos than I am."

"Only a little better," I laughed, feeling a wave of warmth wash over me. It was moments like these that made the worries of my past fade, replaced by the lightness of this burgeoning friendship. "You've got to work on your dog-wrangling skills. They're going to take over the world if we let them."

Max's eyes sparkled with mischief. "I think they're already halfway there. Just look at the way Duke is eyeing those pigeons. He's clearly plotting his next move."

With a mock-serious expression, I glanced over at Duke, who had momentarily paused in his chase, crouched low like a little hunter ready to spring. "Do you think we should stage an intervention?"

"Definitely," he replied, rising back to his full height, "but only if we get to use treats as a negotiating tactic."

"Deal!" I grinned, heart racing as the ease of our banter settled like a comfortable quilt around me. It was as if I had known him for years, even though our encounters had been brief and sporadic. The kind of connection that dances at the edges of friendship, teasing you with the prospect of something more.

As we stood there, laughing over the dogs' antics, a sudden chill swept through the air, sending a shiver down my spine. The autumn leaves rustled above us, painting the ground in shades of amber and gold, a reminder of the changing seasons. Change was something I had been wrestling with for a while, and while my heart felt light in Max's presence, the shadows of my past loomed like stubborn clouds overhead.

"Do you want to grab coffee after this?" Max asked suddenly, his gaze steady and sincere. The question hung in the air, a fragile thing that made my heart race and my stomach flip.

I hesitated for a heartbeat, my mind racing. Coffee could mean casual companionship or the potential for something deeper. What if I let him in, and he saw the cracks in my heart? "I... uh, I'm not sure," I stammered, glancing down at the rambunctious trio still in their wrestling match.

"Hey," he said gently, stepping closer, "no pressure. We can always keep it dog-related. I just thought it could be nice to chat without our furry distractions."

It was the way he said it, with such effortless charm, that made the walls around my heart tremble. "I would like that," I finally admitted, unable to hide the smile creeping onto my lips. "But only if you promise not to judge my coffee order. I have a penchant for the most ridiculous drinks."

"Ridiculous how?" he asked, arching an eyebrow. "Do you add extra whipped cream, sprinkles, and a cherry on top?"

"Worse," I teased, leaning in conspiratorially. "I take my coffee with oat milk, a dash of vanilla, and a splash of cinnamon. It's basically dessert in a cup."

Max chuckled, throwing his head back, his laughter echoing through the park. "I can respect that level of creativity. Plus, I've heard cinnamon has magical properties."

"Exactly! It's practically a health drink," I retorted, feeling buoyed by our playful exchange.

Just as I was about to suggest we finish our walk, a sharp bark interrupted our moment. Charlie had taken it upon himself to initiate a wrestling match with Duke, and before I could react, they both toppled into a nearby puddle.

"Oh no!" I exclaimed, rushing over as they emerged, dripping and muddy, tails wagging with unabashed joy. "You two are going to need a bath."

Max laughed again, his eyes glimmering with amusement as he approached. "Looks like they've found their own version of coffee. Mud lattes, anyone?"

"Ha! If they could drink them, I'd be worried about our sanity levels," I replied, shaking my head, the tension in my chest easing further.

As we cleaned up the chaos, I felt a warmth blossom within me. Max was becoming a constant in my life, and despite my reservations, it felt strangely exhilarating. Yet, I couldn't shake the feeling of vulnerability creeping in, the weight of my past reminding me of its existence.

We made our way to a cozy café that perched on the corner, its warm lights twinkling like a promise against the backdrop of an evening sky. The scent of coffee and baked goods wafted through the air, wrapping around us like a familiar embrace.

As we settled at a small table near the window, the world outside blurred into a soft canvas of autumn hues. Max leaned back in his chair, watching me with a playful glint in his eyes. "So, tell me your deepest, darkest coffee secret."

I laughed, unable to resist the spark of mischief in his gaze. "Well, I once tried to make my own pumpkin spice syrup. Let's just say it did not end well."

"Oh? How bad could it be?" he asked, leaning forward, genuinely intrigued.

"Picture an explosion of spices, a sticky mess, and a blender that nearly met its untimely end," I recounted, weaving the tale with an exaggerated flair. "I was left with something that resembled a science experiment more than a coffee drink."

Max howled with laughter, and for a moment, the worries of the world outside faded away, leaving just us and the sweet aroma of coffee. It was this kind of connection that felt rare, a delightful discovery that brushed away the dust of old heartaches.

"Okay, I promise not to judge your coffee order," he said, wiping a tear from his eye. "But if you ever try that again, you're calling me to help. I have a knack for disaster recovery."

"Noted," I replied, the warmth between us glowing stronger. It felt like standing at the edge of a cliff, the thrill of the unknown tugging at me to take a leap.

The conversation flowed effortlessly, the minutes melting into hours. Every laugh, every shared story, built a bridge over the lingering doubts that haunted me. Just as I was beginning to believe that maybe, just maybe, I could allow myself to feel again, Max leaned in closer, his voice dropping to a soft murmur.

"You know, there's something really special about this," he said, his gaze searching mine, a vulnerability evident in his eyes. "It's like we just click."

The words hung between us, a fragile promise wrapped in the warmth of shared laughter. And for the first time in a long while, I felt the stirrings of hope blossom in the depths of my heart, fighting against the shadows that had long kept it at bay.

The café's ambiance wrapped around me like a well-loved blanket, soft and inviting, with the hum of chatter blending seamlessly with the comforting aroma of coffee. I found myself leaning in, caught in the orbit of Max's magnetic charm. He had a way of making the world feel a little less daunting, his playful nature acting as a balm for the worries that clung to my heart like stubborn vines.

"Clicking, huh?" I echoed, teasing the words from my lips as I stirred my coffee, watching the cinnamon swirl like a tiny galaxy. "That's quite the bold statement for a second meeting."

"Bold is my middle name," he shot back, a roguish grin spreading across his face. "Well, it's actually David, but 'Bold David' doesn't quite have the same ring, does it?"

I laughed, and for a moment, I forgot about everything else—the uncertainties, the shadows of the past that had loomed over me for so long. "Okay, Bold David, let's test that theory. What's your hidden talent? Everyone has one, even if they don't want to admit it."

Max leaned back, feigning deep thought, a twinkle of mischief in his eyes. "Well, I can juggle. But only with items I can eat. I'd have to limit myself to snacks, which isn't really a limitation for me."

"Ah, the classic culinary juggler," I said, leaning closer, intrigued. "But can you really juggle or is this some sort of ploy to impress me with your snack skills?"

"Why not both?" He laughed, a rich sound that bounced between us, making the air feel lighter. "But seriously, I can juggle. You name it: apples, oranges, even those ridiculous little rubber chickens that make squeaking noises when they land."

"Now that's a skill I would pay to see," I replied, picturing him in a circus tent, throwing fruits and rubber chickens in the air with flair. "So, next time we meet, I expect a full performance. Just promise you won't drop anything on my head."

"Deal. But you'd be doing the world a disservice if you didn't share your secret talent," he challenged, his tone shifting slightly, probing. "What's your hidden gem?"

I hesitated, the familiar knots tightening in my stomach. My heart whispered to share something, anything that would make me feel more real in this moment. "I've been told I make a mean chocolate cake," I confessed, trying to sound casual. "But it's more about the chaos that happens in my kitchen than the cake itself."

"Chaos and cake? Now that sounds like a recipe for a good time. Do you have any horror stories?"

"Oh, plenty." I chuckled, recalling the time I had mistaken baking soda for baking powder. "I once made a cake so dense that when it hit the table, I swear it could have doubled as a doorstop. I nearly called it a 'brick cake' and marketed it as a new trend."

Max laughed heartily, and I felt a rush of warmth, his laughter rolling over me like sunshine breaking through clouds. "Let's be real, you'd probably be a viral sensation. 'The Brick Cake: A New Culinary Experience.'"

The conversation danced from one subject to another, each topic weaving a tighter bond between us. I felt myself open up, revealing bits of my life, my dreams, and the hurdles I had faced. Max listened, his attention unwavering, and with each word, the tension I had carried began to loosen its grip.

"I've always wanted to travel, to see the world outside my little bubble," I admitted, my voice softening as I allowed a sliver of vulnerability to creep in. "But there's always been something holding me back—fear, I guess. I get so wrapped up in my work that I forget to live."

Max nodded, a knowing look crossing his face. "You're not alone in that. Sometimes we get so caught up in the day-to-day that we forget there's a whole world out there waiting for us."

"Exactly! I feel like I'm on the edge of something—like there's a big adventure just waiting for me to jump in." The admission felt both freeing and terrifying. What if I leaped and fell? What if I ended up in more chaos than I could handle?

"Why not take that leap?" he challenged, leaning forward, his eyes intense and encouraging. "You've got the dogs, a job you love, and you've already conquered cake disasters. What's the worst that could happen?"

"The worst?" I laughed, though it felt more like a nervous chuckle. "I could end up lost in a foreign city, eating something I can't pronounce, and never find my way home. My mother would have a field day with that."

"But wouldn't that be an incredible story?" he pressed, his enthusiasm infectious. "Life is messy, and sometimes those mishaps lead to the best experiences."

As I sat there, gazing into his earnest eyes, I couldn't help but wonder if he was right. What would it look like to embrace that uncertainty, to let go of the fears that had held me captive for so long? It was an intoxicating thought, but reality pulled at my heartstrings, reminding me of all the reasons I had built those walls.

"Let's start with a mini-adventure," Max suggested, shifting gears and pulling me from my reverie. "What if we plan a day trip? Just us, the dogs, and maybe some cake? It could be a small taste of the wild side."

A day trip? My heart raced at the thought, a mix of excitement and apprehension swirling within me. "A day trip sounds... incredible, but are you sure you're ready for my chaotic crew?"

"Absolutely. I'm ready for anything, especially if cake is involved." His grin was disarming, and my reservations began to melt away, one by one. "What's life without a little chaos, anyway?"

"Okay, I'm in," I said, unable to suppress my smile. "But if we're doing this, we're definitely bringing the treats. You can't have an adventure without snacks."

"Great! I'll bring the juggling fruit, and you can bring the cake," he declared, his excitement palpable. "Just don't be surprised when I challenge you to a bake-off at some point. It'll be the ultimate competition."

"Only if we can film it and send it to the food network for a good laugh."

As we continued to talk and plan, the world outside faded, becoming nothing more than a backdrop to our shared excitement. I felt alive, as if the shackles of fear and past heartbreak were slowly loosening. With every word exchanged, every smile shared, a flicker of hope ignited within me.

But just as I was beginning to believe that maybe, just maybe, this was the turning point I had been waiting for, the café door swung open, and a figure stepped inside.

It was a familiar face—a shadow from my past that sent chills racing down my spine. My heart stuttered, and for a moment, I was frozen in place, staring in disbelief. The past had returned, uninvited, its presence a stark reminder of the hurt I had been trying to escape.

"Is everything okay?" Max's voice broke through my daze, concern etched on his face as he followed my gaze.

I could only manage a nod, my heart pounding in my chest. But as the figure moved closer, I knew that this moment was about to shatter the fragile reality I had begun to build. The tension thickened, and my mind raced, the walls I had just begun to lower threatening to come crashing down once more.

Chapter 3: The Secret Garden

Sunlight streamed through the canopy of twisted branches, casting a dappled pattern of light and shadow across the overgrown path. I followed Max deeper into the hidden garden, a world untouched by the city's relentless pace. The air was thick with the sweet scent of blooming honeysuckle, mingling with the earthy undertones of damp soil and decaying leaves. Each step felt like a whisper, an invitation to explore the secrets woven into this verdant tapestry. As I brushed my fingers against the velvety petals of wildflowers, a sense of belonging washed over me, easing the tension coiled in my chest.

"This place is incredible," I breathed, glancing at Max, who stood a few steps ahead, his silhouette framed by a riot of color. His tousled hair caught the light, making him look almost ethereal, like a character lifted from a storybook. He turned, his grin wide and infectious, and I felt a flutter of something I hadn't experienced in far too long.

"Isn't it?" he replied, his voice low and smooth, like a lazy summer breeze. "I stumbled upon it while jogging one afternoon. It was like finding a forgotten treasure." He stepped aside, gesturing for me to explore. "Go ahead, lose yourself in it."

I ventured further into the garden, my heart racing in rhythm with the gentle hum of nature around me. The chaos of city life faded, replaced by the symphony of chirping birds and the rustle of leaves. It was in this moment, surrounded by the wild beauty, that I felt the walls I had built around my heart begin to crack. The raw honesty of our conversation lingered in the air, an unspoken connection threading through the space between us. I could sense his eyes on me, a steady warmth that sent my thoughts spiraling.

"What did you want to be when you were a kid?" I asked, my voice barely above a whisper as I twirled around, my arms wide as if to embrace the garden itself. I didn't want to think about the future, only the warmth of the moment and the sweet thrill of possibility.

Max chuckled, a sound that danced like sunlight filtering through the leaves. "An astronaut," he said, a playful glint in his eyes. "I thought I could float among the stars, paint them in colors no one had ever seen. But I quickly realized I'd probably just get lost in space."

I laughed, imagining him drifting among the cosmos, paintbrush in hand, swirling galaxies into existence. "You would have turned space into a gallery. But what happened to that dream?"

His smile faltered for a fraction of a second, the spark in his eyes dimming. "Life happened, I suppose," he said, shrugging. "I ended up here, trying to navigate the art world. It's harder than it looks. Everyone has a voice but me."

My heart ached for him, this bright soul hiding behind layers of uncertainty. "You just haven't found your medium yet," I encouraged, stepping closer. "Art isn't just about the final piece; it's about the journey, the process of creating. Sometimes it's messy, but that's what makes it real."

Max studied me, his gaze penetrating, and I felt exposed, like a canvas laid bare before him. "And what about you? What's your dream?"

I hesitated, my past swarming back like shadows creeping in. "I used to want to be a writer," I admitted, the words tasting bittersweet on my tongue. "But life twisted that dream into something I hardly recognize anymore. It feels too far away, like a childhood fantasy."

"Why do you think that is?" he asked, tilting his head as if trying to dissect the complexities of my mind.

I stared into the distance, the garden swirling in vibrant colors around me. "I guess… I lost my way. Life threw some curveballs, and I forgot how to catch them. It's like I was living in a story where the plot got twisted, and I don't know how to rewrite it."

"Maybe you just need a new chapter," he suggested, his voice gentle yet firm, like a grounding force in a storm.

I turned to him, surprised by the depth of his insight. "Easier said than done, don't you think?"

"Sure, but sometimes the best stories come from the most unexpected places." His eyes sparkled with mischief. "Like this garden. It's wild and untamed, but it's also beautiful. There's magic here, and it's all about how you see it."

"Okay, Mr. Philosopher," I replied, rolling my eyes playfully, though his words resonated within me, unraveling threads of doubt. "So what do we do now? Just wander aimlessly, hoping inspiration strikes?"

He grinned, the corners of his mouth curling mischievously. "Why not? Or we could do something more fun. Ever thought about playing a game of 'Truth or Dare'?"

My eyebrows shot up, incredulous. "In a secret garden? What are we, teenagers again?"

He laughed, the sound rich and vibrant. "Why not? It's a perfect setting for secrets and dares. I'll go first. Truth or dare?"

I hesitated, caught off guard by his enthusiasm. "Um... truth."

"Boring choice," he teased, but his eyes sparkled with curiosity. "What's something you've always wanted to do but haven't?"

I gulped, my heart racing. The moment felt electric, charged with potential. "I've always wanted to travel the world, to see the places that inspired the stories I've read. But..." I paused, uncertainty creeping back in. "But I've been too afraid to take the leap."

"Fear can be a suffocating weight," Max said, his expression turning serious. "But what if you let it go? What if you dared to dream again?"

His words resonated deeply, echoing through the chambers of my heart. I looked around at the tangled beauty of the garden, a testament to resilience and growth. The vibrant flowers seemed to nod in agreement, urging me to shed my fears, to let the wildness within me bloom.

"Alright," I said, summoning a newfound resolve. "I dare myself to start writing again."

Max's eyes widened, and I could see the approval dancing in their depths. "Now we're getting somewhere. Your turn! Truth or dare?"

"Dare," I replied, a spark of mischief igniting within me.

"I dare you to climb that tree," he challenged, pointing to a gnarled old oak, its branches stretching like welcoming arms toward the sky.

I laughed, a mixture of disbelief and exhilaration coursing through me. "You're on! Just don't blame me if I break my neck."

With a determined grin, I approached the tree, the rough bark scratching against my palms as I began to climb. The branches felt sturdy beneath my feet, and with each upward movement, I felt a rush of freedom, as if I were shedding my inhibitions along with the leaves brushing against me. When I finally reached a sturdy branch, I looked down at Max, who was gazing up at me with unabashed admiration.

"See? You're a natural!" he called, laughter in his voice.

"Or a fool!" I shot back, but my heart soared. From my perch, I felt invincible, the garden sprawling below me like a canvas waiting for a masterstroke. In that moment, I understood that maybe, just maybe, I could start to reclaim the dreams I had let slip away.

The world felt vibrant, alive with possibilities, and I could almost taste the sweetness of newfound courage on my lips. I breathed in the fragrant air, relishing the sensation of letting go. Beneath the canopy of leaves, everything felt right, as if the garden itself had conspired to awaken the dormant artist within me.

Perched high in the sturdy branches of the ancient oak, I felt as if I were the queen of this hidden realm. The rustling leaves sang a song of freedom, their whispers weaving tales of long-forgotten secrets.

Max's laughter floated up to me, a buoyant sound that echoed my exhilaration. I hadn't felt so alive in years, and it terrified me. With every inch I climbed, I feared the fall more than ever, not just from the tree but from whatever fragile hope was taking root in my heart.

"Look at you, all high and mighty!" he called, leaning against the tree trunk, arms crossed, a teasing glint in his eyes. "What's the view like from up there? Can you see your dreams?"

I squinted down at him, a playful smirk dancing on my lips. "Nope, just a bird's eye view of your embarrassing haircut!"

He feigned horror, clutching his chest in mock offense. "How dare you! This is high fashion, thank you very much!"

"Sure, if the look you're going for is 'I just woke up after a week-long bender,'" I shot back, laughter bubbling up like champagne. As he rolled his eyes dramatically, I felt a sense of connection bloom—a vibrant thread weaving our lives together in the shared absurdity of the moment.

But as I clambered down, the warmth of our banter began to chill. What if this garden was just an ephemeral escape? Would I wake up one day to find it faded like a half-remembered dream? My heart raced with the weight of unasked questions, each one heavier than the last.

"Okay, queen of the tree, your turn," Max said, leaning back and gazing at me expectantly, his eyes twinkling with curiosity. "Truth or dare?"

"Dare," I replied, feeling the thrill of spontaneity surge through me.

"I dare you to... sing something! Right here, right now!"

My heart sank. "Oh no, no, no! That's not happening." I scrambled to come up with an escape route. Singing in public was about as comfortable for me as walking barefoot on hot coals.

"Too scared?" he taunted, a sly grin spreading across his face. "C'mon, I promise I won't throw any tomatoes!"

"Fine!" I sighed dramatically, casting my eyes upward as if searching for divine intervention. "I'll do it, but only if you promise to join me."

He raised an eyebrow, pretending to mull it over. "Deal. But only if you start."

With my stomach in knots, I took a deep breath and began to hum a silly little tune that popped into my head—something my grandmother used to sing to me. The melody twirled around us, infused with the aroma of blooming flowers, and as the notes escaped my lips, I felt a strange weight lift. Max joined in, harmonizing with an exaggerated flourish that made me giggle. We sounded like a pair of deranged birds, but in that moment, it didn't matter. The garden enveloped us like a cocoon, sheltering our ridiculousness.

"See? That wasn't so bad!" he declared as we finished, an exaggerated flourish to his bow. "Next time, we'll bring a whole choir."

"Just what I need, a backup group for my public embarrassment," I shot back, but I couldn't suppress my laughter.

We settled onto the grass, the world around us painted in lush greens and bursting blooms. As the sun dipped lower in the sky, painting everything in hues of gold and soft pink, the magic of the moment settled over us like a warm blanket. But with it came an unsettling thought—a reminder of the walls I had built around my heart.

"Max," I began, the weight of the question heavy on my tongue, "what do you really want from life? You know, besides singing with me in a garden?"

He shifted slightly, the levity in his expression replaced by something more serious. "I want to create art that makes people feel something—anything, really. But I get in my own way. I'm afraid that if I put my work out there, people will hate it."

"That's a real fear," I said softly, my heart aching for him. "But isn't it scarier to never try?"

He nodded, a flicker of vulnerability crossing his face. "Yeah, I guess. But it's easier to hide behind my sketches than to expose myself. You know what I mean?"

I looked at him, a piece of my own heart resonating in his words. "I do. It's terrifying to lay bare your soul, to let others see the real you. But maybe... maybe that's where the beauty lies."

Just as the weight of our confessions hung between us, a rustling in the bushes startled us both. I shot up, ready for anything—an errant squirrel, perhaps, or a particularly bold rabbit. Instead, a small group of children burst into the garden, laughter spilling from them like the petals of the flowers they trampled underfoot.

"Look! A secret garden!" one shouted, pointing directly at us, his eyes wide with wonder.

"Shh!" I hissed, though the instinct felt absurd. "It's supposed to be a secret!"

Max snickered beside me, clearly enjoying the chaos. "Sorry, kids! You've uncovered our hideout! You have to pay the toll," he said dramatically, crossing his arms and adopting a mock-serious expression.

"What toll?" they demanded, their faces painted with curiosity and mischief.

"Your best secret! It has to be good," he challenged.

The children exchanged glances, eyes sparkling with excitement. "I can't tell you my best secret!" one girl said, her voice incredulous. "It's a secret!"

"Then you can't enter!" Max announced, feigning authority.

The kids erupted into a fit of giggles, and as I watched, I realized how easily they tumbled into joy without fear. Their laughter wrapped around me like a warm embrace, nudging me further into the realization that maybe, just maybe, I was also allowed to chase joy.

"Okay, okay," I said, suddenly feeling bold. "If you tell us a secret, we'll give you a tour of the garden. How does that sound?"

The children huddled together, whispering conspiratorially before the oldest boy stepped forward. "I have a secret! I once saw a dragonfly that was as big as my hand!"

"Wow! Really?" I feigned astonishment, leaning closer as if he were revealing the world's greatest mystery.

"Yep! And it could fly through the trees like a rocket!"

"Then you, my friend, have earned your passage!" Max proclaimed, gesturing dramatically for them to enter the garden. They squealed in delight, darting past us and into the heart of the greenery.

As the chaos of children enveloped us, I caught Max's eye, and we shared a moment of laughter that bridged the gap between our guarded hearts. It was chaotic and messy, much like life, but within that mess, there was a glimmer of hope. Perhaps it was possible to let go of the fears that had clung to me for so long, to let the vibrancy of the world seep into the corners of my heart.

I leaned back against the trunk of the tree, the laughter of children echoing around us, and as I watched Max interact with the little ones, something shifted deep within me. Maybe this hidden garden was more than a temporary escape; it was a reminder that life is meant to be embraced, even with its tangled roots and wildflowers. The path ahead might still be uncertain, but for the first time in a long time, I felt the warmth of possibility rising like the sun on the horizon, painting the world in colors I hadn't dared to imagine.

Laughter erupted around us as the children raced through the garden, their energy a vibrant current that pulled me from my introspection. Max knelt beside a particularly curious girl who had latched onto his ankle, asking questions with the fervor of a detective on the trail of a juicy scoop. "What's your favorite flower?" she demanded, eyes wide with expectation.

"Ah, the age-old question," he replied theatrically, stroking his chin. "I would have to say... the sunflower. They're so cheerful, always reaching for the sun, just like I aspire to do."

The girl gasped as if he'd revealed a great secret, eyes sparkling with admiration. "I like daisies!" she declared, spinning on her heel and running off to share her revelation with her friends.

Max turned to me, a smile lingering on his lips. "See? They have the right idea. Daisies are all about joy. They don't overthink it. They just bloom."

His words resonated, and I felt a stir within me, as if the seed of hope he had planted was beginning to take root. But just as I found myself caught in the moment, the children's giggles filled the air with a sense of urgency that felt almost infectious. I watched as they darted between flowers, their voices rising and falling like a symphony, and I could feel the garden alive with possibilities.

"Alright, tiny adventurers," I called, my voice carrying across the colorful chaos. "What do you think we should explore next? We've got an entire kingdom of flowers to discover!"

The children paused, eyes gleaming with mischief. "Let's go find the biggest flower!" shouted the oldest boy, his face smeared with mud and delight.

"A quest!" Max declared, standing tall and pretending to wield an imaginary sword. "Onward, to the land of giant blooms!"

I couldn't help but laugh at his playful antics, the sheer joy radiating from him igniting something deep within me. Perhaps the hesitation that had gripped my heart began to loosen its hold, moment by moment, as we swept into the vibrant chaos of the garden.

The children led us deeper into the heart of the overgrown sanctuary, where sprawling vines draped like curtains over secret alcoves, and the air was thick with the perfume of nectar and earth. I felt as though I had stepped into a world where time ceased to matter, where the constraints of adulthood melted away like wax beneath the sun.

After a short trek, we stumbled upon a small clearing, a sunlit oasis where flowers stood tall, their colors shouting for attention. "Look!" one of the children exclaimed, pointing to a sunflower that towered above the rest, its golden face tilted toward the sun. "That's the biggest one!"

"It's a giant! We should take a picture!" another chimed in, scrambling to pose with their arms around the enormous bloom, laughter bubbling up in joyful chaos.

Max knelt beside the sunflower, his fingers brushing against its velvety petals. "You know," he mused, his voice thoughtful, "these flowers don't care about being the best. They just grow as they are, completely unapologetic."

A pang of realization hit me—how often had I buried my own potential under the weight of expectations? Watching Max, I recognized the beauty in being true to oneself, in allowing the vibrant, untamed parts of life to emerge.

"Can we take a picture too?" I asked, the question slipping out before I could overthink it. The children cheered in agreement, and we gathered in front of the sunflower. Max draped an arm over my shoulder, his warmth radiating into me, and for a fleeting moment, I felt as if we were a small, chaotic family—a quirky tribe bound by laughter and whimsy.

As the camera clicked, I could almost hear my heart shifting gears, but the moment was swiftly interrupted by a distant sound. A rustling echoed through the garden, more ominous than the playful laughter that had enveloped us. I looked around, my senses heightened.

"Did you hear that?" I whispered to Max, my voice barely audible over the chorus of children's chatter.

"What?" he asked, his brow furrowing.

"Something... something doesn't feel right."

Before he could respond, the rustling grew louder, accompanied by a series of thuds, like heavy footsteps crushing the foliage beneath. The children paused, their laughter dying on their lips, eyes wide with confusion and a hint of fear.

"Maybe it's just a raccoon?" one of the kids suggested hesitantly, glancing over his shoulder.

Max and I exchanged glances, our expressions mirroring the same unease. "Let's not stick around to find out," I murmured, my instincts kicking in. "Everyone, back to the entrance! We should go!"

The children, sensing the change in the atmosphere, began to scatter back the way we had come, but I couldn't shake the feeling that something was lurking just beyond our sight. I took a few steps back, scanning the shadows that danced along the edges of the garden, half-expecting a creature to burst through the thicket.

"Stay close!" Max shouted, ushering the children toward the exit. I felt his hand find mine, fingers intertwining, and an electric jolt of connection surged through me, filling me with a strange mix of warmth and trepidation.

"Why is it so dark over there?" one of the girls asked, her voice a trembling whisper as she pointed to the shadows creeping closer, cloaking the garden in an unsettling stillness.

"I... I don't know," I stammered, my heart racing. "Let's keep moving!"

As we hurried back, the sounds intensified, the rustling morphing into something almost tangible, a palpable presence that seemed to reach out for us. The air thickened with tension, and I could feel the weight of unseen eyes watching, waiting.

"Almost there!" Max urged, his grip tightening around my hand, a comforting anchor amidst the mounting fear.

But just as we neared the garden's entrance, the source of the rustling emerged from the underbrush—a figure cloaked in shadows, features obscured. My breath hitched in my throat, and panic surged through me.

"Who's there?" I called, my voice steadier than I felt.

The figure stepped forward, revealing nothing but darkness, a silhouette that seemed to blend into the very essence of the garden. "You shouldn't be here," a low voice echoed, sending chills racing down my spine.

"What do you mean?" I shot back, instinctively stepping in front of the children, my heart pounding.

Max's grip tightened around my hand, grounding me as the tension hung thick in the air. "We were just—"

But before he could finish, the figure took another step forward, and in the twilight shadows, I caught a glimpse of something glimmering—something that looked alarmingly like a knife.

The garden, once a sanctuary, had transformed into a battleground of uncertainty and fear, and I could feel the walls closing in around us, the vibrant colors fading into a haze of confusion and dread.

"Run!" Max shouted, but the word felt like a spell gone awry, and as we turned to flee, the sound of laughter and joy shattered into silence, echoing into the unknown, leaving us with only the darkness and the sense that our hidden paradise was not as safe as we had believed.

Chapter 4: Layers of the Past

Max leaned against the weathered oak bar, a half-empty glass of whiskey in hand, the amber liquid catching the dim light from the flickering neon sign behind him. The bar was a charmingly chaotic blend of mismatched furniture and patrons who seemed to be entangled in their own stories, just like us. I watched him through the haze of the smoke swirling in the air, the scent of aged wood and something slightly sweet—a hint of vanilla from the nearby candle—filling my senses. He was beautiful in a way that felt both familiar and foreign, with tousled hair that fell just above his striking green eyes, which held depths I yearned to explore.

"So, what's the story behind the mysterious Max?" I asked, trying to keep the mood light, my voice a teasing lilt. I leaned forward, resting my chin on my palm, the wooden bar cool against my skin. "Were you once a boy band heartthrob, or just a simple farm boy with dreams of city lights?"

He chuckled, a sound that danced through the din of the bar and settled warmly in my chest. "Neither, I'm afraid. I was more of the 'forgotten art student' type." His smile faded slightly, as if a memory had flitted too close, nudging at the edges of his otherwise lighthearted demeanor. "I fell in love for the first time in high school. Her name was Lily. She had this incredible way of looking at the world, like it was all magic and wonder. Then one day, she just... vanished. No goodbyes, no explanations."

I felt a pang of sympathy, a shared understanding of love lost threading between us like a taut string. "That must've hurt," I said softly, my heart drumming in my chest as I considered how much I was beginning to feel for him.

He shrugged, but the weight of the words lingered in the air. "It did. I think it's why I find it so hard to let anyone in. I keep my heart locked away, afraid it might get broken again."

The honesty in his voice echoed my own guarded feelings. My past was a jumbled mess of trust and betrayal, the shards of which I had never quite managed to piece together again. I'd thought I was ready to dive back into the world of dating after my last relationship, but as he spoke, I realized how unprepared I truly was.

"Funny, isn't it?" I ventured, my lips curling into a wry smile. "We go through life pretending we're tough, but it only takes a little honesty to crack us wide open."

He raised an eyebrow, a playful glint lighting up his eyes. "You think we're tough? Look at us, sharing heartache like it's a cocktail special. We're practically a self-help book waiting to happen."

The banter flowed easily, a comforting current amidst the undercurrents of vulnerability. As I took a sip of my drink—an overly sweet concoction that barely masked the whiskey—I wondered if this was how it always began: with a simple conversation that slowly unraveled the threads of who we were.

"You have this way of making things sound less... tragic," I said, admiring the way he seemed to shrug off his past like a worn coat. "It's almost like you're wearing your scars like badges of honor."

Max laughed, the sound genuine, and I couldn't help but notice how the room seemed to brighten with his mirth. "If only it worked like that. Instead, I'm just the guy who learned to keep his heart at arm's length, and occasionally, I indulge in whiskey and ridiculous conversations."

"I could use more ridiculous conversations," I admitted, letting my gaze drift around the bar. The walls were adorned with vintage photos, snapshots of lives once lived, laughter frozen in time. I wondered about the stories behind them, how many layers of heartache and joy hung in this small space, woven together like a patchwork quilt of shared human experience.

"Tell me about yours," he prompted, leaning in as if I were about to unveil a treasured secret. "What's your heart's history?"

"Ah, it's a classic tale of betrayal and bad decisions," I replied, feigning a theatrical sigh. "I fell for someone I thought was different. The kind of guy who read poetry and wore scarves in the summer. Turns out, he was just a wolf in sheep's clothing, looking for a quick thrill."

His expression softened, and I could see him processing my words, weighing the past against the present. "And now?" he asked gently, as if stepping carefully around the shards of glass. "What does your heart want now?"

I hesitated, the weight of his question lingering in the air. The truth was, I wanted to reach for something real again, to risk the pain for the potential of joy. Yet, the thought of exposing my heart, of letting someone in after all I had been through, was terrifying. "I want to believe that it's possible to find something genuine," I finally confessed, my voice barely above a whisper. "But every time I think I'm ready, I feel that familiar knot in my stomach."

Max nodded, his eyes steady and encouraging, a lighthouse guiding me through the fog of my doubts. "We're all just trying to find our way, aren't we? Maybe we should stop pretending we've got it all figured out."

"Maybe we should just embrace the chaos," I replied, feeling a spark of determination. Perhaps this connection we were building was worth the risk. After all, what was love if not a series of chances taken?

A week passed in a blur of laughter, shared drinks, and moments that felt stolen from the mundane. Each evening, we found ourselves retreating to our corner of the bar, a sanctuary amid the noise and clamor of the outside world. Max's stories flowed as freely as the whiskey, revealing glimmers of his past, each one more intricate than the last, yet I remained an enigma to him—a puzzle box he couldn't quite crack open.

"Okay, your turn," he declared one evening, leaning in with that devil-may-care smile that sent a thrill darting through me. The bar was alive with energy; laughter danced in the air, and the clinking of glasses created a rhythmic backdrop to our conversation. "Tell me something I don't know about you. Something juicy."

I feigned contemplation, swirling the remnants of my cocktail, the ice clinking against the glass as if urging me to share. "I once had a pet iguana named Monty," I said, suppressing a giggle at the absurdity of it. "I thought he'd be the perfect companion, a creature of mystery and grace. But he turned out to be more of a diva than I anticipated. He had this penchant for sunbathing on the couch, and if anyone dared to sit near him, well, let's just say he had a flair for theatrics."

Max threw his head back in laughter, the sound rich and genuine, and I felt warmth bloom in my chest. "Iguanas have flair? I never knew. That's a solid piece of information."

"I know! It was a tragedy when Monty decided to stage his great escape one day, barreling out of the open patio door and into the wilds of my suburban backyard. I never saw him again. Let's just say I've always wondered if he found his calling as a lizard libertine."

Max chuckled, shaking his head as if still processing my revelation. "You're telling me that your pet iguana left you for a life of freedom? I didn't realize he had dreams of becoming the next great explorer."

"Right? Who knew Monty was such a free spirit?" I grinned, feeling the tension ease between us. "But hey, I like to think he's out there, living his best life—maybe he's got a posse of equally ambitious reptiles now."

"Monty, the rebel lizard," he mused, his eyes sparkling. "What a legacy."

As the conversation danced around us, the intimacy of our shared stories created an invisible thread that tugged us closer. The warmth of his presence felt intoxicating, a combination of familiarity and thrill, the kind of feeling you can't quite articulate but know is significant. I shifted my gaze, absorbing the surrounding atmosphere—the bar's walls lined with vintage photographs, each telling a story of its own, echoing the laughter and heartache of the people who had gathered before us.

"So, besides iguana wrangling, what else should I know?" he pressed, his curiosity genuine.

"Hmm, let's see," I mused, pretending to consider deeply. "I may have once participated in a terrible karaoke rendition of 'I Will Survive.' The only thing that kept the audience from booing me off stage was the sheer volume of my enthusiasm. It was like I thought the more I belted out the notes, the less I could hear my own voice cracking."

"Now that sounds like a glorious disaster," he laughed, and I couldn't help but join him, my cheeks flushing with the warmth of embarrassment and nostalgia.

"Glorious is one word for it. I've never been able to look at disco balls the same way since."

Max leaned back, his expression playful yet contemplative. "You know, I think it's these moments—being ridiculous and unafraid—that really make life worthwhile. We take ourselves too seriously sometimes."

"I couldn't agree more," I said, the honesty of his words resonating within me. The past week had felt like a delightful escape, an opportunity to embrace the absurdities of life instead of clinging to the shadows of heartbreak.

A thought flickered in the back of my mind, one I had avoided confronting. "You've been remarkably open with me, Max. What about you? What's the most ridiculous thing you've done?"

He paused, the lightheartedness momentarily slipping from his expression. "Hmm, I might have participated in an underground poetry slam once. It was supposed to be a 'soulful expression of art,' but honestly, I was just trying to impress a girl. My poem was a jumbled mess about lost love and regret, and the only thing that saved me was the fact that I recited it with such dramatic flair. I ended up winning... not for the content, but because the audience appreciated the performance. I think I still have nightmares about that night."

"Now that's impressive," I said, leaning closer. "Dramatic flair has its advantages. Who knows? Maybe you could have a second career as a spoken word artist."

"Only if I can bring Monty along as my hype man," he shot back, his grin infectious.

Suddenly, the air shifted, a chill creeping in as laughter faded into the background noise. A couple at the far end of the bar had fallen into a heated argument, their words punctuated by harsh gestures. My heart quickened, a reminder of the fragility of human connection, the unpredictability of emotions. It was a stark contrast to the warmth that had enveloped us just moments before.

"Do you think they'll be okay?" I asked, unable to tear my gaze away.

Max followed my line of sight, his expression turning serious. "Relationships can be fragile, like glass. One small crack, and everything shatters."

His words hung in the air, heavy with meaning. A knot formed in my stomach, an unwelcome reminder of my own scars. I hesitated, not wanting to darken the moment we had been enjoying. "Yeah, it's a tricky balance," I said finally, trying to keep my tone light. "But, you know, if we don't embrace the chaos, we might miss the good stuff."

Max turned to me, a spark in his eyes. "Exactly. So, let's promise each other—no matter how chaotic it gets, we'll keep this going. Just the two of us against the world. With or without iguanas."

"Deal," I replied, feeling a sense of warmth swell within me, the tension easing into something softer, something that felt like hope. In that moment, I realized that maybe, just maybe, opening my heart wouldn't be the end of the world. It could very well be the beginning of something beautiful.

The night wore on, and the bar buzzed with a delightful mix of warmth and familiarity, a sanctuary from the outside world. We had settled into a rhythm, trading jokes and stories, and I found myself leaning into the comfort Max offered like a soft blanket on a chilly evening. Yet, beneath the laughter, an undercurrent of tension simmered between us, something both exhilarating and terrifying.

Max was mid-sentence, recounting the time he accidentally joined a dodgeball league thinking it was an art class, when I noticed the flicker of something darker in his eyes. His smile faded, replaced by a shadow that flitted across his features like a passing cloud. It was fleeting, but enough to snag my attention.

"Hey, you alright?" I asked, my voice softer than intended, the playful banter faltering.

"Yeah, just..." He sighed, his gaze dropping to the table. "Sometimes the past has a way of creeping up on you, doesn't it?"

I nodded, feeling the weight of his words hang in the air between us. "It does. Like an unwelcome guest at a party, you think you've locked the door, but somehow they still find a way in."

He chuckled weakly, but I could see the tension beneath the surface. "I suppose that's why I've been avoiding relationships," he said, leaning back in his chair, arms crossed defensively. "It's easier to keep things light, to dance around the hard stuff."

"Light is great, but I don't think you can build something real on it alone," I replied, my heart racing as I dared to push a little deeper. "At some point, you have to face the music."

He looked at me, a mixture of appreciation and apprehension in his eyes. "You're right. It's just... I don't want to scare you away. I've been burned before, and it left scars. It's easier to keep my walls up."

"You won't scare me away," I said, surprised by my own conviction. "Honestly, I think it's a bit refreshing to see someone be real about their fears."

With a hesitant smile, he uncrossed his arms. "Okay, then. Here goes nothing."

As he began to peel back the layers of his heart, revealing the raw edges of his past, I listened intently. His stories were like brushstrokes on a canvas—some vibrant and alive, others muted and haunting. He spoke of dreams deferred, of nights spent wondering what might have been if life had unfolded differently. Each confession tugged at my heart, drawing me in closer, binding us in an invisible thread of shared vulnerability.

But just as I began to feel the warmth of his honesty wash over me, a loud crash interrupted our moment. A group of rowdy patrons stumbled through the door, laughter spilling out like champagne from a shaken bottle. They were boisterous, and one particularly loud voice shouted something incoherent, slicing through our conversation like a knife.

"Let's celebrate life!" he bellowed, raising a glass high as if toasting to the chaos he brought with him.

Max and I exchanged bemused glances, the atmosphere shifting abruptly. The laughter and lightheartedness of our conversation dimmed, replaced by a mix of annoyance and curiosity. I could see the frustration etched on Max's face; he was like a carefully tuned instrument suddenly jarred out of tune.

"Perfect timing, huh?" I quipped, trying to lighten the mood as I rolled my eyes at the interlopers.

"Just my luck," he said, a hint of a smile breaking through. "But let's not let them steal our moment."

As the raucous group settled at a nearby table, I felt a ripple of discomfort run through me. I wanted to continue our conversation, to delve into the depths of what was clearly a difficult subject for him. Yet, with the disruption, I could see the walls slowly creeping back up around Max, his expression shifting to something more guarded.

"Hey, want to grab some air?" I suggested, hoping to escape the chaotic scene unfolding before us. The bar's atmosphere had morphed into something too loud and intrusive, drowning out the intimacy we'd built.

"Yeah, I could use a break," he replied, and we slipped out the back door into the cool night.

The moment we stepped outside, the cacophony faded into a soft hum. The air was crisp, filled with the scent of freshly cut grass and the faint hint of smoke from a nearby grill. I leaned against the brick wall, feeling the rough surface against my back as I took a deep breath.

"Much better," I sighed, glancing over at Max. He stood beside me, his posture relaxed but his eyes still reflecting the turmoil that had surfaced moments before.

"Thanks for suggesting this," he said, shoving his hands into his pockets. "I needed a moment to recalibrate."

"Of course. It's nice to be out here where we can actually hear each other." I paused, searching for the right words. "I didn't mean to push you earlier. I just think it's important to talk about the tough stuff."

He met my gaze, his expression shifting to something more earnest. "You didn't push. I'm just... not used to being so open. It's a bit terrifying, honestly."

"Welcome to the club," I said lightly, trying to ease the tension. "I'm not exactly a master at vulnerability either. I've had my fair share of heartaches that make sharing feel like a gamble."

He nodded, his eyes darkening with understanding. "It's funny, though, isn't it? How we meet people when we least expect it, and suddenly they want to unravel all the carefully tied knots we've been holding onto?"

"Life really has a knack for throwing curveballs," I replied, feeling the gravity of our shared experiences weighing heavily on us.

The night stretched before us, punctuated by the distant sounds of laughter and music from the bar. I took a step closer, feeling the warmth radiate between us, a comforting reminder that we were navigating this complex emotional terrain together. But just as I felt a shift in the atmosphere—an invitation to explore deeper—the bar door swung open again, and the group from earlier tumbled outside, spilling laughter and chaos into our moment.

"Hey! You two lovebirds!" one of the rowdy guys shouted, pointing at us with a ridiculous grin plastered on his face. "Come join the party!"

Max stiffened beside me, his eyes narrowing, a mix of annoyance and uncertainty flickering across his features. I felt the moment slipping away, the air between us growing thicker with unspoken words.

"Not really our scene," I said, shooting them a smile that didn't quite reach my eyes.

But the loudmouth wasn't deterred. "Aw, come on! Live a little! Don't let the past drag you down!"

Max shifted, his discomfort palpable, and I could sense the wall coming up between us again.

"Looks like the iguana brigade is calling for you," he joked weakly, but the humor felt forced, and I could see the hesitation in his posture.

"Maybe we should head back inside," I suggested, glancing back at the bar. "I think our moment is officially over."

"Yeah, maybe," he said, though the reluctance in his tone was clear.

But just as we turned to make our way back, a shout erupted from the crowd, drawing our attention. "No way! You can't just leave like that!"

The world tilted as the tension escalated, and I felt a jolt of adrenaline. A fight seemed to break out among the rowdy group, a flurry of fists and bodies colliding as chaos erupted.

"Max!" I gasped, instinctively grabbing his arm, my heart racing. "We should go!"

But before we could react, a figure barreled toward us, and in an instant, everything shifted. I caught a glimpse of a familiar face amidst the turmoil—a face I thought I'd left behind. A face that carried the weight of my past and everything I had tried to escape.

"Julia?" The voice was unmistakable, laced with disbelief and something darker.

I froze, my heart plummeting into my stomach as I faced the ghost I had hoped never to see again.

Chapter 5: A Glimpse of Hope

The rain lashed against the window with a rhythmic insistence, each drop creating a symphony that blended perfectly with the faint hum of chatter in the café. I nestled deeper into the cushy embrace of the worn leather armchair, its creaking frame a gentle reminder of the stories it had witnessed. The warmth of the mug cradled in my hands seeped into my fingertips, melting away the chill that had settled in my bones since the moment I stepped into this intimate haven. The café was adorned with mismatched furniture and eclectic artwork, a cozy maze of corners where conversations thrived like the wild plants creeping up the windowsills. Outside, the world was a tempest; inside, it felt like a sanctuary, fortified by laughter and the sweet aroma of pastries baking in the oven.

Across from me, Evan leaned forward, his dark hair falling into his eyes, and a mischievous grin stretching across his face as he recounted an absurd encounter he'd had with a client during his last gallery showing. "You know, I thought I'd prepared for every possible question, but then she asked me if the painting could talk, what would it say?" His eyes twinkled, and I couldn't help but join in his laughter. "What was I supposed to say? 'It would probably tell you to get a grip and buy me already'?"

I burst out laughing, feeling a delightful warmth spread through me. His passion for art was contagious, igniting something in my chest that I hadn't felt in a long time. I wanted to reach across the table, take his hand, and assure him that his work mattered. That his vision, his vibrant strokes of paint, could change the world in small but meaningful ways. "What would your painting say?" I asked, genuinely curious.

Evan paused, his expression shifting to one of contemplation. "Maybe it would tell stories. About the people who view it, the emotions it evokes. Each layer of paint a new chapter." There was a depth to his words, a hint of vulnerability that invited me to peel back the layers of his persona. I felt a sudden urge to share my own secrets, my dreams and fears, in that warm bubble of intimacy we'd spun around ourselves. But before I could, the café door swung open, and the wind howled in, a frigid reminder of the storm still raging outside.

With the chaotic sounds of rain clattering on the pavement, my phone buzzed violently against the wooden table, shattering the moment like glass underfoot. I glanced down at the screen, my heart sinking as my ex's name flickered to life. "I should—" I started, but Evan's expression turned serious, his smile faltering as he watched my hesitation.

"Do you need to take that?" His tone was casual, but the concern in his eyes was palpable, and suddenly, the air felt thick with unspoken words.

"It's... it's my ex." I winced, the sound of his name sending a ripple of dread through me. "I really don't want to talk to him, but—"

"Hey," Evan interrupted gently, "if it's important, you should answer. But if it's just him wanting to rehash old drama, maybe you should just—"

"Ignore it?" I finished, a nervous laugh escaping my lips. "Sounds easier said than done."

The phone buzzed again, a stark reminder of the tangled past I was trying so hard to escape. I picked it up reluctantly, my heart racing as I swiped to answer. "Hello?" I greeted, keeping my voice steady despite the wave of anxiety crashing over me.

"Where the hell have you been?" His voice was gruff, the kind of tone that could cut through glass. The warmth of the café dimmed, shadows stretching across the walls as memories I had tried to bury bubbled to the surface.

"I've been busy," I replied, keeping my tone measured. "I don't think we need to do this."

"But we have to. You can't just disappear when things get tough." His words were laced with frustration, and I could almost see his scowl through the phone.

"Listen, I'm not disappearing; I'm moving on." I felt the urge to hang up, to toss my phone into the storm outside and reclaim my peace, but the thread of our history kept me rooted.

"Moving on? Really? You think running away will solve anything?"

I could hear the sharpness in his voice, the way he twisted my words like a knife. "This isn't about running away. This is about me finally standing up for myself." The conviction in my voice surprised even me, but Evan's gaze held me steady, a silent support that buoyed my resolve.

"Standing up? You call this standing up? You're just hiding," he shot back, a taunt that tugged at the frayed edges of my patience. "You can't pretend everything is okay when it's not."

"Stop," I snapped, anger flaring in my chest. "You don't get to decide what's okay for me anymore. I'm not your punching bag."

With a final surge of defiance, I ended the call, my heart racing as I set the phone down, the sudden silence ringing in my ears. I met Evan's gaze, his expression a mix of concern and admiration. "Sorry about that," I murmured, suddenly feeling exposed. "I didn't mean to—"

"Hey," he interrupted softly, leaning forward, "you stood up for yourself. That's huge. You should be proud."

The weight of his words settled over me like a warm blanket, the storm outside now a distant memory as I focused on the flicker of determination in Evan's eyes. The café, with its cozy nooks and charming imperfections, transformed into a safe haven, each moment we shared reinforcing the bond we were beginning to forge. Perhaps, just perhaps, this was a turning point, a glimpse of hope amidst the chaos of my past.

The tension from the call hung in the air like a thick fog, palpable and unsettling. I forced myself to take a deep breath, inhaling the rich aroma of cocoa and freshly baked croissants that wafted around us, hoping to ground myself in the moment. Evan leaned back in his chair, his brow slightly furrowed, an expression of concern mingled with admiration still lingering in his eyes.

"Do you want to talk about it?" he asked, his voice low and soothing. "I mean, if you're up for it."

I considered his offer for a moment, feeling the warmth of our earlier laughter slip through my fingers. "Honestly, I don't think talking would help much. It's just the same old story. He thinks I should still care about his opinions and choices like I did when we were together."

Evan nodded, his expression shifting to one of understanding. "Relationships can be like an old sweater, you know? Cozy but full of holes and a little frayed at the edges. Sometimes, you've just got to decide whether to keep wearing it or toss it."

I chuckled, the image of a lumpy, old sweater popping into my mind. "I think I'd rather set it on fire."

"Now there's a dramatic exit," he teased, his eyes dancing with mischief. "But let's be real; it's not so easy, is it? Especially when they keep trying to sneak back in, like that annoying email from your gym you never wanted in the first place."

"Or like a bad sequel to a movie that should have ended after the first one," I replied, warming to the playful banter. "Nobody asked for this version."

"Exactly! Who even thought that was a good idea?" He laughed, and for a moment, the remnants of my earlier discomfort faded away, replaced by a lightness that made me feel almost buoyant. I watched him as he spoke, his hands animatedly illustrating his points, the way he engaged with the world around him igniting something deep within me, a spark I'd thought had long since extinguished.

Just then, a loud crash erupted outside as a gust of wind sent an umbrella tumbling through the air. We both turned to watch as it spiraled down the street, a chaotic dance of fabric and metal, and I couldn't help but laugh. "See? Even the weather can't keep itself together today."

"Right? It's like nature decided to take a personal day. Maybe it's on the verge of a meltdown like the rest of us." He smiled, and I felt a warmth unfurl in my chest, like spring thawing the last remnants of winter.

"Maybe we're all just trying to weather the storm in our own way," I mused, glancing out at the rain-soaked street. "Figuratively and literally."

"Speaking of weathering storms," Evan said, his voice suddenly serious, "how do you really feel about it? I mean, about your ex and everything."

I hesitated, contemplating my next words carefully. The truth was, I felt raw and exposed, still entangled in the emotions of our past, but beneath that was a flicker of defiance. "I guess I'm just tired of living in his shadow. It's like I've been stuck on pause while he's off doing his thing, thinking I'm still pining for him. I need to reclaim my life."

"Reclaim it?" he echoed, tilting his head as if to draw out the weight of the words. "That sounds... empowering."

"It does, doesn't it?" I smiled, feeling the affirmation wash over me. "But the thing is, it's a little scary, too. What if I reclaim it and then realize I have no idea what to do next?"

"Then you'll figure it out," he replied confidently. "I mean, when you're lost in a new city, you don't just sit down in the middle of the street and give up, right? You grab a map or, you know, a local coffee and ask someone for directions."

"Ah, yes, because I'm sure the barista at the corner café has the perfect life advice," I said, rolling my eyes playfully.

"Hey, you never know! They might just hit you with some profound insight about the meaning of life while steaming your milk."

I laughed again, a genuine sound that felt like a long-forgotten melody. "You've got a point there. Maybe I should start carrying a map and asking baristas for life advice."

"Or, you could just keep hanging out with me," he suggested with a grin that made my stomach flutter. "I'm full of surprises. Plus, I make a mean hot chocolate."

As the rain continued its rhythmic serenade, I felt a weight lift. The café transformed around us, a vibrant cocoon against the chaos outside. I found myself leaning in closer, the connection between us forging a bond that felt both exciting and terrifying.

"I think I'd like that," I said softly, my heart racing as I realized how much I wanted to see where this could lead. "Hanging out with you, I mean."

Evan's smile widened, but before he could respond, the door swung open again, a rush of cold air and an unfamiliar figure stepping inside. The newcomer was drenched, shaking off the rain like a dog, and as he turned toward us, I felt my heart drop.

"Hey there, remember me?" My ex's voice cut through the cozy atmosphere like a knife, and the warmth I had just begun to bask in evaporated in an instant. The smile fell from Evan's face, and I could only stare at the man who had walked back into my life, uninvited and unwelcome.

"What are you doing here?" I managed to ask, my voice tinged with disbelief as my heart raced once more. "You can't just show up like this."

"I needed to talk to you. It's important." He stepped closer, and I instinctively shifted in my seat, trying to create some distance.

Evan straightened up, his demeanor shifting to one of protectiveness, and I felt a surge of gratitude for his presence, a reminder that I wasn't alone in this moment. "I think she made it pretty clear she doesn't want to talk," Evan interjected, his tone firm, a wall of support behind me.

"You're not helping," my ex shot back, annoyance flashing in his eyes as he turned to Evan. "This is between me and her."

"Yes, and I think you should respect that boundary," Evan replied, his voice steady.

The air was thick with tension, and I could feel my heart racing as I weighed my options. This was my chance to confront the ghosts of my past, to stand firm in the new life I was trying to carve out for myself. The café, the laughter, the warmth—all of it was on the line, and I couldn't let it slip away again.

The atmosphere shifted palpably as my ex stepped further into the café, shaking off the remnants of the storm like a cat after a bath. My stomach twisted with an odd mix of dread and defiance. I could feel Evan tense beside me, his presence a steady anchor in the swirling chaos of my emotions. I drew a deep breath, grounding myself with the lingering taste of hot chocolate on my lips, trying to summon the courage I so desperately needed.

"Seriously, why now?" I shot at my ex, my voice trembling slightly despite my best efforts to sound composed. "Can't you see I'm busy?"

He glanced between Evan and me, an incredulous expression morphing into a smirk. "Busy? It looks more like you're hiding out. With him." The disdain dripped from his words like the rain cascading outside.

"Excuse me?" I retorted, every nerve in my body sparking. "I'm not hiding. I'm living my life, something you seem to forget I'm allowed to do."

Evan leaned forward, his eyes narrowing slightly, protective energy radiating from him. "Look, it's clear she doesn't want to talk to you right now," he stated firmly, his voice steady. "So why don't you just take a step back?"

"Who the hell are you to tell me what to do?" my ex shot back, his irritation simmering beneath the surface.

I could almost hear the clash of two bulls in a ring, and though my instincts screamed to retreat, I stood my ground. "He's someone who respects me," I said, forcing the words out as a declaration rather than an apology. "Something you've clearly forgotten how to do."

His expression darkened, and for a moment, I caught a flicker of vulnerability behind the bravado. "This isn't over, you know," he warned, his voice low. "You can't just walk away from what we had."

"Oh, I'm not walking away," I replied, my voice gaining strength with each syllable. "I'm running. Running far and fast from a life that stifles me."

The café had grown quiet, the murmurs of other patrons fading into a hush as eyes subtly flickered our way. I could feel the weight of judgment and curiosity resting on my shoulders, but I refused to let it shatter my resolve.

"Is that really what you want?" he pressed, his tone shifting from condescending to something that almost resembled concern. "To throw everything away like it meant nothing?"

"Everything you said meant nothing," I countered, the heat in my words bolstering my confidence. "It's not throwing away a life; it's reclaiming mine."

Evan shot me a look of surprise mixed with admiration, and I felt a surge of gratitude for his silent support. I glanced back at my ex, determination settling in my chest like armor. "And if you think showing up here is going to change anything, you're mistaken."

"You think you've moved on?" he scoffed, crossing his arms over his chest, a barrier I could feel even from across the table. "This isn't over until I say it is."

I could see the desperation creeping into his eyes, a man clinging to the remnants of a relationship he had taken for granted. But it was too late for that. I was done being the one who picked up the pieces while he walked away unscathed.

"I'm sorry," I said, my tone suddenly softer, laced with the finality of a door closing. "But I have no intention of going back. This is my life now, and I refuse to let you dictate it."

With that, I turned to Evan, whose presence suddenly felt like a shield, a bastion against the tempest I had just faced. "Let's go," I said, determination lacing my words. "We can find another place to escape this storm."

Evan's face broke into a supportive smile, but before we could rise, my ex took a step forward, his hand raised in a half-hearted attempt to grab my arm. "Wait! I just want to talk—"

But the moment had passed. I stood up, adrenaline coursing through my veins. "You've had your chance," I declared, my heart racing as I moved toward the door. "Now it's my turn to speak."

As we walked away, I could feel his gaze on my back, a mixture of anger and regret brewing behind me, but I didn't dare turn around. Outside, the rain had lessened to a drizzle, a thin veil that created a world of muted colors and soft sounds. Evan fell into step beside me, his energy palpable as we navigated the slick pavement, and I found myself stealing glances at him, hoping to read his thoughts.

"I didn't expect that," he said finally, his voice warm, filled with an admiration that set my heart racing anew. "You were incredible."

"Thanks," I replied, trying to keep my voice steady, but inside, I felt like a small fire had been ignited, flickering with potential. "I just... I've had enough of being walked all over."

"That was really brave," he continued, his tone serious. "Not everyone has the guts to confront their past like that."

"I'm not saying it was easy," I admitted, the rush of adrenaline beginning to wear off, leaving me a bit shaky. "But it feels good to reclaim my voice."

"Reclaiming your voice is a powerful thing," he remarked, his eyes glinting with sincerity. "So, what's next for you? Do you have a plan, or are you just going to see where the wind takes you?"

A playful smile crept onto my lips. "Honestly? I might just let the wind blow me toward the nearest bakery. I could use something sweet right about now."

Evan laughed, the sound rich and infectious. "Then I'm your guy. Lead the way to pastry paradise."

As we turned a corner, the cozy lights of another café flickered invitingly ahead, but before we could reach it, a familiar figure emerged from the shadows, standing under the awning as if he had been waiting for us. My heart dropped, dread flooding my senses as I recognized the silhouette.

Evan must have sensed my sudden tension because he glanced at me, confusion etched on his face. "What's wrong?"

I didn't have time to respond. The figure stepped forward, the streetlamp illuminating the expression that twisted my stomach into knots. My ex's words echoed ominously in my mind, and just as the figure called out my name, I felt the ground beneath me shift, the world around us teetering on the edge of chaos.

"Wait!" he shouted, and in that moment, I froze, heart pounding as the realization hit me like a wave. This wasn't over. Not yet.

Chapter 6: Echoes of Regret

The sun was setting, drenching the small café where I sat with Max in a cascade of golden hues. The scent of fresh coffee wafted through the air, mingling with the faint sweetness of pastries that seemed to whisper promises of warmth and comfort. Max was animated, his hands punctuating his words as he spoke about his latest hiking adventure, the way the earth felt beneath his feet and the thrill of conquering steep trails. I could feel my heart fluttering at his enthusiasm, an intoxicating blend of admiration and something deeper that I hadn't quite identified yet.

But as his laughter rang like a chime, a shadow fell over my mind. The image of Aaron, standing outside my door with his sheepish grin and the same piercing blue eyes that once felt like home, slipped into the forefront of my thoughts. I bit my lip, attempting to keep my smile plastered on my face as I chewed on the sweet, flaky croissant before me, but the buttery pastry was far less satisfying than the thought of escaping the turmoil in my heart.

"Hey, are you with me?" Max's voice broke through my haze, his brow furrowing with concern. He leaned closer, his gaze locking onto mine, and the warmth of his presence momentarily chased away the chill of my memories.

"Yeah, just... lost in thought," I replied, forcing a grin. "It's just so beautiful here. I love how the light hits everything at this hour."

"Beautiful, huh?" he teased, raising an eyebrow playfully. "I think you might be biased. I mean, look at me." He gestured dramatically, striking a pose that had me chuckling despite myself.

"Oh, right, the absolute embodiment of rugged charm," I quipped, taking a sip of my coffee to mask the tension tightening in my chest. "Just try not to let it go to your head."

Max rolled his eyes, but the glint of mischief in his eyes told me he enjoyed our banter as much as I did. Yet, as I laughed, a pang of guilt flickered within me. Every shared moment with Max felt tainted by the specter of Aaron's call, the weight of unresolved issues pressing down on me like a heavy blanket.

Just as I thought I might be able to push the memories aside, my phone buzzed violently against the table, pulling me from my reverie. The screen lit up, and I saw his name flash across it like an unwelcome sign. I hesitated, fingers hovering over the screen, heart racing as a wave of anxiety washed over me.

"Everything okay?" Max's voice was soft, laced with concern.

"Yeah, just... an old friend," I said, trying to sound casual. I swiped the notification away, but the knot in my stomach tightened. It felt wrong to keep the truth from him, but how could I explain the jagged pieces of my past without unraveling the fragile happiness we had built together?

"An old friend, huh? Sounds mysterious," he said, his smile wavering slightly as he tried to gauge my reaction.

I shifted in my seat, the chair creaking softly beneath me. "It's nothing I can't handle," I replied, a little too quickly. I didn't want to dampen the mood, especially not now, with the way the sun cast a warm glow around us, making everything feel like a fairytale.

"I don't know, I feel like you could use a little more mystery in your life," he teased, leaning back with a mock-serious expression. "But if this friend starts creeping around like some sort of ghost, I'd be happy to step in as your knight in shining armor."

His offer made me smile, but the ache in my heart lingered. Just as the light in the café dimmed, reality crashed back in with a vengeance. How could I let myself dive deeper into this burgeoning relationship when my past was still clawing at my heels?

"I appreciate the thought," I said, attempting to keep my tone light, "but this isn't a fairy tale. Trust me, you'd be better off saving your sword for someone else."

"Not a fairy tale, huh?" he said, feigning disappointment. "You've got the charming prince, a beautiful setting, and the scent of coffee in the air. Sounds pretty fairy tale-like to me."

"It's more like a rom-com with a complicated plot twist," I replied, a note of honesty slipping through. I felt the urge to confide in him, to share the weight of my struggle. "There's just... a lot going on in my head right now."

Max nodded, his expression shifting to one of understanding. "If you ever want to talk about it, I'm here. No pressure, just know that I care."

I felt the warmth of his words seep into the cracks of my heart, a balm against the cold dread that had settled in. "Thanks, Max. Really." I meant it.

Just as we were about to dive deeper into our conversation, the café door swung open, the bell tinkling above it. I looked up to see a figure stride in, and my heart sank into my stomach as Aaron stepped into view, his presence commanding the room with an unsettling familiarity.

Max's laughter faded as he noticed the shift in my demeanor. "You okay?"

I couldn't respond. Aaron scanned the room, and when his gaze landed on me, an array of emotions flickered across his face—confusion, concern, and that infuriating hint of charm that had once made me feel safe. My heart raced as I fought to remain composed, but my hands shook slightly on the table, threatening to betray the calm exterior I desperately tried to maintain.

I felt caught between two worlds—one filled with the promise of new beginnings, the other echoing with the regrets of the past. And as Aaron approached, a storm brewed within me, the distant rumble of confrontation on the horizon. I could almost hear the clock ticking down to the moment when I would have to choose which path to take, and in that instant, the scent of coffee turned bitter in my mouth, and the warmth of the café felt like a distant memory.

Max's expression shifted from playful to serious as Aaron approached, the air thickening with the tension I could almost taste. "You know him?" he asked, his voice low, but the edge of protectiveness was unmistakable.

I could feel my heart hammering in my chest, each thud reminding me that this was not just a bad dream but a reality that was rapidly unraveling. "It's... complicated," I managed, trying to sound casual, but the tremor in my voice betrayed me.

Aaron was only a few steps away now, his hands tucked casually into the pockets of his worn jeans, a semblance of nonchalance that was hard to read. A frown creased his brow as he took in the scene—me, sitting at a small table, the sunlight catching the rich mahogany of the café's interior, and Max, who was now staring at him with an intensity that made the air crackle.

"Wow, this is a surprise," Aaron said, forcing a smile that didn't reach his eyes. "Didn't expect to see you here."

"Yeah, well, I'm busy, you know," I replied, the words escaping before I could filter them. The sarcasm laced in my tone felt like my only defense mechanism, an armor against the vulnerability that Aaron had always managed to pierce.

"Busy? Looks more like you're having a date," he shot back, his tone teasing, but the bite of jealousy was unmistakable.

I felt Max stiffen beside me, his presence a comforting barrier, yet also a reminder of everything I was trying to protect. "This isn't what it looks like," I said, the words tumbling out in a flustered rush. "Actually, it is exactly what it looks like. It's none of your business."

"Hey," Max interjected, his voice calm but firm, "I think you should leave her alone."

Aaron's eyes narrowed, and for a fleeting moment, the room felt like it was teetering on the edge of a confrontation. "You don't get to tell me what to do, man. This is between me and her."

The tension was palpable, the café suddenly feeling much too small, the chatter of patrons around us fading into a dull murmur. I sensed the world shrinking down to this moment, the future hanging in the balance as I watched the two men in my life collide, the weight of my indecision crashing down like a wave.

"Aaron, please," I said, my voice barely above a whisper, but both men were locked in a silent standoff. I had to intervene before this spiraled further. "Let's just talk outside, okay? Just give me a moment."

Aaron's expression shifted to one of surprise, as if he hadn't anticipated my willingness to engage. "You're going to talk to him?" he asked, incredulous.

"It's my choice, isn't it?" I shot back, frustration creeping into my tone. "Look, you called me out of the blue. If you want to say something, let's not do it in front of my... friend."

Max's gaze flicked between us, assessing, a blend of curiosity and concern on his face. "Do you want me to come?" he asked, his voice steady, the offer genuine but laced with an underlying tension.

I considered it for a moment, the warmth of his support a tempting anchor, but part of me knew I had to face this alone, to reclaim my narrative. "No, I'll be fine. Just... give me a second."

Reluctantly, he nodded, and I could see the concern in his eyes, the silent promise that he would be waiting for me to return. With a deep breath, I stood up, my legs feeling slightly unsteady as I moved towards Aaron, my heart racing with uncertainty.

As we stepped outside, the cool breeze felt refreshing against my flushed skin. The chaos of the café faded, replaced by the gentle rustle of leaves and distant laughter. I could feel the tension radiating from

Aaron, an energy that pulled at the remnants of my old feelings, igniting old wounds that had barely begun to heal.

"What do you want, Aaron?" I asked, folding my arms across my chest defensively.

"I wanted to see you," he said, his voice earnest, his blue eyes searching mine for understanding. "I know I messed things up. I've been doing a lot of thinking, and I want to explain."

"Explain?" I echoed, incredulous. "After everything? You think you can just waltz back into my life and make it all better with a few words?"

"Listen," he replied, his tone shifting, frustration creeping in. "I know I hurt you, but I'm different now. I've changed. I just want a chance to prove that to you."

The wind picked up, swirling around us, and for a moment, I was torn between nostalgia and the newfound strength I had gained since we parted ways. "Change isn't just a word, Aaron. It takes time, effort—trust. You shattered that trust. How can I believe you now?"

"I know," he said, running a hand through his hair, a familiar gesture that made my stomach twist. "I'm not asking for everything back. Just... just a chance to talk, to show you. That's all."

A part of me wanted to believe him, to succumb to the comfort of our shared past. Yet another part, the stronger part, whispered reminders of sleepless nights and heartache, of lessons learned the hard way. "I don't know if I can do that," I admitted, my voice wavering as uncertainty clawed at my resolve.

"A chance? That's all I'm asking for," he pressed, desperation creeping into his voice. "I can't change what happened, but I want to try to make things right. You were everything to me, and I messed it all up."

"Maybe I was everything to you," I countered, my heart racing, "but you never considered what I needed. What I wanted."

A silence fell between us, the air thick with unspoken words and memories that clung like a fog. The weight of our shared history bore down heavily, and the longing for the past mingled with the hard-earned freedom I had fought to reclaim.

"Just think about it," he said finally, his tone softening, the hint of vulnerability cracking through the bravado. "I'll wait for you to decide."

With that, he turned and walked away, leaving me standing on the sidewalk, heart racing and thoughts swirling. I felt a whirlwind of emotions—confusion, anger, and a haunting whisper of hope. As I stared at his retreating figure, a sense of finality washed over me, but also a flicker of longing that I couldn't quite extinguish.

Turning back towards the café, I caught a glimpse of Max through the window, his eyes fixed on me with a blend of concern and curiosity. I took a deep breath, feeling the crisp air fill my lungs, steeling myself for the conversation that awaited me. I could sense the delicate balance of my past and present teetering dangerously, and as I stepped back inside, I knew I had to confront the echoes of regret that still clung to me like a shroud.

The moment I stepped back into the café, the vibrant hum of conversations and the rich aroma of coffee swirled around me like a comforting embrace. But I felt untethered, my thoughts still wrapped around Aaron's words. As I approached our table, Max was already waiting, his brows furrowed, worry etched on his handsome features.

"Hey, are you okay?" His voice was soft, yet it carried a weight that made my heart ache.

"I'm fine," I replied, too quickly. I settled back into my chair, my fingers fidgeting with the napkin before me. "Just a little... unexpected reunion."

Max leaned closer, his eyes searching mine. "Do you want to talk about it?"

"Not really," I said, shaking my head, but then a thought crossed my mind. "Actually, maybe I do. But can you promise not to roll your eyes?"

"Not my style," he replied, an eyebrow raised in mock offense. "I reserve that for bad jokes."

I couldn't help but smile, the tension in my chest loosening just a fraction. "So, about the bad joke level of my life..." I paused, gauging his reaction, then continued, "Aaron wants to meet. He says he's changed."

Max's expression turned serious. "Changed how? Is that even possible?"

"Good question," I said, swirling my coffee in a little circle. "Part of me thinks it's just the same old song, a new verse. But another part..." I trailed off, unsure if I should even voice the flicker of hope that had begun to rise.

"What does your gut tell you?" Max asked, his voice steady, offering me an anchor amidst the chaos of my thoughts.

"Honestly?" I leaned in, lowering my voice. "It's a battle between my heart and my head. My head says to run far, far away. But my heart? Well, it's an idiot that's always been a sucker for a good apology."

Max chuckled softly. "I know a thing or two about hearts being idiots. Trust me, they can be real drama queens."

"Drama queens, indeed," I agreed, laughter bubbling up and breaking the tension. "I just don't want to drag you into this mess."

"Too late," he said with a grin, leaning back in his chair. "I'm already knee-deep in your drama. Consider me your personal therapist with a dash of humor."

I couldn't help but appreciate his lighthearted approach, even as the shadows of my past threatened to engulf me. "What if I end up getting hurt again?"

Max leaned forward, his expression earnest. "Then you pick up the pieces, and I'll be right here, ice cream in hand, ready for a binge-watch session of whatever cheesy rom-coms you want."

The warmth of his promise wrapped around me, and for a moment, the darkness receded. "I guess I could use that," I admitted, feeling a little lighter. "But it's just so complicated."

"Life is complicated," he replied with a shrug, his smile infectious. "What matters is how you navigate through it. You've got this."

I wanted to believe him, wanted to push away the uncertainty that wrapped around my heart like a vine, threatening to choke the new beginnings that Max represented. Just as I was about to respond, my phone buzzed again on the table, a message flashing across the screen. I hesitated before glancing down, dread pooling in my stomach.

Aaron's name loomed large against the bright background, a stark reminder of the choice I was faced with. "He's asking if we can talk tonight," I said, my voice barely above a whisper.

Max leaned closer, the light from the overhead fixture casting shadows across his face. "What do you want?"

"I don't know," I said, frustration creeping in. "Part of me wants to tell him to shove it. The other part... well, it's a little more sentimental."

"Sentimental can be dangerous," he cautioned, his tone serious but tinged with the warmth of understanding. "You don't owe him anything. Remember that."

"I know," I replied, trying to sound more resolute than I felt. "But there's a nagging part of me that wants closure, some sort of explanation that might give me peace."

"Closure is overrated," Max said, his voice firm but gentle. "Sometimes you have to create your own. You don't need his permission to move on."

I met his gaze, the sincerity in his eyes grounding me. "You're right. It's just hard to let go of someone who once felt like home."

Max's brow furrowed slightly, a mixture of empathy and frustration flickering across his features. "And what about now? Is he still home? Or just a memory of what you thought was a safe space?"

That hit harder than I expected, and I shifted in my seat, contemplating his words. "You make it sound so simple," I said, the weight of my choices pressing down on me.

"Maybe it is, in its own way," he replied. "You deserve better than ghosts from your past haunting your present. Focus on what makes you happy now."

His sincerity washed over me, and the warmth of his words ignited something deep within. "And what if that happiness involves a messy confrontation?" I asked, glancing back at my phone.

"Then you handle it like the strong woman I know you are," he said, his gaze unwavering. "You've come this far. Don't let him pull you back."

Just then, the café door swung open with a creak, and a cool gust of wind swept through, sending a shiver down my spine. I glanced over my shoulder, the feeling of foreboding creeping in as I noticed a figure lingering outside, silhouetted against the dim light.

My breath caught in my throat as I realized it was Aaron, hesitating just outside the threshold. For a moment, time froze, and all the laughter and warmth from earlier seemed to evaporate, leaving behind a chilling void.

Max must have sensed the shift because he leaned in closer, his voice a low murmur. "What are you going to do?"

I could feel my heart racing, the weight of the decision pressing down on me like a leaden blanket. I wanted to run away, to escape the tangled web of emotions threatening to ensnare me once more. But something deeper urged me to stay, to confront the shadows that had haunted me for too long.

"I don't know," I finally admitted, my voice trembling slightly. "Maybe... maybe I have to face him."

Max's expression softened, understanding passing between us like a shared secret. "Just remember, whatever happens, you're not alone."

I nodded, steeling myself as I pushed back my chair and stood. My heart pounded as I made my way to the door, every step feeling monumental. With one last glance back at Max, who offered me a reassuring nod, I stepped outside, the cool air brushing against my skin.

Aaron's gaze met mine, and for a fleeting moment, I was reminded of the boy who had once made me laugh, who had held my heart in his hands. But that was gone now, replaced by the reality of the man before me.

"Hey," he said, his voice hesitant, almost fragile.

"Hey," I replied, my voice steady, despite the storm of emotions swirling within me.

As I opened my mouth to speak, the ground beneath us seemed to shift. An unexpected sound echoed in the distance—a high-pitched scream that cut through the evening air, sending a jolt of adrenaline racing through my veins.

"What was that?" Aaron and I spoke simultaneously, and our eyes widened in shared alarm as the tension between us crackled with new urgency.

Before I could process what was happening, chaos erupted, the world spinning on its axis as I stood at the precipice of my past and present, uncertainty clawing at my insides. I felt the familiar stir of panic rising, but it was quickly drowned out by the instinct to survive, to face whatever storm was coming my way.

Chapter 7: Painting Shadows

The air inside the gallery buzzed with excitement, a cacophony of laughter and hushed whispers, mingling with the faint scent of turpentine and varnish. I stood against the cool white wall, a glass of Merlot cradled in my palm, watching as Max navigated the sea of patrons with the grace of a seasoned dancer. His laughter rang out, clear and warm, drawing everyone in like moths to a flame. Each brushstroke he'd laid on canvas seemed to pulse with life, a vibrant symphony of color that pulled me in deeper.

Yet, with each gleaming smile he shared, my heart twisted tighter. What if my past, that tangled web of mistakes and regrets, slipped through the cracks of our burgeoning connection? My mind raced, wrapping me in a fog of uncertainty as I tried to breathe through the tightness in my chest. I clutched my glass a little too hard, the edges biting into my palm, reminding me that pain can often be self-inflicted.

I forced myself to refocus on the art, letting the colors wash over me—the fiery oranges and deep ocean blues danced together in chaotic harmony, depicting a landscape that felt both foreign and familiar. It was a world I longed to escape into, yet each brushstroke echoed my own struggles. Shadows loomed behind the brilliance, whispering of the darkness I was trying to shake off.

Max caught my eye, a playful spark igniting in his expression as he gestured toward a particularly vibrant piece—a riotous explosion of color that screamed life. "What do you think?" he asked, leaning closer, his breath a warm caress against my cheek.

"It's… raw," I replied, my voice barely above a whisper, as I caught a glimpse of my own reflection in the glass. "Like you let the chaos flow through you."

"Exactly!" His enthusiasm was contagious, and for a moment, I felt lighter, my worries retreating. But just as I opened my mouth to say more, I felt the hair on the back of my neck prickling.

The gallery's entrance swung open, and a hush fell over the crowd. In strolled Aaron, his presence commanding and unmistakable, the man who had once filled my life with both passion and pain. My heart raced, a wild thing trying to break free. The room felt smaller, the air thicker, as if the very atmosphere was charged with electricity.

"Aaron," I breathed, the name slipping past my lips like a forgotten prayer.

"Wow, look who decided to show up," he said, his voice smooth like honey, but with an edge that cut through the evening's joy. He scanned the room, his gaze landing on Max and me. A glint of recognition sparked in his eyes, and I felt exposed under his scrutiny.

Max, oblivious to the storm brewing within me, stepped forward, extending his hand. "Nice to meet you. I'm Max, the artist."

Aaron's smile widened, but there was a tension in his posture. "I've heard a lot about you." He turned his gaze back to me, and in that instant, the world around us faded. The room, once vibrant, now felt muted, the laughter and chatter transforming into a distant echo.

"Must be all good things," I said, forcing a chuckle, but it sounded hollow even to my ears.

"Depends on your perspective," Aaron replied, his tone laced with sarcasm, making my stomach twist. The warmth of the gallery felt suffocating, the walls closing in as his presence loomed over me like a dark cloud.

Max's smile faltered, sensing the shift in the air. "Well, I hope you enjoy the show," he said, his voice light, though his eyes darted between us, searching for the source of the tension.

I opened my mouth, desperate to explain, to bridge the gap between my past and present, but the words clung to my throat like dry leaves. Instead, I offered a weak smile and turned back to the art, as if it could offer me refuge.

"Isn't that one striking?" I gestured towards a canvas of swirling galaxies, hoping to distract him—and myself—from the conversation that felt poised to explode.

"Sure, if you're into the whole 'drowning in color' thing." His tone was teasing, but there was an undertone of something darker that sent a shiver down my spine.

Max chuckled, and I watched him, marveling at how he remained unshaken. "It's a reflection of chaos, isn't it? Beautiful yet unpredictable."

I could see Max's appreciation for the artwork, his eyes lighting up with every color, and for a fleeting moment, I felt buoyed by the shared passion. But Aaron's shadow loomed large, always lurking just at the periphery.

"I guess it's a bit like life," I said, trying to weave some levity into the moment. "You never know what you're going to get."

"Except in my case," Aaron interjected, his voice dripping with irony. "I knew exactly what I was getting into."

The weight of his words hung in the air, and I felt my heart plummet. It was an accusation veiled in humor, and I was left grappling for a retort that wouldn't reveal how deeply it pierced.

Max shifted, glancing between us, sensing the shift in tone. "Maybe we should all take a step back and appreciate the art." His effort to lighten the mood fell flat, and I could see the concern etched on his face.

"Sure, let's focus on the art," I said, forcing a smile. "There's plenty of it to appreciate."

As we wandered from one painting to another, I felt the tension simmer beneath the surface, a constant reminder of the unresolved past that threatened to suffocate me. Each piece of art felt like a mirror reflecting the chaos I'd tried so hard to escape.

But as the crowd swelled around us, laughter and conversations rising like a symphony, I knew I had to confront the shadows before they consumed me whole.

The air shifted again as Aaron's laughter mingled with the music of the evening, each note a reminder of our tangled history. I tried to concentrate on the bright hues of Max's paintings, searching for solace in the vivid strokes that told stories of love, loss, and everything in between. But with every passing moment, Aaron's presence loomed larger, his smile a beacon that both drew and repelled me.

"I can't believe you managed to drag yourself out tonight," Aaron said, his voice smooth as he leaned casually against a nearby pillar, arms crossed. "Thought you'd be hiding under a blanket, binge-watching whatever drama you've got on repeat."

I scoffed, trying to sound unfazed. "And miss the chance to watch you crash and burn at a fancy art show? Not a chance." I aimed for a light tone, but it dripped with tension, each word laced with the weight of history we both carried.

Max, oblivious to the brewing storm, leaned closer to me, his warm presence a shield. "You're doing great. Just keep breathing," he whispered, his eyes shimmering with encouragement.

I nodded, grateful for his support, but the moment was fleeting. Aaron caught the exchange, his brow furrowing in that way that suggested he was about to turn the knife just a little more. "So, you've moved on to the art world, huh? Looks like you've found yourself a new muse."

Max, ever the charmer, flashed a smile that could brighten the darkest corners. "Just trying to bring a little beauty into the world, one painting at a time." His casual confidence was like a lighthouse in a storm, yet the winds of my past threatened to capsize me.

"Beauty? Is that what you call it?" Aaron's tone was teasing, yet there was an underlying menace that made my heart race. "I suppose it takes a certain kind of talent to turn chaos into something people actually want to pay for."

I felt my stomach twist. "Art isn't about chaos; it's about perspective," I snapped, surprising even myself. "Sometimes you have to embrace the mess to find something beautiful. Kind of like life."

Aaron raised an eyebrow, the corner of his mouth twitching upward. "Ah, I see. So you've embraced the mess, huh? That explains a lot."

A laugh bubbled up from somewhere deep inside me, a genuine one, a rare moment of defiance against his barbs. "You should know all about messes, Aaron. You're practically a walking disaster."

Max chuckled, glancing between us as if witnessing a tennis match. "Wow, we should get a referee in here. Or perhaps a canvas. There's a lot of emotion in the air."

Before I could respond, a woman with a platinum bob and a dress that sparkled like a disco ball glided up to Max, her eyes sparkling with admiration. "Your work is breathtaking! I can feel the energy just radiating off the canvases," she exclaimed, oblivious to the tension simmering just a few feet away.

Max's smile widened, and I felt a pang of jealousy that surprised me. "Thank you! I believe art is meant to evoke emotion, to connect with the viewer in a way that transcends words."

As they engaged in conversation about his inspiration—his travels, his process—I felt like an intruder in their moment, my heart pounding as I silently willed Max to look back at me. But he was lost in the swirl of his art, his passion painting a picture that had nothing to do with me.

I stole a glance at Aaron, who leaned back, arms crossed, a smirk dancing on his lips as he watched the scene unfold. "You know, it's funny how quickly someone can move on. Must be nice to find a new source of inspiration," he mused, his voice dripping with sarcasm.

"Or maybe," I replied, turning to him, "it's just about not dragging old baggage into new places."

"Touché," he conceded, holding up his hands in mock surrender. "But let's be real; no one's perfect. You've got a past, and it's not something you can just paint over with pretty colors."

Max, hearing the edge in my voice, finally turned back to me, his expression softening. "Hey, are you okay?" He took a step closer, the warmth radiating from him like sunshine breaking through a stormy sky.

"Yeah," I said too quickly, forcing a smile that felt more like a grimace. "Just a little... conversation."

Max frowned slightly, concern etched across his brow, and I wanted nothing more than to wipe the worry from his face. "If you need a break, we can step outside for some air."

The offer hung in the air, a tempting escape. But the prospect of retreating felt like defeat, especially in front of Aaron, who would undoubtedly revel in my need to flee.

"Let's just enjoy the evening," I said, my voice steadier than I felt. "There's so much to see."

"Sure thing," Max replied, though the worry lingered in his eyes. "Just know I'm here if you need me."

As the gallery filled with laughter and the sound of clinking glasses, I tried to focus on the art. But Aaron's presence felt like a heavy weight on my shoulders, reminding me of every mistake, every regret that I couldn't escape.

"Did you see the one with the blue and gold?" I asked, pointing toward a large canvas that swirled like a sunset over the ocean.

"Yeah, it's nice," Aaron replied, but his tone lacked enthusiasm. "Though I have to wonder if it's really reflective of the artist's true self. Is it really art if it's not honest?"

"Art is subjective, Aaron," I shot back, my patience wearing thin. "It's about expression, not just reflection."

"Sure, but sometimes honesty hurts," he said, the shadows in his eyes hinting at deeper truths.

"And sometimes that honesty is what sets you free," I countered, my heart racing as I realized we were no longer just talking about art.

Max, sensing the shift in our dynamic, stepped in, his charm turning the conversation. "How about we get another round of drinks?"

"Good idea," I agreed, thankful for the distraction, though I felt the tension still crackling between Aaron and me like static electricity.

As we moved toward the bar, I couldn't shake the feeling that this night was more than just an art show. It was a reckoning, a collision of past and present, and I was caught in the crossfire, desperately trying to navigate the aftermath without losing myself in the process.

With each passing moment, I felt like I was straddling two worlds: one filled with vibrant colors and the promise of new beginnings, the other a murky pool of memories I was afraid to confront. As I stood there, waiting for my drink, I wondered how long I could maintain the delicate balance between these shadows and the light that was beginning to seep into my life.

The moment I turned away from the bar, drink in hand, the atmosphere thickened, weighed down by unspoken words and lingering glances. Aaron's presence flickered at the edge of my vision, an unwelcome specter haunting the bright canvas of my evening. He stood, arms crossed, watching me with a smirk that held all the arrogance of someone who thrived on discomfort. I forced a smile, attempting to wield it like a shield, but it felt more like a paper thin veneer that could be torn apart at any moment.

"Look who's making friends," he drawled, gesturing toward Max, who was deep in conversation with a couple nearby. "What a lovely little soirée you've managed to pull together. Very cultured."

"Don't you have someone else to bother?" I shot back, my voice sharper than intended. The heat of embarrassment crept up my neck, but there was no way I was letting him get to me.

"I'm just admiring your taste, that's all. Looks like you've upgraded from chasing shadows to basking in the limelight," he replied, his tone light but his words heavy with implication.

Before I could think of a suitable retort, Max turned back to us, a dazzling smile lighting up his face like the gallery lights reflecting off polished canvases. "Got us drinks! Cheers!" He raised his glass, oblivious to the charged atmosphere.

I clinked my glass against his, grateful for the distraction. "To art and new beginnings," I said, forcing my enthusiasm to the surface.

Aaron's eyes narrowed, a flicker of annoyance crossing his face. "New beginnings? Sounds like someone's eager to rewrite the script."

"Better than clinging to a faded draft," I countered, my heartbeat quickening. "Some of us prefer to turn the page."

"Oh, I'm sure you've always been the one to turn pages," he quipped, his voice smooth but laced with malice. "How many times have you changed the plot, I wonder?"

Max, ever the diplomat, intervened, raising an eyebrow. "Let's keep it friendly. We're here to enjoy art, right?"

The brief reprieve was welcome, but I felt the tension still simmering beneath the surface, waiting to erupt like a pressure cooker. I turned my attention back to Max, who was animatedly explaining one of his pieces to a nearby couple, the light catching the glint in his eye.

"Can you believe this color scheme? I was inspired by the way the sun hits the ocean at dusk," he said, gesturing to a painting filled with swirling waves of orange and teal.

"It's stunning," I said, genuinely moved. "You really capture the feeling of being there, the warmth and tranquility."

He smiled, a mix of pride and gratitude in his expression. "Thank you. That's what I aim for—transporting people to a different place, even if just for a moment."

As the night wore on, I managed to steal glances at Max, the way he breathed life into each brushstroke, how he made art feel like an intimate conversation. Yet, each time I caught Aaron's gaze lingering on me, the warmth drained from my chest, replaced with that familiar chill of insecurity.

"Max, do you have any plans for your next series?" I asked, genuinely curious, hoping to steer the conversation away from Aaron.

He took a sip of his drink, a glimmer of excitement lighting his eyes. "Actually, I've been toying with the idea of a collection inspired by dreams—how they twist and turn, blending reality and fantasy."

"Sounds intriguing," I replied, picturing ethereal landscapes painted in hues that didn't quite exist in waking life. "But aren't dreams notoriously fickle? They can be beautiful one moment and terrifying the next."

"Exactly! It's that unpredictability that fascinates me," he said, his passion infectious. "Like navigating through life, don't you think?"

Aaron leaned in, clearly unable to resist. "Navigating life is easy if you stick to the well-trodden paths. But sometimes, taking a risk leads you to more interesting places."

"Or more dangerous ones," I shot back, glaring at him, the underlying tension boiling over.

Max's brow furrowed slightly, catching the current of discord. "Hey, we're all friends here, right?" He looked between us, trying to smooth the ruffled feathers, but the damage was already done.

"Right. Friends," Aaron echoed, his eyes darkening. "Friends who know too much about each other, perhaps."

"Is there a point you're trying to make?" I asked, my voice steady but my pulse racing.

"I just think it's funny," he said, taking a deliberate step closer. "How quickly someone can pretend they've moved on, especially when they haven't truly faced what's behind them."

Max glanced at me, concern etched in his features, but I squared my shoulders, refusing to be cowed. "Some of us aren't afraid of our pasts. We're just ready to stop letting them dictate our futures."

"I hope so," Aaron replied, his smile predatory. "Because, you know, the past has a funny way of showing up when you least expect it."

The weight of his words hung in the air, heavy and oppressive. I could feel the walls of the gallery closing in, the vibrant art around us suddenly feeling claustrophobic, each canvas a reminder of everything I was trying to escape.

"I think I need some fresh air," I said, my voice tight as I turned away, trying to mask my rising panic.

"Let's go outside," Max said quickly, following me toward the door.

The night air hit me like a balm, cool and crisp, as I stepped outside into the world that felt so much larger than the suffocating tension inside. I inhaled deeply, the scent of rain-soaked pavement mingling with the faint aroma of blooming jasmine.

"Hey," Max said, concern woven into his voice. "Are you okay? I didn't mean to drag you into that mess."

"I'm fine," I lied, but the tremor in my voice gave me away. "Just… Aaron knows how to push buttons."

"He can be a bit much," Max agreed, leaning against the gallery's entrance, his gaze steady on me. "But you held your own in there. I admire that."

"Thanks. It's just hard sometimes," I admitted, shivering slightly in the cool air. "I thought I was past all of that."

"You are. You're standing here, right now, and you didn't let him get under your skin. That counts for something."

I smiled at him, warmth creeping back into my chest. "You make it sound so simple."

"It is simple. Just don't let him define your worth," Max said, his voice firm but kind.

"Easier said than done," I murmured, wrapping my arms around myself.

"True, but you're stronger than you think. And besides, I'm here," he added, flashing that charming smile that lit up the dark night.

Before I could respond, the gallery doors swung open again, and the chatter from inside washed over us like a wave. Aaron stepped out, his expression deceptively casual, but I could sense the storm brewing behind his calm facade.

"I think it's time to face the music, don't you?" he said, his voice smooth and unsettling.

I felt a rush of cold fear wash over me, the kind that made every instinct scream to run. "What do you mean?" I asked, my heart racing as I exchanged glances with Max, who straightened, ready to confront whatever came next.

"Just that your past isn't done with you yet," Aaron said, his smile widening like a cheshire cat. "And it's coming for you."

The words hung in the air, charged with ominous intent, and in that moment, I knew that whatever shadow I had tried to escape was about to collide with my present in a way I could never have anticipated.

Chapter 8: The Confrontation

The moment Aaron stepped into the café, the air shifted, thickening with unspoken words and memories I had carefully locked away. The doorbell chimed, announcing his presence like a herald of trouble, and I could almost hear my heart stutter in disbelief. He moved with that familiar blend of confidence and uncertainty that always made him feel so magnetic, but I wasn't prepared for the tidal wave of emotions crashing over me. My fingers tightened around the ceramic mug, the warmth barely enough to counter the chill creeping up my spine.

"Hey, can we talk?" His voice was a low murmur, filled with that same pleading tone that used to make my heart race. It didn't work this time. I stood frozen, my pulse a frantic drumbeat drowning out the soft jazz playing in the background. The scent of freshly brewed coffee mingled with the sweet aroma of pastries, but all I could focus on was the storm brewing between us.

Max, seated across the table, shifted slightly, his brow furrowed in confusion. His dark eyes, always so perceptive, darted between us, trying to gauge the temperature of the moment. I felt the weight of his silent support anchoring me. It was as if he was whispering, "You've got this." But did I? Could I really face the man who had once meant everything to me while sitting beside the one who represented my future?

I drew in a breath, trying to mask the chaos swirling in my mind. "What do you want, Aaron?" I managed to ask, my voice steadier than I felt. The question hung in the air, loaded with the gravity of our shared history.

His gaze flickered to Max, then back to me, and I could see the hesitation ripple through him. "I just—" he started, his words trailing off as if they were not enough to bridge the chasm that had opened up between us. "I know I messed up. I didn't mean to just disappear."

"You didn't just disappear; you ghosted me," I shot back, my voice sharper than I intended. "Without a word, without a thought for how it would affect me."

The corner of his mouth twitched, a faint ghost of a smile, and for a split second, I remembered the way he could charm the sun out of the sky. But then reality slammed into me with a force that almost knocked the wind out of my lungs. "I thought we had something real," I continued, feeling the raw edge of my emotions spilling over. "You were everything, and then you just vanished."

He ran a hand through his tousled hair, a familiar nervous gesture that used to endear him to me. "I was scared," he admitted, his voice barely above a whisper, the sincerity in his eyes almost disarming. "Things were getting serious, and I didn't know how to handle it. I panicked."

"Scared?" I echoed, incredulous. "So you decided to take the coward's way out? You left me to pick up the pieces of a life I thought we were building together."

His shoulders slumped as if my words had physically weighed him down. "I know I messed up, and I'm sorry," he said, desperation creeping into his tone. "I've changed. I've been working on myself."

A sardonic laugh escaped my lips, surprising even me. "Is that supposed to make me feel better? You think I'm just going to take you back because you've found a self-help book or attended a few therapy sessions?"

The tension thickened, a tangible thing that wrapped around us like an unwanted blanket. I caught a glimpse of Max's expression—a mix of confusion and hurt—as I hurled my emotions at Aaron like a reckless archer. This wasn't just about Aaron and me anymore; I was dragging Max into this chaotic mess, and I could see the shadows of doubt beginning to creep into his eyes.

"I'm not asking you to take me back," Aaron replied, his voice firming as if the words themselves were gaining weight. "I'm just asking for a chance to explain. I owe you that much."

"Explain?" I scoffed, crossing my arms in a defensive gesture that felt more like a shield than a barrier. "What's there to explain? You walked away when I needed you most."

The hurt in my own voice startled me, and I could feel the tears prickling at the corners of my eyes. This wasn't how I wanted to feel. I was supposed to be strong, resilient. Max had been my rock, the one who stood by me when everything else crumbled. But here I was, unraveling in front of my past, feeling like a ragged tapestry fraying at the edges.

Max shifted in his seat, breaking the tension like a sudden clap of thunder. "Look, maybe we should take a step back," he said, his voice calm but laced with an underlying current of frustration. "This isn't just between you two anymore. You need to consider how this is affecting everyone involved."

"Everyone?" I snapped, my gaze flickering back to Max, whose expression was a mixture of sympathy and resolve. "This is about me and Aaron. You don't get to decide how I handle my past."

"I'm not trying to decide anything for you," he replied, his tone softening. "But I care about you. I don't want to see you hurt again."

Hurt again. The words sliced through the air, a reminder of all the scars I had fought so hard to heal. I felt torn, my heart a battlefield of conflicting emotions. The specter of my past loomed large, but the warmth of Max's steadfastness pulled me back, urging me to stand firm.

I looked back at Aaron, my voice low but unwavering. "You think you can just waltz back into my life and make everything okay? You have no idea what I've been through since you left."

The tension hung in the air like a poorly executed joke, and I could almost hear the collective breath of the café patrons holding their breath as if they were all somehow invested in our mess. Aaron shifted, the muscles in his jaw tightening, and I could tell he was grappling with a blend of regret and resolve, but that didn't absolve him of the pain he'd caused. I glanced at Max, his eyes reflecting a cocktail of concern and something else—something I wasn't ready to unpack. It struck me then that we were standing on a tightrope stretched between my past and my uncertain future, and the slightest misstep could send everything tumbling down.

"You're right," Aaron finally said, his voice low but firm, as if trying to assert control over a conversation that was rapidly spiraling out of reach. "I don't expect you to forgive me just because I showed up. I just—I need you to know I didn't forget about you. Not for a second."

"Really?" I arched an eyebrow, folding my arms tighter across my chest, the gesture both defensive and dismissive. "Because it felt a lot like you forgot everything we built. You didn't just leave; you left a crater where we used to be. So forgive me if I'm not buying the whole 'I've been thinking of you' routine."

A flicker of something—shame, maybe—crossed his face, and for a heartbeat, I felt a surge of sympathy. It wasn't easy to confront your mistakes, especially ones that had left a scar like ours. But that sympathy crumbled under the weight of my memories, memories that played like a slideshow in my mind, each image sharper than the last. The laughter, the dreams we had shared, the plans that now lay in ruins.

Max cleared his throat, a sound that somehow carried the weight of a thousand unsaid words. "You know, this might be better if we—"

"No," I interjected, feeling a mixture of gratitude and frustration at his willingness to step back. "This is my mess, Max. I need to sort it out."

"Fine," Aaron said, his voice raising slightly, laced with irritation. "Then let's sort it out. Let's talk about what happened. Because I owe you that. I owe you everything."

I couldn't help but scoff, the bitter taste of disbelief coating my tongue. "You owe me? You think showing up and tossing around empty promises makes everything okay? You're the one who left. You didn't even bother to say goodbye." The accusation hung between us, each word a barb.

"I know," he replied, his voice cracking under the strain of emotion. "I know. And I can't change the past, but I can tell you that I'm different now. I've spent months trying to figure out who I am and what I want. I just—" He hesitated, his eyes searching mine, vulnerable. "I want another chance to prove it to you."

"Another chance?" I shook my head, a laugh escaping my lips that sounded more like a sob. "You think this is a game? That you can just come back and everything will magically fall into place like some poorly written rom-com?"

"Maybe I'm the fool for trying," he shot back, frustration leaking into his tone. "But dammit, I'm not ready to walk away without trying."

Max shifted in his seat again, and I could feel his internal struggle. He was here for me, yet caught in the crossfire of a war that I didn't want him to fight. I felt the need to protect him from my past, even if it meant shielding myself from it too.

"I can't do this right now," I finally said, my voice barely above a whisper, the weight of my words more profound than I intended. I turned to Max, seeking his support, his calm presence a refuge from the storm. "Can we just go?"

"Not yet," Aaron said, stepping closer, the intensity in his gaze flickering between determination and desperation. "Please, just give me a moment. If I walk away now, I'll regret it for the rest of my life."

"Life? You think you've got the market cornered on regret?" I took a deep breath, trying to ground myself in the chaos swirling within me. "You broke me, Aaron. You don't get to waltz back into my life and act like nothing happened. There are consequences to your choices."

The silence that followed felt heavy, thick with all the unsaid things pressing down on us. Aaron's face paled, and for a moment, I saw the flicker of the boy I once knew—the one who could make me laugh in the darkest of times, the one who had felt like home. But home had crumbled, and now I was standing in the wreckage, clutching onto a flickering hope that maybe, just maybe, I could rebuild.

"I'm here to take responsibility," he said quietly, almost pleading. "I know I don't deserve it, but I want to make it right. I'm ready to do the work if you'll let me."

"Work?" The word hung in the air like a taunt. "You think saying the right things and showing up makes it okay? I'm not a charity case you can rescue with your newfound wisdom."

"I'm not trying to rescue you!" he shot back, exasperation breaking through. "I'm trying to be honest. The last thing I wanted was to hurt you."

The honesty in his voice caught me off guard, and for a heartbeat, I felt the walls I had so carefully built around my heart start to tremble. "You should have thought about that before you left," I replied, trying to steady the ground beneath me. "You don't get to pick and choose when you want to care."

Max cleared his throat, his presence a steady flame in the flickering light of our confrontation. "Maybe we should take a step back," he suggested gently, sensing the intensity of the moment. "This is a lot, and I'm sure you both need time to process."

"No," I insisted, my heart racing. "I don't want to step back. I want answers, and I want to know why I should believe a word you say."

Aaron stepped closer, the vulnerability in his eyes mixed with determination. "Because I want you to know that I'm not the same person I was. I've been working on myself, trying to figure out how to make things right. I can't change the past, but I can show you I've changed."

The sincerity in his voice caused a crack in my defenses, and I could feel the swell of emotions threatening to spill over. Could I really let myself be vulnerable again? Would I be a fool to trust him after everything?

The air hung heavy with unspoken words, a thick fog of unresolved emotions swirling between us. Aaron's attempts at reconciliation dripped with sincerity, but beneath his earnest facade lay the remnants of a past that I had fought hard to escape. The late afternoon sun cast long shadows on the ground, but all I could see was the shadow of our history looming over me.

"Ashley, please," he urged, stepping closer, a hand outstretched as if to bridge the gap between us. "I never meant for it to end like this. I thought—"

"Thought what?" I interrupted, my voice sharper than I intended. "That you could just walk back into my life after disappearing? You left me, Aaron. You vanished into thin air, and I had to pick up the pieces on my own."

His expression faltered, a flicker of regret crossing his features. "I was scared, okay? Scared of what we could become. I thought I was doing the right thing by letting you go."

"Right thing?" The bitterness in my tone echoed like thunder in the silence. "You mean the right thing for you. You didn't think about how it would affect me. You didn't think about anything but yourself."

"Don't make it worse than it was," he pleaded, frustration creeping into his voice. "I was young and foolish. I thought it was a phase—"

"A phase? Aaron, you don't just get to label our relationship as a 'phase' and expect me to swallow that!"

Max shifted beside me, his presence a steady force. I could feel his tension radiating, but he remained silent, letting me take the reins of this storm. I didn't want him to feel responsible for the fallout of my past. But the hurt in his eyes spoke volumes, amplifying the turmoil swirling inside me.

"I'm not here to hurt you again," Aaron said softly, his voice almost a whisper. "I came back because I realized what I lost. You were my everything."

"Funny how you only realize that once it's too late," I shot back, my heart pounding. "I've moved on, Aaron. I've built a life without you. You're the ghost of my past, and I refuse to let you haunt me anymore."

He stepped back, visibly shaken, and for a moment, I thought he might just turn and walk away. But then he squared his shoulders, determination flashing in his eyes. "What if I told you I'm not the same person? That I've changed?"

"People don't just change overnight, Aaron. Change takes time. It takes effort. What makes you think I should just take your word for it?"

"Because I'm willing to prove it," he insisted. "I've done the work—therapy, self-reflection, everything. I know I messed up, and I don't expect you to forgive me right away, but I want a chance to show you I'm better."

The sincerity in his tone tugged at something deep within me, a faint glimmer of the affection we once shared. I had to admit, a part of me was tempted. But then I glanced at Max, whose steady gaze pierced through my conflicted heart. This wasn't just about me; it was about the life I was building with him.

"Don't you dare drag him into this," I warned, pointing at Max with an intensity that surprised even me. "This is between us, and you need to respect that."

Aaron's gaze shifted, and I could see the realization dawn on him. He had underestimated the bond Max and I had formed. "I get it," he said, a hint of bitterness creeping back into his voice. "You've moved on. But what if I told you that something bigger is happening? Something that could change everything?"

My heart raced. "What do you mean?"

"Someone's looking for you, Ash. And they won't stop until they find you. I thought you should know before it's too late."

My mind spun as the implications settled over me like a shroud. "What do you mean, looking for me? Who?"

"I can't say much, but I overheard some people talking. They were saying things that sent chills down my spine. They know about your past, and they're not just going to let it go." His voice was low, filled with urgency.

"Stop playing games, Aaron," I demanded, my voice wavering slightly. "What are you talking about?"

"I wish I was playing. I'm telling you the truth. This isn't just about us anymore. It's bigger than that. I didn't come here to disrupt your life; I came to warn you."

My pulse quickened, adrenaline coursing through my veins. I shot a glance at Max, whose brows furrowed in concern. "This doesn't make sense. Why would anyone be looking for me?"

Aaron hesitated, the weight of his next words hanging heavy in the air. "Because there's something you don't know about your family, Ash. Something you've been kept in the dark about. Something that connects you to this. If they find you—"

"What?" I pressed, my voice sharp and unyielding. "If they find me, what?"

"They'll want to use you. You're not just anyone; you're part of something much larger. And I don't know how deep it goes, but you need to be careful. You need to trust no one."

The ground beneath my feet felt unsteady, as if the very foundations of my life were crumbling. I opened my mouth to respond, but before I could form a coherent thought, a sound shattered the tension—a loud crash echoed through the alley, followed by hurried footsteps approaching from behind.

"What the hell was that?" Max asked, his voice steady yet laced with apprehension.

Aaron's eyes widened, and he grabbed my wrist, pulling me closer. "We need to go. Now."

As the footsteps drew nearer, panic surged through me. Everything I thought I knew felt like a fragile facade, and just as it threatened to shatter, the world plunged into chaos.

Chapter 9: Crossroads of the Heart

The aftermath of the confrontation left me reeling. I couldn't shake the look on Max's face when I had been vulnerable with Aaron. It was a blend of disbelief and something sharper, a hurt that sliced through me like the chill of the night air. Fear wrapped its icy fingers around my heart as I considered what I might have done. Had I pushed him away forever with my careless words? That thought weighed heavily, like an anchor dragging me down into the murky depths of doubt.

I slipped into the shadows of the bustling streets, the city a kaleidoscope of sounds and colors swirling around me. Bright neon lights flickered, bathing everything in an ethereal glow, making the familiar look almost alien. The laughter of strangers mingled with the distant honk of horns, creating a symphony of urban life that felt at once comforting and chaotic. I took a deep breath, allowing the scent of roasted chestnuts and warm pretzels from a nearby cart to fill my lungs, grounding me momentarily before the tidal wave of emotions crashed back in.

My feet moved automatically toward the Hudson River, a place where the world felt larger than my worries. The wind whipped through my hair, tangling it around my fingers, and I embraced the chaos outside, hoping it would drown out the turmoil within. Standing at the water's edge, I watched the river's dark surface reflect the city's skyline, the twinkling lights like stars scattered across a velvet canvas. The lapping water whispered secrets, urging me to make a choice, to find a direction in this winding path I was on.

The echoes of my confrontation with Max replayed in my mind. I had let my guard down with Aaron, and the consequences of that vulnerability had reverberated between us like a sudden clap of thunder in an otherwise clear sky. Max had always been my safe harbor, the one person who understood the layers of my past, yet here I was, risking it all. The thought made my heart race—was it worth it? The truth I had sought felt like a double-edged sword, cutting away the ties that bound me to the past but also threatening to sever the bond I had with Max.

As the water danced before me, a thought struck like lightning: perhaps I had to stop living in fear. The very idea of letting my past dictate my future felt like wearing shackles that bound me to memories I couldn't change. Yes, I had made mistakes—countless ones—but clinging to them felt more suffocating than liberating. Could I really find the strength to embrace love, even when it felt like standing on the edge of a precipice?

With a sigh, I glanced up at the moon, its silvery glow spilling over the surface of the water, illuminating the path ahead. A sudden determination surged within me. I couldn't control how Max felt about me, nor could I manipulate the tides of our relationship. All I could do was be true to myself.

A soft voice broke through my thoughts, pulling me from my reverie. "You look like you could use a friend." It was an older gentleman, his face crinkled in a way that suggested he had lived a life full of stories. He wore a woolen hat pulled low over his brow, and his eyes twinkled with a warmth that felt oddly familiar, like a scene from a favorite movie.

"Or maybe just a good distraction," I replied, a smile creeping onto my lips despite the heaviness in my heart.

"Distractions are good. Sometimes the heart needs a little break from the chaos." He leaned against the railing, gazing out at the river, his posture relaxed yet attentive. "What's troubling you, if you don't mind me asking?"

I hesitated, weighing the wisdom of a stranger against my own tumultuous thoughts. "Just... navigating some tricky feelings. You know how it is."

He chuckled softly. "Oh, I do. Love and its complexities can turn the most ordinary of lives into a Shakespearean drama."

"More like a soap opera," I quipped, feeling a lightness begin to unfurl within me. "One minute everything is blissful, and the next, it's all betrayal and misunderstandings."

He nodded knowingly, his gaze still fixed on the river. "Every good story has its twists. What matters is how you navigate them. Do you want my advice?"

I shrugged, the night air invigorating, as I leaned closer to hear him better. "Sure, I'm all ears."

"Don't be afraid to leap. You might fall, but you might also find wings you never knew you had." He paused, glancing at me with a twinkle in his eye. "And remember, every good leap requires a proper run-up. Think about what you want, not just what you fear losing."

I absorbed his words, each syllable resonating deep within me. It was as if he could see through the fog that clouded my mind, illuminating the path I had to take. "Easier said than done," I muttered.

"True, but sometimes the heart knows what the mind can't accept. Trust it."

As I watched him turn back to the river, something shifted within me. I realized he was right; my heart was a compass, and perhaps it was time to listen more closely. Would Max be receptive to my honesty, or had I already ruined my chances? Only one way to find out, I thought, steeling myself for what lay ahead.

With newfound resolve, I turned my gaze back to the water, feeling the cool breeze against my skin. The city around me pulsed with life, and I was no longer just an observer. I was ready to step forward, to embrace the uncertainty ahead, armed with the belief that love, messy and complicated as it may be, was worth every leap of faith.

The moment I stepped away from the river, a curious urgency propelled me back into the heart of the city. My feet moved with purpose, each step igniting a flicker of determination that had been dimmed by doubt. I wove through the streets, my surroundings blurring into a vibrant tapestry of sound and color, but the only thing that truly anchored me was the thought of Max.

I remembered the way he smiled, that lopsided grin that could shift my whole day from dull to dazzling in an instant. The memory was bittersweet now, laced with the tension of what had happened between us. As I made my way to the little Italian café we often visited, I wondered if I was chasing a ghost of our connection, or if it still flickered beneath the surface, waiting for me to stoke the flames.

The aroma of fresh basil and garlic wafted through the air as I pushed open the café's door, the bell jingling a soft welcome. I spotted a corner table, the perfect little nook for a heart-to-heart, and settled into the chair, hoping the familiarity of the place would soothe my jangled nerves. I ordered a cappuccino, watching the barista craft the foam art like it was some kind of magic. A heart appeared in the foam, and I couldn't help but chuckle softly. If only love were that easy to brew.

My phone buzzed on the table, and my heart raced as I glanced down. A message from Max. The words were simple yet electrifying: Can we talk? Just the thought of his voice sent warmth flooding through me, but I hesitated, the weight of my vulnerability crashing back. What would I say? How would I explain everything I was feeling without sounding like a walking contradiction?

Before I could spiral too deep, I typed back, Yes. Where? I tapped my fingers anxiously against the table, the rhythm matching my racing heart.

A few moments later, he replied, The park near your place in thirty?

I took a steadying breath. The park was our sanctuary, a place where laughter had danced with the rustling leaves, where our most profound conversations had unfolded beneath the canopy of trees. It felt like a good choice, yet the memory of our last encounter there played in my mind like a film loop—full of laughter that faded into tension.

The minutes ticked by slowly, and my cappuccino turned lukewarm, the foam losing its charm as I fidgeted. As I prepared to leave, a sense of resolve settled in. I would go in with my heart open, no walls, just honesty. If this was a leap, then I would fly or fall gracefully, but I wouldn't let fear anchor me down.

The walk to the park felt like an eternity, each step echoing the dialogue I rehearsed in my mind. When I finally arrived, I spotted Max sitting on a bench, the fading light casting a soft glow around him, giving him an almost ethereal quality. My heart stuttered at the sight, a pang of longing crashing through me. He looked up as I approached, and our eyes locked. The world around us faded, leaving just the two of us, suspended in a moment filled with unspoken words.

"Hey," I said, my voice steady despite the nervous flutter in my stomach.

"Hey." He shifted, his expression a mix of hope and uncertainty, and I knew he felt it too—the tension crackling in the air between us.

We both sat in silence for a moment, the sounds of children playing in the distance mingling with the rustle of leaves overhead. The sun dipped lower, painting the sky in shades of pink and orange, a perfect backdrop for a heart-to-heart.

"I've been thinking about what happened," I started, breaking the stillness, my heart thumping loudly in my ears. "And I know I messed up. I didn't mean to…"

"Don't. Just let me say something first," he interrupted, his voice firm but gentle. "I was hurt when I saw you with Aaron. But I realized it wasn't just about that moment. It was about my own insecurities creeping in. I'm sorry if I made you feel like you had to hide from me."

His words hit me like a cool breeze on a sweltering day, refreshing yet unsettling. "Max, I never wanted to hide. You have to understand, I was trying to figure things out on my end too. Being open is terrifying for me. I don't want to lose you."

He leaned forward, the distance between us closing, as if we were bridging the gap of misunderstanding. "Then let's not do that. Let's just be honest, even if it's messy. I don't want to dance around each other anymore."

"I like the idea of honesty," I said, smiling faintly, even as nerves twisted in my stomach. "It's the execution I find daunting."

"Just remember, even if we stumble, we're in this together." He reached across the space between us, his hand hovering just above mine.

With a deep breath, I reached out, letting my fingers brush against his. The contact sent a wave of warmth coursing through me, igniting the flicker of hope that had dimmed in the wake of our previous confrontation. "I care about you, Max. And I want to explore what this is, what we could be. But I need to be clear about my past. It's... complicated."

"Complicated can be good. Complicated means there's depth." He gave me a reassuring smile that felt like sunlight breaking through clouds. "I'm here for all of it—the good, the bad, and the complicated. Let's tackle it together."

In that moment, with the sun setting behind us and a cool breeze carrying the scent of blooming flowers, I felt the weight of my fears begin to lift. Maybe it wouldn't be easy, but this connection we shared was worth every leap into the unknown. As I gazed into his eyes, I knew we were at a crossroads, but this time, I wouldn't be afraid to take the path that led toward him. Together, we could navigate the twists and turns ahead, with honesty as our compass.

The warmth of Max's hand enveloped mine, a gentle reminder that we were still anchored together amidst the uncertainty swirling around us. The park felt alive, as if it were breathing in sync with our budding connection. As the last rays of sunlight dipped below the horizon, shadows stretched across the grass, wrapping us in a cocoon of intimacy.

"I mean it," Max said, his voice steady but low. "I want to know everything—the good, the bad, the chaotic. I'm not going anywhere unless you push me away."

My heart fluttered at his words. "I don't plan on pushing you away. I'm just... I'm scared. My past is messy, and I don't want to drag you into it."

"You won't drag me anywhere. I'm here because I choose to be." He paused, taking a breath, his gaze searching mine. "I want to understand the parts of you that make you... well, you."

I took a moment to gather my thoughts. The air between us crackled with honesty, and I felt compelled to share the shadows that haunted me. "When I was younger, I had a relationship that went south. It shattered my trust. I let someone in, and when they left, it felt like they took a part of me with them. I've been trying to reclaim that piece ever since."

Max nodded, his expression serious. "That sounds rough. But you're not that same person anymore, right? You've grown, and you've learned. That experience shaped you, but it doesn't have to define you."

"I know that intellectually," I admitted, biting my lip. "But emotionally? That's another story. Every time I let someone close, I can't help but hear that voice in my head telling me to run before it gets too real."

"Then let's take it slow. No running, just walking. Together."

His words made my heart swell, a quiet promise that perhaps this time would be different. "Okay," I said, my voice barely above a whisper. "Together sounds nice."

Just as we were settling into a comforting silence, the shrill ring of my phone pierced the moment. I fumbled in my pocket, the sound jarring against the tender atmosphere. I pulled it out to see Aaron's name flashing on the screen. The reality of the situation crashed down on me, and my stomach tightened.

"I should probably—"

"Answer it," Max said, his eyes never leaving mine. "You can't avoid your past forever."

With a reluctant nod, I swiped to answer. "Hey, Aaron." My voice wavered, the name feeling foreign on my lips as I glanced at Max, who wore an inscrutable expression.

"Hey! Sorry to bother you. I just wanted to check in. Things got a little crazy after you left," Aaron said, his tone light but there was an undercurrent of something I couldn't quite place. "We need to talk about the project. Can we meet up?"

I could feel Max's presence beside me, his body tense as he studied my reaction. "Um, sure. When were you thinking?"

"How about tomorrow afternoon? I'll bring the updates, and we can brainstorm a bit."

"Sounds good," I said, trying to keep my voice steady.

"Great! Looking forward to it. See you then!" With that, he hung up, leaving me staring at my phone as if it were a live grenade.

"What was that about?" Max asked, his voice edged with curiosity, or perhaps something sharper.

"It's about work," I said, my voice barely above a whisper. "We've been collaborating on a project, and he wants to discuss some updates."

Max's jaw tightened, the atmosphere shifting like storm clouds rolling in. "And how does that feel for you? Do you want to meet him?"

I felt trapped in a web of my own making, the past and present colliding in a way that was both confusing and suffocating. "I... I don't know. I need to figure out how to handle this without making things worse."

Max shifted slightly, his brows furrowing. "What do you mean by that? You're not obligated to meet him, are you?"

"No, but he's part of my work. And—" I stopped, realizing I was spiraling. "I don't want to hide from the people in my life just because I'm afraid of what they might think."

His expression softened, and he leaned closer. "You're not hiding anything from me, but if Aaron makes you uncomfortable, you need to voice that."

"I know, but it's complicated. I don't want to hurt him, especially after everything."

Max let out a frustrated sigh, running a hand through his hair. "Then maybe you need to be upfront with him about how you feel. You're not responsible for his reactions."

The weight of his words settled on my shoulders, and I glanced away, trying to gather my thoughts. "You're right. I can't keep dancing around this. But what if it doesn't go well?"

"Then you deal with it together, like we said." His tone was firm, an anchor amidst the storm brewing in my heart.

The tension hung in the air, thick and electric, as I wrestled with my feelings. Suddenly, the sounds of the park—laughter, rustling leaves, the distant sounds of traffic—seemed to fade, and the world shrank to just the two of us.

"What if I tell him I need space?" I asked, my voice trembling slightly.

Max nodded, his expression softening again. "Then you tell him that. You deserve to set boundaries. You're not the villain in your own story."

I took a deep breath, feeling a flicker of resolve light within me. "Okay, I can do that. But what about us? I don't want this to affect what we're building here."

Max hesitated, his gaze searching mine. "We can't control how others react, but we can control how we communicate with each other. I'm not going anywhere."

Just as I began to feel a sense of calm returning, the park was suddenly enveloped in a strange hush. The laughter dimmed, the leaves stilled, and a shadow fell over us. I turned to see a figure approaching, a silhouette against the fading light. My breath caught in my throat as the figure drew closer, and I realized it was someone I hadn't expected to see.

"Hey there!" the stranger called, a wide grin spreading across their face. "Long time no see!"

The familiar voice sent a jolt of recognition coursing through me, and suddenly, my heart raced for an entirely different reason. This was someone from my past—someone I hadn't seen in years and never expected to encounter here, not in this moment, not when everything felt so fragile.

"What are you doing here?" I blurted, half in disbelief, half in a panic that swirled inside me, threatening to upend everything I had just begun to rebuild.

Max shot me a questioning glance, confusion flickering in his eyes, but I couldn't pull my gaze away from the approaching figure, the shadows growing long and foreboding. The choices I had made and the ones I would now face felt suddenly as tangled as the branches above us.

"Just passing through," the figure said, a smirk playing on their lips. "Looks like I caught you at a crossroads, huh?"

The air shifted, tension thrumming like a plucked string, and in that moment, I felt the ground shift beneath me, leaving me teetering on the edge of everything I thought I knew.

Chapter 10: Threads of Connection

The scent of freshly brewed coffee enveloped me as I pushed open the door to the bistro, a delightful little spot nestled between a vintage record store and a quirky plant shop. Sunlight streamed through the windows, casting a warm glow on the rustic wooden tables that were scattered about like intimate conversations waiting to unfold. I took a moment to appreciate the eclectic decor—a mix of vibrant art and mismatched furniture, each piece seemingly chosen for its charm rather than uniformity. The chatter of patrons blended into a soft symphony, punctuated by the occasional clatter of dishes and the gentle hiss of the espresso machine.

I spotted Max sitting at a corner table, his dark hair tousled, and his deep-set eyes scanning the menu with that familiar furrowed brow. My heart did an unexpected flip; the sight of him grounded me in a way I hadn't realized I craved. It felt like discovering a hidden garden after wandering through a barren landscape for too long. I made my way over, and as he looked up, a smile broke across his face—one that was utterly infectious. It was like sunlight breaking through clouds, illuminating everything in its path.

"Hey there," he said, his voice warm, wrapping around me like a well-loved sweater.

"Hey," I replied, my own smile widening as I slid into the chair across from him. "You look like you've just stepped out of a music video."

Max chuckled, a sound that ignited something warm in my chest. "Thanks! I was aiming for 'casual yet slightly tortured artist,' but I'll take the music video. How about you? You look like you just walked off a Parisian street."

"I'll take that compliment too," I said, reaching for my water glass and feeling the coolness of the glass against my palm. "I just figured

I'd try to match the ambiance. It's not often I get to eat somewhere that feels like it has a personality."

"I know what you mean. This place is perfect. It's like the universe decided to throw in a little creativity with the caffeine." He paused, his expression shifting from playful to contemplative. "I'm really glad we're doing this."

"Me too," I replied, my heart racing a little as I remembered the tension that had lingered between us since that gallery night. "I've missed our conversations. They feel... easy."

"Easy," he echoed, his brow arched in a way that made me feel as if he were looking right through me. "That's a loaded word."

"Loaded how?" I challenged, leaning in slightly, eager to dive deeper into this unexpected dialogue.

"Well," he began, his voice dropping to a conspiratorial whisper, "'easy' implies there's no depth, no complexity. Life, love, everything in between... it's all tangled up like those cords behind your TV stand."

"Now you're just getting practical," I laughed, shaking my head at his analogy. "But I get what you mean. The messiness is where the real stories lie."

"Exactly. And you, my dear, have a story brewing." He leaned back in his chair, a smirk dancing on his lips. "Care to share?"

For a moment, I considered diving headfirst into the tumult of thoughts that had been swirling around in my mind since our last encounter. But as I met his gaze, I realized the chaos of my feelings was too muddled to articulate. Instead, I took a sip of my coffee, letting the rich flavor settle on my tongue, buying myself time to gather my thoughts.

"Let's just say life's been throwing me curveballs," I replied, choosing to keep it vague, unsure if I wanted to expose the intricate details of my heartache. "But I'm trying to embrace the chaos, you know?"

"Chaos has its charms," Max said, his voice softening. "You can always find a spark of creativity there, if you look closely enough."

"That's one way to see it," I mused, my mind racing through recent memories. "But sometimes, I feel like I'm just stumbling through the dark, waiting for someone to turn on the lights."

He studied me, and the silence stretched between us like an elastic band, taut with unspoken thoughts. I felt my breath hitch slightly as I glanced away, tracing the intricate patterns on the tablecloth. The moment was thick with tension, each second stretching into eternity until he broke it with a gentle nudge.

"Maybe we're meant to be our own light," he said, his voice steady. "You know, like the fireflies that come out in the summer. They may not illuminate everything, but they create magic in the darkness."

I couldn't help but smile at his analogy, the corners of my lips curling upward despite the turmoil swirling inside me. "I like that. But what if the fireflies are too dim to make a difference?"

"Then you add more fireflies. Light is contagious," he replied, his gaze unwavering. "You've got a spark, and I've seen you bring out that light in others. You just need to believe in it yourself."

The sincerity in his words struck a chord deep within me. My chest tightened as his compliment sunk in, pulling me closer to the edge of vulnerability I had been avoiding. It felt disarming, yet invigorating, to have someone see me so clearly.

"Maybe you're right," I said, my voice barely above a whisper. "But what if I don't know how to keep that light burning?"

Max reached across the table, his fingers brushing against mine, sending a jolt of warmth through me. "Then we'll figure it out together. That's what friends are for, right?"

His gaze held mine, and for a moment, everything else faded—the noise, the chaos, even the worries. It was just us, two fireflies flickering in a world that sometimes felt too dark.

The warmth of the bistro wrapped around us like a favorite blanket, but just as the aroma of freshly baked croissants danced in the air, so did the shadows of unspoken words linger between us. I could feel Max's thumb grazing my knuckles, a gentle reminder of his presence, yet the weight of my thoughts tugged at me, urging me to delve deeper into the currents that flowed beneath our laughter.

"Okay," I said, suddenly serious. "Let's talk about those fireflies. How exactly do we gather a swarm?"

Max leaned in, intrigued. "Well, first, we have to start with one. So, what's your spark? What's lighting you up these days?"

I hesitated, the question hanging in the air like a promise. "I've been working on a project. It's a bit ambitious, actually. I'm trying to create a community art program for local kids. Something to bring them together, you know?"

He raised an eyebrow, his interest visibly piqued. "That's brilliant! You've always had a way with kids. What's the theme?"

"Art and nature," I replied, animated now. "I want to take them outside, show them how to find beauty in the world around us. We could even incorporate photography. Imagine their eyes lighting up when they capture something they've never noticed before."

Max nodded, his gaze unwavering as he leaned back, clearly impressed. "You really care about this, don't you? It's like you're harnessing your own light to share it with others."

"Maybe," I murmured, my heart swelling with both pride and trepidation. "But it feels overwhelming at times. I worry about how to fund it, how to get the kids interested. I mean, there's a million ways it could go wrong."

"Sure, but you know what else? A million ways it could go right." He took a sip of his coffee, his eyes sparkling with enthusiasm. "You've always been a dreamer, but you also know how to make those dreams tangible. It's part of your charm."

"Charming?" I scoffed playfully, pretending to toss my hair over my shoulder. "I prefer 'visionary.' But don't let it get to your head."

"Too late," he grinned, leaning forward conspiratorially. "I'm not sure how to handle this newfound charm of yours. It's making me think I should start taking notes."

I laughed, the sound ringing out like a melody among the clatter of plates. Just then, the waitress glided over, her apron adorned with bright splashes of paint, a fitting reflection of the bistro's personality. "Can I get you two something else? More coffee? Dessert?"

"Absolutely!" Max replied, his eyes glinting with mischief. "How about a slice of your best cake? I think we need to celebrate this dynamic duo."

I shot him a playful glare. "Dynamic duo? Really? You're laying it on thick, aren't you?"

"Only because it's true." He winked at the waitress. "Two slices of your finest cake, please. We're forging a new path here."

As she left, I couldn't help but admire the way he effortlessly commanded the space around him. It was a blend of confidence and playfulness that made people gravitate toward him. I, on the other hand, was still figuring out how to shine in my own right.

"Speaking of paths," I ventured, leaning closer, "what's going on with you? I mean, besides charming the waitstaff and finding ways to deflect my self-doubt?"

He sighed, the sparkle in his eyes dimming momentarily. "I'm trying to find my way too, honestly. Work's been… complicated. You know how I've been juggling projects."

"You're still working at that design firm?" I asked, remembering our late-night discussions filled with excitement and aspirations.

"Yeah, but it's not what I expected. It's become this weird corporate machine that stifles creativity. I'm starting to think I need to break free. It's like being in a beautiful cage," he said, running a hand through his hair in frustration. "And I keep asking myself, what am I doing with my life?"

"Break free," I encouraged, feeling a spark of rebellion igniting within me. "You're too talented to stay stuck in a place that doesn't nurture your creativity. You deserve more than just a paycheck."

Max chuckled softly, a hint of appreciation in his gaze. "You make it sound so easy. Just 'break free' like I'm some sort of bird. What if I fall flat on my face?"

"Then you get back up," I said firmly. "But at least you'll be doing something you love, something that lights you up. And trust me, I'll be there cheering you on."

"Even if I take a nosedive?" he challenged, a teasing glimmer returning to his eyes.

"Especially if you take a nosedive," I countered, a grin spreading across my face. "That's when it becomes a great story!"

Just then, the waitress returned, two slices of vibrant red velvet cake perched on her tray. "Here you go, one for each firefly," she said with a wink before placing the plates down.

Max's eyes widened in delight. "Wow, this looks incredible. Almost too good to eat—almost."

"You're such a foodie," I teased, grabbing my fork and eyeing the frosting with an intensity that would make a detective proud. "I swear, you have a food mood."

"It's a talent," he said, taking a bite with dramatic flair. "This is heavenly. The perfect amount of sweetness. I'm convinced dessert can fix anything."

"Dessert and a good friend," I mused, savoring my own bite. "Who needs therapy when you have cake and a charm-filled companion?"

"Now you're just buttering me up for more support with your art project," he said, playfully narrowing his eyes at me.

"Guilty as charged," I admitted with a mock-serious expression. "But I think you secretly enjoy being my cheerleader."

"Only because you keep it interesting. You never know what's going to come out of that creative brain of yours," he replied, leaning back in his chair, a thoughtful look crossing his face. "But you know, I'd love to be part of that project. I can help with the design aspect—make it visually stunning."

"Really?" My heart danced at the thought. "You'd do that?"

"Of course," he replied, his expression earnest. "What are friends for if not to support each other's wild dreams? Just promise me one thing."

"Anything," I said, intrigued.

"Don't let your doubts overshadow your vision. The world needs your spark."

His sincerity enveloped me, and I felt the first inklings of hope unfurling within me. Perhaps we were both on the brink of something new, a shared journey that could ignite our creative fires in ways we never expected. And for the first time in a long while, I felt a flicker of possibility dance on the horizon, ready to guide us into the light.

With our plates empty and the last crumbs of red velvet cake lingering like sweet memories, the conversation took a reflective turn. Max leaned forward, elbows resting on the table, his gaze steady and thoughtful. "So, what's next for your art project? Do you have a plan in place?"

I fiddled with the napkin, twisting it between my fingers, a sign of my swirling thoughts. "I'm still piecing things together. I need to find a community center willing to host the workshops, secure some funding, and figure out how to reach the kids I want to help."

"Have you thought about collaborating with local schools?" he suggested. "They might be open to supporting a program that encourages creativity."

"That's a solid idea," I replied, a flicker of excitement igniting within me. "I hadn't considered schools. They could be the key to reaching the kids who need this the most."

"Exactly. Plus, you could make it a field trip. Kids love being out of the classroom." He grinned, a boyish spark lighting his eyes. "Just imagine—art and nature combined. It's a recipe for fun."

"You make it sound so effortless," I said, shaking my head in disbelief. "You're a real cheerleader, you know?"

"I do what I can," he replied, his expression shifting to something more earnest. "But seriously, I believe in this. You've got a gift for bringing people together."

His words wrapped around me like a warm blanket, and I felt a mixture of gratitude and hesitation. What if I failed? What if this project became yet another dream that crumbled under the weight of reality? Before I could spiral, he reached across the table and squeezed my hand gently.

"Hey," he said softly, "you're not alone in this. We'll make it happen together."

Just then, the bistro door swung open, ushering in a gust of cool air along with a couple of patrons. I turned to glance at the entrance, only to freeze at the sight of a familiar figure. Standing there, her arms crossed and her expression a mixture of disdain and amusement, was Jenna, the art critic who had sparked so much trouble at the gallery. Her presence felt like a bolt of lightning slicing through the cozy atmosphere we'd created.

"Fancy seeing you here," she drawled, her voice dripping with sarcasm as she sauntered over, heels clicking against the wooden floor. "I didn't realize this was a meet-up for the creatively challenged."

"Jenna," I said, my heart racing, "what a surprise."

"Surprise indeed," she replied, her eyes narrowing as they flicked between Max and me. "I didn't know you two were friends. Thought you were too busy drowning in your own mediocrity."

"Charming as always," Max shot back, his protective instincts flaring as he shifted in his seat. "What brings you here? Spreading negativity, or just looking for an audience?"

"Actually, I was just enjoying my day until I stumbled upon this... delightful reunion." She glanced at me, her lips curling into a smug smile. "I hope you're not expecting to find success in this venture of yours. Your last exhibition didn't exactly set the art world on fire."

My pulse quickened, anger bubbling just beneath the surface. "I'm working on something new," I said, keeping my tone steady despite the turmoil within me. "Maybe you should reserve judgment until you actually see it."

Jenna raised an eyebrow, her amusement clearly unshakeable. "Oh, I can hardly wait. Just remember, if you need a critic, I'm more than qualified. And if you think Max can save you, think again. He's too busy pining over a dream he can't grasp."

"Enough," Max interjected, his voice low but firm. "You don't know anything about either of us. So why don't you take your negativity and—"

"—and what? Walk away? I'm not going anywhere." Jenna leaned closer, her gaze challenging. "The art world is about survival of the fittest, and sweetie, you're not it."

As the tension crackled in the air, I glanced at Max, whose expression was a mix of frustration and determination. "You know what? I'm done letting you dictate my worth," I said, my voice gaining strength. "This project isn't just for me; it's for the kids who deserve a chance to express themselves. If you can't understand that, then maybe you should reevaluate what art truly means."

"Such passion," Jenna mocked, a theatrical hand to her heart. "It's adorable, really. But let's be honest—you're all talk and no talent. One more flop and you'll be done for."

"Why do you care so much?" I shot back, feeling the fire within me ignite. "You're just a bitter critic who thrives on tearing others down to feel better about your own failures."

The air between us thickened, and for a moment, I feared the conversation would spiral into a full-blown confrontation. But then, to my surprise, Jenna's expression softened, almost imperceptibly. "You're naive," she said quietly, a flicker of something resembling vulnerability crossing her features. "The art world isn't kind, and it has a way of chewing you up and spitting you out."

"I know it can be harsh," I replied, my voice steadier now. "But I'm ready to face it. This is about more than just art for me; it's about connection. It's about giving kids the opportunity to find their voice when the world tells them to stay silent."

Jenna paused, her expression momentarily inscrutable. Then she shrugged, as if shaking off a moment of honesty. "Well, good luck with that. You'll need it." With a dismissive flip of her hair, she turned on her heel and strode away, her presence evaporating as quickly as it had arrived.

I let out a breath I didn't realize I was holding, my heart pounding in my chest. "That was intense," I said, my voice a mixture of disbelief and exhilaration.

Max shook his head, a blend of admiration and frustration etched on his face. "You handled that like a pro. But don't let her get to you. You're better than her insults."

"I'm trying," I said, feeling a swell of determination replace the remnants of doubt. "But I won't lie; she rattles me."

"Let her rattle," he said, his tone firm. "She doesn't define you or your art. Just remember why you're doing this. Hold on to that."

"Right," I said, a smile creeping onto my lips as the adrenaline from the confrontation faded. "Let's get back to planning this art program. It's more important than her petty jealousy."

Just then, my phone buzzed in my pocket. I fished it out, glancing at the screen. It was a message from an unknown number, but the words sent a chill down my spine: "You should reconsider your project. Someone's watching."

My heart raced as I met Max's gaze, a sense of foreboding hanging in the air. "Max," I whispered, "I think I might be in trouble."

Chapter 11: Embracing Vulnerability

The air was thick with the scent of blooming jasmine, its sweet fragrance mingling with the faint traces of rain from earlier in the day. As I sat on the worn steps of my apartment building, my knees pulled up to my chest and my fingers nervously tracing the rough edges of the weathered wood, I found myself marveling at the comfort of this moment. The evening sun hung low, casting a warm golden hue across the pavement, and I could hear the distant hum of life buzzing around us—children's laughter echoed down the street, the rhythmic tapping of a nearby vendor closing up for the night, and the soft clink of glasses from the café across the way. This was home, in all its chaotic glory, and yet I felt a tension building within me, a restless energy that urged me to let go of the masks I so often wore.

Max sat beside me, his casual demeanor a balm to my anxious heart. He leaned back against the step, his shoulder brushing against mine, grounding me in a way I hadn't anticipated. I had known him for what felt like a lifetime, but there were still layers of ourselves that remained unexplored. It was a strange paradox; while we had shared countless laughs and a few tender moments, there lingered an unspoken weight that tethered us both to our pasts. "You know," I began, my voice tentative, "I've always had this...fear about love." I could feel the words slip from my lips like reluctant confessions, both terrifying and liberating.

Max turned to me, his gaze steady and earnest. "Fear is a natural part of the deal, right?" He arched an eyebrow, a playful grin tugging at the corners of his mouth. "I mean, who wouldn't be scared of something as chaotic as love?"

I chuckled softly, grateful for the lightness he injected into the gravity of our conversation. "True. But for me, it's more than just fear; it's like this constant wrestling match with myself. I've built these walls, and I sometimes wonder if they're strong enough to keep the good out, along with the bad."

He shifted slightly, his expression shifting from playful to contemplative. "Walls can be useful," he said, his voice low and serious. "They protect us from hurt, but they also keep out the people who want to care for us. It's a tricky balance."

His insight struck a chord deep within me. I sighed, letting my shoulders relax just a fraction as I allowed his words to resonate. "I guess I've just seen too many people I care about get hurt. My parents, my friends... I've always thought if I could keep a safe distance, I'd be protecting myself and everyone I love."

Max nodded, his brow furrowing slightly as he processed my words. "That makes sense. But what if the very thing you're trying to protect ends up being what you're missing most?"

The question hung in the air, charged with unspoken potential. I could feel the delicate strands of connection weaving between us, pulling tighter as our hearts dared to lay bare their vulnerabilities. "What do you mean?"

"Love isn't just about the good moments," he replied, his voice rich with sincerity. "It's about being there for each other through everything—the chaos, the heartbreak, the raw and unfiltered life that happens in between."

For a moment, the world around us faded, leaving just the two of us, tangled in our fears and hopes, bare in our honesty. I wanted to reach out, cover his hand with mine, but the weight of years of hesitation held me back. Instead, I ventured deeper. "What about you? What scares you about love?"

He hesitated, his gaze drifting to the sunset, the golden rays illuminating his features in a way that made my heart flutter. "Honestly?" he said, a hint of a smile playing on his lips. "I'm scared of ending up alone. I've seen it happen too many times, and I don't want to be one of those guys who loses everything because he was too afraid to take a chance."

I studied him, searching for signs of bravado behind his confession. Instead, I found a tenderness that only deepened my connection to him. "That sounds lonely," I murmured, the words escaping before I could hold them back.

"It is," he admitted, turning to meet my gaze with a vulnerability that caught me off guard. "But the idea of sharing my life with someone who truly sees me—that's worth the risk, isn't it?"

His words wrapped around me like a warm embrace, igniting a spark within me that I hadn't realized was there. Maybe it was time to let down my guard, to embrace the messy, unpredictable nature of love. After all, wasn't it the very essence of being alive? I felt the gravity of his honesty drawing me closer, urging me to step into a space where fears could coexist with the possibility of something beautiful.

"Max," I began, my heart racing, "maybe we can be brave together. Maybe we can try to break down those walls, one tiny brick at a time."

He smiled, a glimmer of hope igniting in his eyes. "You mean it?"

"I do," I replied, emboldened by the sincerity of the moment. "Let's be a little reckless. Let's dare to be vulnerable."

As the sun dipped below the horizon, painting the sky in vibrant hues of orange and purple, I felt a shift within me—a willingness to embrace the uncertainties ahead. The night felt alive with possibility, and I knew this was just the beginning of something profound.

The next few days felt like we were walking through a haze, each moment tinged with a thrilling anticipation that made even the mundane shimmer with promise. I caught myself glancing at my phone more often than I'd care to admit, a mix of hope and nervousness thrumming in my chest every time I heard the ping of a message. Max had an uncanny ability to turn the simplest texts into little treasures, whether it was a meme that made me laugh out loud or a single line that spoke to the shared intimacy of our last conversation. The barriers we had begun to dismantle now felt like stepping stones, leading us closer together, and I savored each interaction like a fine wine—sipping slowly, afraid of the hangover of reality that might follow.

One Saturday morning, with the sun filtering through my curtains in gentle beams, I decided to venture out for coffee. I needed the caffeine boost, but mostly, I wanted to feel the world alive around me. The streets buzzed with a liveliness that felt contagious; the chatter of people filled the air, mixed with the rich aroma of roasted coffee beans wafting from the nearby café. As I pushed open the door, a bell jingled cheerfully, and I was greeted by the warmth of the place—a comforting refuge from the crisp autumn air outside.

The café was a vibrant tapestry of life. A young couple sat in the corner, their laughter spilling over like the foam on their lattes, while an older gentleman meticulously read the newspaper, the pages crinkling softly under his careful touch. I ordered my usual—an oat milk latte, because apparently, I had decided I was one of those people—and found a cozy spot by the window where I could indulge in my people-watching habit.

Settling in, I took a moment to appreciate the ordinary magic around me. I pulled out my phone, and a flutter of excitement coursed through me at the thought of texting Max. Just as I was about to type a witty remark about oat milk being the elixir of life, the café door swung open with a jingle, and there he stood, tousled hair catching the light, wearing that slightly rumpled jacket that always made my heart skip.

"Fancy seeing you here," he said, a grin spreading across his face as he approached my table, his eyes twinkling with mischief.

"Don't you mean fancy seeing you everywhere?" I shot back, unable to contain my smile. "I'm starting to think you're stalking me."

"Only in the name of love," he replied, dropping into the chair across from me with exaggerated flair, as if he were a dashing hero from a rom-com. "I thought I'd see how my favorite barista was faring in her natural habitat."

"Surprisingly well, considering I've just imbibed the magical elixir," I gestured to my latte, pretending to take a long, indulgent sip.

Max leaned back, an amused expression dancing across his features. "You know, you could save a lot of time if you just admitted you've been waiting for me to show up."

"Or you could admit that you're just as eager to see me, and we can skip the whole dance."

"Touché." His eyes sparkled, and the playful banter flowed easily between us, a delightful rhythm that made the moment feel almost electric.

We talked about everything and nothing, the conversation weaving effortlessly from our favorite books to absurd pet stories. I felt lighter than I had in years, as if the shadows of doubt that had clung to me were finally lifting. It was refreshing, but there was also a gnawing thought at the back of my mind—a quiet whisper reminding me that vulnerability, while exhilarating, came with its own set of risks.

As we lingered over our drinks, the café began to fill with a chorus of voices. I noticed a couple sitting nearby, their conversation taking on a heated edge, words like daggers flung back and forth. It caught my attention, and I found myself drawn into their drama, a morbid curiosity piquing my interest.

"Do you think they'll break up?" I mused, nodding toward them.

Max followed my gaze, his brow furrowing slightly. "I'm hoping they'll find a way to sort it out. I'd hate to think love is so fragile that it can shatter over a disagreement about...whatever that is."

I laughed, "That's a fair point. But you know, sometimes it takes a fight to really dig into the heart of things. It's like they're peeling back layers to get to the truth."

"Or they're just being ridiculous," he shot back, amusement twinkling in his eyes. "But I get what you mean. Sometimes vulnerability looks like chaos."

Our conversation slipped seamlessly back to our own lives, but I couldn't shake the image of that couple from my mind. As I sipped my latte, the foam forming delicate patterns on top, I wondered about our own dynamic. We were still in the early stages of unearthing ourselves, yet here we were, both pushing through the discomfort with laughter and shared secrets.

Suddenly, Max leaned closer, lowering his voice conspiratorially. "I've got an idea," he said, his eyes sparkling with mischief. "Let's do something that scares us."

"Scares us? Like skydiving?" I asked, feigning horror.

"Even better. Let's attend a spoken word night at that little venue on Maple Street."

My stomach twisted with both excitement and dread. "Spoken word? As in, stand up and share your deepest thoughts and insecurities with a room full of strangers?"

"Exactly," he replied, unabashed enthusiasm shining in his expression. "Think of it as an opportunity to practice embracing that vulnerability we were talking about."

I narrowed my eyes, caught between the thrill of the idea and the sheer terror of public speaking. "You do realize I'm a writer, not a performer, right?"

"Precisely! That's why it'll be a great challenge. Plus, I'll be there to support you."

His confidence was infectious, and before I knew it, my heart was racing with the prospect. "Okay, I'm in. But only if you promise to go first."

Max laughed, his joy lighting up the space around us. "Deal. We'll be two brave souls facing the world together."

As the chatter of the café swirled around us, I felt a shift within me, a delicious thrill coursing through my veins. Stepping outside my comfort zone with him didn't seem so daunting anymore. It felt like an adventure waiting to unfold, and for the first time in a long while, I was eager to embrace the unexpected.

The day of the spoken word night arrived with the sort of anticipation that tickled the back of my throat. The sky was a muted gray, promising rain, which felt like the universe's way of adding an extra layer of drama to my already jittery nerves. I paced in my tiny apartment, a whirlwind of excitement and trepidation. Max had texted me earlier, a cheeky message that had me smiling through the anxiety: "Just remember, if you bomb, I'll take full responsibility for this terrible idea. But I'm confident you'll be brilliant."

Despite his humor, the thought of standing in front of a crowd sent my heart racing like I'd just sprinted a marathon. I could envision myself on that stage—my palms clammy, my throat dry, and a spotlight scorching down like an interrogation lamp, highlighting every flaw. But as the clock ticked closer to the event, I couldn't shake the thought of sharing something real, something profound. Maybe this was my chance to dig deeper into those buried fears, to transform the chaotic energy swirling within me into something beautiful.

As I slipped into a pair of comfortable jeans and a cozy sweater, I caught a glimpse of myself in the mirror. My reflection stared back, eyes wide with uncertainty but somehow hopeful. "You've got this," I murmured, giving myself a little pep talk as if I were about to step into a boxing ring instead of a cozy venue full of art and poetry.

When I arrived at the venue, the vibrant chatter of the crowd enveloped me like a warm hug. The space was intimate, with dim lighting and the scent of coffee mingling with the aroma of freshly baked pastries. Fairy lights twinkled overhead, casting a soft glow on the faces around me. My stomach churned with a mix of excitement and anxiety as I scanned the room for Max.

"There you are!" he called out, his voice cutting through the murmur. He was leaning casually against the bar, looking as charming as ever in a fitted shirt that accentuated the strength in his arms. The moment I spotted him, my worries melted away, replaced by a rush of warmth.

"Hey! You made it," I exclaimed, joining him.

"Of course! I wouldn't miss the chance to see you dazzle the crowd," he replied, flashing that boyish grin that made my heart flip.

We chatted as more people filtered in, the energy buzzing with creativity and possibility. It was thrilling to see so many diverse souls gathered in one space, each there to share a piece of themselves. I could feel the weight of the room's collective vulnerability, a sensation that somehow grounded me amid my swirling thoughts.

As the event began, the host took the stage, exuding an effortless charm that drew everyone's attention. She welcomed the audience with a flourish, her enthusiasm palpable. My heart raced as I realized the night was finally underway. With each poet who stepped up, I felt a rush of admiration for their bravery—sharing their truths in front of strangers took guts.

Max leaned in closer, his voice low. "You're up next, just so you know."

"Wait, what?!" I almost choked on my sip of soda. "I thought we were going to play the waiting game until the end!"

"Surprise! It's the 'embrace your fears' plan, remember?"

I shot him a mock glare, but my stomach twisted in excitement. He had a point; this was my moment, whether I was ready or not.

The nerves crawled back up my spine as I watched the previous speaker step down to a round of applause. When they called my name, it felt like time warped, dragging me into the spotlight, the room fading into a blur.

As I approached the mic, a thousand thoughts raced through my mind. "You can do this," I whispered to myself, and for a moment, I felt the supportive energy of the audience. I glanced at Max, who gave me a subtle nod of encouragement, and it fueled me with enough confidence to begin.

"Hi everyone, I'm glad to be here tonight," I started, my voice steadier than I anticipated. "I'm going to share a piece that reflects on the beauty and chaos of love and vulnerability. It's a little scary, but... well, that's the point, right?"

With each word I spoke, I began to feel liberated. I wove in stories of love, loss, and the bittersweet dance of connections. The audience leaned in, captivated, and I could see their expressions shifting as I bared my heart. I had feared rejection, but instead, I found empathy. Each laugh and sigh from the crowd wrapped around me like a warm blanket, lifting me higher.

But just as I reached the climax of my piece, ready to share a vulnerable confession about my own fears regarding commitment, a loud crash echoed from the back of the room.

Everyone turned, startled. I faltered, my heart dropping as the noise sliced through the moment. A man had knocked over a stack of chairs, and chaos ensued as people murmured and shifted in their seats. My focus shattered, and I felt my confidence waver, the moment slipping through my fingers like grains of sand.

"Maybe it's time for me to step back," I muttered, panic creeping in. But then I caught Max's eye. He gave me an encouraging smile, silently urging me to reclaim my moment.

"Focus on your truth," he mouthed, and I drew in a deep breath, grounding myself in the rhythm of my heartbeat.

With renewed determination, I began to speak again, louder this time, trying to drown out the chaos. "As I was saying, vulnerability is terrifying but necessary. It's the bridge that connects us in our most raw forms."

Just as the audience began to settle again, the door swung open violently, and in walked a woman, drenched from the rain, her eyes wild and frantic. "I need help!" she shouted, her voice slicing through the air like a knife.

A hush fell over the crowd, tension thickening the atmosphere as all eyes turned toward her.

"What's going on?" I asked, a mix of concern and curiosity bubbling within me.

"I can't find my brother! He was supposed to be here!" Her voice cracked, desperation threading through her words, causing an unsettling chill to settle over the room.

Max shot up, his brows furrowed in concern. "What do you mean? How long has he been missing?"

"I don't know! He said he would come tonight, and I just... I can't find him!"

In that moment, the warmth of shared vulnerability morphed into something darker, the room brimming with questions and fears of its own. I could feel the impending storm on the horizon, a wave of uncertainty crashing in, overshadowing the evening's celebration of connection.

"Let's figure this out together," I said, suddenly feeling the weight of the situation settle on my shoulders. The warmth of the café was replaced by an electric tension, and I couldn't help but feel that our night of vulnerability had transformed into something that would test us all in ways we had never imagined.

Chapter 12: Under the Stars

The air was thick with the scent of blooming honeysuckle, its sweetness curling around us like a warm embrace as I nestled deeper into the blanket. Fort Tryon Park was a hidden gem in the city, a pocket of tranquility where the frenetic energy of New York seemed to fade into the background. The stars above blinked like mischievous eyes, each one a tiny glimmer of possibility against the velvet sky, and for a moment, I believed we could keep this moment suspended in time.

Max was seated cross-legged beside me, his auburn hair catching the moonlight as he focused on his sketchbook. The faint rustle of leaves danced in the gentle breeze, and I found myself drawn into the rhythm of his concentration, my heart beating in time with the scratch of pencil on paper. It was as if the world had narrowed down to just the two of us, and I reveled in that intimacy, my mind spinning with thoughts I wasn't quite ready to voice. The casualness of our picnic—half-eaten sandwiches and a trail of cookie crumbs—felt like the perfect prelude to something more profound.

"Is that my good side?" I teased, leaning in closer to peer at his drawing. Max's pencil paused mid-air, and he glanced up, a playful smirk stretching across his face.

"Depends on who you ask," he shot back, his voice smooth and laced with mischief. "But for my artistic integrity, I'd say your left profile is a bit more... dramatic."

I laughed, the sound bubbling up like champagne. "Dramatic? Me? I'll have you know I'm the picture of calm."

"Sure, if you count flailing your arms while explaining why you can't possibly do the dishes as calm," he shot back, and I couldn't help but roll my eyes. The light banter felt effortless, a seamless blend of humor and flirtation that I could easily lose myself in. Yet, beneath the laughter, an undercurrent of tension simmered, a whisper of unspoken feelings that hung in the air between us, almost tangible.

His gaze fell back to the sketchbook, and I watched him with rapt attention, mesmerized by the way his brow furrowed in concentration. The lines began to take shape, forming a rough outline of my face. "You're capturing my good side, then," I said, the playful jab punctuating the moment.

"Of course," he replied, glancing back at me, his eyes dancing with mischief. "If I capture your right side, you might just float away into the stratosphere with all that hot air."

I gasped in mock offense, clutching my heart as though he'd delivered a fatal blow. "You wound me, Max!" I declared, feigning despair. He chuckled, the sound deep and warm, wrapping around me like the softest blanket on a chilly night.

As he continued sketching, I leaned back on my hands, my eyes drifting to the star-speckled sky. It was a sight I never tired of—constellations whispering stories of long-forgotten myths and dreams. I longed to weave my own narrative into the fabric of the universe. Max's presence beside me felt like a piece of that narrative, but the weight of my burgeoning feelings hovered like a storm cloud.

With each stroke of his pencil, I felt a surge of courage mixed with apprehension, as if I were standing on the precipice of a cliff, ready to leap but terrified of the fall. The moment stretched, and I felt a palpable shift in the air, a silent plea begging for me to speak. But just as I opened my mouth to share my heart, a siren blared in the distance, slicing through the tranquility like a knife.

"Damn city noise," Max muttered, breaking the tension that had built between us. "Can't even enjoy a moment of peace without being reminded we're still in Manhattan." His voice was laced with disappointment, and I felt my heart sink alongside his.

"Maybe it's a reminder of how precious these moments are," I suggested softly, hoping to reignite the spark we had just moments ago.

Max looked at me, the corner of his mouth twitching as if he were fighting a smile. "Philosopher and comedian, huh? Multi-talented." He leaned back on his elbows, gazing up at the stars, and I could see the way his mind danced between thoughts, each flicker of light igniting a new idea.

"What if we had our own private universe?" he mused, his voice dreamy and distant. "One where the only sirens are the ones calling us to adventure?"

"Are you suggesting we ditch this picnic and run off into the night?" I replied, half-serious, half-teasing. "I'm not sure how far we'd get on these cookies and stale chips."

"Maybe just a short trip to a coffee shop?" He laughed, and the warmth of his laughter wrapped around me, brightening the cool night air. "I could go for some hot cocoa, and I know the perfect place."

His invitation hung in the air, tempting me with the promise of more stolen moments and whispered confessions. The thought of continuing our night filled me with both excitement and dread. What if I couldn't find the words? What if this night ended without me having said what I needed to say?

"Coffee it is, then," I said, a thrill running through me at the prospect of adventure, however small. "But only if you promise to tell me more about your drawing. What do you see in my face?"

"Ah, you mean besides the obvious?" He winked, and I felt a rush of warmth flood my cheeks.

I watched as he gathered our things, that unshakable grin never leaving his face. He was magnetic, this boy who wielded pencils with as much finesse as a painter with a brush, and I found myself craving not just his artistry but the connection we were building, thread by thread, moment by moment.

With the city lights flickering in the distance and the sirens fading behind us, I took a deep breath, steeling myself for the night ahead. Underneath the laughter and easy banter lay an uncharted territory of feelings, and perhaps, just perhaps, tonight would be the night I navigated those waters.

The prospect of coffee drew me away from the enchantment of the park, but as we strolled through the softly illuminated streets, I couldn't shake the lingering warmth of that moment under the stars. Max walked beside me, his fingers brushing against mine in a manner that felt charged, as if the universe had whispered a secret between us. The chaos of the city pulsed around us, each honk of a taxi and clatter of heels on the pavement echoing the rhythm of life, yet somehow, it all faded into a background hum, and all I could hear was the laughter we shared.

"Have you ever thought about how a simple cup of coffee can lead to life-altering revelations?" Max asked, his eyes glimmering with mischief.

"Are we talking about the caffeine or the conversations?" I countered, enjoying the playful banter that felt so natural between us.

"Why not both?" he replied, grinning. "Caffeine to fuel the heart and the chat to fuel the soul. It's a winning combination."

As we approached the coffee shop, its warm light spilled onto the sidewalk, inviting us like an old friend. Inside, the rich aroma of roasted beans enveloped us, and I felt a wave of comfort wash over me. The barista was a familiar face, an affable guy named Leo who seemed to know everyone by name and order, effortlessly weaving through the crowd.

"Max! Fancy seeing you here again!" Leo called out, flashing a smile as he leaned against the counter, a steaming cup in hand.

"Hey, Leo! You know me—never can resist a late-night caffeine fix." Max leaned on the counter, his casual posture making it clear he felt right at home.

"And who's this?" Leo asked, turning his attention to me, curiosity gleaming in his eyes.

"This is my friend, a fellow adventurer in the quest for the perfect coffee," Max introduced me, a hint of mischief in his tone.

"An adventurer, huh?" Leo quirked an eyebrow, clearly intrigued. "So, what's the plan tonight? Conquer the coffee world, one cup at a time?"

I smiled, caught up in the playful exchange. "More like trying not to spill on ourselves while we figure out the meaning of life," I shot back, meeting Leo's gaze with a wink.

"Good luck with that," he chuckled. "But if you figure it out, let me know. I've been dying to get a jump on my New Year's resolutions." He winked and busied himself with our drinks, leaving me with a sense of warmth that resonated far beyond the shop's cozy ambiance.

With our coffees in hand—Max opting for something audaciously espresso-laden while I chose the caramel macchiato, sweet enough to cut through any existential dread—we settled at a corner table by the window. The view outside was alive with city energy; people rushed by, their faces illuminated by the occasional streetlight, each one a story I felt privileged to observe.

"Okay, let's get philosophical," Max said, leaning forward, his elbows resting on the table. "If you could ask the universe one question right now, what would it be?"

I took a moment, letting his question swirl in my mind. "What is the secret to happiness?" I finally answered, my tone more serious than I intended.

"Ah, a classic! The eternal quest for the meaning of life," he replied, raising his cup in mock salute. "But seriously, what if the secret is simply to not take life too seriously?"

I laughed, enjoying the way his playful demeanor lightened the weight of my thoughts. "So, you're saying I should quit my job and become a professional pillow fluffer?"

"Absolutely. There's a great demand for that," he replied, his eyes twinkling with mischief. "You'll be rolling in the cash, not to mention the comfort. Just think—people napping on your fluffy pillows, thanking you for their dreams!"

"Sounds like my kind of gig," I said, my laughter bubbling over. The way he could weave humor into even the most mundane topics left me feeling lighter, my worries momentarily suspended.

But as our laughter faded, an unfamiliar weight settled in the air. The shift felt almost palpable, as if the universe had shifted its gaze back to us, reminding me of the confessions I was still holding close. I wanted to plunge into the depths of my feelings, to throw caution to the wind and spill my heart out, but doubt lingered like an uninvited guest. What if my words shattered the fragile connection we were building?

Max seemed to sense the change, his smile softening. "You okay?" he asked, his voice sincere, and I felt a rush of warmth that made my heart ache.

"Just thinking," I replied, my tone evasive, hoping to sidestep the moment.

"About the meaning of life?" he prodded gently, tilting his head in a way that made my resolve waver.

"More like what it means to take chances," I admitted, my words spilling out before I could filter them. "Sometimes I feel like I'm standing at the edge of something huge, and I'm terrified to jump."

Max studied me, his expression shifting from playful to serious, and for a moment, the world outside the window blurred into the background. "You know," he said softly, "jumping doesn't have to mean falling. Sometimes it's just about trusting that you'll land where you're meant to be."

The weight of his words hung in the air, heavy with meaning, and I felt the pulse of possibility racing through me. Perhaps the night would hold more than I had anticipated, more than just coffee and laughter. Maybe it was the prelude to something monumental, an awakening I hadn't dared to hope for.

"Do you ever get scared?" I ventured, my voice barely above a whisper.

"Every day," he confessed, and there was a vulnerability in his tone that sent a shiver down my spine. "But I think that's what makes the leap worthwhile. It's the fear that makes us human."

His honesty pierced through the veil of uncertainty, and I realized that perhaps I didn't have to carry this burden alone. The revelation felt like a breath of fresh air, invigorating and frightening all at once.

"Maybe we could leap together," I suggested, a spark of courage igniting within me.

Max's gaze locked onto mine, and in that instant, the weight of our unspoken feelings hung in the air, electric and alive. "I'd like that," he said, his voice low and earnest.

In the midst of the bustling café, with our hearts laid bare and the weight of the world temporarily suspended, the night transformed into something more than just a fleeting moment. It became a canvas, waiting for us to paint our dreams and fears onto its expansive surface, and for the first time, I felt ready to dip my brush into the colors of possibility.

The warmth of our conversation enveloped me, yet a thrilling uncertainty lingered just beneath the surface, crackling like static electricity in the air. I had opened a door to vulnerability, and Max, with his steady gaze and genuine curiosity, was right there, ready to step through with me. The world outside the coffee shop continued its frenetic dance, but within this little haven, time felt almost elastic, stretching to accommodate the deepening connection between us.

"So, about this leap," Max prompted, leaning in, his elbows resting on the table, inviting me to share my thoughts. "What's stopping you from taking it?"

I sipped my caramel macchiato, the sweetness swirling with warmth in my chest, but my heart raced at the thought of my unspoken truth. "Fear, mostly. You know, fear of failure, of making a fool of myself."

"Ah, the classic. But you know what? Every leap comes with the risk of falling, but it also comes with the potential for flying," he replied, his eyes glinting with enthusiasm. "You just have to figure out what you want to soar toward."

As he spoke, I felt something shift within me, a combination of hope and apprehension that ignited a flicker of courage. "And if I'm afraid of falling flat on my face?" I asked, letting the vulnerability seep through my words.

Max chuckled, the sound rich and comforting. "Then you invest in a good pair of landing pads. Seriously, though, failing isn't the end of the world. It's just a pit stop on the way to figuring out what works for you."

His words washed over me, a soothing balm against my insecurities, yet an underlying tension remained, a realization that our conversation was building to something deeper. "What about you? Are you afraid?"

He paused, the smile slipping from his lips for just a moment, revealing a flicker of vulnerability. "Every day. But I think I'm learning to embrace it. If you're not scared, you're probably not challenging yourself enough."

"Nice save," I quipped, trying to lighten the mood, but the truth of his admission settled between us like a shared secret.

"What can I say? I've been working on my philosophy skills." He grinned, but there was a depth in his eyes that suggested he wasn't just talking about coffee shop banter. "Let's make a pact. We leap together. No backing down, no second-guessing."

The intensity of his gaze sent my heart racing, a combination of exhilaration and the thrill of the unknown. "You're really going to hold me to that?"

"Absolutely. I'm not letting you slip away without taking that leap," he declared, his tone light yet unwavering.

The barista called out a customer's name, pulling me momentarily from our bubble of shared aspirations. Outside, the world continued to swirl, oblivious to the intimate pact being forged over coffee. I couldn't help but wonder what that leap would look like for both of us. What if it meant confronting feelings that had been simmering beneath the surface, waiting for the right moment to boil over?

"I'll take you up on that," I said, my voice steady, infused with determination I hadn't expected. "But let's make it interesting. If I leap, you have to jump too."

Max's grin widened, revealing the playful spark I'd come to adore. "Challenge accepted. But if we're jumping, let's make sure it's into something worth diving into. I'm thinking something epic—like an art project or a crazy adventure."

"Or a secret career change?" I suggested, feeling a boldness wash over me. "Maybe we both reinvent ourselves as part-time professional pillow fluffers."

"Now you're talking! We can fluff our way to the top of the pillow empire," he replied, chuckling. "Imagine the fame! The glory!"

As laughter spilled between us, I felt the weight of my unspoken feelings, heavier now, pressing against my chest. We were dancing around something monumental, and I was terrified to take that final step into the unknown.

"Max," I began, hesitating as I searched for the right words, the perfect moment to unravel my heart. But just as I gathered my thoughts, a commotion erupted outside, pulling our attention to the window.

A group of people had gathered near the entrance, their voices rising in a mix of excitement and alarm. "What's going on?" I asked, my curiosity piqued.

Max leaned closer, his brows knitting together in concern. "I don't know, but it looks like something's happening."

We both rose, leaving our half-empty cups behind as we moved to the window. The city's energy pulsed around us, a sudden wave of urgency crackling in the air. A man was standing on a bench, gesticulating wildly, drawing a small crowd.

"Listen! Listen!" he shouted, his voice rising above the crowd. "Something big is happening downtown! You won't believe it!"

Max turned to me, his expression a mix of intrigue and worry. "Do you think we should check it out?"

"What if it's a performance art piece? Or a spontaneous flash mob?" I suggested, a playful lilt in my tone.

"Or what if it's something serious?" His eyes darted back to the gathering, and I could see the tension building beneath his calm exterior.

Just then, the man on the bench raised his arms dramatically, and the crowd fell silent. "They've announced it!" he proclaimed, his voice echoing in the night. "They're closing down Broadway for a secret event! Tonight!"

"What?" Max exclaimed, glancing at me, his eyes wide with excitement and disbelief. "A secret event? We have to go!"

Before I could respond, the man continued, "Grab your friends, your lovers, anyone you can! This is a chance to be part of something unforgettable!"

Max's expression shifted, and I could feel the energy buzzing between us. "Julia, this could be our leap," he said, his voice filled with urgency. "What do you think?"

Heart pounding, adrenaline coursing through my veins, I felt the thrill of adventure calling my name. "Are we really going to do this?"

His grin was contagious. "Why not? We're already here, living on the edge of something great!"

With a deep breath, I nodded, my decision made. "Let's do it!"

We pushed through the door and joined the throng of excited strangers, the anticipation electrifying the air around us. As we made our way toward the unfolding chaos, I felt a heady mix of fear and exhilaration, a spark of potential igniting within me.

But just as we reached the street corner, a sharp crack echoed through the air, cutting through the excited chatter. The crowd gasped collectively, and I turned, my heart sinking. A shadow loomed in the distance, a figure moving through the crowd with an intensity that sent shivers down my spine.

And in that moment, as the night teetered on the brink of something extraordinary, I couldn't shake the feeling that we were about to plunge into a darkness neither of us had anticipated.

Chapter 13: Fractured Promises

The fluorescent lights flickered above me in the grocery store, casting a sterile glow over the aisles lined with neatly arranged products. The smell of fresh produce wafted through the air, mingling with the slightly metallic scent of the shopping carts. I stood in front of the cereal aisle, mentally debating the merits of gluten-free oats versus sugary flakes, when I felt a familiar presence behind me.

"Fancy seeing you here," Aaron's voice slid into my ears like velvet, smooth and enticing yet laced with an undercurrent that made my skin prickle. I turned, and there he was—his dark hair tousled just so, a stubble of indecision on his jawline, and those striking blue eyes that had once felt like home but now were a riddle wrapped in a mystery I wasn't sure I wanted to solve.

I clenched my jaw, the box of gluten-free oats forgotten in my hand. "What are you doing here?" I asked, my voice steadier than my insides felt. The last thing I needed was a reminder of the chapter I had struggled to close.

He shrugged, hands tucked casually into the pockets of his fitted jeans. "Just grabbing some essentials. You know how it is." His smile, that infuriatingly charming smile, twitched at the corners, teasing memories I thought had faded into the recesses of my mind.

"Yeah, I suppose everyone needs to eat," I replied, an edge creeping into my tone. I forced myself to look around, as if scanning for escape routes rather than grappling with the gravity of this sudden encounter. The customers flowed past us, oblivious to the emotional storm brewing in the cereal aisle.

"I've been thinking about you," he said, his voice dropping, making it sound almost conspiratorial. "I thought it was time we talked. Really talked."

I narrowed my eyes, a wave of disbelief washing over me. "Talk? Is that what you call it now?"

His gaze sharpened, and I could see the conflict lurking behind his calm facade. "You know what I mean. Closure. I owe you that much."

Closure. The word echoed in my mind, laden with unfulfilled promises and half-hearted apologies. I had spent countless nights tossing and turning, replaying the moments that had led us to this precipice of hurt. The intimacy we had once shared now felt like a delicate glass ornament—beautiful yet dangerously fragile.

"Closure is just a fancy term for digging up the past," I countered, my heart thumping in defiance of the memories that threatened to pull me in. "You don't get to choose when it's convenient for you."

He opened his mouth as if to argue but quickly snapped it shut. The silence stretched between us, heavy with unspoken words. I could feel my resolve teetering, a tightrope walk over an abyss of old feelings and buried heartache.

"Let's get coffee. Just to talk," he suggested, a glimmer of hope flickering in his eyes. "I'll even buy you your favorite. What was it? Caramel macchiato with extra whipped cream?"

My heart stuttered at the memory of those cozy afternoons, spent lounging in our favorite café while rain drummed against the windows. I had savored those moments, treasuring the simplicity of being together. But those memories were now a bittersweet melody, played on a broken piano.

"I don't think that's a good idea," I replied, my voice firmer now. "I've moved on."

"Aren't you with Max?" His tone shifted, probing.

The mention of Max, my steady anchor in the storm of my emotions, sent a jolt through me. I had fought hard to build a life without Aaron, to embrace the warmth and safety Max offered. Yet here I was, standing in a grocery store, battling with the shadows of my past.

"Yes, I am," I affirmed, lifting my chin defiantly. "Max is everything I need right now."

Aaron stepped closer, the scent of his cologne wrapping around me like a fog. "But is he everything you want?"

That question hung in the air, a whisper that dripped with uncertainty. I felt the walls I had built start to tremble, fissures cracking beneath the weight of old affection and lingering doubt. Had I truly banished Aaron from my heart, or was I merely shoving him into a dark corner, pretending he no longer existed?

"Aaron," I began, struggling to keep my voice steady, "this isn't just about you and me anymore. It's about what I've built. I can't keep looking back."

"Why not?" he challenged, his tone shifting from smooth to intense, the edge of desperation creeping in. "You act like moving on means erasing the past. But it doesn't. It shapes who we are."

I could feel the heat rising in my cheeks, a mix of anger and confusion. "And what are you suggesting? That I just forget everything Max and I have built because you want to revisit old wounds?"

"I'm not asking you to forget. I just think we owe it to ourselves to confront it. To understand what happened."

With a deep breath, I closed my eyes for a moment, trying to drown out the clamor of my racing thoughts. I had spent so long battling the ghost of us, trying to lay it to rest. The idea of reopening that chapter felt like cracking open a door to a storm I had painstakingly weathered.

"I need to think," I finally said, turning away to gather my scattered thoughts, my heart pounding with the urgency of decision. I felt his gaze linger on my back, the weight of his presence pressing against me as if trying to pull me into his orbit once more.

I took a step away, pushing my cart toward the exit, but the invisible tether held firm. The struggle between the past and the present danced in my chest, a delicate balance that felt poised to tip into chaos.

Just as I reached the sliding doors, I paused, glancing back at him. Aaron stood rooted in place, a fleeting shadow of vulnerability crossing his features. "I just want to understand," he said, his voice barely a whisper, filled with a sincerity that broke through my defenses.

And in that moment, I was caught between two worlds—one that had shaped me and one that was just beginning to unfold, both vying for my heart and my trust.

The air outside was crisp, a welcome contrast to the sterile chill of the grocery store. I stepped out into the world, feeling the sun's warmth bathe my skin, but it did little to thaw the chill settling in my bones. My thoughts spun in a chaotic whirlwind, each one colliding with the next, tugging at my heartstrings like a well-rehearsed symphony gone rogue. I leaned against the cool metal of my car, my breath forming little clouds of frustration, trying to gather my thoughts into something coherent.

Aaron's face lingered in my mind, not the way I remembered him—youthful and vibrant—but rather as a specter of my past, a reminder of the heartache I had fought so hard to escape. I dug my keys out of my pocket, the metallic clinking grounding me momentarily, and tossed them into the air, catching them in my palm.

I shook my head, willing myself to push thoughts of him aside. Max was waiting for me. He was dependable, patient, and brought a steady rhythm to my life that I had desperately needed after the chaos Aaron had wrought. I had to remember that. As I climbed into the car, I gripped the steering wheel, the leather cool against my palms, and took a deep breath, letting the sweet aroma of vanilla from the air freshener fill my lungs.

The drive home was a blur, my thoughts tangled in a web of memories and emotions. I replayed the moment in the grocery store over and over, as if I could dissect it piece by piece, making sense of the disarray. What did he mean by wanting to understand? Did he really want closure, or was this just another ploy to reel me back into his orbit?

Pulling into my driveway, I parked and took a moment to gather my thoughts, staring out at the neat rows of flowers I had planted in the spring. The vibrant yellows and pinks were a stark contrast to the turmoil brewing inside me. I wanted to find comfort in their beauty, but every blossom felt like a taunt, a reminder of the happiness I had fought to reclaim.

Max's laughter rang out from the backyard, pulling me from my spiraling thoughts. I walked through the house, taking in the familiar scents of grilled vegetables and herbs wafting from the kitchen. He was always experimenting with new recipes, a passion that had blossomed in the months we'd spent together.

"Hey there, chef extraordinaire!" I called, stepping outside to find him standing by the grill, flipping marinated zucchini with an ease that made me smile. His hair was tousled, a few strands sticking up in a way that made him look boyishly charming. He glanced over at me, his eyes lighting up as they always did.

"Perfect timing! I just threw on the last batch," he said, flashing a grin that sent a rush of warmth through me. "Care to lend a hand, or should I be worried about your culinary skills?"

"Oh, come on," I laughed, joining him by the grill. "You know I can cook. I just prefer to keep my talents for special occasions."

He raised an eyebrow, leaning casually against the grill. "So, you're saying my cooking isn't special?"

"Not at all! It's just... consistently excellent," I replied, rolling my eyes playfully. "Why would I compete with that?"

"Fair point." He smirked, flipping the zucchini again. "But if you're just going to stand there and praise my genius, you could at least fetch the drinks from the fridge."

"Fine, but only because you're so good at making me look bad," I retorted, heading back inside, the laughter still bubbling in my chest.

As I rummaged through the fridge, the cold air hitting my face, my mind wandered back to Aaron. What had I really wanted from that encounter? I poured two glasses of iced tea, the sweetness a stark reminder of simpler times. Max was right; I had been dragging the weight of my past around like a worn-out backpack, and now it felt like I was at a crossroads—between a future I had begun to build and a past that refused to stay buried.

Returning to the patio, I set the glasses down on the table, my resolve solidifying. Max deserved all of me, unblemished by the shadows of my former relationship. I watched as he plated the food, the way he focused intently on each detail, and felt a flicker of hope.

"Dinner's served!" he announced, the pride in his voice evident as he brought everything to the table. I took a seat, the cool breeze wrapping around us like a comforting shawl. "What do you think?" he asked, presenting the plate with a flourish.

"It looks incredible! Almost too pretty to eat," I said, eyeing the vibrant colors of the vegetables arranged artistically.

"I aim to impress." He grinned, digging into his own meal with gusto. "So, how was your day? Besides running into your ex, of course."

The casual mention of Aaron felt like a raw nerve, but I appreciated Max's easy-going nature. "Oh, you know, the usual. Cereal debates at the grocery store," I replied, trying to keep my tone light. "Nothing too scandalous."

"Just a day in the life of a grocery connoisseur?" He chuckled, clearly enjoying my attempt at nonchalance.

I took a deep breath, my heart hammering as I weighed my words. "Actually, I did see Aaron."

Max's fork paused mid-air, his expression shifting from playful to serious in an instant. "Oh? How did that go?"

"Not great, to be honest. He wanted to talk. To have closure," I admitted, feeling a twinge of guilt as I met Max's eyes. "I told him it wasn't a good idea."

Max studied me, his gaze unwavering, and I could see the wheels turning in his mind. "You're sure you want to leave it in the past? It sounds like you two have unfinished business."

"I don't want to revisit that part of my life," I insisted, my voice rising slightly. "I've moved on, and I'm happy with you."

His eyes softened, and he reached across the table, his fingers brushing against mine. "I get that, but it's natural to feel conflicted when someone from your past resurfaces. Just make sure you're not pushing away your feelings."

I opened my mouth to respond, but the honesty in his tone left me momentarily speechless. The weight of the moment settled around us like a warm blanket, and I found myself grappling with the realization that my past was a tangled thread woven into the fabric of my present.

"Can we just enjoy dinner?" I finally said, trying to lighten the mood. "Let's not analyze my emotional baggage over grilled zucchini."

"Fair enough. But you owe me a full debrief later," he replied, a playful spark returning to his eyes.

"Deal," I laughed, grateful for his ability to pivot so effortlessly back to lightness. As we ate, the tension eased, and the flavors danced on my palate, each bite reinforcing the warmth of the moment. Yet, in the back of my mind, the nagging questions about Aaron and my feelings swirled, creating an undercurrent I couldn't quite shake. The balance between my past and present hung precariously, and while I wanted to immerse myself in the joy of the here and now, a part of me remained tethered to that grocery store encounter, caught in a web of nostalgia and confusion.

Even as I laughed with Max over dinner, a current of unease thrummed beneath the surface. The flickering candlelight danced between us, casting shadows that wavered and flickered like the memories of my past. Each delightful bite of grilled zucchini felt like a reminder of the simplicity I craved, yet a part of me was still tangled in a conversation that had left my heart unsettled.

"Do you think you can survive without dessert?" Max asked, feigning horror as he cleared our plates. "I mean, this is practically a crime against culinary art."

"Oh, you know I have a special relationship with sweets," I replied, feigning innocence as I waggled my eyebrows at him. "But I thought we were trying to keep this a guilt-free meal."

"Guilt-free? With my cooking? That's rich." He chuckled, his eyes sparkling. "Dessert is non-negotiable in my kitchen, and you know it. What do you want? Chocolate cake? Ice cream? Both?"

"Is that even a question?" I laughed, the tension from earlier starting to dissipate. "I'll take the cake and a scoop of that overpriced vanilla bean ice cream that's hidden in the back of your freezer."

Max saluted me with a spatula, and I couldn't help but admire the way he threw himself into the task of dessert, like a musician composing a symphony. The kitchen was filled with the comforting scent of chocolate as he prepared the cake, a sweet note that blended perfectly with the savory remnants of our dinner.

"Tell me more about your day while I whip this masterpiece up," he called over his shoulder, his focus laser-like as he melted chocolate.

I thought about the emotional whirlwind of the day, about Aaron standing in that grocery store, and my heart fluttered with hesitation. How much of my day should I share? Would it burden

Max with my unresolved feelings? The thought felt heavy, like dragging a suitcase filled with rocks.

"Well," I started, keeping my voice light, "I had an unexpected visit from Aaron, which was... interesting."

He paused, the spatula hovering mid-air, before he turned to look at me, his expression shifting to something more serious. "Interesting how? Did he cause trouble?"

"No trouble, just a nostalgic walk down memory lane," I replied, the bitterness of those words sticking in my throat. "He wanted closure, or at least claimed he did."

Max's eyebrows knitted together, and he put down the spatula, his attention fully on me. "Closure? And you want to go down that road? With him?"

"It's not like I'm planning to rekindle our romance," I said defensively. "But he's part of my past, and it's hard to just forget about that."

"Is he worth the emotional rollercoaster? You've worked so hard to move on."

"Believe me, I know." I sighed, frustration creeping into my voice. "I'm just trying to sort out what this means for me now. What if I'm not as over him as I thought?"

"Don't give him that power," Max said, stepping closer and placing a hand on my shoulder, grounding me with his presence. "You're with me. I'm here."

The reassurance in his voice sent a wave of gratitude coursing through me. "You're right. I just... I didn't expect to see him, and it threw me off."

"Then let's focus on us. What do you want for dessert?"

I grinned, feeling the heaviness lift a little. "Anything with chocolate, as long as it's made by you."

As he returned to his culinary creation, I felt a warmth wash over me, but it was swiftly followed by a pang of guilt. I should have been fully present in this moment, enjoying our easy banter, but my mind kept drifting back to that grocery store encounter. My heart battled between two worlds, each tugging at me with a different kind of longing.

"Okay, dessert is served!" Max announced dramatically, placing a slice of chocolate cake topped with a lavish scoop of vanilla ice cream in front of me. "I call this a 'sweet distraction.'"

"More like a delightful victory," I laughed, savoring the sight of my favorite dessert.

As we dug in, the rich flavors enveloped me in warmth. The chocolate was decadently smooth, the sweetness perfectly balanced by the creamy ice cream melting on top. I lost myself in the indulgence, grateful for Max's presence and the comfort he brought. Yet, somewhere deep inside, the thought of Aaron loomed like a dark cloud, a thunderstorm just waiting to break.

After dessert, we moved to the living room, where the faint glow of the lamp created a cozy atmosphere. We snuggled onto the couch, and Max switched on the television, flipping through channels until he found a classic romantic comedy. The lighthearted banter and silly antics on screen filled the air, and for a moment, laughter drowned out my worries.

"This is my kind of night," I said, leaning against him.

"Good to know I'm doing my job right." He grinned, wrapping an arm around my shoulders.

But just as I began to relax, a sudden buzz from my phone disrupted the moment. It was a text from an unknown number. My heart skipped a beat as I glanced at the screen.

"We need to talk. I'm sorry for how things ended. Let's meet."

My breath caught in my throat. I recognized the number immediately. It was Aaron.

"What's wrong?" Max noticed my change in demeanor, the warmth of our moment slipping away like sand through fingers.

"It's Aaron," I whispered, my heart racing, the tension from earlier crashing back like an unwelcome wave. "He wants to meet."

Max's expression hardened, a flicker of concern darkening his features. "What does he want? I thought you said you weren't going to let him back in."

"I don't know," I stammered, panic clawing at my insides. "I didn't respond."

"You should ignore it," Max said firmly, leaning forward. "You don't owe him anything. You've moved on."

"I know," I replied, torn between the need to protect what I had with Max and the overwhelming curiosity about what Aaron wanted.

"Then don't meet him," Max insisted, his eyes searching mine for assurance.

"I—" The words caught in my throat as a mix of emotions swirled within me. "What if this is my chance to really close the door?"

Max shook his head. "Or it could open a whole new can of worms. You really want to go down that path?"

The weight of his words hung heavy in the air, a moment of decision that felt monumental. As I stared at my phone, the screen glowing ominously, I could feel the world around me shift. The past and present collided in a dizzying whirl, and for a heartbeat, I stood on the precipice of choice, a riptide pulling me one way while the safety of my relationship with Max tugged me the other.

"I have to think," I finally said, my voice barely above a whisper, the flickering light of uncertainty casting shadows on my heart.

Max nodded, the worry still etched on his face, but I could see a flicker of resolve there too. "Just remember, you're not alone in this," he said softly, his words a balm against my chaos.

And as I sat there, the silence stretching between us, I felt the weight of the decision pressing down on me, a storm brewing just on the horizon. What if this was a turning point? A chance to redefine everything I thought I knew about myself, about Aaron, and about the love I was building with Max?

With my heart pounding in my chest, I knew I had to choose—stay safely within the walls I had built or step into the unknown, where shadows lurked but also where clarity might await. And as the moment hung in the air, I realized the decision could change everything.

Chapter 14: Tides of Doubt

Every time I glanced at Max, a wave of warmth flooded through me, like sunlight breaking through the trees on an autumn afternoon. His laughter filled the air, a sweet melody that danced around the park, mingling with the rustling leaves. We strolled side by side, the crunch of gravel beneath our feet punctuating the easy rhythm of our conversation. But there, nestled within the ease, lay an unshakable weight—a familiar ache that made my heart stutter and falter.

I stared out at the lake, its surface reflecting the dappled light like a shattered mirror, each glimmer a reminder of the fractures within me. As much as I wanted to lean into the comfort of Max's presence, I felt the ghosts of my past hovering at the edges of my thoughts. Aaron's laughter echoed in my mind, a bittersweet reminder of a time when happiness seemed just within reach, only to slip away like sand through my fingers. The warmth of Max's affection was intoxicating, yet it scared me, too. What if I was unworthy of such love? What if the shadows lurking in my heart grew bolder, threatening to consume everything we'd built together?

Max turned to me, his brow furrowing with concern, his hazel eyes searching mine. "Hey, are you alright?" His voice, smooth like honey, broke through my spiraling thoughts. "You've been quiet lately."

I smiled, though it felt more like a fragile mask than a genuine expression. "Just... lost in thought, I guess." My words were a fragile barrier against the storm brewing inside me, a flimsy excuse for the tumult I could hardly comprehend myself.

"You know, you can talk to me, right?" His fingers brushed against mine, a fleeting connection that sent shivers up my arm. "I'm here."

Those three words hung in the air, a lifeline I longed to grasp, yet I hesitated, caught in a tug-of-war between vulnerability and self-preservation. My heart ached with the truth I didn't dare share. The tide of emotions swelled, and I felt like I was standing on the edge of a cliff, staring into the abyss. I could jump into his arms and let him catch me, or I could pull back, retreat into the safety of my carefully constructed walls.

"I know," I said, my voice barely a whisper. "It's just... complicated." The word itself felt like a lead weight, the kind that sinks straight to the bottom of the ocean, dragging down everything in its wake.

"Complicated how?" He nudged, the hint of a smile playing on his lips. "Are we talking tangled shoelaces or the kind of complicated that requires a PhD?"

I couldn't help but chuckle, a small burst of laughter that surprised me. "More like the PhD, I'm afraid."

"Ah, I see." His eyes sparkled with mischief. "Well, I've been known to dabble in advanced emotional mathematics. What's the formula for happiness? A pinch of trust, a dash of communication, and maybe a sprinkle of late-night pizza?"

I loved this side of him—the playful, teasing nature that brought lightness even to my darkest thoughts. But that moment of levity quickly faded, and the heaviness settled back in like a fog.

"Max," I started, my voice shaking as I tried to weave my heart into words. "I—"

Before I could unravel the tangle of feelings, my phone buzzed in my pocket, shattering the fragile moment. I pulled it out, glancing at the screen. A text from Aaron. My breath caught in my throat. Why now?

"Is everything okay?" Max asked, concern etched on his face as he watched me go pale.

I swallowed hard, the words catching in my throat. "It's just..." I hesitated, unsure of how to explain the turmoil. I opened the message, the familiar twinge of anxiety swirling within me. "It's from Aaron."

"Ah." The understanding in his voice was laced with something unnameable, a mix of concern and perhaps a flicker of jealousy.

I turned the phone away, not ready to invite the past back into my present. "It's nothing important," I lied, though the weight of the truth felt like a leaden anchor in my gut.

"Doesn't sound like nothing." His tone shifted, the playful banter fading into something more serious. "If it bothers you, I want to know."

A pulse of warmth flickered within me, but it was quickly swallowed by the anxiety that clung to my thoughts. I could feel the fissures deepening, the cracks widening between us. How could I explain that Aaron was a specter in my life, a reminder of the mistakes that haunted me?

"It's just... old baggage," I managed, forcing a smile that didn't quite reach my eyes. "You know how it is. Some people just don't know when to let go."

Max stepped closer, the warmth radiating from his body comforting yet intimidating. "And what about you? Are you letting go?"

The question pierced through me, as sharp as a knife. I wanted to scream, to confess all my fears and doubts, to lay bare my heart for him to see. But instead, I clutched my phone tighter, a lifeline to my past that I wasn't ready to sever.

"Let's just enjoy the day, okay?" I said, the plea slipping from my lips like a secret I wasn't prepared to share.

He nodded, though the worry in his eyes remained. "Alright, but just know I'm here when you're ready."

As we continued our walk, the tension simmered beneath the surface, a quiet storm threatening to break. I could feel the weight of my choices pressing down on me, the struggle between past and present tangling like the roots of the trees surrounding us. My heart raced with each step, the fear of losing Max mingling with the dread of facing my own truths.

In that moment, surrounded by the vibrant colors of autumn and the crisp scent of fallen leaves, I couldn't help but wonder if I was strong enough to confront the tides of doubt crashing against the shores of my heart.

The following days unfolded like a well-rehearsed play, where I was both the lead and the reluctant understudy, caught between scenes that refused to blend harmoniously. Each morning, the sun crept through my bedroom window, illuminating the shadows that had nestled into my heart. I would stare at my reflection, seeking reassurance in my own eyes, yet all I found were the flickering doubts that had anchored themselves there. The laughter we once shared felt like echoes from another lifetime, each joyful note now tainted with the unresolved complexities of my heart.

The park had become our regular escape, a haven where we could momentarily forget the world outside. Yet with each visit, my heart weighed heavier, entangled in a web of hesitation and fear. Max, ever attuned to my moods, tried to draw me out. His questions, gentle yet probing, lingered in the air like a delicate perfume, sweet yet suffocating.

"Do you think ducks ever get bored just floating around?" he asked one afternoon, plopping down on a bench beside me, his easy smile a beacon of warmth.

"Probably," I replied, forcing a lighthearted chuckle. "But their lives seem so simple. Swim, quack, and occasionally waddle around looking for bread crumbs. Sounds delightful."

He raised an eyebrow, that playful spark igniting in his gaze. "You're telling me you wouldn't trade your complicated life for a couple of carefree quacks?"

"Let me think about that..." I mused, tapping my chin dramatically. "You might just be onto something. Less emotional baggage for sure."

Max leaned closer, the light breeze tousling his dark hair. "And what would you do with all that free time?"

"I don't know. Maybe start a duck-themed podcast? 'Quacking Up with Kelsey' has a nice ring to it, don't you think?"

He laughed, and for a brief moment, I felt the tension dissolve into the atmosphere like mist in the morning sun. But as quickly as it lifted, the heaviness returned, a storm brewing behind the façade of my smile.

"What's really going on?" His voice softened, the playful banter slipping away to reveal the genuine concern that lay beneath. "You know you can talk to me."

The sincerity in his eyes sent a shiver through me. I wanted to unburden my heart, to spill the chaos brewing inside, but my throat tightened as I recalled the message from Aaron. The past was a jagged stone lodged in my heart, refusing to budge, and it threatened to fracture the fragile connection I was beginning to cherish with Max.

"I'm just... figuring some things out," I replied, avoiding his gaze, my fingers absently tracing patterns on the bench. "It's not you. It's just... everything."

"Everything can be a lot to handle," he said, nodding. "But you don't have to carry it alone."

The warmth in his words wrapped around me like a soft blanket, and I wanted so desperately to lean into it. Yet, the echo of Aaron's name loomed over me, a shadow that refused to dissipate.

A soft breeze rustled the leaves above us, casting dappled shadows on the ground. "Maybe I need a ducking intervention," I said, trying to deflect the conversation back to lighter territory. "You know, a chance to float away from all this heaviness."

His lips twitched with amusement, but the concern didn't leave his eyes. "Well, let me know if you need a fellow quacker."

A genuine smile broke through my facade, and for a moment, the world felt lighter. We continued to talk about trivial things—favorite childhood cartoons, the best pizza toppings (an eternally contentious debate), and the absurdity of reality TV. But as the sun dipped lower in the sky, painting the world in golden hues, I couldn't shake the gnawing anxiety clawing at my insides.

The next evening, I stood in front of my mirror, running a hand through my hair, considering the cascade of emotions that had become my new normal. I was restless, a caged bird that longed to soar yet feared the open skies. Just as I was about to give in to the urge to message Max, my phone chimed again.

This time, it was a notification from my social media. A post from Aaron popped up, showcasing a new venture he was diving into—a project that radiated the kind of excitement I had once felt alongside him. The caption was innocuous enough, a simple invitation to join him at a launch party. But beneath the surface, it felt like a tug of war, a siren call beckoning me back into the past.

Max's laughter from earlier echoed in my mind, and the thought of his warm smile brought a flutter of hope. I stared at Aaron's post, the warmth of nostalgia mixing with an unsettling chill of fear. Would attending this launch party mean inviting the chaos of my past back into my life? Or would it simply be a chance to confront the specter that haunted me?

Before I could overthink it further, I opened a new message to Max. I hesitated, the words hanging heavy on my fingertips. I wanted to tell him everything, but the fear of shattering our fragile peace kept me rooted in silence.

But as I considered retreating back into my shell, another notification broke the stillness. It was from Max, his name lighting up my screen like a beacon in the dark. "Hey, just checking in. Want to grab dinner tomorrow? I found a new Thai place that I think you'll love."

My heart raced, caught in a delightful whirlwind. The offer was simple yet filled with the promise of connection, a chance to escape the heavy thoughts that had become my constant companions.

"Sounds perfect," I replied, my fingers moving with newfound urgency. "I could use some delicious distraction."

"Great! What time works for you?"

"Anytime. I'm flexible."

"Alright, then. Seven it is. Just promise you won't order anything spicy to prove a point."

"Ha! No promises."

I could almost hear his playful chuckle, a sound that wrapped around me like a warm hug. As the conversation flowed, I felt a flicker of hope ignite within me. Maybe this dinner could be the bridge I needed to cross the chasm of doubt that had threatened to pull me under.

As I set my phone down, a smile danced on my lips. Perhaps the evening would shed some light on the shadows lurking in my heart. After all, every moment spent with Max felt like a step towards discovering the joy I had almost forgotten. Yet as the twilight deepened outside my window, I couldn't shake the feeling that the shadows were still watching, waiting for the perfect moment to make their presence known.

The night of our dinner felt electric, charged with a mixture of anticipation and anxiety that made my stomach flutter like a swarm of butterflies trying to escape a jar. I had chosen a simple, yet striking, black dress—something that would hopefully mask the turmoil roiling within. As I stood before the mirror, I felt both hopeful and slightly ridiculous, as if I were preparing for a battle in an arena I didn't quite belong to. The idea of facing Max, the light in my otherwise tumultuous life, filled me with both excitement and fear.

Walking into the restaurant, the aroma of Thai spices enveloped me, a fragrant embrace that offered a semblance of comfort. I spotted Max at a cozy table in the corner, a soft glow of candles flickering around him, highlighting the way his hair curled just slightly at the ends, like he'd just rolled out of bed and forgotten to tame it. He caught my eye and grinned, a dazzling smile that chased away the last remnants of my nerves.

"Look at you," he said, standing to pull out my chair with a flourish. "You're radiant. Are you sure this isn't a 'quack' event?"

I laughed, the tension in my shoulders easing as I slid into the chair. "If it were, I'd definitely be the most overdressed duck in the room."

Max settled across from me, his eyes twinkling with delight. "Well, it's a good thing you're not trying to impress a flock of ducks then. I'm pretty sure they'd just honk at your shoes."

We shared playful banter as the evening unfolded, laughter punctuating the air, mingling with the clinking of dishes and the low murmur of conversation surrounding us. The menu was an adventure of its own; the moment I mentioned my indecision, Max leaned in, an earnest expression lighting his features.

"Okay, here's my expert recommendation: the Pad Thai is a classic, but if you're feeling daring, try the green curry. It's spicy enough to make you question your life choices but worth it."

"Daring, huh?" I mused, pretending to mull over it. "I'm in a risky mood. Let's do the green curry."

"Brave choice," he replied, nodding in approval. "I admire your courage. Just don't blame me if you end up breathing fire."

The banter flowed seamlessly, and with each passing moment, I felt the walls I had built around my heart begin to crumble. The fear and uncertainty that had shadowed my every thought started to dissipate, replaced by a sense of clarity that felt almost intoxicating.

"Tell me something," Max said, his expression shifting to something more serious as we waited for our food. "What's the most ridiculous thing you've ever done for love?"

I raised an eyebrow, considering the question, which held an undertone of deeper inquiry. "Are we talking romantic love or the 'I-will-eat-a-whole-pint-of-ice-cream-for-my-friends' kind of love?"

"Both. I'm curious about your spectrum of ridiculousness."

"Okay, for romantic love, I once drove four hours just to surprise a boyfriend at a concert. It turned out he was dating someone else, and I walked into the wrong section, and he was right there, making out with her."

Max winced, his eyes widening in sympathy. "Ouch. That's brutal."

"Right? But I'm pretty sure I got an A in the 'awkward exits' department." I chuckled, shaking my head at the memory. "And for friend love? Well, I might have once tried to convince my best friend to get matching tattoos that say 'Besties for Life.' Thankfully, she had more sense than I did."

"Hey, I'd totally support that," he grinned, leaning back in his chair. "I think it shows commitment."

We laughed together, the warmth of his presence washing over me, erasing the doubts that had gnawed at my heart. Yet, just as I felt the barriers crumbling, my phone buzzed on the table. The screen lit up with an unexpected notification, the name 'Aaron' flashing before me like a warning sign.

I froze, staring at the screen as my heart raced. "Oh, no."

"What is it?" Max asked, his tone shifting to concern as he leaned forward.

"It's a message from Aaron," I replied, the words slipping out almost in a whisper.

"Do you want to read it?"

I hesitated, my heart caught between the thrilling connection I felt with Max and the pull of the past that had unexpectedly surfaced. "I... I don't know."

"Do you think it's something that needs to be dealt with? You said he was old baggage."

"You're right, but... it feels like opening a can of worms."

"Then let's not open it just yet," Max said gently, his eyes locking onto mine, grounding me in the moment. "Focus on us tonight. Whatever it is can wait."

With a deep breath, I pushed the phone aside, forcing my thoughts back to the present. "Okay, you're right. Let's enjoy our dinner."

Our food arrived, vibrant colors spilling onto the table—crimson curry, bright green herbs, and steaming jasmine rice. I took a tentative bite, and my taste buds exploded in a fiery symphony. The heat washed over me like a tidal wave, immediate and intense, causing me to gasp for air.

"Welcome to daring," Max said, his laughter bubbling over as he watched my reaction. "How are we feeling about the life choices now?"

"I think I might need a fire extinguisher!" I replied, laughing between bites, but beneath the humor lay an undercurrent of unresolved tension, a fragile barrier threatening to collapse.

We dove into deeper conversations as the meal continued, sharing stories of childhood mishaps, favorite travel memories, and future dreams that painted the world with hope. Yet, just as the evening felt perfect, my phone buzzed again, this time more insistently.

I glanced at the screen, dread pooling in my stomach as I saw that it was another message from Aaron. My heart raced, the thrill of the evening suddenly clouded by uncertainty. "I can't believe he's messaging me this much," I said, almost to myself.

"Are you sure you want to keep ignoring it?" Max asked, a mixture of concern and curiosity in his voice.

I looked at him, torn between wanting to shield him from my past and needing to be honest about my reality. Just as I opened my mouth to respond, my phone buzzed again. This time, it was a call from Aaron, the screen lighting up with his name, demanding attention I wasn't sure I was ready to give.

The atmosphere shifted, a heavy weight settling between us as the sound of his name echoed like a haunting melody. I could feel the tension in the air as if it were a living thing, waiting to pounce.

"Maybe you should take it," Max suggested, his expression a mix of concern and support. "If it's bothering you this much..."

I hesitated, my heart pounding, the decision hanging in the balance like a pendulum. Should I answer and invite the chaos of my past back into my present? Or should I silence it, preserving the fragile connection I was building with Max?

I pressed my lips together, glancing between the phone and Max's hopeful gaze. "But what if it changes everything?"

"Then you'll deal with it together," he said softly, an unwavering strength radiating from him.

The call kept ringing, each chime punctuating the tension that hung like a thick fog. I took a deep breath, my heart racing. In that moment, I realized I was standing at a crossroads, one path leading to the past I thought I had left behind, and the other—into the uncertain embrace of a future I yearned to explore.

I reached for the phone, my fingers hovering over the screen, and just as I was about to answer, the call ended. A mix of relief and anxiety washed over me. I turned to Max, whose expression reflected my own uncertainty, a silent acknowledgment of the weight of the moment.

Suddenly, my phone buzzed again, another message illuminating the screen. "You need to see this."

I froze, my heart thundering in my chest, a sense of foreboding creeping in. "What does he want?"

Max leaned closer, his brow furrowing with concern. "Open it."

With trembling hands, I tapped the message, and as the words appeared before me, the world around us faded away, leaving only the stark reality of what lay ahead.

Chapter 15: Beneath the Surface

The rain drummed a soft, chaotic rhythm against the glass, a symphony of nature that seemed to seep into every crevice of the tiny art supply store. As I wandered through the narrow aisles, the scent of linseed oil and fresh canvas swirled around me like a warm embrace. Each step stirred up a blend of colors, an array of reds, blues, and yellows that beckoned me closer. I could almost hear the whispers of the artists who had come before me, each one leaving a piece of their soul behind in the very fabric of these walls.

My fingers grazed the rough texture of a canvas, and an electric spark shot through me. I could almost envision the masterpiece hidden within, waiting to escape the confines of my mind. Painting had always been a distant dream, an idle thought that lingered in the background of my chaotic life, but today felt different. Today was the day I would finally dive headfirst into the vibrant world that lay just beyond my fingertips.

I meandered toward the paint section, where tubes of color glistened under the soft glow of the overhead lights. I selected a few, each one promising to bring my emotions to life. With every brushstroke, I would strip away the layers I had built around myself. There was something terrifying yet exhilarating about the prospect of laying bare my innermost thoughts and fears, turning them into a kaleidoscope of color on a canvas. With a determined heart, I headed home, the weight of the world suddenly feeling lighter.

Once inside my apartment, I laid the canvas against the easel, the blank surface taunting me like a blank page in a diary. I took a deep breath, the air thick with anticipation. I squeezed out dollops of paint, the vibrant colors mixing on my palette like my own jumbled feelings. As the first brush made contact with the canvas, a surge of energy coursed through me. The brush glided across the surface, creating sweeping strokes of azure that mirrored the restlessness within my soul. Each movement became a dialogue between me and the canvas, a silent exchange where vulnerability met creativity.

Hours melted away as I immersed myself in this artistic reverie. The rain continued to patter against the window, a gentle reminder of the world outside, but inside, I was wrapped in a cocoon of color and emotion. Deep reds morphed into fiery oranges, swirling together like the passion and frustration fighting for dominance in my heart. I let the colors bleed into each other, the paint blending as my thoughts began to coalesce into something tangible. I was no longer just a woman in an apartment; I was a tempest of dreams, fears, and hopes, all screaming for attention.

As the evening deepened, I realized I had created something unexpected, a reflection of not just my turmoil but also of my resilience. I stood back, surveying the canvas, my breath catching in my throat. It was messy yet beautiful, a tapestry of emotions I had long buried. I felt alive, invigorated by the rawness of my creation, and the thought of sharing it with Max sent an exhilarating jolt through me.

Max, with his charming smile and quick wit, had always been a grounding force in my chaotic life. I could still remember the first time we met—his laughter echoed like music, breaking through my shell. He had a way of seeing through the surface, of peeling back the layers until he revealed the core of who I was, and the idea of sharing this piece of myself with him filled me with equal parts excitement and dread.

I texted him, my fingers trembling as I typed, "Come over! I have something to show you." The seconds stretched into eternity as I awaited his response, my heart pounding like a drum. When he finally replied with a simple, "On my way," a mix of relief and anticipation washed over me.

I prepared myself, tidying the apartment in a flurry of activity, as if I could organize the chaos within me by straightening cushions and wiping countertops. I placed my palette and brushes aside, trying to still the nerves that threatened to bubble over. What if he didn't get it? What if he looked at my canvas and saw only a mess? I shushed those thoughts away, reminding myself that this was about honesty, about sharing my world with someone I cared about.

When he knocked on the door, I felt a rush of adrenaline. I opened it to find him standing there, drenched from the rain, his dark hair sticking to his forehead in a charmingly disheveled way. "Nice weather we're having," he quipped, a smirk playing at the corners of his mouth.

"Right? Just what I needed—an indoor adventure," I replied, stepping aside to let him in. He took off his shoes, leaving them in a haphazard pile at the door, and I couldn't help but smile. There was something so endearing about his effortless charm.

"I can't believe you dragged me out in this weather. What's so important?" he teased, but his eyes glinted with genuine curiosity.

"Just... come see," I said, leading him to the small nook where my easel stood. I could feel my pulse quickening, a mixture of excitement and anxiety thrumming through me. When he finally laid eyes on the canvas, his expression shifted from playful to contemplative. He stepped closer, his gaze scanning the colors and shapes, each stroke of paint telling a story I was about to unfold.

"It's... incredible," he said slowly, his voice thick with sincerity. "What inspired this?"

The question hung in the air, heavy with meaning. This was the moment to be vulnerable, to let him into the depths of my world. I took a breath, the weight of my emotions spilling out. "It's a representation of everything I've been feeling lately. The chaos, the confusion, the moments of clarity. It's me."

He looked back at the canvas, and for a moment, the room was filled with silence—an intimate, sacred moment where the outside world faded away.

The silence hung between us like a well-tuned string, vibrating with unspoken words and lingering questions. Max stepped closer, tilting his head as if the angle would unlock the secrets swirling within the swathes of color. "You've captured a lot here," he finally said, his voice low, almost reverent. "What does this red mean? It looks like it's ready to leap off the canvas."

I followed his gaze, the deep crimson almost pulsing with a life of its own. "That's anger," I said, surprising myself with the clarity of my answer. "Or maybe frustration. It's all the times I felt trapped, like I was screaming underwater, but nobody could hear me." I bit my lip, suddenly feeling exposed. "And the blue? That's sadness. It felt like a storm brewing inside, churning and swirling."

Max nodded, his expression shifting as he absorbed the weight of my words. "You're better at this than you give yourself credit for," he said, his tone teasing yet sincere. "You might have to give up that day job and start painting full-time."

I laughed, a little too loud, a little too bright, and the sound bounced off the walls, filling the space with warmth. "Right, because starving artist sounds so appealing." The levity in my voice masked the unease that bubbled beneath. I wanted to feel validated, yet the thought of truly exposing myself made my stomach twist. "But seriously, I've never really done this before. I mean, really done it. It's one thing to doodle in a sketchbook and another to bare your soul on canvas."

"Who knew you were hiding this artistic soul under that practical exterior?" he quipped, a playful glint in his eye. "I feel like I'm getting to know a whole new side of you. What else are you hiding? A secret stash of treasure maps?"

I rolled my eyes, but the lightness in his tone made my heart flutter. "If I had a treasure map, I'd be more interested in finding some hidden beaches than painting," I replied, my voice half-serious.

"And maybe a boat. I've always thought the sea would be a good escape."

Max's brow furrowed in thought, and he crossed his arms. "So, you're telling me if you could run away anywhere, it would be to the ocean?"

"Not just the ocean," I said, feeling a spark of adventure ignite within me. "Somewhere with soft sands, the kind that makes you forget about everything else. Maybe a little beach shack with mismatched furniture and a porch swing. Just me and the sound of the waves. It sounds perfect, doesn't it?"

"I'd say it sounds like a cliché waiting to happen," he countered, but his smile revealed he was charmed by my vision. "But I get it. A little escape from reality isn't the worst idea."

"Reality, right?" I echoed, the weight of those words pressing down on my chest. "But then again, where does that leave us? I mean, is it enough just to paint our dreams or our fears? What happens when the paint dries, and we're left with the mess we created?"

He stepped back, contemplating the canvas, and I held my breath, waiting for him to respond. "I think the mess is part of the beauty. Sometimes, the things we don't want to show are the things that resonate most with people. It's the imperfections that make life interesting."

I studied him, a spark of something I couldn't quite name igniting in my chest. "Wow, when did you become a philosopher?" I teased, but inside, his words burrowed deep.

"Must be all those late nights watching documentaries," he joked, shrugging. "But really, I think people connect over shared struggles. It's like finding common ground on a shaky foundation."

My heart pounded in my chest. Max was right; there was beauty in the imperfections, and maybe, just maybe, I didn't have to hide behind the curtain of my chaos. My fears, my hopes, my paintings—they all mattered. The thought of embracing the mess, both on the canvas and in life, felt exhilarating and terrifying all at once.

"Alright, Mr. Philosopher, let's see how much deeper you can dive into the rabbit hole." I gestured toward a blank canvas sitting beside the easel. "Are you ready to create a masterpiece of your own?"

His eyes widened, a mix of surprise and mischief igniting in his expression. "You want me to paint? Like, really paint? You realize I once thought a stick figure was a complex art form?"

"Exactly! You're the perfect candidate," I laughed, the sound bubbling out of me. "Let's see how profound you can get with a brush in your hand. Just promise me you won't draw a stick figure, or I might cry."

He took a deep breath, pretending to summon his courage. "Fine, but if this goes south, I'm blaming you for my inevitable embarrassment."

"Deal!" I said, tossing him a paintbrush, which he caught with a look of mock triumph. I could feel the energy shift as he approached the canvas, eyes glinting with determination.

Max squirted some paint onto his palette, the colors mixing in a vibrant splash, and for a moment, he looked surprisingly focused. "What should I paint?" he asked, glancing over his shoulder, the corners of his mouth twitching in a grin.

"How about something that represents you? What's the first thing that comes to mind?"

He paused, tapping the brush against his chin as if deep in thought. "A coffee cup, obviously. My entire personality can be summed up in caffeine."

I couldn't suppress a laugh. "That sounds about right. Go for it. Let's see how you express your inner barista."

He launched into it with surprising zeal, paint flying as he gestured animatedly. Each stroke was a mix of wild abandon and childlike enthusiasm, the laughter spilling out of us like music. As his "coffee cup" took shape—a wildly abstract swirl of browns and creams—I realized this was more than just painting; it was about connection, a shared moment that transcended the messiness of life.

"Behold, my tribute to the liquid motivation that drives me," he announced with mock grandeur, stepping back to admire his creation.

I studied it, feigning seriousness. "It's magnificent. I'm moved, truly. Who knew you had such depth hidden beneath those coffee grounds?"

His laughter filled the space, a sound I wanted to capture and hold onto. "I'll take that as a compliment. But seriously, this is actually... fun."

"Right? Who knew therapy could be so colorful?" I grinned, feeling the air around us shift as we played with colors and words, dancing between lighthearted banter and something deeper.

But just as I was losing myself in the moment, that nagging fear whispered back, nudging me, reminding me of the layers I was still afraid to peel away. What if this connection was fleeting? What if, like my art, the colors would fade, leaving behind only the shadow of what could have been?

As we continued to paint, the atmosphere between Max and me crackled with a vibrant energy, weaving itself into a tapestry of laughter and playful banter. I watched as he wrestled with his brush, his brow furrowed in concentration, while splashes of paint erupted around him like fireworks. The smell of paint filled the air, mingling with the warmth of our shared moments, creating an intoxicating blend that made me feel as if we were cocooned in our own little world.

"Alright, Picasso, what's next?" I called out, leaning back against the wall, arms crossed and a teasing smile playing on my lips.

He glanced back at me, a mischievous grin spreading across his face. "You mean I'm not just a barista anymore? I'm an artist too? This is a real career breakthrough."

"Oh, absolutely! I see a future exhibit in our local coffee shop showcasing your work. 'A Caffeine-Inspired Journey Through Brushstrokes.'"

"Only if you promise to write the press release," he shot back, his voice dripping with mock seriousness. "Something like, 'Join us for a taste of rich espresso and even richer art.'"

I laughed, the sound bouncing around the room, blending seamlessly with the artistic chaos we'd created. But just as I was about to respond, my phone buzzed on the table, breaking the spell. I grabbed it, glancing at the screen, and my stomach dropped.

"Hey, it's just my mom," I said, trying to sound nonchalant as I thumbed through the text. But the words felt like a heavy weight in my hands. We need to talk.

Max watched me, the playful light in his eyes dimming slightly. "Everything okay?"

I hesitated, caught between the urge to brush it off and the reality of the knot tightening in my stomach. "Yeah, just... family stuff."

"Ah, the ominous 'family stuff.' My favorite." He said it lightly, but I could see the concern flickering in his gaze.

"More like the kind of stuff that gets dropped into conversations at family dinners and spirals into two-hour debates," I replied, trying to keep my tone light, but the weight of it clung to me. "I'll just... deal with it later."

He nodded but didn't look convinced. The moment hung there, charged and uncertain, before he turned back to his coffee cup painting, a hint of tension settling between us. I fought the urge to dig deeper, to lay my worries bare, but I couldn't shake the feeling that something was looming on the horizon.

Max's brush moved in rhythmic strokes, but his gaze flicked back to me. "You know, you can talk to me about anything, right?"

I hesitated, the truth trembling on my lips. "I know. It's just... complicated."

"Complicated tends to be my middle name." He turned, the paintbrush poised dramatically like a sword. "What's more complicated than an artist with a vivid imagination? Tell me your worst fear. Go ahead, spill your heart."

I chuckled softly, appreciating his effort to lighten the mood, but I wasn't ready to divulge the tangled threads of my worries. Instead, I shrugged, deflecting. "I'll take the 'worst fear' question under advisement. But let's focus on your work of art instead. How's that coffee cup coming along?"

He huffed a laugh, rolling his eyes. "I'll have you know this masterpiece requires intense concentration and deep thought. You don't just throw paint around; it's about feeling."

"Feeling, huh? Is that what we're calling it now?"

"Absolutely! Art is subjective, after all. I'm currently on an emotional roller coaster, navigating the highs and lows of my coffee cup."

"Sounds like a thrilling ride," I teased, but my heart wasn't in it. The weight of my mother's message still lingered, casting a shadow over the laughter we shared.

He moved closer, eyes searching mine. "You know, sometimes the thing we think is complicated isn't really that complicated at all. It's just a matter of perspective."

My heart raced, caught between the warmth of his gaze and the impending storm of family dynamics that loomed over me. "It's just—" I began, but the words stalled in my throat, and I looked away, staring at the canvas as if it could offer me answers.

Max shifted, placing his hand gently on my shoulder, grounding me. "Hey, whatever it is, I'm here. Just remember that, okay?"

I nodded, appreciating the weight of his presence, the unwavering support that felt like a shield against the outside world. "Thanks, Max. That means a lot."

We shared a moment, silence wrapping around us like a comforting blanket, until the doorbell rang, slicing through the intimacy of the space.

"Who could that be?" I asked, glancing toward the door.

"Maybe it's the art critics, here to praise my brilliance." He flashed a grin, but I could sense the tension creeping back into the air.

I walked to the door, my heart pounding a little faster. As I opened it, the sight that greeted me sent a chill down my spine. Standing there, framed in the doorway, was my mother, her expression unreadable, her presence a storm cloud hovering over our painted oasis.

"Mom?" I stammered, trying to process the sudden twist of fate. "What are you doing here?"

Her gaze flickered over my shoulder, landing on Max, who stood behind me, concern etched across his features. "I need to talk to you," she said, her voice steady but heavy with something unspoken.

"Can't it wait?" I replied, forcing my voice to remain calm, even as a sense of dread pooled in my stomach.

"No, it can't," she insisted, her eyes narrowing slightly. "This is important."

I felt the air shift around us, a palpable tension charging the atmosphere as I glanced back at Max, who looked caught between concern and confusion. "Can you give us a moment?" I asked, the words tumbling out before I could think them through.

He nodded, but the look he shot my way was one of worry, one that sent a jolt of apprehension through me. I stepped outside, closing the door behind me, and immediately felt the weight of her gaze pin me to the spot.

"What's going on?" I asked, my voice steadier than I felt.

She took a breath, her posture rigid, and I braced myself for the words that were about to change everything. "It's about your father," she said, and the moment felt like a raw nerve exposed to the world, the tension tightening around us as I prepared for whatever revelation would follow.

Chapter 16: Colors of Truth

The paint on my palette was a riot of colors, a tempest of emotion swirling in the depths of my mind. Each hue whispered secrets, coaxing me to release my heart onto the canvas, where its raw truth could dance in the light. Max stood beside me, the late afternoon sun casting a golden glow through the studio windows, illuminating the chaos that surrounded us. The air smelled of linseed oil and turpentine, mingling with the faintest hint of lavender from the sachets I kept in the corners, hoping to inspire serenity in my creative chaos. As he leaned closer, I caught the warmth of his presence, an anchor amidst the storm of colors.

"Is that a hint of cobalt blue I see? Or is it merely your mood?" he teased, a playful grin tugging at the corners of his mouth. His eyes sparkled with mischief, and for a moment, the weight of my thoughts slipped away, replaced by the lighter burden of shared laughter.

"It's definitely a reflection of my mood," I shot back, rolling my eyes as I swirled the paint on my palette. "Cobalt blue for my existential dread, and maybe a splash of cadmium red for the frustration that accompanies it." I pointed my brush at him, pretending it was a sword, the bristles poised dramatically in the air.

"Ah, the classic painter's dilemma—too many emotions, not enough canvas," he quipped, folding his arms as he leaned against the doorframe, clearly enjoying our banter. "So, what's next? A thousand-yard stare to symbolize your longing for clarity?"

I laughed, the sound bubbling up unexpectedly, the kind of laughter that feels like sunshine breaking through a cloudy sky. "I could capture that, but I'd rather channel it into something a bit more... vibrant."

Max stepped closer, his gaze sweeping over the chaotic beauty I had created, the wild strokes of color that mirrored the tempest within me. "It's beautiful," he murmured, his voice softening as he took in the myriad of emotions woven into each brushstroke. "I can see the pain and hope here. It's like you've poured your soul onto the canvas."

His words stirred something deep within me, a mix of pride and vulnerability that settled in my chest. The walls I had built around my heart began to tremble as I saw the truth in his eyes—a reflection of my own struggles, an acknowledgment of the battles I fought in silence. I hesitated, grappling with the urge to share the fears that had kept me at arm's length, the secrets that clung to me like shadows.

"Art has always been my way of processing things," I began, my voice barely above a whisper, "but it's also a way to hide. Each stroke, each color, it's all part of a narrative I'm scared to speak aloud."

Max nodded, his expression earnest, inviting me to continue. The afternoon sun streamed through the windows, bathing us in warmth, a gentle reminder that we were cocooned in this moment together, safe from the outside world.

"I've always felt like I had to keep my struggles to myself, like sharing them would somehow lessen their weight. But looking at this—" I gestured towards my canvas, "it feels different. It feels like I'm finally ready to let someone in."

"Then let me in," he replied, his voice steady, holding my gaze as if it were a fragile thing, a treasure that needed care. "I promise, I won't run away."

There was a sincerity in his words that broke through the last of my defenses. The truth of my emotions swelled within me, a tide that demanded to be released. "There's a part of me that feels like I've always had to be strong, that vulnerability is a weakness. But I'm tired of pretending."

As I spoke, I felt the heaviness in my heart lift, like the clouds parting to reveal a bright blue sky. I revealed the fears that had kept me at a distance—the anxiety of being unworthy, the shadow of past failures, and the struggle to be seen beyond my art. With every word, I felt the connection between us deepen, the invisible thread that tied our souls together strengthening.

Max stepped closer, the warmth radiating from him wrapping around me like a cocoon. "You're not alone in this," he said, his voice barely above a whisper. "I've felt those same fears, the weight of expectations. It's exhausting to carry it all by yourself."

I looked up, searching his eyes for the truth in his words. The vulnerability etched into his expression mirrored my own, and for the first time, I didn't feel like I was burdening him with my struggles. Instead, I felt like we were forging a bond, a shared understanding that ran deeper than mere words.

The evening unfolded in a tapestry of stories, our voices weaving a narrative that was both personal and universal. We spoke of dreams and aspirations, our artistic visions intertwined like the colors on my canvas. Max shared tales of his own struggles, how he had found solace in painting, how he had once felt lost in a world that seemed to demand perfection at every turn.

"I painted my way through heartbreak," he confessed, a hint of a smile playing on his lips. "It was either that or drown in my own self-pity, and I'm terrible at swimming."

"Same," I admitted, unable to contain my laughter. "My only lifeguard is my paintbrush, and even that gets a bit soggy sometimes."

As the sun dipped below the horizon, casting a warm glow across the studio, I felt a shift within myself, a blossoming hope that perhaps letting him in wasn't just a risk, but a chance to embrace something beautiful. In the sanctuary of our shared vulnerability, I realized that it wasn't just my story I was painting—it was a tapestry of our truths, each brushstroke a testament to the strength found in openness.

As twilight draped its velvet cloak over the world outside, the studio transformed into a sanctuary of warmth and connection. The vibrant chaos on my canvas mirrored the rising warmth in my chest, a sense of camaraderie blooming like the flowers I had painted in a riot of colors. Max lingered, leaning against the easel as if it were a bar counter where we were sharing secrets over cocktails, only we were pouring our souls into words instead.

"So, what's the next big masterpiece?" he asked, his eyes sparkling with a blend of mischief and curiosity. "Something depicting the tragic fate of the last paintbrush? Or perhaps a grand mural of me, the misunderstood artist, bathed in chiaroscuro light?"

I snorted, laughter bubbling up unbidden. "Oh, definitely the mural. Your visage deserves a place on the Sistine Chapel of Heartbreak."

"Ah, but will there be a halo?" he shot back, feigning a seriousness that was utterly at odds with the twinkle in his eye.

I considered this for a moment, tapping my chin in mock contemplation. "Only if it's made of glitter. A subtle nod to your dazzling personality."

He laughed, a sound that filled the room and bounced off the walls, igniting a warmth that lingered in the air. "Then I'll settle for that, but I'm demanding a gallery opening when you're done. Complete with red wine and an absurd amount of cheese."

"Cheese? The true artist's fuel," I agreed, savoring the way our playful banter felt like stepping onto a well-worn path, familiar yet exhilarating. There was a lightness to our exchanges, a dance of words that felt like we were weaving an invisible thread between our hearts.

As we settled into a comfortable rhythm, our laughter flowed easily, but there was an undercurrent of something deeper, a hint of uncharted territory that beckoned just beyond the horizon of our conversations. I could feel it in the way he shifted closer, the subtle brush of his arm against mine, igniting a warmth that spread through me like a sunbeam on a winter's day.

"Tell me," he said, his tone suddenly more serious as he studied my expression. "What's the story behind that one?" He pointed at a canvas tucked in the corner, a swirling mass of reds and blacks that seemed to pulse with an energy all its own.

I followed his gaze, my heart tightening as I remembered the emotions that had birthed that particular piece—a culmination of heartache, frustration, and a longing for something just out of reach. "That one was born out of a breakup," I admitted, my voice dropping to a hush. "It's... well, it's a bit of a mess, much like the relationship."

"Messy emotions make for the best art," he encouraged, tilting his head slightly as if he were studying a complex puzzle. "What were you trying to convey?"

I paused, searching for the right words, the vulnerable truth buried beneath layers of paint and memories. "I think I was trying to capture the feeling of drowning in emotions, of being caught in a storm where everything feels chaotic and out of control. It's like standing on the edge of a cliff, knowing you might fall but unable to move."

Max nodded slowly, his expression thoughtful. "And now?"

"Now?" I echoed, letting the weight of his question settle over me. "Now I feel like I'm finally learning how to swim."

He smiled, the corners of his mouth lifting in a way that made my heart do an unexpected flip. "Then you've already won, haven't you? The ocean can be brutal, but it can also be a place of discovery."

Our conversation shifted, the night deepening as we shared more of our lives—stories of triumph and defeat, moments that had shaped us, and those that had almost broken us. With every confession, I felt the barriers I had constructed around my heart crumbling, revealing the raw and tender parts of myself that I had kept hidden for far too long.

"I always thought that being vulnerable was a weakness," I confessed, my voice softening as I spoke. "But now, I'm starting to see it differently. Maybe it's a strength, a way to connect with others."

"It is," he affirmed, his eyes reflecting the flickering light of the candles I had lit, creating an atmosphere that was both intimate and safe. "And it's what makes you a fantastic artist. You're not afraid to bare your soul, even when it's terrifying."

I met his gaze, a rush of warmth flooding through me at his compliment. The moment felt electric, charged with a tension that was both exhilarating and terrifying. "And you? What do you hope to create?"

"I want to create art that makes people feel," he said, his voice steady, unwavering. "Art that draws them in, that resonates with their own experiences. I want to be part of a community where we all share our truths, where vulnerability is celebrated."

I leaned back, letting his words wash over me like a soothing balm. There was something powerful in the way we were peeling back layers, discovering the heart of each other through art and honesty. "That sounds like a beautiful dream," I replied softly. "But isn't it also risky? What if they don't resonate?"

He shrugged, the movement casual but his eyes serious. "What matters is that we try. If we share our truths, we create a space for others to do the same. And who knows? Maybe we'll inspire someone else to pick up a brush or a pen."

I considered this, the notion settling in my mind like a puzzle piece falling into place. It felt good, this connection we were nurturing, the seeds of something deep taking root in the fertile ground of our shared dreams.

"Here's to our messy truths," I said, raising an imaginary glass.

"To messy truths," he echoed, a smile dancing on his lips.

Just then, the quiet hum of my phone broke the moment, its screen lighting up with a message from my sister. A fleeting look of annoyance crossed my face before I realized I hadn't checked in with her all day. I glanced at the screen, ready to dismiss it, but something held me back.

"Go ahead, see what it is," Max encouraged, a knowing smile on his face. "I'll just admire the chaotic beauty of your workspace while you do."

I chuckled, grateful for his understanding. "Right, because nothing says art like a studio covered in paint splatters and glitter."

As I read the message, my heart sank. "Can we talk?" it read, followed by a string of anxious emojis. A wave of unease washed over me, a sudden reminder of the turbulent waters I had tried so hard to leave behind for the night.

"What's wrong?" Max asked, concern etching his features as he caught the change in my demeanor.

"It's my sister," I admitted, anxiety knotting in my stomach. "She wants to talk. It's... complicated."

He studied me for a moment, the warmth of his presence providing a grounding force as I processed the sudden shift in my emotions. "Do you want to talk about it?"

I hesitated, torn between the comfort of our evening and the unsettling gravity of my sister's message. But looking into Max's eyes, I realized that perhaps this was the moment to embrace my vulnerability, to let him in even further. "Maybe I do."

The gentle vibration of my phone echoed in the quiet space, breaking the tranquil spell woven between Max and me. As I processed my sister's message, a familiar knot tightened in my stomach, the anxiety creeping back in like an unwelcome guest crashing a cozy gathering. I took a deep breath, reminding myself of the warmth we'd just shared, the blossoming connection that felt like a breath of fresh air after a long winter.

"What's it about?" Max asked, his concern palpable, a tether to reality amidst my rising turmoil.

"It's... complicated," I admitted, biting my lip. The last thing I wanted was to pull him into the drama that often accompanied family. "She tends to call when things are going wrong."

"Sounds like she needs you," he said softly, the weight of understanding in his voice. "Is it serious?"

I considered my answer, weighing the chaos that had become our family dynamic against the serene sanctuary we had created here in the studio. "I don't know. It could be. Or it might just be her usual melodrama. Either way, it feels like I've been balancing on a tightrope, and one slip could send me tumbling."

Max stepped closer, his presence grounding me. "You don't have to do it alone. You can share the load, you know."

The sincerity in his words washed over me like a soothing balm, but the gnawing uncertainty of my sister's situation remained. "It's hard for me to let people in, especially when I'm not sure what they want. My sister can be a lot... more than I can handle sometimes."

"Then let's tackle it together," he offered, his tone unwavering, even as I felt my resolve slipping. "We can take it one step at a time. You don't have to carry the weight of her worries alone."

There was something incredibly reassuring about his offer, the way he seemed to promise he would be there, ready to help navigate whatever storm lay ahead. I appreciated the gesture but felt an urge to protect him from my family's chaos, that old instinct to shield others from my burdens. Yet, the idea of facing this alone felt far worse than the thought of dragging him into the fray.

I nodded slowly, my resolve strengthening. "You're right. Maybe it's time I stop pretending everything is fine and just... face the mess head-on."

"Exactly." He smiled, that easy, disarming grin that made me feel both seen and understood. "Plus, I could use a good story. All this art talk has me itching for some real drama."

I chuckled, a lightness returning to my chest. "I can guarantee you a story worthy of a soap opera. Just wait."

I reached for my phone, hesitating for a moment, the weight of my sister's previous dramas lingering in the air. With a deep breath, I opened the message and began typing a response.

"Hey, what's up? I saw your message. I'm here if you need to talk."

Just as I hit send, the atmosphere shifted, an unsettling energy coursing through the room like a chill breeze. Max watched me intently, his eyes filled with curiosity and concern.

"Are you sure you want to dive into this tonight?" he asked, the lightheartedness of our earlier banter giving way to a more serious tone. "We could keep this going, you know. Art, laughter... it might be just what you need."

"I know, but it's calling me," I said, unable to shake the urgency rising within me. "I can't just ignore her."

"Fair enough," he replied, stepping back slightly, giving me space to breathe while remaining a comforting presence. "Just remember, you're not alone in this. Whatever happens, I'm right here."

The sincerity of his words lingered in the air like an unspoken promise as my phone chimed again, jolting me back to reality. I glanced at the screen, my heart dropping as I read my sister's reply.

"I need you to come home. There's something you need to know."

The gravity of her words hit me like a tidal wave. Home had always been a double-edged sword, a place of both comfort and chaos, memories wrapped in love and turmoil. I glanced at Max, who looked at me with a mixture of concern and understanding, as if he could sense the tumultuous storm brewing just beneath the surface.

"I need to go," I said, my voice steadier than I felt.

"Want me to come with you?" he asked, his offer genuine and heartfelt.

I hesitated, torn between the comfort of his presence and the need to handle my family's business on my own. "I don't want to drag you into my family's mess," I admitted, the tension creeping back into my voice.

He shrugged, his expression unwavering. "You wouldn't be dragging me in. You'd be inviting me along, and I'm all for it if it means supporting you."

The sincerity in his voice warmed my heart, but the weight of my sister's message loomed large, pressing against my chest like a heavy stone. I took a deep breath, steeling myself for the inevitable plunge into chaos. "Okay, let's do this."

Together, we stepped into the evening, the cool night air wrapping around us like a cloak as we made our way to my car. The quiet of the street contrasted sharply with the whirlwind of emotions swirling within me. The stars glittered overhead, indifferent to the turmoil unfolding beneath them.

As we drove, the silence was thick with anticipation, punctuated only by the soft hum of the engine and the distant sounds of the city. My thoughts raced, replaying every moment that had led to this. Would my sister's revelations alter everything I had fought so hard to build?

"What do you think she wants to tell you?" Max broke the silence, his voice steady, grounding me as we approached my childhood home, a place rich with memories and complexities.

I bit my lip, my stomach a twisting knot of nerves. "I'm not sure. But knowing her, it's probably something dramatic."

He chuckled lightly, attempting to lighten the mood, but I could feel the tension crackling in the air. "Dramatic is good. It keeps life interesting, right?"

"Unless it's the type of drama that shatters everything," I murmured, my voice barely above a whisper.

Just then, I spotted the silhouette of my sister standing on the porch, her figure outlined against the soft glow of the porch light. The sight sent a jolt of apprehension through me. There was something in her stance—tense, almost expectant—that sent my heart racing.

Max squeezed my hand, a gentle reassurance as I parked the car. "You've got this. Remember, you're not alone."

I nodded, my heart pounding as I stepped out into the night, the familiar scent of rain-soaked earth filling the air, mingling with the bittersweet aroma of nostalgia. The moment stretched before me like a vast canvas waiting to be painted, and I could almost feel the colors of my emotions swirling within me, ready to burst forth.

As I walked toward her, the weight of uncertainty settled heavily on my shoulders. "What's going on?" I called out, my voice echoing slightly in the stillness.

She stepped forward, her expression serious, eyes glistening with unshed tears. "I didn't know how to tell you, but..."

And then, just as she opened her mouth to continue, the sudden screech of tires interrupted the moment. A figure stepped into view from the shadows, and my heart dropped as a wave of recognition washed over me, freezing me in place.

"Surprise!" The voice was all too familiar, a jarring note in the evening's fragile harmony, sending shockwaves through the air.

Chapter 17: Chasing Dreams

The air was thick with the scent of paint, mingling with the late afternoon sun that spilled through the open windows of the community center. I stood before a wall that had once been a drab beige, its surface cracked and lifeless, an eyesore in a place meant for joy and connection. Max was beside me, his laughter ringing out like music against the monotony, his fingers splattered with a riot of colors. Together, we were embarking on a journey of transformation, not just of the wall but of ourselves.

"What if we start with a tree?" he suggested, tilting his head to gauge my reaction. "A giant one, roots sprawling out across the wall, a testament to strength and growth. We can fill the branches with all sorts of birds, symbolizing freedom."

"Birds?" I raised an eyebrow, a playful smirk tugging at my lips. "So we're just going to make a sanctuary for feathered friends? What are we, a wildlife refuge?"

He grinned, his blue eyes sparkling with mischief. "You'd be surprised how well a tree could serve as a metaphor for our dreams. They start small, just like us, but with the right care, they reach for the sky."

A rush of warmth surged through me as I studied him. Max had a way of turning the ordinary into the extraordinary, his thoughts flowing like the paint on our brushes, vibrant and alive. With a nod, I picked up a brush and dipped it into a rich brown hue. The first stroke felt electric, the bristles dancing across the wall, and I couldn't help but smile as the outline of the trunk began to take shape.

Hours slipped away in a blur of color and laughter. We lost ourselves in the rhythm of creation, our playful banter punctuated by the occasional splash of paint that somehow found its way onto our clothes or into each other's hair. I caught him once, mid-laugh, with a smear of emerald green across his forehead. I couldn't help but lean in, my lips curving into a teasing grin. "You've got a little something there. Did you mean to start a fashion trend?"

He feigned innocence, his expression exaggeratedly serious. "Clearly, I'm just trying to channel my inner Picasso. You wouldn't understand—art is about the unexpected." Then, without warning, he flicked a wet brush in my direction, the paint splattering across my cheek. "Oops! Guess I'm more Jackson Pollock than I thought!"

As I wiped the paint from my face, I felt a giddy rush, the tension from my everyday life fading like the brush strokes we laid down on the wall. This was a sanctuary, our sanctuary, a moment suspended in time where worries dissolved into laughter and creativity. Each brushstroke carried a whisper of hope, a promise of brighter days to come.

Yet, in the quiet corners of my mind, shadows of doubt lurked, remnants of a past I was desperate to escape. I'd spent years pushing away those I cared about, fearful of the kind of vulnerability that came with opening my heart. But as I mixed colors and lost myself in the splashes and swirls, I began to understand: vulnerability was not a weakness; it was a vibrant palette, waiting to be explored.

"Look at that!" Max exclaimed, stepping back to admire our work. The tree was taking shape, its trunk strong and commanding, branches stretching out like arms embracing the sky. "It's alive! I can almost hear it whispering to the clouds."

"Can trees actually whisper?" I mused, teasing him lightly. "Or are you just being melodramatic again?"

He shrugged, a glimmer of mischief in his eyes. "What's life without a little drama? Besides, I believe they do. Every time the wind rustles through the leaves, it's their way of speaking. They've got stories, you know."

As the sun began to dip below the horizon, casting a golden glow across the room, I found myself lost in his words. Perhaps we all had stories etched into our souls, waiting for the right moment to be shared. The idea sent a ripple of excitement through me, stirring a longing to uncover my own tale, to weave it into the vibrant tapestry we were creating together.

"Okay, Mr. Tree Whisperer," I said, glancing at him with newfound determination. "Let's add some colors to those birds. They should be just as full of life as our tree."

Together, we began to paint the birds, each one bursting with color and personality, representing the dreams we dared to chase. I chose a bright yellow for one, a nod to optimism and new beginnings, while Max selected a deep blue, embodying the depths of our aspirations.

"This one," I said, pointing to a particularly plump little bird, "is the one that'll sing the loudest when we finally go for our dreams. I think we should name it 'Courage.'"

Max chuckled, his paintbrush dancing in the air as he added intricate details to the wings. "And this one," he said, gesturing to a bird soaring high above the tree, "is 'Adventure.' It'll lead us to places we've only dreamed about."

I was swept up in the moment, feeling a sense of unity with Max that was both exhilarating and terrifying. This mural was more than just paint on a wall; it was a manifestation of our hopes, dreams, and fears, swirling together in a chaotic yet beautiful mix. As the colors dried and the sun faded, I knew that this was just the beginning. We were standing at the edge of something magnificent, ready to take flight into the unknown.

With the sun settling into a lazy embrace behind the horizon, we stepped back to admire our handiwork. The vibrant tree loomed majestically on the wall, its branches reaching for the heavens, adorned with the cheerful birds we'd brought to life. I felt a swell of pride mingling with the paint on my hands, a symbol of our shared effort and budding connection.

"Who knew we'd be modern-day Picassos?" Max teased, leaning against the wall, his arms crossed, a satisfied smile gracing his lips.

"More like amateur impressionists," I shot back, feigning seriousness. "Though I could get used to this artist lifestyle. No one really expects you to be neat."

He chuckled, the sound warm and inviting. "True, though I think they're starting to expect the second coat on the tree anytime soon."

I glanced at the partially completed mural, a patchwork of colors. "Fine. But only if you promise to bring snacks next time."

"Deal!" he replied, his smile widening. "I can already picture it—paint, laughter, and snacks. It'll be the perfect trifecta of creativity."

As we cleaned up, the lingering scents of paint and fresh wood mingled with the slight chill of evening air. My heart raced with a strange mix of excitement and something deeper—a connection that felt as tangible as the paint on my skin. It was as if the colors had woven a bond between us, blurring the lines of our individual stories into a shared narrative.

"So," Max began, his voice casual but laced with curiosity, "what's the deal with you? I mean, you're a mystery wrapped in a paint-splattered hoodie."

I laughed, shaking my head as I rolled the last paintbrush in the bucket. "What's there to know? I'm just your average mural enthusiast, trying to add a splash of color to a dreary life."

"Average?" he scoffed playfully. "You're definitely not average. You don't just leap into projects like this without some serious thought. What's your story?"

Caught off guard by his sincerity, I hesitated. The question hung in the air, heavy with unspoken secrets and untold dreams. "Okay, maybe I'm not entirely average," I admitted. "But my story is... well, it's messy. Kind of like this wall before we started."

He leaned in, his expression earnest. "Messy can be good. Sometimes the best stories come from chaos."

"True enough," I said, my heart racing. "I've been chasing dreams since I can remember. For a long time, it felt like I was running in circles, never getting anywhere. But lately, I think I'm starting to figure it out."

"Figuring it out is a journey," he said, his voice softening. "Trust me; I know all about the winding paths."

For a moment, the atmosphere shifted, and I sensed an invisible wall between us crackling under the weight of shared understanding. His eyes held a depth that made my breath catch, as if he was inviting me to peel back the layers of my own story, exposing the raw edges I had kept hidden.

"I used to think that if I just followed the rules, I'd end up where I wanted," I confessed, a nervous laugh escaping me. "But the more I tried to fit into the box, the more I felt like I was suffocating. It wasn't until I embraced the chaos that I started to see a clearer path."

He nodded, a thoughtful look on his face. "That's exactly it. Life doesn't come with a manual. We have to paint our own picture, even if it means going outside the lines."

His words resonated deeply, and I felt a connection to him grow, a spark of shared ambition igniting my thoughts. "What about you? What's your chaotic journey?"

"Ah, my chaos is more like an accidental adventure," he chuckled, running a hand through his hair. "I stumbled into the art world by accident. One day I was studying finance, and the next, I was painting a mural on the side of a coffee shop, trying to impress a girl. Spoiler: it didn't work out with the girl, but here I am, stuck in the paint."

The honesty in his voice made me grin. "A classic tale of love lost and art found. I admire that."

"Thanks! But it's a work in progress. I still haven't quite figured out what I want to be when I grow up," he admitted, his eyes glinting with mischief. "I mean, it's hard to choose between a muralist and a finance wizard, right?"

"Such a tough choice," I teased. "Maybe you should go for both. Just imagine the fascinating conversations you'd have at parties!"

He burst into laughter, the sound rich and infectious. "Yes! 'So, let's talk about market trends, but first, have you seen my latest mural?' It's the best of both worlds!"

I could feel the tension between us loosening, replaced by an easy camaraderie. We finished cleaning the brushes in comfortable silence, the occasional glances exchanged laced with unspoken words. There was something electrifying about the chemistry crackling in the air—a dance of words and laughter that felt as natural as breathing.

"Hey, let's grab dinner," he suggested suddenly, brushing the last remnants of paint from his hands. "I know a great little diner nearby. Best milkshakes in town."

"Milkshakes?" My eyebrows shot up in mock surprise. "Well, now you've got my attention. What kind of milkshakes are we talking about here?"

"The kind that come with sprinkles and whipped cream that could rival a small mountain," he replied, his grin widening. "A glorious concoction that makes life just a little sweeter."

"How can I resist?" I agreed, the warmth in my chest blooming anew.

As we stepped outside, the cool evening air wrapped around us like a familiar blanket. Streetlamps flickered to life, casting a golden glow over the sidewalk, illuminating the path ahead. I felt a flutter of anticipation as we walked side by side, our shoulders brushing together, an unintentional reminder of our newly forged bond.

"Tell me," I said, glancing at him sideways, "do you always go around splattering paint on unsuspecting walls, or is this a special occasion?"

"Only for special people," he replied, his tone earnest, yet playful. "I might have to start charging for my services if I keep this up."

I laughed, a genuine sound that echoed through the quiet street. "I'll keep that in mind. Maybe I can be your agent, handling the contracts while you provide the art."

He stopped mid-stride, turning to face me with a feigned look of seriousness. "Just so you know, my art comes with a hefty price. Emotional support is not included."

"Good thing I have plenty of that to spare," I quipped back, my heart dancing with the thrill of our banter.

As we continued down the street, I realized this was more than just an evening out. It was the first chapter of a new story, one where paintbrushes and laughter intertwined, painting a picture of something beautiful yet uncertain. In this moment, as laughter echoed into the night, I dared to imagine the possibilities that lay ahead, and for the first time in a long while, it felt like I was exactly where I was meant to be.

The diner was a cozy little nook tucked away on a quiet street, a relic of simpler times with its red vinyl booths and chrome accents that glinted under the warm glow of yellowed lights. As we stepped inside, the sweet aroma of grilled cheese and chocolate syrup enveloped us, making my stomach rumble in enthusiastic agreement.

Max slid into a booth, a casual ease in his movements that made me feel oddly at home. "You'll love this place," he said, flipping through the menu. "They serve milkshakes that practically have their own zip code."

"Is that even legal?" I quipped, sliding into the seat across from him. "Shouldn't we have a warning label or something?"

"Only if they come with a side of fries," he grinned, clearly unfazed by my sarcasm. "But trust me, it's worth the risk. You'll never look at a milkshake the same way again."

We ordered our shakes and a plate of fries to share, the playful banter continuing as we swapped stories and laughter, the comfortable rhythm of our conversation weaving an invisible thread that pulled us closer. It was easy to lose track of time, each moment flavored with wit and the kind of chemistry that felt electric.

"So, what do you think our mural will look like once it's finished?" I asked, leaning forward, intrigued by the vision we were creating together.

"Picture this," he began, his hands animated as he spoke. "A brilliant sun rising in the corner, casting golden rays that dance across the tree, and under it, a meadow of flowers. It'll be like a glimpse into a hopeful future, all painted in vibrant colors. And maybe a few quirky elements—like a cat lounging in the grass, because why not?"

"A cat?" I laughed, picturing a lazy feline lounging in the sun. "That's quite the artistic statement."

"Absolutely! It'll represent the importance of taking it easy. You know, balancing hard work with moments of relaxation," he said, his eyes sparkling. "And let's not forget a quote or two sprinkled in. Something inspiring, like 'Chase your dreams' or 'Life is what you make it.'"

"Or 'Eat dessert first,'" I suggested, feigning seriousness. "That's always been my motto."

He chuckled, and I felt my heart race at the sound. "That's a solid life philosophy. I think we can incorporate that somewhere."

When the milkshakes arrived, they were indeed monumental—a tall, frosty glass topped with a swirl of whipped cream and a cherry that seemed to defy gravity. "This," he said, lifting his shake in mock reverence, "is the moment we've all been waiting for."

With our shakes raised high, I felt a rush of exhilaration, a warmth that extended beyond the sugar and cream. "To dreams and messy murals," I proclaimed, grinning at him.

"To dreams," he echoed, clinking his glass against mine. The sweetness of the milkshake was like liquid joy, a perfect accompaniment to our burgeoning friendship, and I found myself wanting to linger in this moment, to savor every drop of laughter and connection.

As we continued to drink our shakes and devour the fries, I noticed a subtle shift in the atmosphere around us. Laughter echoed in the diner, but a knot of tension slowly formed in my stomach, creeping in like a shadow that threatened to eclipse the light of our fun.

"Hey," Max said, his voice cutting through my thoughts. "You okay? You went all serious on me there."

I took a breath, weighing my response. "Just... thinking about the future. It feels uncertain sometimes, doesn't it?"

His brow furrowed, genuine concern etched on his features. "Yeah, it does. But isn't that part of the adventure? The uncertainty makes it interesting."

I nodded, appreciating his perspective. "True. I guess I'm just afraid of taking the wrong turn and ending up somewhere I don't want to be."

"Look, I get it. We all have our fears," he replied, leaning closer, his voice dropping to a whisper. "But it's how we handle those fears that defines us. We've already taken a leap by creating this mural. You've got to trust that we're moving in the right direction."

There was something grounding in his words, a shared understanding that bridged the gap between our experiences. But before I could respond, a commotion erupted at the entrance of the diner.

A man burst through the door, his expression frantic, eyes scanning the room as if searching for someone—or something. My pulse quickened as he locked eyes with Max, and I could feel the tension in the air shift dramatically.

"Max!" the man shouted, his voice rising above the low hum of conversation. "We need to go. Now!"

"What's going on?" Max shot to his feet, concern etched across his face.

"There's no time to explain," the man urged, his eyes darting nervously. "They're coming for you."

My heart raced, a surge of adrenaline pulsing through my veins as I tried to comprehend the sudden shift. "Who? What do you mean?"

Max's gaze flickered to me, a mixture of urgency and fear. "I don't know how they found me, but we need to leave. Now!"

"Leave? What are you talking about?" I was bewildered, feeling as if I'd been thrust into the middle of a thriller without any warning.

"There's no time!" the man insisted, glancing toward the door, his expression a mask of dread. "You don't understand the danger you're in!"

Panic coursed through me as I glanced around the diner, feeling the weight of the moment hang in the air. What danger? And why was Max at the center of it?

With a sudden resolve, I stood up. "I'm not leaving him," I declared, my voice trembling yet determined.

Max reached for my hand, his grip firm and reassuring. "You shouldn't be involved in this. It's too dangerous."

"Too late for that," I said, my heart pounding in my chest. "I'm not letting you face whatever this is alone."

The man's expression shifted, a flicker of respect mixed with disbelief. "Fine. But if you're coming, we need to move—now!"

As we rushed toward the exit, a cacophony of voices rose behind us, and I couldn't shake the feeling that our lives were about to spiral into something far more complicated than a simple mural and milkshakes. Outside, the cool night air hit me like a slap, and I could feel the weight of uncertainty and danger lurking in the shadows, leaving me with one nagging question: what had I really gotten myself into?

Chapter 18: The Unraveling

The aroma of freshly brewed coffee mingled with the sweet scent of pastries wafting from the corner bakery, wrapping around me like a warm embrace. The community center hummed with life, laughter spilling from the gymnasium where children darted in a chaotic flurry, their shrieks of joy punctuating the air. I leaned against the wall, a half-empty cup cradled in my hands, watching the chaos unfold as I took a moment to breathe and ground myself in the now. Just a week ago, I had felt like a phoenix, rising from the ashes of my past, confident and reborn alongside Max, whose unwavering support became the bedrock of my newfound clarity. But clarity, it seemed, was about to waver like the flickering candle on the table beside me.

A figure emerged through the front doors, framed by the harsh daylight that streamed in, transforming him into a silhouette of memory and regret. Aaron. My heart lurched, stumbling over itself as memories I had buried rushed back, flooding my mind with a bittersweet tide. He strolled in with that same cocky stride, all arrogance and charm wrapped up in a designer jacket that surely cost more than my monthly grocery bill. In that moment, all my hard-earned peace felt like a fragile soap bubble, ready to pop at the slightest touch.

"Aaron," I breathed, and the name fell from my lips like a spell that had been cast. I had thought I'd rid myself of him, but here he was, lurking in the shadows of my life once again. He caught my eye, a crooked smile breaking over his face, one that had once made me weak in the knees and now stirred a blend of nostalgia and annoyance.

"Look at you," he said, closing the distance between us with a confidence that felt both infuriating and intoxicating. "You look... good. Happy." His gaze danced over me, as if he were trying to memorize every detail, every change that had taken root in my being since I'd kicked him to the curb. "I miss this place," he added, gesturing to the colorful murals on the walls, vibrant with stories and hopes. "You always knew how to bring the good vibes."

I felt a surge of irritation. "You have a funny way of showing it, Aaron," I replied, my tone sharper than I intended. "You disappeared without a trace when things got tough."

He held up his hands, palms outward in a mock surrender. "I know, I know. But that's the past, right? I'm here now. I want to make amends."

The sincerity in his voice almost caught me off guard, and for a brief second, I contemplated the possibility of reconciliation. But a flicker of memory reminded me of the nights I spent waiting for a text that never came, the silence that echoed in the absence of his presence.

"Amends?" I laughed, a hollow sound that seemed to bounce off the walls. "What does that even look like, Aaron? A few coffee dates? Some heartfelt apologies?"

His expression hardened, the easy charm slipping away to reveal a trace of vulnerability beneath. "Maybe more than coffee," he replied softly, his eyes searching mine for something—a spark of recognition, a glimmer of the past we once shared.

Just then, Max appeared, his broad shoulders filling the doorway as he approached with that same effortless grace that had me enamored since our first meeting. My heart fluttered in a way I hadn't expected, a reminder that I had someone here with me who was genuine, kind, and above all, present. "Hey," he said, glancing between us, his brow furrowed in that adorable way that suggested he was trying to decode a riddle.

"Aaron," I said, the name feeling foreign on my tongue, like a relic of an old world I was trying to forget. "This is Max. My—"

"Boyfriend?" Aaron interjected, a trace of disbelief coloring his tone as he eyed Max with a mix of challenge and surprise.

"Something like that," I said, crossing my arms defensively, a sudden need to protect what I had built with Max. "And you're just here to…what? Drop a bombshell and expect me to roll over?"

Max's presence offered me strength, grounding me against the swell of old emotions that threatened to wash over me. I could feel his warmth beside me, a reassuring anchor against the storm that Aaron's unexpected arrival had unleashed.

"I know we're just getting started, but I'm not going anywhere," Max said, his voice steady and firm. The confidence in his words sent a thrill through me, reminding me why I had been drawn to him in the first place.

Aaron scoffed lightly, folding his arms across his chest. "Look, I didn't come here to stir up drama. I just want to talk. About us."

"Us?" I echoed incredulously, my voice rising an octave as the indignation bubbled over. "You mean the 'us' that you ghosted when things got tough? That us?"

Max stepped slightly in front of me, his protective stance radiating a palpable energy. "Listen, Aaron," he said, his voice calm but laced with an underlying tension. "You've resurfaced after vanishing for ages. You can't just waltz back into her life and expect everything to be sunshine and rainbows."

The sharpness in Max's tone sent a thrill of appreciation through me. It was comforting to have someone willing to stand up for what we had created, even when it meant facing the specter of my past.

"Maybe I'm not looking for sunshine and rainbows," Aaron said, his voice dropping an octave, the charm waning as sincerity bled through. "Maybe I just want a chance to make things right."

I stood in that charged space, torn between the warmth of Max's unwavering support and the flickering light of familiarity that Aaron brought. The weight of my decision pressed heavily against my chest, a relentless drumbeat that grew louder with each heartbeat. Would I let my past dictate my future, or was it time to carve a new path, one that might lead me to a deeper understanding of what I truly wanted?

The air thickened with tension, a delicate balance of longing and resolve. The community center buzzed around us, a cacophony of laughter and chatter, yet in this moment, it felt like we were suspended in a bubble, the world outside fading into insignificance. Choices loomed ahead, and I could feel the inevitability of confrontation with my own heart—one that would either bind me to the safety of the known or propel me into the uncertain, exhilarating unknown.

As Aaron leaned against the wall, that infuriating smirk still plastered on his face, I could feel the tension crackling like static in the air, thick enough to slice through. Max stood firm beside me, his eyes narrowed with concern, as if he could sense the unsteady ground I was teetering on. I wanted to scream, to shake some sense into Aaron, to remind him that he didn't get to stroll back into my life like he was the hero of some grand romance novel. I could almost hear the pages turning—his grand reentrance, complete with a soundtrack of soft piano music. But this wasn't a fairy tale. It was messy and complicated, riddled with sharp edges that threatened to cut deep.

"Why now?" I finally asked, the words escaping me before I could think them through. "What makes you think I'd even consider letting you back in?"

He pushed off the wall, his posture shifting from casual to earnest. "Because I've been doing some thinking. Life's too short to live with regrets, don't you think?"

Max scoffed, crossing his arms tighter over his chest. "Is that your idea of an apology? Just 'thinking' about it?"

"Actually, yes," Aaron shot back, his voice laced with a mix of irritation and desperation. "I've realized how much I took for granted. You were always the one who understood me."

"And yet you still disappeared," I pointed out, my heart racing as the familiar sting of betrayal resurfaced. "You left when I needed you most. Why should I believe anything's changed?"

The corner of Aaron's mouth twitched, a flash of frustration flickering in his eyes. "People change, you know. I'm not the same guy you used to know."

"Is that supposed to make me feel better?" I snapped, anger bubbling to the surface. "You think I'm just going to take your word for it? Look, I've moved on. I've found someone who actually shows up."

Max's hand brushed against mine, the warmth of his touch sending a calming wave through me. I glanced at him, grateful for his steady presence. In contrast, Aaron's absence had always been like a void—one I had struggled to fill.

"Someone?" Aaron echoed, his voice tinged with a bitterness that dripped like honey from a spoon. "Is that really what you want?"

I took a breath, grounding myself in the moment. "Yes, Aaron. I do. And if you truly want to make amends, you need to respect that."

A pause fell over us, thick and heavy, the world around us fading into a distant hum. Max stepped forward, his gaze never wavering from Aaron's. "You need to understand that you can't just drop back into her life and expect everything to be okay. You've got some serious making up to do, and it doesn't start with charm and promises."

"Wow, knight in shining armor much?" Aaron quipped, rolling his eyes.

"More like a guy who's tired of watching someone he cares about get hurt," Max shot back, his voice firm but steady, a protective edge woven into each word.

"Touché," Aaron said, a begrudging respect creeping into his tone. "But I came here to talk to her, not you."

"Fine," I said, my heart racing. "So talk."

He took a step closer, and I held my ground, fighting the urge to retreat. "Look, I know I messed up. I know I hurt you," he admitted, the bravado slipping away, leaving a raw honesty in its place. "But I've spent the last few months reevaluating everything. I'm not asking for your forgiveness right now; I just want you to know I'm here to listen. Whatever you need to say, I'm ready."

"Listening is a start," I replied cautiously. "But you know what they say about actions and words."

Aaron nodded, his expression serious. "I get that. Just give me a chance to prove I'm different."

Max shifted beside me, his muscles tense, a silent warning that sent shivers of uncertainty down my spine. I could feel the tug of familiarity in Aaron's plea, a call back to simpler times when his smile could make me forget the world. But those times were marred by memories of late-night fights, tears shed in the dark, and the ghost of dreams that had turned to ash.

"Why should I?" I asked, crossing my arms defiantly, my heart still reeling. "You had your chance and you blew it. What's different now?"

Aaron hesitated, his jaw working as he searched for words. "Because I know I was wrong," he finally said, voice low. "I didn't realize what I had until it was gone. It's like waking up from a bad dream and seeing the sunlight after being trapped in darkness. I know I don't deserve a second chance, but I want to earn it."

A fleeting glance at Max revealed the tension etched in his face, a mix of skepticism and support. He wasn't going to interfere; he trusted me to navigate this storm, even as the winds howled around us. I felt the weight of the decision pressing down, like a hand gripping my heart. I could either give in to the familiar lull of nostalgia or choose the uncertain but thrilling path that awaited me with Max.

"I don't know if you can earn it," I admitted, my voice softening just a fraction. "You've given me a lot to think about, but I'm not promising anything."

"Fair enough," Aaron said, his expression turning thoughtful. "I'll take what I can get. Just remember, I'm not the enemy here."

"Then what are you?" I challenged, the vulnerability in my heart clashing with my anger.

"A guy who messed up and wants to fix it. But I can't do it alone."

The sincerity in his eyes wavered, leaving a trace of uncertainty lingering in the air. I glanced at Max, who remained steadfast, his support grounding me in the whirlwind of emotions swirling around us. "If you want to be a part of my life again," I said, my voice stronger now, "you need to understand it's not going to be easy. There are no shortcuts or magic words."

Aaron nodded slowly, his expression shifting from cockiness to something resembling genuine hope. "I'm willing to do whatever it takes."

And just like that, the landscape shifted, a precarious balance hanging in the air between the known and the unknown. The door to the past cracked open, just a sliver, inviting the chaos in while also leaving room for the new. I could feel the storm brewing within, the conflicting emotions clashing like waves against the shore, ready to reshape everything I had built.

The hum of laughter faded further into the background as I stood at the precipice, torn between the life I had fought to build with Max and the shadow of a past that refused to stay buried. The light flickered around us, illuminating the crossroads of my heart, and I could only hope that when the dust settled, I would emerge with a clearer vision of who I was meant to be.

The air between us buzzed with an unspoken challenge, as if the universe itself were holding its breath, waiting for my response. I felt the familiar flutter of doubt settle in my stomach, a disquieting mix of anxiety and anticipation. Every second stretched, the moment teetering on the edge of something profound. Aaron's presence was like a fog creeping in, clouding the clarity I'd found with Max, blurring the lines of my heart.

"I want to know everything," Aaron pressed, the sincerity in his eyes almost disarming. "What have you been doing? Who have you become?"

Max cleared his throat, breaking the spell that seemed to grip us. "That's not the point, Aaron. It's not about what she's done since you left. It's about what you did."

"Look, I get that you're protective," Aaron said, frustration creeping into his tone. "But I'm not the same guy who walked away. I'm trying to show that I've changed."

"Changed? You think a few heartfelt words are enough?" I shot back, my emotions bubbling over like a pot left unattended on the stove. "You broke me, Aaron. It's not that easy."

There it was again, that old familiar ache—the one that had haunted my nights and whispered in my ears during the quiet moments when I had convinced myself I was finally over him. Aaron shifted uncomfortably, the facade of confidence faltering. I wondered if he could see the turmoil in my eyes, the conflict gnawing at my insides.

Max's grip on my hand tightened, his warmth anchoring me as I prepared to dive into a conversation that felt like an ocean with no visible shore. "Look, you want a chance to prove yourself? Then start by respecting her and what she's built with me. It's not just about you anymore."

"Yeah? And what do you think I'm here for?" Aaron countered, defensiveness creeping into his voice. "I'm trying to make things right. You think I want to hurt her again?"

A brittle silence descended, heavy with tension. I could feel the churning inside me—a mix of anger, confusion, and something that resembled longing. I hated that, despite everything, I still wanted to believe that maybe, just maybe, he could change.

"I don't want to be part of your games," I said, my voice steadier now. "This isn't a reality show where you can just swoop back in for dramatic effect."

"Dramatic effect?" Aaron's laughter rang out, laced with disbelief. "I'm not here for ratings, I'm here for you. Just let me explain."

"Okay, explain," I said, my tone daring him to strip away the bravado and show me something real.

He drew a breath, the air thick with vulnerability. "After everything that happened, I realized I was living in my own little bubble, afraid to face reality. I thought I could escape it by running away, but all I did was create a bigger mess."

"Is that supposed to make me feel better?" I challenged, crossing my arms tightly over my chest, shielding my heart from his words. "You're justifying abandoning me because it was easier for you?"

"No, no!" he rushed to clarify, his hands gesturing as if he could physically lift the weight of my hurt. "I'm saying that I was a coward. I know it sounds cliché, but I've grown up. I can't change the past, but I can try to be a better man moving forward."

Max shifted beside me, his expression skeptical but supportive, the silent strength I had come to rely on. "What does that look like, Aaron? What are you really willing to do to show that you've changed?"

"I'll be here," he replied, looking me directly in the eyes. "I'm not expecting to walk back into your life like nothing happened. But I want to be part of it again, even if it means starting from scratch."

"And what about me?" I asked, my heart aching with the weight of the decision that loomed before me. "What if I'm not ready to have you back in my life? What if I'm happier without the past haunting me?"

"I'll take whatever you're willing to give," he answered, his voice softening. "Even if it's just a conversation here and there, a chance to show you I've changed."

A rush of emotions overwhelmed me, swirling in a maelstrom that left me dizzy. I wanted to believe him, but the fear of betrayal tightened around my chest like a vice. I shot a glance at Max, who wore a look of quiet determination, as if he were ready to fight whatever battle lay ahead, be it against Aaron or my own wavering heart.

"Can you honestly say you're prepared for that?" Max asked, addressing Aaron, his gaze unwavering. "To respect her boundaries, to be patient? She deserves that, and more."

"I can," Aaron replied, a flicker of sincerity igniting in his eyes. "I'm done playing games. I'll respect whatever she needs."

"I'm not asking for a dramatic reunion," I said, the words tumbling out as I searched for clarity amid the chaos. "I just want to make the right choice for me."

Silence settled again, thick with anticipation. I could feel the tension crackle between the three of us, a palpable energy that hinted at the monumental shift happening in my life. I was caught in a web of emotions, each strand pulling me in different directions.

"Okay, here's the deal," I said, my voice firming as resolve replaced uncertainty. "You get to show me that you've changed, but it's on my terms. I need space, and if I decide I want you in my life, I'll let you know."

"Deal," Aaron replied, a hint of relief washing over his features, though his eyes flickered with an intensity that told me he was ready to fight for this chance.

"Fine," I said, turning my focus back to Max. "And I hope you understand my need for time."

"I get it," Max said, squeezing my hand lightly, the warmth radiating between us a comforting balm. "Whatever you need, I'm right here."

As I stood at this crossroads, the gravity of my decision sank in. The weight of the past had shifted, leaving me teetering on the edge of an uncertain future. Just as I thought I had found my footing, an unexpected voice sliced through the air.

"Sorry to interrupt," a soft, melodic voice chimed in from behind us. "But I think we need to talk."

Turning, I found myself staring into the eyes of someone I hadn't seen in years—a face I had thought I would never have to confront again. The woman looked just as I remembered, her hair cascading like a waterfall over her shoulders, her expression a mix of regret and determination.

My heart raced, confusion settling in like a heavy fog. "What are you doing here?" I demanded, my pulse quickening.

"I came to set the record straight," she replied, a fierce intensity in her gaze that sent a shiver down my spine. "There are things you don't know—things about Aaron that change everything."

As her words hung in the air, a cold wave of dread washed over me, and I realized that this was just the beginning of an unraveling I never anticipated.

Chapter 19: Crossroads of the Heart

The sun hung low in the sky, painting the world in hues of amber and rose, casting long shadows across the cobblestone street. Each step I took towards the café where I had agreed to meet Aaron felt like I was wading through syrup. The air was thick with an unspoken heaviness, a tangible reminder of all that had transpired between us. My heart thudded against my ribcage, a traitor betraying my calm exterior. As I approached the familiar façade, memories swirled around me like autumn leaves caught in a whirlwind, memories that once filled me with warmth but now chilled my bones.

Inside, the café buzzed with life. Baristas shouted orders over the hiss of espresso machines, and the scent of freshly baked pastries mingled with the rich aroma of coffee, creating a welcoming cocoon. Yet, it felt foreign to me, as if I were a ghost haunting the remnants of a past life. I spotted Aaron at a corner table, his posture a mix of anxious energy and desperate hope. He ran a hand through his tousled hair, a familiar gesture that used to make me weak at the knees. But today, it only ignited a simmering anger within me.

"Hey," I said, taking a seat across from him. I fought the urge to let my eyes soften, to indulge in the pull of nostalgia. Instead, I steeled myself, crossing my arms as if to shield my heart from the tidal wave of emotions threatening to crash over me.

"Thanks for coming," he said, his voice tentative, like a child approaching a wild animal. "I didn't know if you would."

I gave a slight nod, my fingers drumming impatiently on the table. "You know why I'm here, Aaron. We need to talk."

His eyes darkened, shadows playing across his features as if the weight of unspoken words loomed over him. "I know. I just... I've missed you. I'm sorry for everything that happened."

Those words, so sweetly uttered, dripped with syrupy regret, yet they felt like poison on my tongue. I forced myself to maintain eye contact, determined to stand firm in the tempest swirling around us. "Sorry doesn't change what you did. You left me without a word, Aaron. I was... I was shattered."

His gaze dropped to the table, a pained expression crossing his face. "I was scared. I thought I was doing the right thing—"

"By disappearing?" I interrupted, my voice rising slightly, drawing the attention of a nearby couple. "You thought running away would solve everything?"

"I thought it would protect you!" His voice rose too, but there was an earnestness in his eyes that made my resolve waver. "I was a mess back then. I didn't know how to be what you needed."

With every beat of my heart, the walls I had built around myself cracked just a little more. I could see the boy I once loved in the man before me, the same boy who had made me laugh until I cried and who could make me feel like the center of the universe. But with that boy came the pain, the heartache, and the betrayal. I couldn't let myself be pulled back in, not now when I had finally begun to breathe again.

"I've moved on, Aaron," I said, the words tasting bitter. "I've found someone who respects me, who sees me. Max—he's everything you weren't."

A flicker of something—anger? Jealousy?—crossed his face, but he masked it quickly. "And what? You think he's perfect? Everyone has their flaws."

"Unlike you, he doesn't run away when things get tough," I shot back, the heat rising in my cheeks. "He stands beside me. He makes me laugh. He challenges me." I paused, feeling the weight of my own words settle into the space between us. "He's real."

Aaron leaned back, the tension in his shoulders visibly relaxing, as if he were processing a painful truth. "I don't want to fight, okay? I just... I want to explain. Can you give me that?"

I hesitated, my mind racing with images of Aaron—how he used to hold me when storms rattled the windows and how his laughter used to fill my world with light. The past surged like a tide, threatening to drown me in its familiarity. But I couldn't ignore the present, the steady warmth of Max's presence in my life, the way he looked at me as if I were the only one that mattered.

"Fine," I said, my voice steadying, "but make it quick. I don't have all day."

Aaron took a deep breath, his blue eyes searching mine for something I wasn't sure he'd find. "I was young and reckless. I didn't know how to handle what we had. I was afraid of losing myself, and I thought leaving would make it easier. But it didn't. It just made everything worse. I regret hurting you. I really do."

His sincerity, layered with remorse, tugged at my heartstrings, creating a symphony of conflict within me. I could feel my defenses weakening, the cracks widening as I listened. But amidst the tangled emotions, one thing remained clear: the wounds from our past were not easily healed.

"I don't want to go back to that place, Aaron," I replied, my voice softer now, yet resolute. "I'm not the same person you left behind. I've grown, and I need to keep moving forward."

"I know," he said quietly. "I just wish we could start over, maybe be friends again. I can't change what I did, but I'd like to be in your life somehow."

The idea hung in the air, tempting and terrifying all at once. A part of me wanted to believe in the possibility of redemption, of forgiveness, but the scars ran deep, etched into my very being. As I studied his face, the boyish charm mingled with the shadows of regret, a complex portrait of a man grappling with his past.

I shook my head slowly, gathering my thoughts. "We can't just pretend nothing happened. I can't go back to being the person I was with you. I have to protect what I've built."

A silence enveloped us, thick with unresolved tension and unspoken words. The world outside the café blurred into a swirl of colors as I wrestled with the bittersweet reality of the moment. I realized that standing at this crossroads, the weight of my choices pressed down harder than ever, demanding clarity and resolution.

The silence between us stretched, taut like a wire pulled too tight. I could see the myriad of emotions playing across Aaron's face, each flicker a reminder of the tangled history we shared. He was looking at me, really looking, and for a fleeting moment, the warmth of those old feelings crept back in, only to be swiftly smothered by the weight of reality.

"I need you to understand something," I said, letting out a breath I hadn't realized I was holding. "It's not just about you and me anymore. I have someone else in my life now. Someone who makes me feel... alive." The words tumbled out, both a declaration and a shield, a way to protect the fragile space I'd carved for myself.

Aaron opened his mouth to respond, but I raised a hand, cutting him off. "Please, just hear me out. I can't keep revisiting this history like it's a favorite novel. It's more like a horror story, and I'm done reading it."

He grimaced at my words, a flicker of pain crossing his features. "I get it. I really do. I just thought—"

"Thought what?" I shot back, my irritation rising again. "That you could sweep in and say a few nice things, and I'd just fall back into your arms like nothing happened?"

"No! I—" His frustration matched mine, and for a moment, we both paused, taking stock of where we were. "I just wanted you to know how sorry I am. That I've changed. I'm not that same guy anymore."

"Good. Then I hope you've also learned that people can't just be picked back up like a dropped phone." The edge in my voice surprised me, a sharpness that reminded me of how protective I had become over my own heart. I watched him absorb my words, the reality of my rejection sinking in.

We fell into another silence, this one more contemplative. I could see Aaron's wheels turning, calculating his next move, his defenses crumbling like the scones that sat untouched on the table. I couldn't help but feel a mix of pity and frustration; he had broken something precious between us, and here he was, expecting me to help him put it back together.

"Okay, I won't push," he finally said, his voice low and measured. "But can we at least agree that it was real? What we had, I mean. It wasn't just... nothing."

His vulnerability was disarming, and I could feel the walls I had built start to sway. "It was real," I admitted, my voice softening despite my best intentions. "But so was the hurt. It's just hard to reconcile the two."

"Fair enough." He leaned back in his chair, his fingers tracing the rim of his coffee cup, lost in thought. "And what about Max? Is he... good to you?"

"Max is everything I need and more," I said, unable to suppress the smile that crept onto my lips at the thought of him. "He listens, he supports me, and he makes me laugh in ways I didn't think were possible. There's a warmth with him that I never had with you."

Aaron looked away, the corner of his mouth twitching into something resembling a smile, though it didn't quite reach his eyes. "Sounds like you've really moved on."

"Yeah, I have," I said, my heart tightening a little as I considered how true those words were. "And that's why I can't sit here and pretend we can go back to the way things were."

"Then what do we do?" he asked, his tone shifting to one of resignation. "Do we just walk away, act like we were never here?"

"It's complicated," I admitted, and the truth stung. "I don't want to erase our history, but I can't let it dictate my future."

As we both pondered the impossibility of our situation, a sudden burst of laughter drew my attention to a table nearby. A couple sat close together, their fingers intertwined, the joy between them a vivid contrast to the tension swirling around us. I felt a pang of longing for that kind of effortless connection, the kind that didn't come with the weight of regret.

"I guess that's love, right?" Aaron said, glancing over at the couple. "Full of twists and turns, laughter and pain. It's messy."

I chuckled softly, the warmth in my chest thawing the heaviness that had settled there. "Love is definitely messy. But it's also exhilarating, like a rollercoaster you can't get off once you're strapped in."

"Have you told Max all this?" he asked, looking at me earnestly. "About me? About us?"

I hesitated, the question hanging in the air like the last note of a symphony. "Not all of it. I didn't want to burden him with ghosts from my past."

Aaron nodded, as if he understood. "I get that. But he deserves to know what he's stepping into. It's only fair."

"Maybe," I said, but unease slithered through me. What if sharing my history with Max only muddied the waters? "But I also want to protect what we have. I don't want to jeopardize anything."

"Not every story needs to be retold," Aaron conceded, his voice gentle but firm. "But it's a part of who you are. You can't erase that."

The ache in my chest deepened, a familiar weight that threatened to crush the new life I had begun to build. "You're right," I whispered, the admission tasting like ash on my tongue. "But I'm still trying to figure out how to make it all fit. The past and the present."

The café around us seemed to blur into the background, the sounds fading into a dull hum as we both grappled with the enormity of what lay ahead. For a moment, we were just two people caught in a whirlwind of emotion, standing at the intersection of nostalgia and hope.

"What if we keep it simple?" Aaron suggested, breaking the silence again. "What if we just agree to leave things as they are? No more meetings, no more heavy conversations. Just... let it be."

"Let it be," I echoed, the idea settling over me like a warm blanket. "Maybe that's the best option. For both of us."

As I looked into his eyes, a mixture of relief and sorrow washed over us. We were two souls navigating a storm, and while we couldn't rewrite the past, we could at least chart a course for the future. In that moment of shared understanding, the weight of our choices hung in the air, but it felt a little lighter somehow, as if a bridge had been built to the other side.

A silence settled between us, thick as molasses, and the air crackled with unsaid words and uncharted feelings. I could sense the storm brewing just beneath the surface, each pulse of tension sending ripples through the cozy café atmosphere. Aaron leaned back, his gaze drifting toward the window, where the golden light filtered through the leaves, casting dappled shadows on the floor. I followed his gaze, wondering if he was looking for something—perhaps a sign that would untangle the knot binding our hearts together in this moment.

"Maybe we don't need to have all the answers," I finally said, breaking the heavy silence. "Maybe it's okay to just... exist here, right now, without a plan."

"Exist, huh?" he mused, a hint of sarcasm coloring his voice. "Sounds like the motto of someone who's too scared to commit."

"Or someone who's learned to keep her heart intact," I retorted, rolling my eyes playfully. "You've got to admit, there's something to be said for self-preservation."

"Fair point." He smirked, and for a brief second, the tension dissipated, replaced by a flicker of the camaraderie we once shared.

"Self-preservation is great until it turns into self-sabotage. Trust me; I've been there."

The truth of his statement lingered in the air between us, weaving its way through the bittersweet nostalgia. The man across from me was still the boy who had once whispered promises under the stars, but those promises had been buried under layers of hurt and misunderstandings.

"Tell me about Max," Aaron said suddenly, his tone shifting from playful to serious. "What makes him so special?"

The question caught me off guard, and I couldn't help the smile that spread across my face. "Max is... well, he's the kind of guy who thinks the world is full of possibilities. He has this infectious enthusiasm that makes me want to chase every dream I've ever had."

"And here I thought you were the dream chaser," Aaron shot back, his eyes sparkling with mischief. "What's he got that I don't?"

I leaned in, my voice dropping to a conspiratorial whisper. "He can make pancakes that don't taste like rubber."

Aaron barked out a laugh, and it warmed the air around us. "Touché. I concede that's a strong point in his favor."

As our laughter faded, the moment settled back into something more contemplative. I could see the shadows creeping back into Aaron's eyes, a reminder of the weight he still carried. "But really," he said, his voice softer now, "do you love him?"

The question hung in the air like a tightrope waiting for me to step onto it. I felt the ground shift beneath me, the answer poised on my tongue, but I hesitated. What did love even mean? I had thought I loved Aaron, but that love had crumbled under the pressure of betrayal. I had rebuilt my heart piece by piece, and now I had to grapple with the implications of that word.

"I care about Max deeply," I finally replied, choosing my words carefully. "He makes me feel safe and seen, and I've never felt that before."

"Sounds like love to me," Aaron said, his voice tinged with resignation. "I don't want to mess that up for you, you know? I just wanted to know if there was still a chance for us."

A bitter laugh escaped me, the truth gnawing at my insides. "A chance? You walked away, Aaron. You took your chance when you left me without a word."

"I know, and I'm sorry," he said, his eyes pleading for understanding. "But people can change. I can change."

The determination in his voice ignited a flicker of hope in my chest, quickly drowned by the heavy weight of doubt. I didn't want to be that person again—the one who believed in second chances without knowing the cost. But here we were, dancing on the precipice of what could be, while I clung to the security of what I had built with Max.

"Maybe we need to redefine what we mean by 'chance,'" I suggested. "I don't think going back is an option. But that doesn't mean we can't find a way forward."

Aaron seemed to consider this, the tension in his shoulders easing slightly as he nodded. "Forward... I can live with that."

We fell into a thoughtful silence, the café buzz fading into the background as we both lost ourselves in thought. My mind flickered back to Max—his bright smile, the way he challenged me, and how he had stood by me when I was at my lowest. The contrast between my past with Aaron and my present with Max became stark, like two sides of a coin, each one valid yet impossibly different.

As I gazed out the window, the setting sun painted the sky in strokes of orange and pink, a kaleidoscope of colors swirling together, creating a breathtaking view that reminded me of the beauty in uncertainty. I turned back to Aaron, ready to speak, but my words caught in my throat as I saw the expression on his face.

Before I could process what was happening, the door to the café swung open, and a figure stepped inside, silhouetted against the fading light. I squinted, my heart racing as recognition washed over me, stealing my breath.

Max stood at the entrance, his eyes scanning the room until they landed on me, filled with a mix of confusion and concern. The cheerful aura that usually surrounded him dimmed slightly, replaced by an unsettling tension as he took in the scene before him.

"Uh, hey," he said, his voice even but laced with an undercurrent of uncertainty. "What's going on here?"

The moment hung in the air, a fragile bubble that threatened to burst at any second. My heart raced, panic fluttering in my chest as I looked between Aaron and Max, two pivotal figures in my life standing at the same crossroads.

"Max—" I began, but the words died on my lips as the weight of the situation settled like a heavy fog, obscuring everything I had worked so hard to build. In that heartbeat, I realized how quickly everything could unravel, and I stood at the precipice of choices that could change everything.

Chapter 20: Echoes of the Past

The gentle hum of chatter filled the café, punctuated by the soft clinking of ceramic cups and the hiss of the espresso machine, crafting a symphony of daily life that seemed both comforting and surreal. As I settled into the familiar nook by the window, the sun spilled across the table like honey, warming my skin and offering a fleeting sense of security. Max, with his unruly hair and easy smile, looked up from his steaming mug, a silent invitation for me to lay bare my tangled thoughts.

"Alright, spill it," he urged, his voice steady, yet laced with a playful curiosity that always managed to ease my nerves. "I can practically see the gears turning in your head, and trust me, I'm not in the mood for a caffeine buzz without some juicy drama to accompany it."

I couldn't help but chuckle at his attempt to lighten the mood. The corners of my mouth twitched upward, but the laughter felt hollow against the storm brewing in my chest. "It's just... everything with Aaron. I thought I was over it. I really did." My fingers fidgeted with the edge of the tablecloth, the fabric soft and worn, much like my resolve.

Max leaned in, his expression shifting from playful to serious, the warmth of our banter replaced by the gravity of my admission. "But now he's back. How does that feel? Are you excited? Anxious? Both?"

"More like a cocktail of emotions that I can't quite place." I glanced out the window, where the world bustled on, oblivious to my internal chaos. "Seeing him again brought back so many memories, both sweet and bitter. It's like flipping through a photo album where some images make you smile, and others leave you with an ache in your heart."

"Sounds complicated," Max remarked, his tone softening, the teasing edge of his voice retreating. "Have you talked to him? I mean, really talked?"

"No, and that's part of the problem," I admitted, my voice dropping as I traced the rim of my cup with my fingertip. "Every time I think about it, I freeze up. I want to confront him, to understand why he left without a word, but I'm terrified of what I might find. What if the answers aren't what I want to hear?"

Max's brow furrowed thoughtfully. "But isn't knowing better than lingering in uncertainty? It could help you move on, or... you know, figure things out."

"Moving on feels like the easy way out, and that scares me." I took a deep breath, the rich aroma of the coffee suddenly overwhelming as if the scent alone could ground me. "Part of me still feels tied to him, and the other half wants to cut those ties completely. Maybe I'm just afraid of being disappointed again."

He studied me for a moment, the warmth of his gaze providing a stark contrast to the chill that had settled in my bones. "You know, you're allowed to be scared. But you're also stronger than you think. You've faced worse than a chat with an ex."

"True," I said, the words tumbling out before I could catch them. "But this feels different. Aaron is not just an ex; he was... everything. He knew me in ways I didn't even know myself."

As I spoke, a wave of memories crashed over me—warm evenings spent wrapped in each other's arms, quiet laughter shared over midnight snacks, and the heady thrill of first love, alive and tangible. Those moments pulsed through me, each a reminder of what was lost and what might never be found again.

"What if he's changed? What if I have?" I continued, my voice barely above a whisper. "What if we're not the same people anymore?"

"Then that's something to discover," Max replied, his voice steady and reassuring. "You're allowed to explore that. Besides, it's not like you're signing a contract to get back together. Think of it as... an inquiry into your past. Who knows what you might find?"

His words hung in the air, a gentle nudge toward a path I had been too fearful to tread. I swirled my coffee, contemplating the swirling darkness within the cup, a metaphor for my own chaotic feelings. What if this conversation was the push I needed to confront my past, to unravel the knots of unresolved emotions that had been tying me in circles?

"Okay, maybe I need to stop avoiding him," I finally said, my voice gaining a hint of resolve. "But what if I go to talk, and he's still the same Aaron I remember? What if all those feelings come rushing back and I lose my footing?"

Max chuckled, the sound warm and inviting. "Then you'll just have to be ready to stand your ground. And if it gets too overwhelming, you can always blame the coffee." He winked, and I couldn't help but laugh, the tension in my chest easing slightly.

"I could always say, 'Sorry, I'm too caffeinated to think straight,'" I quipped, the absurdity of the idea sending a ripple of laughter between us.

"Yes! That's perfect! It's a foolproof excuse!" he replied, his laughter mingling with mine, and for a moment, the weight of my worries lifted, if only slightly.

Our banter softened into a comfortable silence, the world outside fading away as I leaned back, allowing the warmth of his presence to wash over me. Max was right; confronting my feelings didn't have to be an all-or-nothing endeavor. It could be a series of small steps—conversations filled with uncertainty and discovery, perhaps sprinkled with a little bit of humor to lighten the burden.

And as I prepared to take that leap, I knew that I had a steadfast ally by my side, ready to catch me if I stumbled. But deep down, I also felt the stirring of something stronger—a budding courage that reminded me that sometimes, the only way to heal was to embrace the echoes of the past and weave them into the tapestry of my future.

The café buzzed with life, its atmosphere a harmonious blend of rich coffee aromas and soft, murmured conversations. I watched as baristas weaved between tables, balancing lattes and pastries, their movements fluid and practiced. With every sip of my coffee, the world felt just a little more manageable, the warmth creeping into my bones like a favorite old sweater. Yet beneath this comfortable facade, my thoughts churned with anticipation and uncertainty.

"So, have you thought about what you want to say to him?" Max asked, breaking through my reverie. His brow was slightly furrowed, a telltale sign of his earnest concern.

"I have," I admitted, rolling the words around in my mind like marbles in a jar, colorful yet clashing. "But every time I try to formulate something coherent, it all falls apart. What do you even say to someone who walked away without a word?"

"Start with hello. It's a classic," he replied, the corner of his mouth quirking into a half-smile. "Or you could jump straight into the deep end and ask him why he vanished like a magician's rabbit. That might get the ball rolling."

"Right, because nothing says 'let's reconnect' like diving into the trauma of the past," I shot back, a hint of sarcasm dripping from my words. But he had a point. Addressing the elephant in the room—an elephant that had been dancing around me for far too long—was essential.

"I could always use the classic 'Why did you ghost me?'" I mused, my voice tinged with a mix of humor and frustration. "Or perhaps, 'Hey, do you remember me? The person you abandoned like last season's trend?'"

"Now we're talking!" Max laughed, a bright sound that made a few heads turn. "See, you've already got the start of a conversation. Just keep that wit up, and you'll be golden."

"Wit isn't the problem," I said, shaking my head. "It's the heart part. I can throw around sarcasm like confetti, but underneath it all... I'm terrified. What if he's still the same? What if I'm still the same? Will we just slip back into old patterns, or will it be as if we're two strangers trying to build a bridge over a river of unresolved feelings?"

Max leaned back, tapping a finger against his chin as if pondering my predicament. "Why not see it as an opportunity to redefine things? Maybe you're both different now, better equipped to handle what you couldn't before."

His words hung in the air, and I found myself nodding slowly. Perhaps that was the key. Instead of letting the past dictate the present, I could reshape it into something new, something that could potentially fill the gaping void he had left behind.

"Okay, so maybe I'll try that," I said, taking a deep breath as a wave of determination washed over me. "But where do I even start?"

"Start with coffee," he said, his expression serious, yet playful. "Offer him a drink. Make it casual. If he shows up with a pumpkin spice latte, that's your cue to run. Just kidding! Kind of."

I laughed, imagining the horror of Aaron walking in with the seasonal drink that had become synonymous with autumn. "God, I hope he hasn't fallen prey to that trend. I mean, what's next? Sweater vests and UGG boots?"

"Don't knock the sweater vests. They're making a comeback," he said, his eyes sparkling with mischief. "But seriously, keep it light. You can ease into the heavy stuff once the ice is broken. You know how to do this."

"I guess I could use a little help from my friends," I mused, my heart racing at the thought of reaching out. The idea of reconnecting with Aaron was as thrilling as it was terrifying, a tightrope walk between the familiar and the unknown.

As we continued to talk, I felt the weight of my emotions shift, as if someone had lifted the heavy drapery that had cloaked my heart for far too long. We reminisced about past escapades—those ridiculous road trips, late-night conversations that turned into dawn, and the ridiculous bets we placed over who could finish a plate of nachos first.

"I'm still convinced you cheated," I said, feigning indignation.

"I prefer to think of it as strategy," Max replied, raising an eyebrow. "You have to play to win, my friend. Besides, I'd never cheat against you. We're too evenly matched."

"True," I conceded, a smile breaking free. "Except for the nachos. You totally rigged that competition."

Just then, the bell above the café door chimed, pulling my attention away from our playful banter. I glanced over my shoulder, and my breath caught in my throat as I spotted Aaron standing just inside the entrance, his familiar silhouette framed by the sunlight streaming through the glass. My heart raced, pounding in my ears like a wild drum, each beat reminding me of our history.

He looked older, yet somehow the same, his tousled hair catching the light, giving him an almost ethereal quality. I felt a surge of emotion—a cocktail of longing and uncertainty, excitement and fear. Was this what I had been waiting for, the moment where the past met the present?

"Speak of the devil," Max said softly, nudging my arm gently. "There's your chance."

My mouth went dry, my heart clamoring to leap out of my chest. "What do I do?" I whispered, my panic rising.

"Just breathe," he replied, his calm demeanor anchoring me for a fleeting moment. "You've got this. Just remember to be honest. And maybe don't mention nachos right away."

I took a deep breath, steadying myself against the tide of emotions threatening to pull me under. With a shaky smile, I pushed my chair back and stood, feeling a rush of resolve flooding my veins. This was it—my moment to reclaim my narrative. No more running, no more hiding.

As I stepped toward him, the world around us faded into a blur. The clatter of dishes, the soft laughter of patrons, even the tantalizing scent of freshly baked pastries vanished, leaving only the two of us in sharp focus.

"Aaron," I breathed, my voice steadying with each step I took. This was my opportunity to confront the echoes of the past, to engage with the man who had once held my heart in his hands and, for better or worse, had shaped my present. And as our eyes locked, I could feel the electricity crackling between us—a reminder that some connections never truly fade, no matter how much time has passed.

As I stood there, caught in the magnetic pull of Aaron's gaze, I felt time stretch and contract around us. The café, once bustling and filled with chatter, faded into a muted backdrop, leaving only the thundering of my heart in my ears. He looked exactly as I remembered, yet there was a shadow of uncertainty flickering in his eyes, a mixture of surprise and something deeper that I couldn't quite decipher.

"Hey," I managed to say, my voice barely above a whisper, but somehow, it felt monumental—a soft declaration that reverberated between us.

"Wow," he said, taking a tentative step forward, his expression shifting from shock to something softer, a cautious smile blooming. "I didn't expect to see you here."

"Neither did I," I replied, a teasing note edging into my voice despite the fluttering in my stomach. "I thought I might run into the ghost of my past, but I see it's just you."

"Ha! Not a ghost yet, but I appreciate the heads-up." He chuckled, his laughter a balm against the rawness of our history. It had a familiar warmth that drew me in, igniting memories I had tried to bury beneath layers of time.

"What are you doing here?" I asked, shifting slightly, trying to catch a glimpse of the man I once knew under the layers of uncertainty that now cloaked our interaction.

"Just grabbing a coffee, like everyone else." His shrug was casual, but there was a tension threading through his demeanor, a tightrope walk between what had been and what could be. "I—uh, I heard about your new project. Congratulations."

"Thanks!" I beamed, the unexpected compliment igniting a flicker of pride. "I didn't expect you to be keeping tabs on me."

"Guilty as charged," he admitted, running a hand through his hair, the gesture as familiar as it was disarming. "It's hard to forget someone who made such an impact on your life, you know?"

The weight of his words settled between us, heavy and undeniable. "I could say the same," I replied, my heart pounding as I attempted to bridge the chasm that time and silence had created. "I've thought about you—about us—more times than I'd like to admit."

There it was, out in the open, a confession that felt like both a release and a risk. I held my breath, waiting for his reaction. Would he recoil, or would he lean in, eager to explore the echoes of our shared past?

His gaze softened, and he took a half-step closer, a movement that felt charged with unspoken possibilities. "I never meant to leave things the way I did. I thought about reaching out so many times, but... life got in the way."

"Life, huh?" I said, forcing a laugh to mask the trepidation creeping in. "Isn't that what they always say? I guess we're all just victims of our busy schedules."

"Yeah, but it's more than that," he replied, a note of urgency creeping into his voice. "I needed time to figure things out, to grow. But I never wanted to hurt you. Not like that."

My heart fluttered at the vulnerability he revealed, each word a thread weaving a tapestry of understanding between us. "And did you figure things out?" I asked, my voice steady, though every fiber of my being was on edge, yearning for answers.

He hesitated, the weight of the moment palpable as the café buzzed around us, oblivious to the tension crackling between two souls attempting to navigate the ruins of their history. "I think so. I've changed. I'm not the same person who left."

"Neither am I," I said softly, a strange mixture of nostalgia and hope coloring my tone. "But the question remains—can we find a way back to each other? Or are we just going to keep reliving this cycle of awkward encounters?"

His eyes searched mine, a deep well of emotions swirling just beneath the surface. "I want to try," he finally said, a fierce determination flashing in his expression. "I'm here now. Let's not waste this chance."

Before I could reply, a loud crash resonated from the other side of the café, drawing our attention. A chair had toppled over, and a group of people erupted into laughter, their carefree energy slicing through the fragile moment we had created. The levity was almost jarring, pulling us back from the precipice of intimacy we had been teetering on.

"Maybe we should get a quieter table," I suggested, a hint of nervous laughter bubbling up as I gestured toward the corner booth, hoping to recapture the bubble of connection we had built.

"Good idea," he agreed, and as we maneuvered through the throng of patrons, a familiar thrill pulsed through me. It felt as though we were entering a new chapter, one filled with possibility.

Once settled in the booth, I took a moment to collect my thoughts, the previous conversation swirling around in my mind. I could sense that we were on the brink of something significant, yet I also felt the weight of the past anchoring us. "So, what was it that kept you from reaching out?" I asked, genuinely curious.

"I was scared," he confessed, his voice barely above a whisper. "I was afraid that if I reached out, it would just reopen old wounds. And I didn't know if we could ever go back to what we had."

"Or if we could move forward," I finished, my heart racing as I looked deep into his eyes. "But maybe that's what we need to figure out together."

"Yes, exactly," he said, the urgency in his tone underscoring the gravity of our conversation. "We could start with lunch, maybe work our way up to... I don't know, a picnic? Something low-pressure."

"A picnic? Oh, that sounds romantic," I teased, trying to lighten the mood, even as the weight of our conversation pressed down on me.

"Hey, if we can't be romantic, what's the point?" He smirked, his eyes twinkling with mischief. "But really, I'm serious about this. I want to see where it goes, even if it takes time."

"Time is something I can do," I said, matching his intensity. "But I need to know you're all in. No more running."

"I promise," he said, his voice steady and sincere. "No more ghosts."

The air between us felt electric, each word a step toward something new. Just as I opened my mouth to respond, my phone buzzed violently on the table, startling both of us. I glanced at the screen, my heart sinking as I read the message.

"Shit," I muttered, my stomach knotting. "It's my boss. Something's gone wrong at work. I have to take this."

"Go ahead," Aaron said, concern etching his features. "We can pause."

But as I looked up, ready to give him a reassuring smile, I caught sight of something—or rather, someone—over his shoulder. My breath caught in my throat as I recognized the figure slipping through the café door. It was Lydia, my former best friend, the one person whose unexpected return could complicate everything I was trying to navigate with Aaron.

"Uh, Aaron, wait..." But it was too late; she had already spotted us, her expression shifting from surprise to something sharper, more possessive.

As she approached, I felt the ground shift beneath me, the bubble of connection with Aaron suddenly feeling fragile and precarious. The look on Lydia's face told me this was about to get very complicated. "Well, well, if it isn't the two lovebirds," she said, her voice dripping with sweet sarcasm. "What a cozy little reunion."

And just like that, the moment we had been building together began to unravel, and I was left standing on the edge, wondering which direction the fall would take me.

Chapter 21: Fragments of Trust

The café bustled around us, the scent of freshly brewed coffee mingling with the sweet notes of pastries cooling on the countertop. Max sat across from me, his emerald eyes reflecting a blend of vulnerability and strength that pulled me in like the tides. I could see his fingers fidgeting with the edge of his napkin, a subtle reminder of the unspoken words hovering just beneath the surface. The soft jazz playing in the background was a stark contrast to the storm brewing within my heart, a cacophony of emotions battling for dominance.

"I've been burned before," he said, his voice low and laced with a hint of gravel. "Trust isn't just given; it's earned." He paused, as if gathering the courage to share a piece of himself. "There was this girl in college. She had a laugh that could light up the darkest room, but when I needed her most, she vanished like smoke in the wind."

I leaned in closer, the urge to comfort him washing over me. "That sounds painful," I murmured, searching his face for any sign of lingering hurt. I wanted to bridge the gap that had formed between us, to dissolve the remnants of our past that still clung to us like stubborn shadows.

Max chuckled softly, a sound that sent warmth through my chest. "Painful is an understatement. It was like being socked in the gut and then watching her waltz away with my trust. I spent years building walls, convinced they were for my protection." His gaze shifted toward the window, where a group of laughter-filled friends walked by, oblivious to the weight of the world we carried.

"I know how that feels," I admitted, the truth spilling from my lips like an unguarded confession. "After Aaron, I didn't just lose faith in him. I lost faith in myself. I thought if I wasn't enough for him, then who could I be enough for?"

Max's fingers brushed against mine, his touch igniting a spark that danced between us. "But you are enough. Trusting yourself is the first step." His earnestness felt like a balm, soothing the jagged edges of my heart.

Before I could respond, my phone buzzed insistently on the table, the screen lighting up with Aaron's name. It felt like an unwelcome ghost haunting our moment, a reminder of the chains that still bound me. "Ugh, it's Aaron," I said, my voice dripping with exasperation. "He wants to meet again."

Max's expression shifted, the flicker of concern playing across his features. "Are you going to?"

I hesitated, the weight of my choices pressing down on my chest. "I don't know. Part of me wants closure, but the other part..." I trailed off, unsure of how to articulate the turmoil churning within me. "I'm scared of what it might do to us."

"Us?" He arched an eyebrow, a teasing glint sparking in his eyes. "You're already planning for us?"

A rush of heat flooded my cheeks, and I quickly diverted my gaze to the table. "That's not what I meant. I just—"

"Relax," he chuckled, his voice smooth as silk. "I'm teasing you. But really, I think you should go. Face him, confront whatever demons are lurking there. You deserve that for yourself."

The sincerity in his voice sent a shiver down my spine. It was strange how quickly he had become a steady presence in my life, a lighthouse in the fog. "But what if it messes things up between us?"

Max leaned forward, his intensity wrapping around me like a warm embrace. "You won't know unless you try. Just remember, I'm here. Whatever happens, we'll face it together."

His reassurance wrapped around my heart, momentarily pushing away the specter of doubt. I breathed in deeply, the aroma of coffee intertwining with the scent of freshly baked croissants. "Okay, I'll meet him. But I'll keep my guard up."

"Good," he said, his fingers tightening around mine. "And don't forget that you have me in your corner."

We spent the next few minutes lost in conversation, a comfortable rhythm taking over as we navigated the murky waters of our pasts and dreams for the future. Laughter bubbled between us, a symphony of shared experiences and light-hearted banter that reminded me how good it felt to be seen and heard. But the lurking shadow of Aaron loomed over our connection, a palpable tension that made me acutely aware of the fragile line I was walking.

As we finished our coffee, the café gradually emptied, leaving us in a cozy cocoon of warmth. Max brushed a stray hair behind my ear, the simple gesture igniting a flicker of hope. "Just remember, you're not alone in this."

I nodded, holding onto the promise of his words like a lifeline. The world outside began to dim, the sunset spilling rich hues of orange and pink across the sky. "I should get going," I said reluctantly, the thought of leaving his presence hanging heavy in the air.

"Right. Confront the past and all that," he replied, a playful smile tugging at his lips. "But don't forget to come back to the future."

With a soft laugh, I stood, feeling the weight of his gaze as I prepared to step back into the chaotic world outside. The night awaited, and as much as I dreaded facing Aaron again, I felt a flicker of courage igniting within me. I took one last look at Max, a silent promise exchanged between us, and stepped outside, the cool air washing over me as I ventured into the unknown.

The walk to the park was a blur of autumn colors, the leaves swirling around me in vibrant shades of gold and crimson. Each crunch beneath my feet felt like a reminder of what I was about to face. I pulled my scarf tighter around my neck, wishing it could shield me from the thoughts creeping in like a chill in the air. The remnants of my conversation with Max echoed in my mind, his warmth a stark contrast to the anxiety knotting my stomach. "Face him," I had told myself, but the word "face" felt far too gentle for what I was preparing to do.

Aaron had suggested the park, a place that held memories I had tried so hard to forget. As I approached the familiar entrance, the soft sounds of laughter and playful barks mingled with the distant strumming of a guitar, wrapping around me like a blanket. I took a deep breath, the crisp air filling my lungs, momentarily easing the unease. But with every step, my resolve wavered, uncertainty sneaking in like a mischievous sprite.

I spotted him sitting on a bench, his dark hair tousled in the gentle breeze, looking every bit the charming rogue I once knew. Aaron's blue eyes were trained on his phone, but they flicked up as I approached, and I could almost see the gears turning in his head as he processed my presence. "Hey," he said, his voice laced with an easy familiarity that sent a jolt through me.

"Hey," I replied, forcing a smile that felt more like a mask than a genuine expression. I plopped down beside him, the space between us charged with unspoken tension. "So, what's this about?"

He glanced sideways at me, an eyebrow raised in mock innocence. "You act like I summoned you for some sinister plot."

I couldn't help but roll my eyes. "It feels like I'm walking into a trap. You do know I have a history of being lured into awkward situations, right?"

"Only the best kind," he quipped, grinning as he leaned back against the bench. "But seriously, I wanted to talk about us."

The word hung in the air like a heavy fog, thick with memories and regrets. "What do you mean by 'us'?" I asked, my tone sharper than intended.

He shifted, suddenly serious, his laughter replaced by a somber expression. "I've had time to think. I messed up, and I know that. But I want to make it right. Can't we just—"

"Make it right?" I interrupted, incredulous. "You mean like how you just... disappeared? How do you plan to make it right? With flowers? A public apology?"

"Okay, okay," he conceded, raising his hands in mock surrender. "Let me rephrase. I want to talk about what happened. Understand what went wrong."

I leaned back, crossing my arms defiantly. "Understand? It felt pretty clear to me. You walked away when things got tough. I had to pick up the pieces, and now you expect me to sit here and discuss our tragic love story like it's some rom-com?"

His gaze softened, but I could see the flicker of frustration in his eyes. "I wasn't the only one at fault, you know. You shut me out too."

"Shut you out?" The incredulity spilled from my lips, and I leaned in closer. "You weren't exactly making it easy to let you in! Every time I tried to reach out, it was like talking to a ghost."

"Because I was trying to protect you!" he snapped back, the anger lacing his words piercing through the air between us. "I thought I was doing the right thing."

"Protect me? By disappearing?" My heart raced, the conversation spiraling into an argument I had hoped to avoid. "That's your idea of protection? Just cutting me off?"

"Can we just stop for a second?" he said, his voice softer now, tinged with desperation. "I know I made a mistake. I just thought if I distanced myself, it would help you focus on what you needed."

"What I needed?" I echoed, disbelief flooding my veins. "What I needed was you to stick around, not pull away like you were being chased by a pack of wolves."

The silence stretched between us, thick with unprocessed emotions. I could see the struggle in his eyes, the regret that flickered just beneath the surface. "You were always so strong, so capable. I thought maybe you didn't need me. I thought I was doing what was best for you."

"That's not how it works, Aaron!" I exclaimed, frustration boiling over. "You don't get to decide what I need. That's not trust; that's control."

He flinched, and for a moment, I could see the walls he had built around his heart begin to crack. "I know that now. I'm not asking for your forgiveness, but I want you to understand why I did what I did."

The wind picked up, rustling the leaves overhead, as if the world itself was waiting for me to respond. My heart raced, caught in a battle between the past I couldn't quite shake and the future I dared to imagine. "Understanding doesn't magically erase the pain you caused, Aaron. I don't want to just understand; I want to heal."

He leaned closer, his voice barely above a whisper. "And I want to help you heal. Can we start over? Just... try to be friends?"

The weight of his request hung in the air, heavy with implications. My heart felt like it was caught in a vice, squeezing tightly as I weighed my options. Could I trust him again? The very thought made my stomach churn, yet beneath the layers of hurt lay a flicker of something I couldn't quite define—curiosity, perhaps?

"I don't know if I can be just friends," I finally admitted, my voice trembling with uncertainty. "Not yet. You're asking me to put aside the scars that still sting."

Aaron nodded, the understanding in his eyes giving me pause. "Then let's take it slow. I'll give you the space you need, but I'm not going anywhere. I mean it."

I could see the sincerity etched in his features, the vulnerability that cracked through the bravado he had wrapped around himself like a shield. Maybe it was naive to hope for a different outcome, to consider that perhaps we could forge a new path, one where trust wasn't a fragile whisper but a solid foundation.

"Alright," I replied, the word feeling foreign on my tongue. "Let's take it slow."

As we sat there, the sun dipping below the horizon, casting long shadows across the park, I felt the fragile threads of trust begin to weave their way between us once more, a tenuous start amidst the wreckage of our shared history. The road ahead was uncertain, fraught with challenges, but for the first time in a long while, I felt a glimmer of hope.

The following days felt like navigating a dense fog, my thoughts swirling around Aaron's proposal to take things slow. I tried to concentrate on my work, but every time I glanced at my phone, my heart raced with the thought of his name lighting up the screen. I hadn't expected my emotions to spiral back into turmoil. Max's presence lingered in my mind, a steady pulse of warmth and encouragement, yet here I was, grappling with a history I thought I could finally leave behind.

The next weekend unfolded with a vibrant autumn chill that danced through the air, sending leaves tumbling down like confetti. I found myself wandering through the farmer's market, its colorful stalls bursting with produce and handcrafted goods. The laughter of children filled the space, and the scent of spiced cider mingled with baked goods, wrapping me in a warm cocoon. My senses began to relax, and for a fleeting moment, I thought of calling Max to share this delightful scene, to invite him to join me in savoring the moment.

As I rounded a corner, my thoughts took a nosedive when I spotted Aaron across the way, his sandy hair tousled by the gentle breeze. He stood at a stall, examining apples as if they held the secrets of the universe. My heart flipped uncomfortably in my chest. Just as I was about to turn away, hoping to avoid an awkward encounter, he caught sight of me and flashed a grin that sent a rush of conflicting feelings coursing through my veins.

"Fancy meeting you here!" he called, striding over with a confidence that belied the tumult I felt within. "I was just thinking about how I owe you a coffee. It's the least I could do after our last chat."

"Is that so?" I replied, crossing my arms defensively. "You seem awfully confident for someone who's trying to rebuild trust."

He laughed, a genuine sound that was somehow both endearing and infuriating. "Touché! But seriously, how about it? Just a coffee, as friends."

I hesitated, my mind racing. This was exactly what I had agreed to—a casual friendship, no strings attached—but with every tick of the clock, my heart began to argue with my mind. "Fine. But just coffee," I finally relented, waving off the sudden swell of warmth that spread through me at the thought of spending more time with him.

We made our way to a nearby café, the smell of roasted beans wrapping around us like a familiar embrace. As we settled into a cozy corner, I glanced at him, trying to discern if this was just an act or if he genuinely wanted to make amends. His playful banter was a thin veil over the lingering shadows of our past.

"So, how's life treating you?" he asked, stirring his coffee absentmindedly, his eyes flickering with a hint of something deeper.

"It's good," I replied, keeping my tone even. "Busy with work and trying to figure things out. You know how it is."

He nodded, but the crease between his brows deepened. "Yeah, I get it. I'm trying to figure my own life out, too. Just trying to be a better version of myself."

"Good luck with that," I shot back, a teasing lilt in my voice to lighten the mood. "You know what they say: you can't teach an old dog new tricks."

Aaron laughed, but there was a glimmer of sincerity in his eyes that caught me off guard. "I guess I'm hoping to be a young dog who learns some new tricks."

Our conversation flowed surprisingly well, punctuated by laughter and occasional moments of silence that felt less awkward and more comfortable. Just as I began to let my guard down, he leaned forward, his voice dropping to a serious tone. "I want you to know that I really am sorry for everything that happened. It wasn't just you; I messed up, too."

"Yeah, you did," I replied, my voice steady, though my pulse quickened. "But saying sorry doesn't fix everything."

"I know. But I want to try, really try, to earn back your trust. I don't expect it overnight."

His earnestness tugged at something deep inside me, a mix of old affection and new skepticism. "It's going to take time," I warned, unable to ignore the flicker of hope blossoming despite my reservations.

"I can wait. As long as you're willing to meet me halfway," he said, a hopeful smile gracing his lips.

Just as I was about to respond, a familiar voice broke through the moment, slicing through the fragile bubble we had created. "There you are!"

I turned to see Max standing at the entrance of the café, a casual yet slightly concerned look on his face. His eyes darted between Aaron and me, a flash of realization crossing his features. "I didn't expect to find you here," he said, forcing a smile that didn't quite reach his eyes.

"Max!" I exclaimed, a wave of surprise washing over me. "What are you doing here?"

He stepped closer, his body language shifting as he took in the scene. "Just grabbing a coffee before heading to the art exhibit. I thought you might want to join me."

I glanced back at Aaron, whose expression had shifted from surprise to guarded curiosity. The air between us crackled with unspoken tension, the warmth of the café suddenly feeling stifling. "I... I can't. I mean, I'm already here with Aaron," I stammered, feeling the weight of the moment pressing down on me.

"Right," Max replied, his tone even but tinged with something I couldn't quite place—disappointment, perhaps? "I didn't mean to interrupt."

"No interruption," Aaron chimed in, his voice too bright, a hint of defensiveness creeping in. "Just catching up."

Max's gaze lingered on me, searching for answers in my eyes. "I see. Well, I hope you enjoy your coffee," he said, attempting nonchalance, but the undercurrent of tension was palpable.

"Thanks," I managed to say, my heart racing as I felt the weight of the decision looming over me. "Maybe I'll catch you later?"

"Sure," Max said, but the smile didn't quite reach his eyes as he turned to leave, the door chiming softly behind him.

As the door closed, the air felt charged, a bubble of tension settling between Aaron and me. "This is awkward," I said, breaking the silence.

"Yeah," Aaron agreed, rubbing the back of his neck. "Do you think he'll be okay?"

I shrugged, not entirely sure. "He's a big boy. He'll figure it out."

But as we resumed our conversation, I couldn't shake the feeling that the fragile thread connecting us was about to unravel. My phone buzzed, pulling my attention away from Aaron. I glanced down to see a new message from Max: We need to talk.

My heart sank. "What does that mean?" I whispered, dread pooling in my stomach.

"What is it?" Aaron asked, leaning closer, concern flickering in his eyes.

Before I could respond, my phone buzzed again, this time with a call. I answered it, my heart pounding. "Hello?"

"Hey, it's me," Max's voice was strained, urgent. "You need to come to the gallery. Now."

"What's going on?" I asked, but the line went dead, leaving me with an icy chill running down my spine.

"I need to go," I said, my heart racing.

"Go where?" Aaron asked, confusion etched across his features.

But I couldn't answer; I was already halfway out the door, an uneasy sense of foreboding clawing at my insides. Whatever awaited me at the gallery could change everything, and the feeling of unease loomed like a storm cloud ready to unleash its fury. As I stepped outside, my breath hitched in my throat. The world around me felt like it was shifting, and I couldn't shake the sense that I was about to walk into something far beyond my control.

Chapter 22: Winds of Change

The bar hummed with a cacophony of laughter and clinking glasses, a vivid tapestry of life unfurling around me. The scent of spiced rum and citrus lingered in the air, mingling with the heady aroma of roasted garlic from the kitchen. Dim, golden light spilled from antique sconces, casting a warm glow over the worn wooden tables and the eclectic crowd. I spotted Aaron in a corner, his familiar silhouette outlined against the backdrop of swirling conversations and the thrum of jazz playing softly from a vintage jukebox.

As I approached, I noticed the way he leaned back, a casual confidence wrapping around him like a well-worn leather jacket. He caught my eye and flashed that signature grin—the one that had once made my heart flutter. Now, however, it felt like a red flag waving in the wind, a signal of something I no longer wished to engage with. I steeled myself, reminding myself of the strength I had fought so hard to reclaim.

"Hey," I said, sliding into the chair opposite him, the wood cool beneath my palms. "Thanks for meeting me."

"Of course. You look... different," he replied, his gaze tracing the curve of my jaw and the way my hair tumbled over my shoulders. "Stronger."

I let out a short laugh, the sound sharper than intended. "Stronger, yes. Wiser? I'm getting there." I studied him, trying to discern the truth behind those deep brown eyes that once held so much allure. "I hope you've brought more than just compliments tonight."

He shifted, his casual demeanor wavering for the briefest moment. "I want to be honest with you. I've been working on myself, on everything we talked about." His words flowed out with practiced ease, but I could see the underlying tension in his shoulders, the way he avoided direct eye contact as if the truth was something he feared would spill from his lips.

I folded my arms, leaning back in my chair, the cool wood pressing against my skin grounding me. "Working on yourself? That's great, Aaron, but I'm here for answers, not reassurances. What do you mean by that?"

He took a deep breath, his fingers fidgeting with the edge of the tablecloth, a nervous habit I'd always found endearing. "I realized that I've been selfish, and I want to change that. I'm trying to figure out what it means to be a better person, not just for me, but for those around me. For you."

The sincerity in his voice caught me off guard. It was tempting to let my defenses slip, to allow his charm to weave its way back into my heart. But I couldn't. Not anymore. "That's a nice sentiment, but I can't be part of your self-discovery journey, Aaron. I've spent too long being someone's project."

His eyes darkened, the playfulness shifting to something more serious. "You think I see you as a project? That's not—"

"It's exactly what it was," I interjected, feeling the familiar rush of frustration bubble to the surface. "You had a way of making me feel special while always keeping me at arm's length. I don't want to be your experiment in empathy."

A silence hung between us, thick and heavy like the humidity before a storm. I could almost see the wheels turning in his mind, processing the reality I was laying out before him.

"I didn't mean it like that," he said, his voice softer now, almost pleading. "I'm not asking you to be part of my journey; I'm just trying to explain what I've been through. I want to be someone you can trust again."

"Trust?" The word hung there, a bitter echo. "You can't just ask for trust like it's a magic trick you can perform. You have to earn it, and right now, it feels like I'm standing on a tightrope over a pit of uncertainty."

He looked pained, as if my words struck a chord deep within him. "I get it. I've hurt you, and I know that's not something you just forget. But I want to be different. I want you to see that I'm trying."

"Trying isn't enough, Aaron. It never was." I felt my heart quicken, a flutter of anger mingling with the sadness that had settled there. "People can change, but I can't keep waiting for you to become someone I can rely on. I've done too much work to unearth my own worth."

The tension thickened, our gazes locked, each of us wrestling with unspoken emotions. I could see the flicker of something in his eyes—was it regret or desperation? Perhaps both.

"Can we at least agree that we had something real?" he asked, his voice low, nearly drowned out by the laughter and music swirling around us.

"Yes, we had something. But that doesn't mean I want to go back to it," I replied, feeling my voice tremble slightly. "What we had was tangled and complicated, a rollercoaster of emotions that left me dizzy. I'm not that person anymore, and I refuse to go back to a love that felt like a constant negotiation for affection."

He leaned closer, the scent of his cologne—a hint of cedar and something sweet—pulling me momentarily back to the days when his presence could anchor me. "You really believe that we can't find a way to salvage this?"

"Salvage?" I repeated, incredulous. "I don't want to be in a salvage yard picking through the remnants of what we used to be. I want to build something new, something authentic. But I can't do that with you hovering in my past."

For a moment, the world around us blurred into the background. It was just me and him, two souls entangled in a web of unfinished business and memories that clung to us like mist. But the air was electric with a sense of finality, and I felt the weight of my own resolve solidifying. I wouldn't let him pull me back into the darkness I'd fought so hard to escape.

The conversation hung in the air like smoke, thick with unresolved feelings and unspoken words. As I pushed my chair back, the screech of wood against the floor echoed my desire to break free from the past. I glanced one last time at Aaron, his expression a mixture of hope and something that looked suspiciously like despair. There was a flicker of the old charm I had fallen for, but this time it felt like a mirage, shimmering just out of reach.

I stood and slipped my coat on, the fabric a comforting weight against my skin. "I hope you find what you're looking for," I said, my voice steady. "But I can't be part of it."

As I turned to leave, the bar buzzed with laughter and clinking glasses, a stark contrast to the storm brewing inside me. Each step away from him felt liberating and terrifying in equal measure. The sidewalk was damp from an earlier rain, the scent of wet asphalt rising to meet me as I made my way toward the subway station.

The night air was crisp, a reminder that autumn was on the cusp of fully claiming the city. Leaves crunched underfoot, their vibrant reds and oranges a celebration of change that mirrored my own journey. With each step, I felt lighter, the burden of our conversation dissolving into the night like fog before the dawn. I couldn't deny the thrill of reclaiming my independence, but a shadow of doubt clung to me. Had I really made the right choice?

The subway rattled and swayed, the rhythmic clattering of wheels a perfect accompaniment to my swirling thoughts. I leaned against the cool metal pole, staring at the flickering lights above as the train lurched forward. My mind danced back to the moments I had spent with Aaron, each one layered with laughter, anger, and the inevitable heartbreak. It had been a whirlwind romance, one that swept me off my feet but left me gasping for air in the aftermath.

The train screeched to a halt, and I hopped off, my heart pounding with a mix of exhilaration and uncertainty. I didn't know where I was going, only that I needed to keep moving. As I stepped onto the platform, I felt a sudden urge to call my best friend, Lila. She was my grounding force, the steady rock who always knew how to pull me back from the brink of self-doubt.

"Hey, are you busy?" I asked when she answered, trying to keep my voice light.

"Busy? Me? Never! What's up?" Her cheerful tone instantly brightened my mood.

"I just had a conversation with Aaron," I admitted, taking a seat on a nearby bench.

"Ah, the infamous Aaron. The one who nearly gave you an existential crisis? Spill it!"

I chuckled, grateful for her ability to lighten even the heaviest of burdens. "It was intense. He claims he's been working on himself, wants to be better. But I just... I can't go back. I'm not ready for a rerun of our old drama."

"Good! Stick to your guns! You deserve someone who lifts you up, not someone who keeps you down," Lila replied, her voice firm. "What are you thinking? Are you going to see him again?"

"Not if I can help it," I sighed, staring at the worn tiles beneath my feet. "It's just so complicated. I thought maybe we could be friends, but I don't know if I can handle that yet. I need space to breathe."

"Space is good. It sounds like you're finally putting yourself first. You go, girl! Just promise me you won't let him back in too easily. Remember how much you struggled before?"

"I promise. I'm not looking for a repeat performance," I said, feeling a wave of determination wash over me. "I want to focus on me for a while, find out who I am without him."

"Exactly! You're like a butterfly breaking free from a cocoon. Let the world see your colors! Speaking of colors, do you want to meet for brunch tomorrow? I found this adorable little café that does the best avocado toast."

The thought of brunch made me smile. "Count me in. I need a hefty dose of caffeine and your fabulous company."

"Perfect! It'll be a date," she chirped. "And you can tell me all about how you're going to take the city by storm."

I hung up, my heart lighter than it had been in months. Just as I was about to leave the bench, a flicker of movement caught my eye. A flash of dark hair and a familiar green jacket appeared in the distance, and my stomach twisted. Aaron was walking toward me, his expression unreadable as he spotted me sitting there.

My breath caught in my throat, and for a split second, I felt the old instinct to run. But I reminded myself of my newfound resolve. I wouldn't let him intimidate me this time. He approached, and I stood my ground, drawing in a steadying breath.

"What are you doing here?" I asked, my voice steady despite the turmoil brewing inside.

"I was hoping to catch you before you left," he said, his eyes earnest. "I didn't mean to upset you tonight. I just wanted to explain myself better."

I shook my head, crossing my arms defensively. "We said what we needed to say, Aaron. I'm not interested in any more explanations. I need to move on."

His face fell, and for a moment, I felt a pang of sympathy. "Can't we at least have a civil conversation? I want to understand you, to show you that I can be better."

"Better?" I repeated, incredulous. "You think that's just a switch you can flip? This isn't about you anymore. It's about me learning to stand on my own two feet."

He paused, the tension crackling like static in the air. "Then let me help you stand. I'm not asking you to jump back into what we had; I just want the chance to show you that I can support you as a friend. Maybe we can figure this out together?"

I hesitated, the warmth of his words a double-edged sword. I wanted to believe him, but the scars of the past still throbbed beneath the surface. "I need time, Aaron. If you truly want to change, then you have to respect my space. I won't be your safety net while you find your way."

His expression shifted, a flicker of understanding crossing his face. "I can do that. I'll give you space. Just know that I'm here when you're ready to talk."

With that, he stepped back, giving me the distance I craved. The night stretched before me like a blank canvas, the future unwritten. I took a deep breath, tasting the crisp autumn air, and with it, a sense of possibility. Change was here, and I was ready to embrace it, even if it meant stepping into the unknown alone.

With Aaron's figure fading into the distance, I felt a strange mixture of relief and lingering apprehension settle over me. The city was alive, the night air charged with the pulse of energy, and I found myself walking toward the park that lay just beyond the bustling streets. Each step echoed the new resolve within me, a mantra that reminded me I was in control of my own narrative now.

The path was dappled with light from the street lamps, casting soft pools of yellow against the darkened grass. I settled onto a weathered bench, taking in the scene—a couple strolled by hand in hand, their laughter bubbling like champagne, while a group of friends huddled over their phones, sharing ridiculous memes. It felt like life was moving on, and I was a spectator on the sidelines, waiting for my cue to jump back in.

My phone buzzed in my pocket, a jarring reminder of reality. I fished it out and smiled at the text from Lila: How'd it go? Did you crush him with your newfound strength?

I couldn't help but chuckle, my fingers flying over the screen as I replied, Not quite a crushing, but definitely a solid "No, thanks."

Excellent! You've taken the first step to liberation. Celebrate with ice cream tomorrow?

Definitely! You know me too well. I'm ready to indulge in all the flavors of freedom.

The thought of spending the next day with Lila, bingeing on ice cream and laughing until our stomachs hurt, filled me with warmth. I could almost taste the strawberry swirl and chocolate fudge already. My phone buzzed again, and as I read her message, a sharp gasp escaped my lips.

Oh, by the way, Aaron's going to be at the same café tomorrow. Just a heads-up.

My heart dropped. Suddenly, the freedom I had just embraced felt like a cage with invisible bars. I stared at the screen, my thoughts a tangled mess. Of course, he'd choose a place I loved, a spot that had been a sanctuary for me long before he ever entered my life. I tapped my fingers on the bench, considering my options. I could cancel, retreat into my bubble of safety, or I could face him again, this time on my terms.

I took a deep breath, letting the cool night air fill my lungs. "What's the worst that could happen?" I murmured to myself. My mind was racing with possibilities, a mix of dread and excitement. Each heartbeat echoed the rhythm of the decision before me.

"Maybe a verbal sparring match?" a voice interrupted my thoughts, light and teasing. I looked up to find a tall figure standing a few feet away. It was a man in a casual leather jacket, the collar turned up, a playful grin dancing on his lips. "Or perhaps an awkward silence over the last piece of cake?"

"Excuse me?" I raised an eyebrow, half-amused and half-confused by the intrusion.

He sauntered closer, his eyes sparkling with mischief. "Just trying to gauge the atmosphere. Seems like you're either in the middle of a deep existential crisis or contemplating a duel over dessert."

I laughed, surprised by his unexpected presence. "Well, it's a bit of both, actually. You could say I'm trying to find the balance between self-discovery and avoiding confrontation."

"Ah, a classic dilemma. But here's the thing—life is too short for half measures. If you're going to face a fear, might as well do it with style." He gestured theatrically, his hands weaving through the air as if orchestrating a symphony. "And if there's ice cream involved, even better!"

I tilted my head, intrigued by this stranger's bravado. "And who are you, the ice cream savior?"

"Call me Ryan," he said, extending a hand with an exaggerated flourish. "Your guide to unearthing the joys of life and embracing your inner badass."

I couldn't help but smile, his energy infectious. "Well, Ryan, I appreciate your enthusiasm. But I think I can manage my own battles. I'm just trying to navigate the aftermath of a rather complicated relationship."

"Complicated relationships are like complicated recipes—sometimes they require a pinch of chaos to make them interesting." He leaned against the bench, confidence radiating off him. "But seriously, if Aaron is your past and you're ready to step into your future, don't let him pull you back. You're stronger than that."

The honesty in his words hit home, resonating deep within me. "You're right," I admitted, a flicker of determination sparking in my chest. "But how do I handle seeing him tomorrow?"

Ryan shrugged, his expression light. "Show up, own your space, and if he tries to pull you back into old patterns, just laugh it off.

You're not the same person he used to know. You're a version of yourself that's ready to reclaim her narrative."

I considered his words, a smile creeping onto my face. "Maybe you're right. Maybe it's time I stopped viewing Aaron as a threat and started seeing him as just another part of my story."

"Exactly! Think of it as a new chapter where you're the heroine who wields a sword made of self-respect. It's going to be epic!"

I chuckled, feeling buoyed by his enthusiasm. "A heroine with a side of ice cream, of course. What's a good story without dessert?"

"Now you're talking!" He straightened up, his posture radiating excitement. "I'll bet you're going to be the most dazzling woman in that café tomorrow. And if you need backup, I'm just a text away."

"Thanks, Ryan. You've turned my evening around," I said, appreciating his light-heartedness. "But I think I'll manage on my own. If I can stand up to Aaron, I can handle anything."

With that, he nodded, a mischievous grin still on his face. "Just remember, you've got a fierce spirit within you. Let it shine, and you might just surprise yourself."

As he strolled away, the vibrant city around me felt a little brighter, each twinkling light echoing the sense of empowerment coursing through me. I could face tomorrow, and whatever it brought.

The night deepened, and I rose to leave the park, feeling ready for the challenge ahead. Just as I turned to walk away, my phone buzzed in my pocket again. Pulling it out, I saw a message from Lila. Just saw Aaron's name trending on social media! Something big happened—check it out!

Curiosity tugged at me, and I opened the app to find a flood of notifications. My breath caught in my throat as I read the headlines: Local Businessman Caught in Controversy—Exposes Cheating Scandal! My heart raced as I realized the implications.

Could this really be about Aaron? My mind whirled, grappling with the sudden shift in the narrative. I needed to know more. I stepped into the night, propelled by an urgency I hadn't felt before, the city buzzing with secrets just waiting to be uncovered. The taste of uncertainty lingered on my tongue, a thrilling reminder that tomorrow would hold more than just ice cream—it would reveal the truth hidden behind the man I thought I knew.

Chapter 23: Blossoms of New Beginnings

The sun dipped low on the horizon, casting golden rays that danced on the vibrant colors of our mural. Each evening, as I stood beside Max, my heart fluttered with a mix of excitement and apprehension. The once-barren wall of the old community center had transformed into a vivid testament to our shared dreams. We painted together, our laughter ringing out like music, drowning out the faint sounds of the bustling park around us. Families strolled by, their children tugging at their parents' hands, captivated by our work. Little ones pointed, eyes wide with wonder, while the adults paused, smiles breaking across their faces, as if our creation was a spark of hope in their busy lives.

"Can you believe we started with a single brushstroke?" Max said one evening, standing back to admire our progress. The colors glimmered against the fading light—swirls of turquoise and coral intertwined with sun-yellow rays that seemed to radiate warmth. "Now look at it. It's like a rainbow exploded."

"More like a carefully orchestrated explosion," I replied, arching an eyebrow playfully. "But I'll take credit for the precision of my splatters." I tossed him a mischievous grin, and he laughed, his voice rich and warm.

Our playful banter wove seamlessly into the fabric of our collaboration, a tapestry of teasing and shared visions. With every moment spent in his company, my affection for Max deepened, weaving its way through my thoughts like the vibrant colors splashed across our mural. He was more than just a friend; he was a muse, sparking creativity I hadn't known resided in me. There was an ease about him, a rhythm that matched my own, and every time our hands brushed as we reached for the same paint, a thrill shot through me, making my cheeks warm.

As the project progressed, we transformed the wall into a vivid collage—a phoenix rising from the ashes, flowers blooming from the concrete, and stars scattered across a deep blue sky. Each element spoke of renewal, resilience, and the beauty of beginnings. I found myself pouring my heart into the art, a catharsis of sorts. The paintbrush became an extension of my emotions, my hopes swirling into the colors and patterns, while Max's deft strokes and creative flair breathed life into our vision.

One afternoon, as we stood side by side, I found the courage to voice my thoughts. "Max, do you ever think about what comes next? I mean, after the mural is done? What happens when the colors dry?"

He paused, the brush hovering above the canvas, and I felt my heart race. "Honestly? I try not to think about it. I love the process too much." He turned to me, eyes glinting with a hint of mischief. "But if you're talking about our next artistic endeavor, I'm ready for anything. I hear there's a fountain downtown that could use a bit of pizzazz."

I laughed, a bubbling sound that filled the air between us. "Are you suggesting we turn a fountain into a unicorn?"

"Only if you're on board with a sparkly rainbow tail," he shot back, his grin wide and contagious.

Our laughter echoed in the afternoon air, and for a moment, everything felt perfect—until a shadow crossed over my heart. The reality of our situation loomed like a dark cloud threatening to rain on our parade. Max had a life beyond our mural, a world I wasn't part of yet, a world filled with unanswered questions and the specter of what might happen if I let my feelings bloom.

As the sun began its descent, painting the sky with hues of lavender and rose, I turned to him, the words I had practiced forming on my tongue. "Max, can I tell you something?"

His brow furrowed, curiosity piqued. "You can tell me anything."

My heart raced as I searched for the right words, the right moment. But before I could speak, a familiar voice interrupted our sanctuary. "There you are!" Amy, my overzealous friend, came barreling toward us, her ponytail bouncing in rhythm with her hurried steps. "I've been looking for you everywhere."

"Hey, Amy," I said, forcing a smile, the weight of my unspoken words slipping away like sand through my fingers.

"Are you two seriously still at it? The mural looks amazing!" She leaned in, her eyes gleaming with admiration. "But we need to talk about the gallery opening next week. I can't believe you didn't mention it."

"Yeah, about that," I said, trying to sound nonchalant while my stomach twisted in knots. "I've been a bit... preoccupied."

"Preoccupied? More like lost in your own world!" She nudged me, her excitement palpable. "You and Max are practically an artistic power couple. I'd ship it if I had a boat."

"Hey now," Max chimed in, raising his hands in mock defense. "I'm just here to help her unleash her inner artist."

"Sure, sure," Amy teased, a knowing smile dancing on her lips. "But seriously, the gallery needs your touch. You can't hide behind the mural forever."

As they bantered, a part of me wanted to slip away, to reclaim that moment before the interruption, before the tension coiled in my stomach like a spring. I watched as Max and Amy sparred with playful words, his laughter mingling with hers, and in that instant, I realized I was at a crossroads. My feelings for Max were burgeoning like the flowers we painted, and I couldn't let fear dictate the canvas of my life.

When the sun finally dipped below the horizon, leaving a canvas of stars in its wake, I took a deep breath, determined to face my truth. As laughter and light danced around us, I felt a shift in the air, a promise of new beginnings waiting just beyond the veil of my hesitation.

As the days unfolded like a well-loved book, I found myself wrapped in the warmth of summer evenings spent with Max. The park transformed into our sanctuary, a vibrant backdrop to our creative escapades. With each brushstroke, I felt more alive, as if the colors we spread across the wall were seeping into my very soul. Max's laughter was like music, a sweet harmony that echoed through the air, making the mundane extraordinary. Our playful banter was a dance of wits, each comeback sharper than the last, leaving me breathless and exhilarated.

One evening, as the sun dipped beneath the horizon, painting the sky with hues of orange and lavender, we stood side by side, contemplating the mural's next phase. I had just dipped my brush in a rich indigo when Max leaned in closer, his shoulder brushing against mine. "What if we added a giant sunflower here?" He pointed, his enthusiasm lighting up his eyes. "Something bright to symbolize growth, you know?"

"A sunflower?" I laughed, imagining the sheer size of it. "Do you mean a sunflower or a sun-titan? Because I'm pretty sure that's going to need its own zip code."

"Just think about it! It could represent all the positive vibes we're sending into this community," he insisted, a grin playing on his lips. "And maybe—just maybe—it could draw in more art lovers, a sunflower spectacle to rival any flower festival."

His passion was contagious, and soon I found myself caught up in the vision of a sunflower as grand as my dreams. "Alright, let's make it the biggest sunflower this town has ever seen! But you know what that means? We're going to need a ladder and probably a few extra cans of paint."

"Consider it done!" Max declared, already calculating the logistics as he swung his arms dramatically. "I'll pull a few strings at the local hardware store. I think I've charmed the guy behind the counter enough with my endless questions about paint sheens and finishes."

With our plans solidified, we launched into action, each stroke of the brush feeling like a step toward something bigger. I let the excitement of the sunflower bloom in my mind, but beneath the surface, a shadow of doubt lurked. What would happen when our mural was complete? Would this newfound bond remain, or would it fade like the colors on the wall, memories fading into the backdrop of life?

The thought twisted in my stomach as I watched him work. Max was absorbed in his own world, his brow furrowed in concentration, a focused artist lost in the rhythm of creation. He had his dreams, his aspirations, and I felt like a secondary character in a narrative I wasn't sure I belonged to.

"Earth to Amelia!" His voice broke through my spiraling thoughts, snapping me back to the present. "Are you going to help me with this, or just stand there daydreaming about giant sunflowers and the meaning of life?"

"Life is much more complicated than a sunflower, my friend. But I'm here," I replied, forcing a smile as I dipped my brush into the golden paint. "Let's create a masterpiece."

As we painted, the sun sank lower, bathing the park in a warm glow. The colors swirled together, and with each stroke, the mural began to take shape—our sunflower sprouting proudly in the center, surrounded by swirls of blues and greens that flowed like a river around its roots. I felt exhilarated and terrified, riding the waves of creativity that came with collaborating so closely.

"Just look at this!" Max exclaimed, stepping back to admire our work. "It's like nature itself is joining in on our little project. I think we've officially created the happiest wall in the city."

"I might argue that it's the happiest wall in the world," I said, my heart swelling with pride. "And it's all thanks to you."

Max met my gaze, and for a moment, the air crackled with unspoken words. A flicker of something deeper danced between us, igniting a warmth that threatened to spill over into the open. But before I could voice the swelling emotion in my chest, Amy swooped in again, her presence like a sudden rainstorm disrupting a sunny day.

"Guess what?" she chirped, her cheeks flushed with excitement. "I just heard from the gallery, and they want to feature our mural as part of the local arts festival!"

"Are you serious?" I gasped, my heart racing. "That's amazing! But—"

"No buts! This is a huge deal!" she interrupted, practically bouncing on her heels. "This could be our chance to shine, Amelia. To get your name out there and put this project on the map!"

"But I wasn't really thinking about getting involved in all of that," I said, feeling a rush of nerves. The idea of our work being showcased sent a thrill through me, but it also felt daunting. What if it failed? What if I wasn't ready for that level of exposure? "I mean, it's a mural. It was supposed to be our little project, just for fun."

Amy rolled her eyes, clearly unimpressed by my hesitance. "Amelia, this isn't just a mural anymore. It's a symbol of everything you've been working toward. It's not just paint on a wall; it's hope, creativity, and the beginning of something beautiful."

I glanced at Max, his expression unreadable as he absorbed Amy's words. Would he want to continue this venture with the weight of public scrutiny? What if he didn't?

"Okay, okay! Let's do it," I finally said, swallowing the lump in my throat. "But we need to make sure we prepare for it. This mural deserves to be seen properly."

"Now you're talking!" Amy beamed, and I could see the gears turning in her head, plotting our next steps. "We'll need a launch event, maybe some live music, a few snacks. I can get some local businesses on board. The works!"

Max stepped closer, an impish grin spreading across his face. "And a sunflower crown for the queen of the mural, of course."

I scoffed playfully, yet my heart raced at the idea of making this vision a reality. "Alright, just so we're clear, if there's a sunflower crown involved, it better not be too big. I have a reputation to uphold."

"Trust me, it will suit you perfectly," he replied, laughter dancing in his eyes.

The evening wore on with plans buzzing in the air, excitement palpable. I found myself swept up in the whirlwind of possibilities, each idea igniting a spark in my chest. But beneath the excitement, a deeper fear simmered. Would our vibrant mural, and the bond we were building, withstand the scrutiny of the outside world?

As I painted that night, the sunflowers slowly taking shape against the backdrop of swirling colors, I knew that whatever happened, I was ready to step into the unknown—if only to see where this adventure with Max would lead.

The days rolled into each other like waves on a shore, a rhythmic cadence of laughter and paint. Our mural had blossomed into a stunning work of art, each detail more intricate than the last. Sunflowers towered like sentinels, vibrant and proud, while swirling blues and greens framed the scene, breathing life into the concrete jungle. The park had become our stage, a place where our creativity unfurled, and I felt like I was part of something magical.

One balmy evening, as the sky blushed in shades of peach and gold, I stood back to admire our work. The fading sunlight illuminated the mural, casting a warm glow over the colors. Max stood beside me, his shoulder brushing against mine as we both took in the sight. "It's unbelievable how far we've come," he murmured, his voice thick with awe.

"Unbelievable? More like a miracle!" I replied, feigning seriousness. "I mean, look at that sunflower—it's practically a celebrity now. I wouldn't be surprised if it starts charging for autographs."

Max chuckled, a soft, infectious sound that sent butterflies fluttering in my stomach. "What can I say? Sunflowers are in demand." He paused, his expression shifting to something more contemplative. "You know, this mural is more than just paint on a wall. It's a part of us, a reflection of what we can achieve together."

The weight of his words settled between us, and I felt my heart race. Was he suggesting something more? Our connection had deepened, but the fear of ruining what we had held me back. "I think it's a testament to your artistic genius," I said lightly, trying to mask the vulnerability that threatened to spill over. "Without you, it would be a wall of sad little splashes."

"You're selling yourself short, Amelia. You've put your heart into this. We both have." He turned to me, sincerity radiating from his gaze. "And I wouldn't want to share this experience with anyone else."

Just then, the unmistakable sounds of chatter and laughter pierced our little bubble. A group of familiar faces approached, led by Amy, her excitement palpable as she waved her arms in greeting. "There you two are! We were starting to think you'd turned into paintbrushes!"

"Now that's a thought," I joked. "The world needs more sentient paintbrushes. Imagine the adventures we'd have."

"I'd settle for a sentient ladder," Max added, a twinkle in his eye. "Imagine the vantage point we could get for our next mural."

Amy rolled her eyes, but I could see the amusement bubbling beneath the surface. "Enough about ladders and paintbrushes. The gallery wants to showcase the mural this weekend! We have to prepare!"

"Wait, this weekend?" My heart raced, a cocktail of excitement and anxiety swirling in my chest. "That's—"

"Perfect timing! We can promote it as part of the arts festival!" Amy cut me off, clearly caught up in her own whirlwind of enthusiasm. "We need to gather supplies, get our promotional materials ready, and maybe a few cute outfits—"

"Cute outfits? I thought we were artists, not fashionistas," I said, trying to rein in the chaos.

"Art is all about presentation!" Amy insisted, her hands animatedly gesturing as if she could sculpt the perfect plan from thin air. "We'll need banners, maybe a little stage for speeches. We'll really need to sell this."

Max leaned closer, a teasing grin on his face. "And by 'sell this,' you mean you want to convince everyone to show up just to see the sunflower crown I promised Amelia?"

"You'll wear it with style," Amy chimed in, giving him a playful nudge. "Now let's talk about snacks. We need something to keep the crowd happy."

As they discussed logistics, my mind wandered back to the mural and the unspoken words I had left hanging between Max and me. Our bond felt electric, charged with possibility, yet the thought of addressing it under the scrutiny of an audience felt daunting. The festival would draw attention—not just to our artwork but to the dynamics we shared. Could I handle that kind of exposure?

"Amelia?" Max's voice cut through my thoughts, pulling me back. "What do you think? Should we incorporate live music into the event?"

"Definitely!" Amy exclaimed. "Maybe even invite some local musicians. We could have a mini concert! People love that."

"Or a sunflower-themed dance-off," I suggested, surprising myself with the idea. "Get everyone involved, celebrate the mural with some fun!"

"I like it!" Max said, grinning. "Picture it: a wall of sunflowers, surrounded by a crowd dancing their hearts out."

"Or tripping over their own feet," I quipped. "But let's be real, the idea is to keep them smiling. Just no one tripping over the ladder, alright?"

As the excitement built around us, my heart fluttered at the prospect of our mural being showcased to the community. It felt like a leap into the unknown, a chance to show the world not just our art, but what we had created together.

The week passed in a flurry of preparation, filled with late nights spent organizing, painting final touches on the mural, and brainstorming ideas for the event. Each passing moment drew me closer to Max, and with every brushstroke, the tension between us grew, a current that buzzed just below the surface.

Finally, the day of the festival arrived. The park transformed into a vibrant gathering of artists, musicians, and community members, each contributing to the tapestry of creativity. The air was thick with the scent of fresh flowers and the sound of laughter echoed around us. I stood before the mural, my heart racing as I took it all in. The sunflowers seemed to shine even brighter, almost alive with excitement.

"Are you ready for this?" Max asked, standing beside me, his gaze fixed on the crowd.

"Ready as I'll ever be," I replied, my voice barely above a whisper. "This is it, isn't it?"

"Yes, it is." His eyes sparkled, and for a moment, the world around us faded, leaving just the two of us and the mural that had become a symbol of our journey. "No matter what happens today, we did this together."

"Together," I echoed, and I felt a surge of emotion welling inside me.

As the crowd began to gather, the energy shifted, and the reality of what we were about to do hit me hard. Suddenly, a loud voice rang out, pulling our attention.

"Amelia! Max!" Amy shouted, her eyes wide with excitement as she approached. "You won't believe it! There's someone here from the local news who wants to do a feature on the mural!"

My breath caught in my throat. "A feature? On us?"

"Yes! They want to interview you guys and film the event!" Amy's enthusiasm was infectious, but panic clutched at my heart.

"Uh, wow. That's... big," I managed to say, my mind racing.

"Just be yourselves," Max encouraged, a reassuring hand resting on my shoulder. "You've got this."

But before I could process his words, the crowd surged, and a sense of urgency flooded through me. Just as I opened my mouth to speak, a figure broke through the throng, making a beeline toward us. The crowd parted like the Red Sea, revealing a woman in a crisp blazer, her expression a mix of determination and enthusiasm.

"Excuse me!" she called, her voice carrying above the murmurs. "I'm here to see the artists behind this incredible mural."

As she reached us, I felt the world shift beneath my feet. The moment was monumental, yet it hung precariously in the balance, and in the whirlwind of excitement, a realization struck me. The fear I had kept buried began to claw its way to the surface, whispering doubts that echoed louder than the cheers of the crowd.

The woman's gaze flickered between us, and I could see the gears turning in her mind, the anticipation building. "You've created something truly remarkable," she said, her eyes gleaming. "I think this could really put you on the map."

In that instant, with my heart pounding and the weight of possibility pressing down on me, I glanced at Max, who stood resolute beside me. The energy between us crackled like electricity, a silent agreement passing between us. I had a choice to make. Would I take this leap, embrace the chance to share our story and my feelings, or would I retreat into the safety of the colors on the wall?

Before I could find my voice, the woman leaned closer, her expression suddenly serious. "I need to ask you something, both of you. Are you ready for what this could mean? Because I have a feeling your mural—and the story behind it—could resonate far beyond this park."

My pulse quickened, the weight of her words sinking in. The spotlight was on us, and the possibility of what lay ahead was exhilarating and terrifying all at once. As the crowd cheered, the tension crackled in the air, and I took a deep breath, ready to step into the unknown.

But before I could respond, a sudden commotion erupted nearby. Shouts filled the air, and I turned to see a child in tears, pointing at the mural. The crowd shifted, and all eyes turned to the sunflower, where something strange and alarming was happening. My heart dropped as the colorful petals began to blur and smear, a wave of panic crashing over me.

"Max, what's happening?" I gasped, the exhilaration of the moment replaced by dread.

"I don't know," he said, his voice tight. "It looks like

Chapter 24: The Art of Letting Go

The air was thick with the scent of freshly painted walls and the sweet, earthy aroma of spring blooms. As twilight descended, the golden glow of string lights cast a warm halo over our mural, the colors swirling and dancing like a festival of life. I adjusted my hair, a few rebellious strands slipping from the careful knot I had fashioned earlier, and glanced at Max, who was busy adjusting the snacks on a table. His enthusiasm radiated like the sun, and I couldn't help but smile at how his presence seemed to brighten the entire evening.

"It's like a dream, isn't it?" he said, stepping back to admire the mural's vibrant colors, a kaleidoscope of emotions that had poured from our hearts and onto the canvas of that old community center wall.

"It really is," I replied, my voice barely above a whisper. The pride swelled within me, a buoyant sensation mingling with the nervous flutter of uncertainty. I felt like an artist, a creator, even if I had initially just been a girl trying to escape the shadows of my past. But beneath the surface of my joy, something darker lurked—an uninvited guest to my celebration.

As laughter and chatter filled the air, punctuated by the clinking of glasses and the rustle of snacks being devoured, I spotted Aaron at the periphery. My heart raced, the rhythm quickening as panic clawed its way up from the pit of my stomach. He stood there, a silhouette against the vibrant scene, his expression inscrutable but magnetic. It was a pull I could neither ignore nor entirely trust.

"Who's that?" Max asked, following my gaze, his brow furrowing slightly.

"No one," I said too quickly, my throat tightening.

"Right. Because no one looks that good in a T-shirt and jeans," he teased, nudging me playfully, his eyes sparkling with mischief.

"It's complicated," I sighed, turning my back to the scene unfolding outside of our carefully curated celebration. I busied myself with adjusting the decorations, arranging the flowers as if their placement could shield me from the storm brewing in my heart.

"Complicated is my middle name," Max said, grinning. "But tonight is for celebrating, remember? Don't let old ghosts ruin this."

He was right. I took a deep breath, inhaling the mingled scents of paint and blossoms, letting them anchor me to the moment. The laughter around me wrapped like a comforting blanket, urging me to loosen the tight grip of my worries. As I turned back to the mural, I found myself staring at the swirls of color—each stroke a part of my journey, a reflection of resilience, of hope.

But just as I was about to engage in conversation with the gathering crowd, Aaron stepped closer, a determined expression on his face. His presence felt like a sudden chill on an otherwise warm evening, and every bit of courage I'd summoned began to dissipate.

"Can we talk?" he asked, his voice low, a slight urgency woven through his words.

"Now? Here?" I replied, my heart pounding. The vibrant colors of the mural dulled for a moment, the laughter fading into a distant hum. I could feel everyone's eyes on us, the world shrinking down to just him and me, caught in a moment that felt achingly heavy.

"Please. Just for a minute," he insisted, his gaze piercing through my defenses. I could see the hope flickering in his eyes, and despite everything, it tugged at something deep within me.

"Fine," I finally relented, leading him away from the prying eyes and laughter of the party, the weight of my own hesitation heavy on my shoulders. We stepped outside, the cool breeze wrapping around us like a protective veil, and I could hear the distant sounds of our friends mingling inside, blissfully unaware of the tension swirling just outside their happy bubble.

"What do you want, Aaron?" I asked, the bite in my tone belying the tumult of emotions roiling inside me.

"I came to apologize," he said, the sincerity in his voice almost disarming. "For everything. For how I left things between us. It was unfair."

"Unfair? You mean, like how you just disappeared?" I shot back, my frustration spilling over. "Do you have any idea how that felt? One day, you were there, and the next—nothing. No explanation, no warning."

"I was a coward," he admitted, running a hand through his hair, a gesture I recognized as one of his vulnerabilities surfacing. "I thought I was doing the right thing by disappearing. I was scared, Amelia. I didn't want to drag you down with me."

"Drag me down? Is that what you think you were doing?" I couldn't help but scoff, a bitter laugh escaping my lips. "I was trying to lift you up, to be there. But you walked away, and I—"

"And I should have stayed," he interjected, his voice firm now, like he was fighting against something much larger than the two of us. "I see that now. But I've changed. I'm different, and I want to make things right."

There was a vulnerability in his tone that made my heart waver. Memories flooded back, of laughter shared under the stars, whispers exchanged in the dead of night, and the warmth of hands clasped together. But the shadows of the past loomed larger, casting doubt on the hope he dangled before me.

"Making things right isn't as easy as just showing up and saying you're sorry, Aaron," I replied, feeling a knot tighten in my chest. "Trust doesn't come with a snap of your fingers."

"I know," he said, stepping closer, the earnestness in his gaze unwavering. "But I'm willing to try. Just give me a chance to prove it."

The air between us crackled with unspoken words, the tension tangible. I wanted to scream, to shake him until he understood the gravity of his actions, but all that emerged was a silence that enveloped us both. In that moment, as the laughter from our friends echoed around the building, I felt the weight of the mural behind me, a testament to my growth, my struggle, and the courage to let go of what once was.

As I stood there, caught in the storm of emotions, I knew that whatever choice I made next would either tether me to the past or set me free.

The cool night air was laced with the sweet scent of blooming jasmine, each breath a reminder that life, much like the mural we'd painted, was a tapestry of color and complexity. I could hear the muffled sounds of laughter spilling from the community center, mingling with the soft strumming of a guitar played by a local musician—a cheerful tune that only highlighted the dissonance within me. Aaron's presence felt like a knot in my stomach, tight and unyielding, as I shifted my gaze from him back to the warmth of our celebration.

"Hey, don't let him steal your spotlight," Max said, leaning in closer, his breath warm with the scent of homemade lemonade. "This night is about your hard work, not some ghost from the past."

I forced a smile, appreciating his attempt to lighten the mood, but it felt more like a band-aid over a wound that was refusing to heal. "Right, the spotlight. Got it." My voice was laced with a humor I didn't feel, the strain evident as I plastered on a grin.

"I mean it, Amelia. You've poured your heart into this. I've watched you bloom through every stroke of paint. Don't let him dim that light."

Just then, laughter erupted from the crowd, pulling my attention back. People were gathered around, their eyes sparkling with joy as they admired our mural—a riot of colors swirling together, depicting the essence of our small town and the dreams we dared to dream. I could see faces illuminated by the soft glow of the fairy lights, their expressions a mix of awe and inspiration, and for a moment, I felt the swell of pride again, pushing against the tide of doubt that threatened to drown me.

But the moment was fleeting. Aaron shifted closer, his voice barely above a whisper, cutting through the noise that surrounded us. "Amelia, please. Just give me a chance to explain."

The warmth of Max's encouragement faded as I turned fully to face Aaron. "Explain what exactly? How you disappeared without a word? How you left me hanging while I was trying to figure out my own mess?"

"It wasn't like that," he insisted, his voice strained. "I thought it was for the best. I was spiraling, and I didn't want to pull you down with me."

"Nice of you to think of me," I snapped, crossing my arms defensively. "But news flash: I'm not a porcelain doll that shatters at the first sign of trouble."

His eyes narrowed, and I could see the conflict swirling within them. "You're right. You're stronger than that, and I've always known it. That's why it hurt so much to leave. I thought I was protecting you."

"Protecting me? By ghosting me?" The incredulity in my tone felt justified, but beneath it lay a pang of hurt I couldn't fully mask. "You don't just walk away and think that's okay. You don't take the easy way out when things get tough."

The music shifted to a softer melody, the strumming gentle against the tension simmering between us. I could feel the crowd behind us, their laughter and camaraderie fading into a distant echo as the world narrowed to just the two of us, locked in this unresolved dance.

"I'm not asking for forgiveness," Aaron continued, taking a step closer, the sincerity in his eyes piercing through my defenses. "But I am asking for the chance to show you that I've changed. I want to be a part of your life again, if you'll let me."

"A part of my life?" I echoed, my heart racing at the thought, half wanting to leap into his arms and half wanting to shove him away. "And what exactly does that look like? You can't just stroll back in and expect everything to be the same. I'm not the same girl you left behind."

"I don't want everything to be the same," he replied earnestly, his voice firm but gentle. "I want to build something new. Something better."

I hesitated, the swirling emotions threatening to sweep me under. Memories flashed through my mind—sunsets shared, secrets whispered, and the way he used to look at me as if I were the only person in the room. But those moments were tainted now, shadows cast over the brilliance of what we once shared.

"Look, I appreciate the sentiment, I really do," I said, my voice softening despite my resolve. "But you've got to understand that I've worked hard to reclaim my life since you left. I've built something new here. With Max, with this mural, with this community. I don't want to risk all of that because you've suddenly decided to re-enter the picture."

"I get that," he said, his eyes darkening with a mix of determination and regret. "But I'm not asking you to forget what happened. I just want a chance to prove I can be better—for you, for us."

"Us?" The word slipped from my lips before I could stop it, the weight of it heavy between us.

"Yes, us. If you'll let me," he urged, the desperation palpable in his voice. "I know I messed up, but I've thought about you every day since I left. I can't just walk away now. Not when I see you thriving."

I glanced back at the community center, the laughter and light spilling out like a promise of happiness. "And what if you end up leaving again? What if I put my trust in you and you just vanish?"

"Then I'll let you throw paint at me," he replied, a grin breaking through the tension, and for a moment, the heaviness lifted, replaced by the flicker of old familiarity. "Or maybe we can work on that mural together. Consider it a trust-building exercise."

I laughed, the sound unexpected and free. "As tempting as that sounds, I'm not sure I want to risk my paintbrushes on you just yet."

"Okay, how about we start with coffee? Just two friends catching up?" His earnestness tugged at the corners of my heart, and despite my better judgment, I felt myself softening.

"Fine. Coffee," I relented, a reluctant smile creeping onto my face. "But no promises. And if you mess this up, I reserve the right to throw paint at you."

"Deal," he said, the relief washing over him was palpable.

As we walked back toward the festivities, a new kind of tension hung in the air—a mixture of hope and uncertainty, like the first hints of dawn peeking over the horizon. I could feel the warmth of the celebration beckoning us forward, the soft glow of string lights illuminating a path that was both familiar and foreign. Perhaps I wasn't ready to let go entirely. Maybe, just maybe, I could hold on to a piece of the past while carving out a new future.

The soft glow of string lights wrapped around the community center, casting a golden hue over the faces of familiar friends and strangers alike. As we wove through the crowd, I tried to focus on the vibrant chatter and the laughter that danced around us. Max nudged me playfully, pulling me from my spiraling thoughts. "Look at them, Amelia. They love it!" He gestured toward a small cluster of kids, eyes wide with wonder as they pointed at our mural, their imaginations ignited by the vibrant colors and swirling forms.

"They really do," I replied, a sense of warmth creeping into my chest. But in the back of my mind, the knot Aaron had tied in my stomach refused to loosen. I couldn't help but glance at him, standing just outside the sea of laughter. He was a contrast to the joy around us, an anchor pulling me into deeper waters.

"Hey, don't zone out on me now," Max said, elbowing me gently. "This is your moment. Let's celebrate."

"Right, my moment," I echoed, forcing a bright smile as we approached the snack table. The spread was a chaotic mix of homemade goodies, each dish a testament to the community's love. As I helped myself to a cupcake topped with fluffy frosting, my eyes darted back to Aaron. He caught my gaze and offered a tentative smile, one that tugged at something deep within me. I couldn't shake the feeling that he was waiting for me to make a choice—one that could change everything.

"Want to head over?" Max asked, catching my eye and noticing my lingering gaze. "It'll be a fun reunion. Who knows? Maybe he's brought you a peace offering."

"More like a heart-wrenching reminder of everything I'm trying to forget," I muttered under my breath, but I followed Max nonetheless. As we approached Aaron, the noise around us faded into a muted backdrop, the atmosphere charged with a mix of anticipation and uncertainty.

"Nice mural," Aaron said, his voice smooth but tinged with an edge of nervousness. "You've really outdone yourself."

"Thanks," I replied, my tone clipped as I glanced away, trying to mask the turmoil brewing inside me. "It's been a team effort."

Max chimed in, flashing a smile that felt both supportive and a bit mischievous. "And it's not just paint; it's a masterpiece of emotions. Every stroke tells a story."

"Exactly," I said, eager to redirect the conversation. "We wanted it to resonate with everyone, not just us."

"I can see that," Aaron said, his gaze holding mine for a fraction longer than comfortable, a hint of something unspoken lingering in the air. "You've created something beautiful."

"Beauty comes from chaos," I quipped, unable to resist a jab. "I should know—I've had plenty of practice dealing with emotional disasters."

Max laughed, the sound a welcome reprieve. "You could say we're the chaos specialists, really."

Aaron's expression shifted, a shadow passing over his features as he processed my words. "I never meant to add to your chaos, Amelia. I just..."

"Thought you could walk back in and everything would be just fine?" I interjected, the bite in my voice sharper than intended. "You can't just show up and pretend nothing happened."

"Can we at least talk about this somewhere private?" he asked, his tone dropping to a whisper, earnestness replacing the earlier bravado. "I promise I won't take long. Just a few minutes."

"Right now?" I said, glancing back at Max, who was watching with a mix of concern and amusement.

"Let's be real," Max said, his grin widening. "You two have some unfinished business, and I, for one, am not opposed to a little intrigue at our unveiling party. I'll grab some more snacks. You handle the drama."

Before I could protest, he vanished into the crowd, leaving me facing Aaron, a mixture of hope and hesitation swirling between us.

"I'm not sure this is a good idea," I said, glancing around as if the vibrant mural might somehow provide an escape.

"Please," he implored, taking a small step closer. "I'm not asking for forever. Just a moment to explain why I did what I did. And then we can go back to pretending this never happened if that's what you want."

"Pretending never really worked for me," I replied, crossing my arms. Yet, against my better judgment, I found myself nodding. "Fine. Let's talk."

We stepped away from the jubilant atmosphere, moving toward a quieter corner of the community center where the shadows loomed a little thicker. The laughter faded, replaced by the distant echo of music, allowing the tension to tighten like a drawn bowstring. I leaned against a wall, the cool surface grounding me even as the heat of his presence engulfed my senses.

"Why did you really leave?" I asked, my voice steady but betraying an edge of vulnerability. "I deserve more than just excuses."

Aaron ran a hand through his hair, the familiar gesture bringing back memories that made my heart ache. "It was a mess, Amelia. I was drowning in my own problems. I thought leaving would protect you. I didn't want you to see me like that."

"Like what?" I pushed back, my pulse quickening. "Like someone who runs when things get tough?"

"Like someone who couldn't keep their life together," he replied, the honesty in his tone striking a chord deep within me. "I was scared. Scared of what I felt for you and scared of dragging you down with me."

"Scared or selfish?" I countered, crossing my arms tighter. "Because there's a fine line between protecting someone and running away when the going gets tough."

"Maybe both," he admitted, his voice dropping to a whisper. "But I want to make it right. I've been working on myself, on everything. I'm not that guy anymore."

My heart wavered, caught between the weight of his words and the fear of repeating past mistakes. "You say that, but how do I know this isn't just another attempt at sweet-talking your way back into my life?"

"Because I'm standing here, ready to face the consequences," he said, the earnestness in his eyes holding me captive. "If I wanted to manipulate you, I would've done it a long time ago."

Just as I opened my mouth to respond, the unmistakable sound of a crash echoed through the community center, jolting both of us from our moment. I turned, the cheerful atmosphere now marred by an air of confusion and concern.

"What was that?" I asked, my heart racing as I stepped away from the wall.

Aaron's expression shifted, concern flashing across his features. "I don't know, but it didn't sound good. Let's check it out."

As we hurried back toward the source of the commotion, the vibrant colors of our mural faded in the backdrop of my racing thoughts. The laughter had turned to hushed murmurs, faces drawn in worry as people gathered near the entrance. I could see Max, his expression a mixture of curiosity and alarm.

"Amelia! Aaron!" he called out, waving us over.

"What happened?" I asked, my stomach tightening as I squeezed through the crowd, Aaron right behind me.

"Someone just knocked over the food table," Max explained, but as I looked closer, my heart sank. The vibrant spread of treats lay scattered across the floor, but it wasn't just the snacks that drew my attention. Amidst the chaos, a figure stood at the entrance, shadowed by the fading light, their face partially hidden.

The moment our eyes met, a chill washed over me. I recognized that silhouette, the weight of my past crashing into me like an unforgiving wave. It was a figure I never thought I'd see again—one that had haunted my dreams, twisting my heart into knots.

"Amelia," the voice called, breaking through the din, heavy with familiarity and a hint of danger. "We need to talk."

My breath hitched, the world around me narrowing as uncertainty flooded my senses. I glanced at Aaron, whose expression mirrored my own disbelief, and the tension twisted tighter, anchoring me in a moment that felt as if it had the potential to unravel everything.

Chapter 25: Shattered Illusions

The afternoon sun draped its warm embrace over the bustling café, casting a golden hue on the mismatched furniture that lent the place its charm. The faint hum of conversation mingled with the rich aroma of freshly brewed coffee, and I felt momentarily buoyed by the lively atmosphere. But as I stepped inside, the momentary comfort was shattered by the sight that met my eyes—Aaron, leaning casually against the counter, a lopsided grin spreading across his face like butter on warm toast. My stomach twisted, knotting with a mixture of dread and something resembling anger.

"Fancy seeing you here," he said, his voice smooth as honey, as if he hadn't just barged back into my life unannounced.

"Really? I thought this was a place for people who actually care about the coffee," I shot back, crossing my arms tightly against my chest, a futile attempt to shield my heart from the remnants of our past.

Aaron's smirk faltered for a split second, and in that moment, I found a flicker of the strength I had been cultivating since I met Max. It was as if the ground beneath me had shifted; the air around us crackled with unspoken words and unresolved tension. I had envisioned this confrontation, but the reality of it felt like walking a tightrope over a chasm, each step precarious and fraught with uncertainty.

"A little harsh, don't you think?" he replied, feigning a nonchalance that only grated on my nerves. "I was just grabbing a coffee before heading out of town."

"Right. Of course, you were." My voice dripped with sarcasm, thick enough to cut through the insincerity in his tone. I stepped closer, allowing the warmth of the café to wrap around me like a protective cocoon, urging me to stand firm. "What's the real reason? Did you come here to play games again?"

His expression shifted slightly, the playfulness replaced by something deeper, more earnest. "I just wanted to talk, Jess. We have unfinished business."

"Unfinished business?" I echoed, letting the words linger in the air between us like the acrid scent of burnt coffee. "You mean the kind where you vanish without a trace, leaving me to pick up the pieces? That kind of business?"

He opened his mouth to respond, but I didn't give him the chance. "You need to leave. I'm done with your drama, Aaron. My heart—my life—belong to someone else now."

The words felt like a declaration, ringing out against the backdrop of the café chatter. I felt an electric thrill coursing through me, a vibrant affirmation of my newfound independence. I was finally stepping into my own light, shedding the shadows of the past.

"Who?" he asked, his brows knitting together in confusion. "Is it that guy? Max?"

The mere mention of Max made my heart swell, a beacon of hope amidst the darkness. I had fought too hard to carve out this new path, and I wasn't about to let Aaron derail me. "Yes, it is," I asserted, letting my voice rise above the din. "Max is everything you're not—steady, reliable, and he respects me. Unlike you."

Aaron's expression morphed into one of incredulity, as if my words had struck him with the force of a rogue wave. "You're serious?"

"Dead serious." I held my ground, the memories of our tumultuous past swirling in my mind like autumn leaves caught in a brisk wind. "You think charm and empty promises can keep me? Newsflash: they can't."

He took a step back, his bravado faltering for the first time since I'd walked in. The hint of vulnerability in his eyes made my heart flutter with uncertainty, but I refused to let it sway me. This was my moment to shine, to reclaim my narrative.

With a deep breath, I turned on my heel, determined to seek solace in Max's presence. I wove through the crowd, the clinking of cups and laughter filling my ears like a familiar symphony, each note urging me forward. I could feel Aaron's gaze lingering on my back, but I refused to look back, my heart set on the warmth and steadiness I found in Max.

When I reached the patio, the cool breeze kissed my cheeks, clearing the remnants of tension that had been tightening my chest. I spotted Max at our usual table, his back to me, engrossed in a book, the sunlight catching the tousled strands of his hair. Just the sight of him sent a wave of relief washing over me. He was my anchor in the storm, my safe harbor amidst the chaos.

"Hey," I said softly as I approached, unable to suppress the smile that spread across my face.

He looked up, his expression shifting from concentration to pure delight. "There you are! I was beginning to think you'd gotten lost in all that coffee chaos."

"I had a little... detour," I admitted, plopping into the chair across from him, feeling the weight of the world begin to lift. "Let's just say that my past has a way of showing up when I least expect it."

Max leaned in, concern etched on his features. "Is everything okay?"

I took a deep breath, grateful for the steady calm he exuded. "Yeah, I just ran into Aaron."

His brow furrowed. "Did he say anything?"

"Just the usual—trying to charm his way back in. But I stood my ground. I told him I'm done with him, that my heart is with you."

Max's face brightened, the corners of his lips curling into that smile that could ignite the dimmest of days. "You did? Jess, that's amazing!"

"I mean, I had to. I can't let him manipulate me anymore. You deserve better than my half-heartedness."

His smile faded slightly, replaced by a thoughtful look. "You know, I never want to be the reason you feel like you have to cut ties with your past. I just want you to be happy."

His words sent a rush of warmth through me. It was a stark contrast to Aaron's bravado, grounding me in a reality where my happiness mattered. "You are my happiness, Max. This is my choice."

"Then let's make sure it's a choice we celebrate." He raised his coffee cup, the sunlight dancing through the mug, creating a halo of light. "To new beginnings, Jess."

I clinked my cup against his, the sound ringing out like a promise. As the warmth of the coffee seeped into my fingers, I felt a sense of possibility, a stirring in my chest that whispered of all that was yet to come.

The sun dipped lower in the sky, casting long shadows across the cobbled streets as I and Max lingered over our coffee. The warmth from the cup in my hands mirrored the flutter of something new taking root within me. My thoughts flickered back to Aaron's stunned expression, but as I focused on Max, I felt the edges of my anxiety dull into a gentle hum of anticipation.

"Okay, spill," Max said, leaning forward, his elbows resting on the table, the playful glint in his eyes dancing with curiosity. "What did the illustrious Aaron want this time? Another half-baked apology?"

"Something like that," I replied, stirring my coffee, the sound of the spoon clinking against the porcelain offering a kind of rhythmic comfort. "He has a flair for the dramatic, you know. He really thought he could just walk back into my life and—poof!—everything would be fine again."

Max raised an eyebrow, a smirk tugging at the corners of his lips. "And did he have a grand speech prepared? Maybe some roses or a song?"

"Just a whole lot of hot air." I couldn't help but chuckle, the tension easing as I recalled the look of disbelief on his face when I'd stood my ground. "I didn't give him the satisfaction of playing along. I told him I was done, and my heart belonged to someone who actually appreciated it."

"Damn right," Max said, his voice low and earnest, and I felt a thrill at his approval. "You're a force, Jess. You deserve someone who sees all of you, not just the parts that are convenient."

I savored his words, letting them wrap around me like a warm blanket. "And you do see me, don't you? The good, the bad, the coffee-stained T-shirts?"

"Especially the coffee-stained T-shirts," he teased, his smile brightening the fading light. "It's all part of your charm."

I rolled my eyes but couldn't hide the grin creeping across my face. Just then, the café door swung open, letting in a gust of wind that tousled my hair and brought the scent of freshly baked pastries with it. My heart raced momentarily, thinking it might be Aaron again, but my tension eased as a familiar face appeared.

"Hey, lovebirds!" shouted Melanie, my best friend, her fiery curls bouncing as she approached with a swagger that only she could pull off. "Hope I'm not interrupting anything too mushy."

Max raised his cup in mock salute. "Not yet, but you might just ruin the moment."

Melanie plopped down beside me, her eyes sparkling with mischief. "Oh, please! I thrive on chaos. What's the scoop? I heard whispers of Aaron causing drama. Should I bring the popcorn?"

I laughed, the tension from earlier fading further into the background. "He was here, but I put him in his place."

"Atta girl!" she exclaimed, and I couldn't help but bask in the camaraderie. "I swear, you're like a superhero. What's your power? Kicking exes to the curb?"

"More like finding new ones that don't require the curb," I shot back, and the three of us burst into laughter, the sound bright and infectious.

"So, what's the plan now? Are we celebrating your newfound freedom?" Melanie leaned in, her tone conspiratorial. "Because if you're ready to move on, I say we hit the town tonight!"

"Tonight?" Max questioned, his brow furrowing slightly. "But don't you think we should take it easy? I mean, you've just had a confrontation and everything."

"Oh, come on! Let her live a little!" Melanie protested, her enthusiasm unwavering. "You're too sweet for your own good, Max. Jess needs to kick up her heels and dance a little."

The prospect of an impromptu night out sent a shiver of excitement coursing through me. It had been too long since I had let loose, and the idea of swirling through the city, vibrant lights twinkling like stars, felt intoxicating.

"Okay, I'm in," I said, throwing caution to the wind. "Let's celebrate freedom and the end of all things Aaron."

"Now you're talking!" Melanie clapped her hands, her energy contagious. "Let's hit that new bar downtown—word on the street is they have the best cocktails and a dance floor that's begging for you to grace it with your presence."

I shared a glance with Max, the slight concern on his face overshadowed by an unmistakable glimmer of excitement. "What do you say, partner? Are you ready for a little chaos?"

"Only if it involves some amazing cocktails," he replied, his lips quirking into that adorable smirk that always made my heart skip.

We all stood up, our chairs scraping against the floor, and I felt a sense of lightness sweep over me. The coffee shop, once a sanctuary of familiarity, faded behind me as we stepped out into the world, the sky tinged with hues of orange and pink—a perfect backdrop for new beginnings.

The walk to the bar was filled with laughter and stories, our voices rising above the city's symphony. Melanie regaled us with tales of her latest dating misadventures, each one punctuated with her signature flair for the dramatic. I found myself grateful for the ease of her company, the way she could make the mundane feel electric.

As we arrived at the bar, the bass thumped through the walls, pulsating with energy that beckoned us inside. The dim lighting flickered with warmth, casting playful shadows as patrons swayed to the rhythm of the music. I felt a surge of adrenaline as we navigated through the throngs of people, the air thick with the mingling scents of sweet cocktails and the promise of a night well spent.

"What do you want?" Max shouted over the music, leaning close so I could hear him.

"Something fruity and strong!" I shouted back, and he nodded, heading toward the bar while Melanie and I claimed a small table near the dance floor, the vibrant atmosphere wrapping around us like a warm embrace.

"What's the plan after drinks?" Melanie asked, her eyes gleaming with mischief as she scanned the crowd. "A little dancing, perhaps? Or are we just going to sit here like old ladies?"

I leaned back in my chair, my confidence surging with every beat of the music. "Oh, we're definitely dancing. Let's show the world what it means to let loose!"

With that, we raised our glasses high, a toast to newfound strength, laughter, and the promise of what lay ahead. I felt the lingering shadows of my past begin to fade as the music enveloped us, drawing me into a world filled with possibility. I was ready to embrace every moment, to savor the sweetness of this new chapter, and let the rhythm guide me into the night.

The pulsing energy of the bar enveloped me as I stepped onto the dance floor, the beat thrumming through my veins like a living pulse. Colors swirled around me—dancing lights and laughter mingling in the air. I felt the weight of the world begin to lift as I surrendered to the rhythm, letting the music weave through my thoughts and erase the remnants of Aaron's presence.

Max had disappeared to the bar, but I knew he wouldn't be far behind. Melanie and I swayed to the music, our laughter bubbling up like champagne, sweet and effervescent. The beat was infectious, and soon enough, I found myself lost in the moment, my worries melting away with each twist and turn of my body.

"You look like you're ready to take on the world!" Melanie shouted over the music, her voice ringing with exuberance.

"Maybe I am!" I replied, spinning in a circle, my dress twirling like a kaleidoscope of colors around me. The sheer joy of the night felt like a warm embrace, lifting my spirits higher than I thought possible.

"Then let's conquer it together!" she declared, and we danced like no one was watching, our bodies moving in sync to the intoxicating rhythm. The room was a blur of faces, all lost in their own moments, but we were a force, radiating laughter and confidence that felt almost electric.

As the song transitioned into a slower tune, I felt a slight tug at my heartstrings. It was a love song, filled with longing and promises, and I could practically feel the weight of memories seep into the air around us. I closed my eyes for a moment, letting the melody wash over me, but then I sensed someone approaching. My heart skipped a beat as I opened my eyes to find Max standing there, a wide grin plastered across his face, two vibrant cocktails in hand.

"Sorry, it took a bit! They're out of the good stuff," he said, handing me a bright pink drink that sparkled like it was infused with stardust. "But this should help you forget about your ex and bring back some cheer."

"Or make me forget my name!" I laughed, taking a sip. The sweetness danced on my tongue, and I could feel the tension from earlier dissipating with every drop.

"Here's to not looking back!" he proposed, raising his glass.

"To not looking back!" I echoed, clinking my glass against his with a determined smile.

We sipped our drinks and continued to sway, and the air around us filled with the promise of adventure. The evening stretched out like a canvas, each moment waiting for us to paint it with laughter, spontaneity, and maybe just a touch of mischief.

"Let's go outside," Max suggested suddenly, his eyes sparkling with mischief. "I need to feel that breeze and not sweat through my shirt."

I chuckled, feeling a surge of warmth at his playful spirit. "Lead the way, Captain!"

As we stepped outside, the cool night air washed over us, refreshing and full of possibility. The city lights flickered like stars overhead, illuminating the street in a warm glow. We leaned against the railing, our drinks in hand, watching the life of the city unfold before us.

"This is perfect," I said, taking a deep breath and savoring the moment. "Just us, the stars, and no drama."

Max nodded, his expression thoughtful. "It's nice to see you like this, carefree. You deserve it."

"Thanks, Max. Really." I meant it from the bottom of my heart. He had brought me out of a darkness I hadn't even realized was consuming me.

Just then, Melanie burst through the door, her eyes wide with excitement. "You won't believe what just happened!"

"What?" I asked, intrigued.

"I saw Aaron talking to some guy in the corner!" She leaned in closer, her voice lowering conspiratorially. "He looked pretty intense. You know how he gets when he's trying to stir up trouble."

My heart raced at the mention of Aaron, that nagging feeling creeping back in. "What do you mean?"

"I couldn't hear everything, but it looked like they were plotting something," she said, her tone laced with concern. "You might want to keep an eye out."

I felt a chill run down my spine, the carefree moment suddenly overshadowed by the thought of Aaron lurking in the background. "I thought I'd seen the last of him tonight."

"Maybe it's not over yet," Max said, his brow furrowing as he scanned the crowd, his protective instincts kicking in. "We should keep our distance."

"Great idea, but what do we do if he shows up?" I asked, anxiety bubbling beneath the surface.

Before anyone could respond, a loud shout erupted from the entrance. The music dimmed momentarily as heads turned, and I felt my breath hitch in my throat. There stood Aaron, flanked by the guy Melanie had seen him with. He cut an imposing figure, his stance radiating an unsettling mix of confidence and arrogance that made my stomach churn.

"Perfect!" Melanie muttered, rolling her eyes. "Guess the universe loves a good plot twist."

"Let's just avoid him," I whispered, already regretting my decision to come out tonight. I felt the warmth of the evening fade into an uncomfortable chill as I held tightly to my drink, wishing it could shield me from the inevitable confrontation.

"Too late for that," Max said, his voice firm as he stepped slightly in front of me, a silent protector ready to defend my space.

"What a coincidence running into you all here," Aaron called out, his voice smooth yet edged with sarcasm. "Looks like the party is just getting started!"

I forced myself to look up, meeting his gaze head-on, determination swirling within me. "Not interested in your games, Aaron. Just let it go."

He laughed, a sound that made my skin crawl. "Oh, I'm just getting started, Jess. You think you can walk away that easily?"

I felt Max tense beside me, and I knew I wasn't the only one feeling the weight of Aaron's words.

"What's that supposed to mean?" I shot back, my voice stronger than I felt.

Aaron stepped closer, his companion standing silently by his side, watching with an inscrutable expression. "Let's just say, it's a small world, and I happen to know a few things about your new love interest."

Max's jaw tightened, and the atmosphere shifted, the excitement of the night evaporating as the tension thickened like fog. "Don't you dare threaten her," he said, his tone low and steady, but I could sense the storm brewing beneath the surface.

"Oh, it's not a threat, my friend. It's just a friendly reminder that everything you think you know might not be what it seems."

With that, Aaron stepped back, a smirk playing on his lips as he exchanged a knowing glance with his companion. I felt a shiver run down my spine, the darkness of his words lingering in the air like a heavy fog.

Max looked at me, a mixture of concern and determination etched on his face. "What did he mean by that?"

Before I could answer, Aaron turned on his heel and sauntered away, leaving behind a tense silence that echoed in my ears.

I felt my heart race, the weight of uncertainty pressing down on me. "I don't know," I said, my voice barely a whisper. "But I have a feeling we're not done with him yet."

Just as I was about to suggest we leave, the door swung open again, and another figure stepped through. I felt my breath hitch as I recognized the face—one I never expected to see again.

The night was just beginning, but as shadows danced around us, I couldn't shake the feeling that the past wasn't done chasing me.

Chapter 26: Embers of Emotion

The mural, a riot of colors sprawling across the once-barren wall, drew the evening sun into its embrace, casting playful shadows that danced around us. Each brushstroke felt like a heartbeat, a pulsing testament to our shared vision and countless hours spent pouring our souls onto that surface. It was more than paint on plaster; it was a mosaic of hopes and fears, triumphs and trials. I could almost hear the whispers of the community that gathered, their laughter mingling with the fading daylight, filling the air with a palpable warmth. But even in this cocoon of creativity and joy, something flickered at the edges of my mind, a nagging thread of unease that tugged at my heart.

"Can you believe it?" I said, my voice giddy with excitement as I stepped back to admire our work. "Look at how the colors come alive in the sunset. It's like the mural is breathing."

Max turned, his eyes shining brighter than the paints we had used, a mixture of pride and something more layered—something I couldn't quite place. He pulled me close, the world around us fading into a soft blur as he cupped my face, his thumb brushing against my cheek in a tender gesture that ignited something within me.

"I knew you were capable of greatness, but this... this is magic," he said, his voice low and filled with sincerity. I leaned into him, allowing myself a moment of vulnerability. The chaos of emotions that had churned inside me since the unexpected encounter with Aaron bubbled to the surface.

"Max, can we talk?" I asked, pulling back just enough to look into his eyes, searching for understanding. "It's about Aaron."

The flicker of happiness that had danced in his gaze dimmed slightly, replaced by a shadow of concern. "What did he want?"

I inhaled sharply, the air thick with memories I had tried to lock away. "He just... showed up. I thought I had put that part of my life behind me. I thought I was done with it."

Max's grip tightened on my hand, grounding me. "You are not defined by your past, you know that, right? You're a different person now."

The warmth of his words wrapped around me, a protective blanket against the chill of my insecurities. "I know, but it feels like a ghost. Every time I think I've moved on, he finds a way to haunt me again."

"Then don't let him," he replied firmly, his gaze unwavering. "You have a choice. Your past doesn't get to dictate your future. You've created something beautiful here, and you're stronger than you think."

His confidence in me lit a spark, igniting a flicker of determination. I nodded, the fear that had gripped my heart loosening its hold, even if just a little. "You're right. It's just... some days, it feels overwhelming."

Max stepped closer, his breath warm against my skin, as he drew me into his embrace. "Then lean on me. You don't have to carry it all alone. I'm right here."

We stood there for a moment, wrapped in a cocoon of warmth, as the voices of the community echoed around us, laughter punctuating the air. I felt lighter, like I could finally breathe again. The past may linger like a stubborn shadow, but in this moment, with Max by my side, I felt an undeniable sense of hope.

As the sun dipped lower on the horizon, painting the sky in hues of pink and orange, I couldn't help but notice how beautifully the mural captured that fleeting light. It was alive, just like the emotions swirling within me. I turned back to it, running my fingers over the vibrant paint, feeling the energy radiating from every stroke. "This mural, it's more than just art. It's a declaration of who we are now," I said, my voice thick with emotion.

Max nodded, his expression softening. "Exactly. It's a testament to growth and resilience. You've turned pain into beauty. That's something to be proud of."

A laugh bubbled up from within me, light and free, momentarily banishing the darkness of my past. "I can't believe I painted that huge sunflower. It's so... optimistic."

"It's you," he replied, a teasing smile playing at the corners of his mouth. "A little quirky, a lot beautiful, and utterly full of life."

"Quirky, huh? Is that your way of saying I'm a weirdo?" I teased back, playfully nudging him.

"Only in the best possible way," he shot back, his grin infectious. "Besides, weird is just another word for unique. And trust me, the world needs more unique people."

"Coming from you, I'll take that as a compliment," I said, my heart swelling with affection. There was something about the way he spoke that made me feel seen and appreciated, quirks and all.

As we stood there, laughter fading into the soft whispers of evening, I felt the tension between us shift, a current of unspoken words hanging in the air. The comfort of the moment coiled around us, but I could sense something else brewing, a deeper current beneath the surface.

"Max," I began, my voice barely a whisper, "what happens if I can't keep moving forward? What if the past really does catch up with me?"

He turned to me, his expression serious yet tender. "Then we face it together. Whatever comes, you won't have to face it alone."

The sincerity in his eyes pulled me in, a promise binding us together. Just as I was about to reply, the sound of laughter erupted from the gathering crowd, cutting through the moment. It was a reminder that life continued, that we weren't alone in this. I turned back toward the mural, a sense of belonging washing over me, feeling like a part of something larger than myself.

The laughter and chatter of the community swirled around us, enveloping the evening in a warm embrace as twilight deepened. I watched as people approached the mural, their expressions transforming from curiosity to delight, their eyes sparkling with the vibrant hues we had poured onto the wall. A sense of accomplishment washed over me, the kind that settled in the bones and whispered promises of potential. Yet, amid the festivities, a faint unease nagged at the edges of my thoughts, the shadow of my past flickering like a candle's flame, threatening to extinguish my newfound light.

"Hey, look at that family," Max said, nodding toward a group of kids running excitedly towards the mural, their laughter ringing like wind chimes in a summer breeze. "They're going to remember this moment forever."

"Just like us," I replied, a smile tugging at my lips. "This is our legacy—somewhere out there, a kid will point at that sunflower and think it's the best thing ever."

"Just wait until they grow up and realize it's a symbol of your 'quirkiness,'" he teased, arching an eyebrow in mock seriousness.

"Quirky? I prefer 'extraordinarily unique,' thank you very much," I shot back, crossing my arms playfully. "At least that sounds less like I have a collection of cat figurines."

"Hey, nothing wrong with a good cat figurine," Max countered, a grin breaking through the playful banter. "It adds character. And you're already filled to the brim with it."

His words wrapped around me, a warm reminder that maybe I wasn't as lost as I sometimes felt. As the sun dipped below the horizon, the mural glowed softly under the flickering fairy lights we'd strung nearby. I caught glimpses of smiles, shared stories, and the occasional squeal of delight that pierced the warm evening air.

Yet, my heart still wavered, teetering on the edge of confidence and trepidation.

"Want to grab a drink?" Max asked, his voice pulling me from my reverie. "We could toast to our masterpiece and plot our next big adventure."

"Are we planning on conquering the art world next? Or is this more of a local coffee shop kind of situation?" I laughed, appreciating how effortlessly he lightened the mood.

"Why not both? We can take the world by storm one latte at a time," he said, winking.

As we made our way toward the makeshift refreshment table, a wave of nostalgia washed over me. I could still remember my first art exhibit, standing in a similar setting, surrounded by friends and family who showered me with encouragement. It had been a different life then—one where shadows lingered longer and memories seemed to choke me. But now, with Max beside me, it felt as if I were breathing fresh air for the first time in years.

I grabbed a glass of lemonade, its tangy sweetness a refreshing counterpoint to the heaviness of my thoughts. Max filled his cup with something bubbling and bright, the fizz rising like the hopeful energy we'd conjured with our mural.

"To creativity, resilience, and all the quirks that make us who we are," he declared, raising his glass in a toast.

I clinked mine against his, a soft chime echoing our shared resolve. "And to not letting the past dictate our future." The words lingered between us, a fragile promise buoyed by the warmth of the evening.

As we sipped our drinks, I watched as the community interacted with the mural, pointing and chatting with one another, lost in the art. My heart swelled with a fierce pride, only to be momentarily pierced by a sharp jab of doubt when I caught sight of Aaron standing at the back of the crowd, his gaze fixated on us. The air felt heavier, charged with something unnameable that sent my stomach into knots.

"Are you okay?" Max asked, his voice laced with concern as he followed my gaze.

"Just... an old ghost," I admitted, my voice a mere whisper. "I didn't expect him to come here."

"Do you want me to talk to him?" Max offered, the tension in his jaw tightening like a drawn bowstring.

"No, that's okay. I can handle this," I said, even as my heart raced, a wild stallion unwilling to be tamed. "I just need to breathe."

He nodded, stepping closer, a silent promise of support. I focused on the laughter around us, letting it wash over me, when Aaron suddenly approached, a grin that felt more like a mask than genuine joy plastered across his face.

"Look at you, painting the town, literally," he said, his voice smooth but lacking the warmth I had once known. "Impressive work. I see you're still chasing dreams."

"Some dreams are worth chasing," I replied, my tone firm, not wanting to let him slip into my thoughts.

"I see you've upgraded your taste in company too," he quipped, his eyes darting to Max, who stood a step behind me, a protective wall that felt both reassuring and intimidating.

"Max is more than just company; he's my partner," I said, the words tasting sweeter than I had anticipated. The truth of it resonated within me, like a fresh breeze breaking through a stifling room.

Aaron's expression flickered for a moment, and I caught a glimpse of something—regret, perhaps? But it was gone before I could fully grasp it. "Good to know you've moved on," he said, though his tone suggested otherwise. "Some people just don't know how to let go, do they?"

"Some people don't realize how to take responsibility for their actions," I replied, holding my ground. The tension hung thick in the air, but there was a newfound strength surging within me, tethered to the very art I had created.

"I didn't come here to cause trouble," he said, feigning nonchalance, but I could sense the undercurrent of defensiveness. "Just wanted to see how you were doing."

"Well, now you know," I stated, crossing my arms in a gesture of finality.

"Interesting choice in words," he said, the sarcasm dripping from his voice like rain from a leaky roof. "But it doesn't mean you're free from the past."

"Maybe not. But I'm free to choose who I let into my life now," I countered, feeling the weight of his gaze lift as I stood taller.

Max stepped forward, a protective energy radiating from him. "I think it's time for you to leave," he said, his voice calm yet firm, a quiet storm ready to unleash.

"Wow, how noble," Aaron scoffed, but the bravado faltered in the face of Max's unwavering gaze.

With one last glance, I watched as Aaron turned and walked away, the energy around us shifting back into something lighter, something vibrant. As I exhaled, the air felt clearer, unencumbered by the weight of unspoken words.

"Thanks for having my back," I said to Max, relief flooding my veins.

"Always," he replied, his smile reassuring. "Now, let's go celebrate the fact that we just stood our ground. We'll show this community how to really make some noise."

With that, we clinked our glasses again, laughter spilling into the night, echoing the joy that surrounded us, as the mural glimmered like a beacon of hope—a vivid reminder that the past may whisper, but it would never drown out the beauty we were creating together.

As the last rays of sunlight melted into the horizon, we found ourselves caught in a whirlwind of chatter and laughter, a tapestry of voices weaving through the crisp evening air. The mural, our labor of love, stood proudly against the backdrop of a dusky sky, its colors a testament to our resilience. I reveled in the camaraderie surrounding us, each smile a reminder that the community we had hoped to inspire was thriving. But just as quickly as joy blossomed, I felt an unwelcome weight in the pit of my stomach, a lingering unease that couldn't shake free.

"Let's grab some food," Max suggested, his eyes scanning the array of snacks set out on a nearby table. "I think I need to refuel after this monumental achievement."

"Monumental indeed. I mean, who knew we had the talent for creating such a spectacle?" I grinned, teasing him lightly. "It's practically world-renowned art now. Maybe I should start charging admission."

"Oh, definitely. We could sell tickets and call it a 'Mural Extravaganza,'" he replied, his tone dripping with mock seriousness. "Though I fear you might be underselling your talents. 'World-renowned' feels like a stretch, even for you."

"Excuse me? I'll have you know that my sunflower alone is ready for the Louvre!" I shot back, nudging him with my elbow.

Max laughed, and for a moment, the chaos of the event faded, leaving just the two of us amidst a sea of colors and laughter. But as we neared the food table, the shadows seemed to shift, and I caught sight of Aaron once more. He stood off to the side, arms crossed and expression inscrutable, as if he were a storm cloud threatening to rain on our parade.

"Why is he still here?" I muttered under my breath, irritation bubbling beneath the surface.

"I don't know, but let's not give him the satisfaction of knowing he's affecting us," Max replied, his voice steady but laced with a hint of tension. "Focus on the good stuff—the food, the mural, the people who are actually celebrating with us."

I nodded, trying to shake off the unease that had nestled back into my chest like an unwanted guest. We loaded our plates with an assortment of finger foods—mini sliders, colorful skewers, and a rather suspicious-looking dip that I hoped was guacamole and not something more adventurous.

"Do you think that dip is made from real avocados or just a clever ruse?" I asked, raising an eyebrow at the slightly greenish substance.

"Ah, the age-old question of community events: to trust or not to trust the dip," he said with a chuckle. "Let's just live dangerously. A little risk never hurt anyone."

"Except, you know, for the people who are violently allergic to whatever that is," I quipped, carefully dipping a chip into the concoction. "But for the rest of us, bottoms up!"

As I took a tentative bite, the flavor exploded in my mouth—a perfect blend of creaminess and zesty spice. "Okay, this dip is officially my new best friend. I might even write it a poem."

"Please don't," Max laughed, shaking his head. "The last thing I need is a heartfelt ode to snack foods. We'll never hear the end of it."

Our laughter bubbled over, a shared moment that felt pure and uncomplicated. But as I scanned the crowd, the joy faded slightly when my gaze landed on Aaron again, who was now striding purposefully toward us, his demeanor different—more aggressive than before.

"Great," I murmured, my stomach sinking. "Here we go again."

"Remember what we talked about? Just breathe. I'm right here," Max reassured me, stepping slightly in front of me as if to shield me from whatever confrontation loomed ahead.

"Impressive work, really," Aaron said, his tone far too polished for my comfort. "You've turned that wall into quite the masterpiece.

Almost makes me wonder why you didn't invite me to collaborate. After all, we had some great moments together, didn't we?"

"Moments, yes. But I'm not sure I'd call them great," I replied, my voice firm but controlled. "They were more like cautionary tales."

He smirked, and something dark danced behind his eyes. "Is that so? Funny how the past can come back to bite you, isn't it?"

"Not if you learn from it," I shot back, feeling Max's presence steadying me.

"I'm all for learning, but sometimes people forget what they've left behind," he said, leaning closer, the challenge in his voice palpable. "Sometimes, it's not the past that haunts you; it's the people who refuse to let you forget."

The air around us thickened, tension snapping like a taut string, and I felt my heart race. "I'm done being haunted. I have a life now, a community, and—"

"Max," Aaron interrupted, cutting me off with a glance that felt like ice water. "You're going to need to step back. This isn't your fight."

Max's expression hardened. "This is absolutely my fight. You may think you can waltz back into her life and—"

"Waltz? How charming. But we both know it's more complicated than that," Aaron countered, a cocky grin breaking through, like he relished this exchange more than I did. "She's been living in my shadow for far too long."

"Stop right there," I said, a surge of defiance welling up within me. "I'm not in anyone's shadow. Not anymore. I'm creating my own light, and it has nothing to do with you."

"Oh, I can see that," he said, his voice dripping with sarcasm. "But you know, light can also cast shadows, and sometimes, the past has a way of creeping back in."

Before I could respond, the crowd shifted as a commotion erupted nearby, laughter turning to startled gasps. People parted, and

I caught sight of a group of children racing towards us, but it wasn't their joy that struck me as odd; it was the erratic movement of the adults behind them, concern painted on their faces.

"What's happening?" I asked, my pulse quickening as I turned to Max, who was already straining to see past the crowd.

"Let's check it out," he said, instinctively taking my hand.

As we moved closer, a knot of dread tightened in my stomach. I could feel Aaron's presence behind me, a dark weight that pulled at my focus, but I shoved it aside. The murmurs around us grew louder, a mix of fear and confusion, until finally, we broke through the throng.

What we saw left my heart racing in a completely different way. A young girl stood frozen, clutching a balloon, her wide eyes trained on something just out of view. The adults were circling protectively around her, their expressions shifting from confusion to panic.

"What happened?" I asked a woman nearby, her face pale and drawn.

"It's... It's there, in the bushes," she stammered, pointing toward a shadowy area behind the mural.

Before I could process her words, a figure emerged from the darkness, stepping into the dim light cast by the fairy lights. My breath caught in my throat as the familiar silhouette materialized, sending shockwaves through my body.

Aaron stepped forward, a knowing smile creeping onto his face as he turned to me, the shadows of the past resurrected in a way I had never expected. "Looks like the past isn't quite done with you yet."

And just like that, I stood frozen, the weight of uncertainty pressing down on me, caught between the comfort of the present and the looming specter of everything I thought I had left behind.

Chapter 27: Breaking Down Walls

The night wrapped around us like a velvet cloak, the kind that whispers secrets and wraps the city in a warm embrace. Neon lights flickered against the damp pavement, casting a kaleidoscope of colors that danced in our eyes as we strolled through Manhattan. I could feel the pulse of the city—the laughter spilling out from the bars, the distant sirens wailing like lost souls, and the chatter of people weaving through the streets, each with their own story to tell. It was intoxicating, this city, and even more so with Max by my side.

He walked with that familiar grace, hands shoved deep into the pockets of his worn leather jacket, his silhouette illuminated by the glow of a nearby café. I couldn't help but admire how the light caught the edges of his tousled hair and how his eyes sparkled with unspoken thoughts. We passed a street musician playing a haunting melody on a saxophone, the notes curling around us, inviting us to lose ourselves in the moment. The world faded away, leaving just the two of us cocooned in our bubble of shared dreams and unfiltered laughter.

"Tell me your deepest fear," I suggested, letting the words tumble from my lips like a dare, a challenge. I had noticed how he often danced around the subject of his art, as if it was a loaded gun he was afraid to touch. The air thickened with unspoken tension as he paused, his expression shifting from the lightness of the moment to something deeper, darker.

He stopped walking, his gaze drifting to the distant skyline, where the skyscrapers stretched like fingers clawing at the stars. "You really want to know?" he asked, a wry smile playing on his lips, but there was an edge of uncertainty in his voice.

"Absolutely," I replied, my heart racing. There was something thrilling about peeling back the layers, digging deep into the soul of the man I had come to cherish. I wanted to understand what made him tick, what shadows haunted him when the lights dimmed and the world turned quiet.

Max let out a soft sigh, the kind that sounded heavy with the weight of his thoughts. "I guess... I fear I'm not good enough." He ran a hand through his hair, the gesture so familiar it felt like a private joke between us. "Every time I finish a piece, there's this nagging voice in my head telling me it's not worthy. That it won't resonate with anyone. It's exhausting, really."

His confession hit me like a tidal wave, washing away the easy banter that usually filled the air between us. I could see the rawness in his eyes, a vulnerability that made my chest tighten. "But your art is incredible, Max. I mean, have you seen the way people react to it?" I wanted to reach out, to bridge the chasm that seemed to widen between us. "You create beauty out of chaos. Isn't that worth something?"

He turned to face me, his expression unreadable. "It's not enough," he murmured, his voice barely above a whisper. "Sometimes I wonder if I'm just fooling myself, chasing a dream that was never meant to be mine."

I felt a flicker of frustration flare within me. This wasn't the Max I knew—the one who laughed too loud, who made jokes even when the punchline fell flat, who could bring a room to life with just a few strokes of his brush. "You're not a fool," I insisted, stepping closer, my heart racing with the urgency of my words. "You're an artist, and every artist questions their worth at some point. But you have to fight that voice. Let me help you."

He looked down at the cobblestones, a storm brewing in his eyes. "How? How do I silence the doubts that feel so much louder than the praise?"

I reached out, placing my hand on his arm, feeling the warmth of his skin through the fabric. "By believing in yourself, and by letting me remind you how incredible you are. You've touched people in ways you can't even imagine." My heart ached for him, for the battles he fought alone in the silence of his studio. "You don't have to do this alone, Max."

The silence that followed felt like a fragile thread stretching between us, but he finally met my gaze, and the air shimmered with an electric tension. "You really mean that?"

"Of course," I said, my voice steady. "I'm here, every step of the way. And maybe—just maybe—if you let me in, we can conquer those fears together."

He chuckled softly, the sound a balm to my spirit. "You make it sound so easy."

"Nothing worthwhile ever is, but you've already taken the first step by opening up to me." I smiled, hoping to lighten the weight in the air. "Just think of me as your artistic cheerleader—complete with pom-poms and questionable dance moves."

Max laughed, the tension breaking like a wave crashing against the shore. The sound was music to my ears, a reminder that even in our darkest moments, light could seep through the cracks. "I'm not sure the world is ready for that," he teased, but his eyes sparkled with a newfound warmth, a flicker of hope igniting within him.

As we continued our walk, I felt a sense of triumph, a sense of closeness that hadn't been there before. I could see the walls he had built around himself beginning to crumble, brick by brick. And in that moment, I realized that our journey was just beginning.

The neon lights of Manhattan pulsed like a heartbeat, vibrant and alive, as we wandered down the bustling streets. The air was thick with the scent of roasted chestnuts and the faint, sweet aroma of bakery treats wafting from a nearby shop, drawing me in like a moth to a flame. As we walked, I caught snippets of conversations, laughter spilling from sidewalk cafés, and the occasional shout of exuberance from groups celebrating a special moment. In this concrete jungle, where dreams collided and chaos reigned, I felt a sense of belonging as I navigated this world beside Max.

We found ourselves in front of a cozy café, its warm glow spilling out onto the sidewalk. "How about a coffee?" I suggested, hoping to prolong our evening. The thought of sitting together, our knees brushing under the table, filled me with a delightful anticipation.

Max shrugged, a hint of a smile dancing on his lips. "Only if they serve something stronger than just coffee. I could use a little liquid courage."

With a playful nudge, I led him inside, the bell above the door chiming softly to announce our arrival. The café was a treasure trove of eclectic decor, filled with mismatched furniture that looked as if it had been collected from different eras. Vintage posters adorned the walls, each telling a story, while the barista skillfully crafted drinks behind the counter, steam swirling like wisps of magic in the air.

We settled into a corner table, the ambiance warm and inviting. As I sipped my cappuccino, the frothy foam clinging to my upper lip, I couldn't help but steal glances at Max. He leaned back, stretching his long legs, and I marveled at the way his energy filled the room, a silent magnet drawing the attention of everyone around us.

"So, tell me more about your art," I prodded, determined to peel back the layers I sensed still lingered beneath the surface. "What really drives you to create?"

He shifted in his seat, the shadows of doubt creeping back into his gaze. "It's a bit like walking a tightrope. One moment you're soaring, feeling inspired, and the next, you're teetering on the edge, wondering if you'll fall flat." His voice was laced with honesty, a thread of vulnerability weaving through his words.

"I can't imagine it's easy," I said, leaning in, my heart racing at the intensity of our conversation. "But isn't that part of the beauty? The risk of falling only makes the moments of flight more exhilarating."

"True," he mused, a glimmer of thoughtfulness flickering in his eyes. "But what if the fall is too hard to recover from?"

"Then you dust yourself off and get back up," I replied, a confident smile playing on my lips. "Besides, if you ever need a hand getting back up, I'm a pretty decent lifeguard."

Max chuckled, the sound lightening the heaviness that had settled in the air. "I appreciate that. Just don't wear a whistle; it'll ruin the vibe."

We continued to banter, but the deeper currents of our conversation never faded. It was exhilarating, uncovering the layers of his creativity, the fears that plagued him like persistent shadows. Yet, beneath his charming facade, I sensed a storm brewing—a mixture of desire and anxiety that made the air thick with unspoken truths.

As the evening stretched on, the café began to empty, the barista cleaning up as the last few patrons trickled out. I glanced at the clock and realized how much time had passed, yet I felt as if we had only just begun to scratch the surface. "Max," I said, my voice softening, "can we talk about your dreams? The ones that keep you awake at night?"

He fell silent for a moment, his fingers tracing the rim of his cup as he contemplated my question. "I dream of showing my work in galleries, of people connecting with my pieces on a deeper level," he admitted, a distant look in his eyes. "But I also fear that I'll just be another face in a crowd of artists, lost among the masterpieces that make the world stop and stare."

"That's the risk we all take," I replied, leaning closer, my heart thumping in my chest. "But don't you see? You're not just another face. You have a unique voice, a perspective that's yours alone. Your art deserves to be seen, to be felt."

He met my gaze, his eyes glimmering with something I couldn't quite decipher—hope, perhaps, or the glimmer of a dream half-formed. "You really believe that?"

"Absolutely," I said, a smile breaking across my face. "I've seen your work. It tells stories—stories that deserve to be shared with the world."

His lips curled into a small smile, a flicker of gratitude softening the lines of worry etched on his forehead. "Thank you. It's nice to hear that from someone who gets it."

The moment felt electric, the air crackling with possibility. As I watched him, I felt a rush of warmth flood through me. I wanted to be the anchor in his storm, the one who reminded him of his worth when the world tried to convince him otherwise.

Just then, the café door swung open, a gust of chilly air rushing in. I turned to see a figure step inside, their silhouette casting a long shadow across the floor. My stomach twisted into knots when I recognized the familiar face of Chloe, an ex-girlfriend of Max's. She strode over with an air of confidence, her presence radiating a mixture of allure and arrogance that made the hairs on the back of my neck stand up.

"Max! Fancy seeing you here," she said, her voice dripping with a playful sweetness that masked the intent behind her eyes. I felt the air shift, a sudden tension crackling between the three of us like an electric current.

"Chloe," he replied, his voice cautious, eyes flickering with an emotion I couldn't quite place. "What are you doing here?"

"Oh, just grabbing a late-night pick-me-up," she said, glancing at me with a raised eyebrow, the kind that dripped with unspoken judgment. "And who's this?"

I forced a smile, holding her gaze with a steely resolve. "I'm the one keeping Max company," I said, my voice unwavering.

Chloe's lips curved into a smirk, her eyes glinting with mischief. "I hope you're not distracting him from his art. He's got enough on his plate without added distractions."

The words hung in the air, sharp as a knife, slicing through the fragile moment we had been cultivating. I could feel Max's tension radiate as he shifted in his seat, a flicker of discomfort crossing his features.

"We were just talking about dreams and creativity," I said, trying to defuse the tension with a casual bravado. "You know, the stuff that fuels life."

Chloe's laughter rang out, a sound that felt more mocking than lighthearted. "Right, because dreaming is all it takes to make it in the art world. Good luck with that."

Max shot me a glance, a silent plea buried within those depths. I could see the battle raging inside him, and in that moment, I vowed not to let her disrupt the connection we were building.

The café felt suddenly stifling, a bubble that threatened to burst under the weight of Chloe's presence. Her laughter was a discordant note in our symphony, jarring and out of place. I felt Max tense beside me, his body language shifting from relaxed to guarded in the blink of an eye.

"Well, Max, I see you've traded up," Chloe continued, her eyes flicking between us with an analytical precision, like a hawk sizing up its prey. "This one doesn't look like the usual canvas for your angst."

"Funny," I replied, keeping my tone light, even as my insides churned. "I thought the usual canvas was reserved for artists like you. But what do I know?"

Max shot me a sideways glance, a hint of admiration mingling with concern. I could sense his hesitation, torn between wanting to defend me and not wanting to escalate the tension.

Chloe's smile was a practiced thing, sweet as honey but with a sting that could make your mouth pucker. "Oh, I'm just here to offer a friendly reminder of reality. It's tough out there, and art isn't a game for the faint of heart. Right, Max?"

"Right," he said slowly, the word hanging in the air like a promise he was afraid to keep.

I could feel the unease radiating off him. "You know, I really admire anyone brave enough to follow their passion," I said, forcing my voice to maintain an upbeat lilt. "And, uh, if you need any advice on how to do it well, I'm sure Max would be happy to help."

Chloe smirked, clearly not buying the friendly act. "I'm sure he would, especially if it means postponing the inevitable day he has to decide whether to pursue this art fantasy or get a real job."

Max shifted again, an uncomfortable laugh escaping him. "Chloe, that's not really fair," he said, but his voice lacked the conviction I had hoped to hear. "Art is my job. It's what I do."

I could see the conflict warring in his eyes, the desire to defend himself battling the deep-rooted fear of failure that had started to surface in our earlier conversation. My heart sank as I realized how deeply Chloe had dug her claws into his psyche. "If this is how you see it, maybe you should reevaluate your priorities," she continued, turning her focus back to me. "After all, you never know when the art scene will dry up, leaving you high and dry."

I opened my mouth, ready to retort, but Max beat me to it. "You're really not helping, Chloe." His voice was firm now, a hint of steel creeping in.

"I'm just saying what needs to be said. Sometimes the truth is hard to swallow, but it's better than living in a fantasy." She leaned closer, her eyes narrowing. "You really think the world needs more mediocre art? Or a mediocre artist?"

"Hey!" I interjected, the words escaping me before I could filter them. "Maybe what the world needs is a little kindness instead of judgment."

Her expression twisted into a faux innocence that did nothing to mask her true intentions. "Kindness won't pay the bills, darling."

"Neither will negativity," I shot back, my heart racing. "If you're here to boost his spirits, I suggest you try being supportive instead of trying to slice him down. It might be a radical concept for you."

Max looked between us, a silent plea in his gaze, but Chloe didn't seem deterred by our exchange. Instead, she leaned back, an amused smirk on her lips as if she was enjoying the show. "You're quite the firecracker, aren't you? But let's be real—Max needs someone who understands the business of art, not someone who's just looking to play house in the big city."

"Let's not pretend you care about his well-being, Chloe," I replied, anger simmering just below the surface. "You're just here for the drama."

Her laughter was cold, a sharp knife cutting through the air. "Oh, sweetie, you've got it all wrong. I'm here for entertainment. Watching him fail would be quite the show."

Max clenched his jaw, his discomfort palpable. I reached out, placing a hand on his arm, hoping to ground him. "You know what?" I said, standing up. "I think we're done here. Enjoy your coffee, Chloe." I shot her a glare that could have burned a hole through steel and turned to Max, hoping he'd follow my lead.

"Let's get out of here," I said softly, my heart pounding.

Max hesitated for a moment, his eyes flickering between me and Chloe, who now wore a triumphant expression, as if she had successfully played her part. "Yeah, let's go." His voice was steady, and I felt a rush of relief as he rose from his seat.

We slipped out into the night, the cool air a welcome contrast to the suffocating atmosphere inside. The city enveloped us again, the distant sounds of laughter and music a balm to my frayed nerves. As we walked, I glanced sideways at him, trying to gauge his mood.

"That was... intense," he finally said, his tone a mix of exasperation and disbelief.

"Intense is one way to put it," I replied, trying to lighten the mood. "More like watching a circus act without a safety net."

He laughed, the sound easing the tension between us, but I could still see the shadows lurking in his eyes. "I'm sorry you had to deal with her," he said quietly. "Chloe has a talent for knowing just how to push my buttons."

"Clearly," I replied, my heart aching for him. "But you're stronger than that. You don't need to let her get into your head."

He sighed, running a hand through his hair. "I know. It's just hard when she knows my history. I thought I was past it, but sometimes the past has a way of creeping back in, doesn't it?"

"Only if you let it," I said, determination rising within me. "You can't allow her to dictate your self-worth. You have so much to offer the world, Max. You have to trust that."

He looked at me, a flicker of gratitude crossing his features. "Thanks for standing up for me. It means a lot."

I smiled, the warmth of our connection wrapping around me like a cozy blanket. "I'd do it again in a heartbeat."

As we strolled along the sidewalk, the city lights twinkling above us like stars, I felt the bond between us deepen. But just as I began to feel hopeful, the night took an unexpected turn.

From across the street, I spotted a figure watching us—a familiar face that sent a jolt of recognition through my veins. My heart sank as I realized it was Derek, Max's former mentor, the man who had once seemed like a guiding light in his life. But I could see something in Derek's eyes now, a glimmer of something dark and unsettling.

"Max," I whispered, my voice barely breaking through the din of the city. "Look over there."

He turned, his expression shifting from curiosity to confusion. "What's wrong?"

I pointed discreetly, my pulse quickening as Derek stepped forward, a predatory smile curling on his lips. "Well, well, if it isn't my favorite artist and his little cheerleader," he called out, his voice dripping with sarcasm.

Max stiffened beside me, his earlier confidence wavering. "What do you want, Derek?" he asked, a hint of wariness in his tone.

Derek shrugged, feigning innocence. "Oh, just wanted to check in on my star pupil. Heard you were having a little creative crisis."

My heart raced, dread pooling in my stomach. "We don't have time for your games," I said, stepping closer to Max, instinctively wanting to shield him.

Derek's gaze flicked to me, a wicked smile playing on his lips. "Games? Oh, sweetheart, this isn't a game. This is just the beginning."

Max's hand clenched into a fist at his side, and I could feel the tension radiating off him. "What do you mean by that?"

Derek leaned closer, his voice lowering to a conspiratorial whisper. "Let's just say the art world can be a little cutthroat, especially for those who think they can play it safe."

A chill raced down my spine as the implications of his words settled in. The night had shifted from a moment of connection to one steeped in uncertainty, and I could sense a storm brewing on the horizon.

Chapter 28: Fading Shadows

The sun dipped below the horizon, casting a golden hue over the city, where shadows danced playfully along the cobblestone streets. As Max and I wandered through the lively marketplace, the aroma of freshly baked bread mingled with the sweet scent of roasted chestnuts, drawing us closer to a food stall adorned with vibrant decorations. I watched as the vendor expertly twisted strands of dough, his hands a blur of motion. Max nudged me with a teasing grin, his eyes sparkling with mischief.

"Care to taste the dough artist's masterpiece?" he asked, a playful lilt in his voice. "I hear it's the best thing to hit the market since... well, ever."

With a mock-serious nod, I stepped forward, clutching my purse. "I'm always in for a culinary adventure, especially when it involves dough. But if this is a scam to get me to pay for your dinner again, you'll be hearing from my lawyer."

Max chuckled, leaning against the stall as I engaged in a delightful barter with the vendor. The laughter of children echoed in the background, intermingling with snippets of cheerful conversations. My heart felt light, almost buoyant, as I savored the simple pleasure of the moment. The world around me was alive with color and sound, a stark contrast to the shadows that had once loomed over my life.

As I took a bite of the warm, flaky pastry, the sweet filling burst forth, enveloping my senses. "This is incredible!" I exclaimed, delight dancing in my eyes. Max leaned closer, his gaze intense, and for a heartbeat, it felt like we were the only two people in this bustling universe.

"Just wait until you try the chocolate-dipped version. It's a game changer," he said, his tone rich with playful conviction.

I rolled my eyes, knowing full well that this was likely another one of his schemes to push my taste boundaries. "You and your bold claims. What's next, a hot pepper pastry?"

"Oh, I wouldn't dream of it," he replied, feigning innocence. "Though I could be convinced if it meant seeing that adorable scrunch of your nose."

"Adorable?" I sputtered, half-laughing, half-offended. "You've been spending too much time with the local cats."

"Can you blame me?" He smirked, then turned serious, his voice dropping a notch. "But really, you deserve to enjoy these moments. You've earned every smile."

His words hung between us, warm and genuine, weaving a connection deeper than I had anticipated. It was in these fleeting moments of levity that I began to grasp the profound shift happening within me. The darkness that had once defined my narrative was gradually loosening its grip, allowing fragments of light to seep through.

But just as I began to embrace this newfound liberation, the persistent ping of my phone broke through the tranquility. The screen illuminated with Aaron's name, sending a chill through my spine. My heart raced, its rhythm clashing with the joyful atmosphere around me. The laughter of nearby friends faded into a dull roar as anxiety crept in like an unwelcome guest.

"Everything okay?" Max asked, his brows furrowed with concern.

I hesitated, torn between wanting to shield him from my past and the unrelenting urge to confide in him. "It's... it's Aaron," I admitted, my voice barely a whisper.

"Do you want to answer it?" He reached for my hand, grounding me amidst the brewing storm of my emotions.

I shook my head vehemently, my grip tightening around my phone. "No, I don't want to be pulled back into that world. Not when I've just begun to find my way out."

"Then don't," Max said, his tone firm yet gentle. "You've come so far. You don't owe him anything. This is your life, and you get to choose how it unfolds."

His unwavering support ignited a spark of courage within me, but a nagging doubt lingered in the back of my mind. What could Aaron possibly want? Would he try to drag me back into his chaotic web, weaving a narrative of guilt and regret? The ghosts of our history loomed like shadows, threatening to eclipse the vibrant memories Max and I were building.

"Maybe I should at least see what he wants," I murmured, grappling with the implications of that decision. "But what if—"

"What ifs can paralyze you," Max interjected, his eyes locking onto mine with an intensity that silenced my worries. "But what if you find the closure you need? What if it's not about him at all? What if this is just another chapter in your story?"

I took a deep breath, inhaling the scents of the market, grounding myself in the present. "You make it sound so simple."

"Maybe it is," he replied, his voice softening. "Maybe you just need to reclaim your narrative."

As I looked into Max's eyes, a wave of gratitude washed over me. His unwavering belief in me was like a balm for my frayed nerves. We had forged a connection that felt as natural as breathing, yet the specter of my past loomed large, threatening to unravel the tapestry we were weaving.

In that moment of quiet contemplation, I recognized the beauty of our journey. We were creating something new, a life that shimmered with potential. But the shadows were relentless, and as I scrolled through the messages from Aaron, I felt their weight pressing down on me, reminding me that the past never truly fades.

"Okay," I said, my voice steadying. "Let's do this." I tapped the screen, preparing to dive into the conversation that could change everything, not knowing how far down the rabbit hole I would fall.

I stared at my phone, heart racing, as Max watched me with an intensity that felt both comforting and daunting. The marketplace buzzed around us, life continuing its vibrant dance while I stood frozen, my mind wrestling with a thousand scenarios. What could Aaron possibly want? The simple truth of it gnawed at me: some things should remain buried, untouched by the chaos of the past.

Max shifted closer, his warmth an anchor in the turbulent sea of my thoughts. "You know, if you want to ignore it, we could dive into that bakery again," he suggested, gesturing toward the stall bursting with colorful pastries, the air rich with the scent of vanilla and cinnamon. "I hear they have a chocolate croissant that could put the finest French baker to shame."

His lightheartedness coaxed a reluctant smile from me, a brief reprieve from the anxiety twisting my insides. "You really think carbs can solve all my problems, don't you?" I shot back, attempting to shake off the gravity of the situation with humor.

"Absolutely," he replied with mock seriousness, "and if they can't, we'll just have to drown our sorrows in gelato. That's practically a proven method of therapy."

With a chuckle, I finally hit 'reply,' my fingers shaking slightly. "I'll think about it," I typed back, the cursor blinking as if daring me to take the plunge. But before I could summon the courage to hit send, the screen lit up again, a new message flashing from Aaron. "Can we meet?"

The words felt like a trap, and suddenly, I was back in that dark place, where every decision felt like a misstep, every choice laced with regret. "What did I do to deserve this?" I mumbled, barely aware that I'd voiced my frustration aloud.

"Maybe he just wants closure," Max suggested, his tone gentle yet insistent. "You said you were ready to confront your past. This could be part of that process."

"Or it could be a minefield," I countered, fighting against the swell of memories that threatened to drown me. "It's not like he ever played fair."

As if sensing my internal battle, Max placed his hand on my shoulder, grounding me with his presence. "You're not the same person you were when you were with him. You've grown, you've changed. Whatever he throws at you, you can handle it."

His confidence was a soothing balm, and as I looked into his earnest eyes, I felt a flicker of hope ignite within me. "Okay," I said slowly, "let's meet."

As I typed out my response, I couldn't shake the feeling of impending doom. Aaron had a knack for twisting conversations, turning even the simplest encounters into something sinister. My heart raced as I sent the message, and a knot of anticipation coiled in my stomach. "Where and when?"

Max was quiet for a moment, his gaze thoughtful. "How about somewhere public? A coffee shop, maybe? That way, if things go south, you have an escape plan."

"Right, because nothing says 'I'm ready to confront my ex' like sipping a mocha in a bustling café." I rolled my eyes but appreciated the idea. "Okay, coffee it is. I'll suggest our usual spot."

"Perfect. And remember, I'll be nearby if you need backup. Just send a text, and I'll swoop in like a caffeinated superhero," he promised, a grin breaking across his face.

I snorted, the image of Max bursting through the door in a cape made entirely of coffee sleeves brightening my mood. "Noted. Just don't wear your cape when you show up; it might draw too much attention."

The nervous energy surged through me as we continued our stroll through the market, laughter mingling with the fragrant air, the sweetness of the pastries lingering on my tongue. We explored the various stalls, each vibrant display beckoning us closer, and for a moment, I managed to forget the looming confrontation.

Then, as if orchestrated by fate, we arrived at a stall selling handcrafted jewelry, shimmering in the afternoon sun. I stopped, entranced by a delicate silver bracelet adorned with tiny charms. "Look at this!" I exclaimed, reaching out to touch the intricate designs. "It's beautiful."

Max leaned closer, inspecting it with exaggerated seriousness. "Ah, the perfect accessory to commemorate your war against your past. A talisman, if you will."

"Or a distraction," I shot back, playfully nudging him. "But let's be real; I'm probably going to need all the luck I can get."

He chuckled, stepping aside to let an elderly woman examine the bracelets. "I'll buy you one if you promise to wear it during your meeting with Aaron. Maybe it'll give you the strength of a thousand warriors."

"Or at least a tiny shield against his charm," I quipped, trying to suppress the swell of anxiety bubbling up again. "But I don't think a bracelet can ward off emotional damage."

"Why not?" Max countered, his expression lightening. "I mean, have you seen some of those charms? They're practically magical."

I couldn't help but laugh at his unwavering enthusiasm. "Okay, you've convinced me. But only if you find something equally ridiculous for yourself."

As we bantered back and forth, I felt a renewed sense of resolve. Maybe I couldn't erase the past, but I could equip myself for whatever came next. I purchased the bracelet, the delicate charm resting in my palm like a promise.

Later, as the evening deepened, I found myself at the coffee shop, nerves dancing like fireflies in my stomach. The chatter of patrons swirled around me, a comforting backdrop as I waited for Aaron. I took a deep breath, reminding myself of Max's words. I was stronger now.

The bell above the door chimed, and my heart skipped as I saw Aaron step inside, his familiar figure cutting through the crowd. Time had altered him; he seemed older, wearier, as though he'd carried the weight of the past just as I had. But there was a certain determination in his eyes, a flicker of the man I once knew.

As he approached, I straightened in my chair, clutching my new bracelet like a lifeline. The moment felt charged, and I knew then that this encounter would test the very limits of my resolve. The shadows were gathering once more, and for better or worse, I was ready to face them head-on.

The moment Aaron approached, the air felt charged, as if the entire café held its breath in anticipation. He was the familiar stranger I had once loved, yet now he carried an air of uncertainty that left me questioning everything. The shadows of our shared history clung to him like a second skin, and for a fleeting second, I wondered if he sensed how far I had come.

"Hey," he said, his voice softer than I remembered. He glanced around, his gaze catching on the busy baristas, the scent of freshly brewed coffee weaving through the room like a familiar embrace. "Thanks for agreeing to meet."

"Thanks for giving me a heads-up," I replied, my tone steadier than I felt. "What's so important that it couldn't be discussed via text?"

A wry smile tugged at his lips, but it didn't reach his eyes. "It's... complicated." He motioned to the seat across from me, and I nodded, forcing myself to remain composed as he settled in.

Silence draped over us, thick and uncomfortable, broken only by the distant clatter of cups and laughter from a nearby table. I could feel my heart thudding loudly in my chest, the sound echoing my swirling thoughts. Had I really agreed to this? My fingers absentmindedly traced the charm on my bracelet, grounding myself in the present.

"So, how have you been?" Aaron asked, his voice a mix of genuine curiosity and something else—was it regret?

I narrowed my eyes, my mind racing. "You know how I've been," I shot back, feeling the walls I had worked so hard to dismantle threatening to rise again. "The last few months have been... transformative. I've been focusing on myself, moving forward."

He leaned back, the weight of my words sinking in. "I'm glad to hear that. You deserve it."

A part of me wanted to believe him, but another part—a more wary part—reminded me of the times his words had been nothing more than smoke and mirrors. "What about you?" I replied, shifting the focus. "You didn't reach out just to make small talk."

Aaron's expression shifted, a flicker of something unnameable passing over his features. "You're right. I needed to talk about something that's been bothering me for a while." He paused, his gaze dropping to the table, as if the surface held answers. "It's about us. About what happened... between us."

I braced myself, unsure whether to lean in or pull back. "It's been a long time, Aaron. I don't think going over the past is going to help either of us."

He raised his eyes, and I caught a glimpse of vulnerability that sent a pang through my chest. "I know. But I've had time to think, and I realized I made some terrible mistakes. I treated you poorly, and I'm sorry."

The sincerity in his tone caught me off guard, stirring the embers of resentment and the bittersweet memories that had settled within me. "Apologies don't erase the past," I said, my voice steady yet edged with steel. "You hurt me. You broke my trust."

"I know," he admitted, his voice thick with emotion. "And I've regretted it every day since."

Something shifted in the atmosphere between us, a tension that was both familiar and foreign. I could see the flickering candlelight reflected in his eyes, highlighting the shadows of doubt and remorse. Part of me wanted to reach across the table, to offer him a chance at redemption, but another part screamed to guard my heart.

"And now you want forgiveness?" I challenged, my brows knitting together in disbelief. "Is that really what this is about?"

"It's not just about forgiveness. I need to explain something to you. There's a reason I acted the way I did," he replied, his voice barely above a whisper.

Curiosity piqued, I leaned in despite myself. "What do you mean? What could possibly justify what you did?"

He hesitated, his expression a mix of regret and hesitation. "It's about the night we broke up. There were things I didn't tell you. Things that affected my choices."

My heart raced, both intrigued and alarmed. "What are you talking about?"

Just then, a loud crash from the café's kitchen broke through our conversation, the noise startling both of us. I glanced toward the commotion, my heart pounding. When I looked back at Aaron, he seemed even more agitated, his gaze darting around as if searching for an escape.

"Can we go outside?" he asked suddenly, his voice urgent. "I'd rather not discuss this here."

I hesitated, the instinct to bolt rising within me. "What are you so afraid of?"

"It's not about fear. It's about keeping this conversation private. Please." His eyes locked onto mine, pleading for understanding.

Against my better judgment, I nodded, rising from my seat. As we stepped outside, the cool evening air wrapped around us, a stark contrast to the heated moment inside. I could feel the weight of our unresolved issues pressing down on us, an invisible force that demanded to be acknowledged.

We walked a few steps down the sidewalk, away from prying eyes and ears. I could hear the distant murmur of voices and the occasional laugh floating out from the café, but here, beneath the golden glow of the streetlights, it was just the two of us.

"Okay, we're outside. Now, what's this big revelation?" I said, trying to sound braver than I felt.

Aaron ran a hand through his hair, frustration etched across his features. "I don't know how to explain this without sounding insane, but there's something you need to know about my family. It's complicated, and it's the reason I was... the way I was with you."

"Spit it out, Aaron. I don't have all night."

He took a deep breath, his expression solemn. "My family has a history of—well, let's just say it's not all sunshine and rainbows. My father... he's been involved in some things. Things that have impacted my choices, my behavior, even our relationship."

I crossed my arms, skepticism creeping in. "What kind of things? You can't just drop a bombshell like that without context."

"I didn't want you to be involved in my mess. I thought it would be easier for you if I pushed you away," he said, his voice low and intense. "But now I see how selfish that was. I thought I was protecting you, but I only hurt you more."

I blinked, grappling with the flood of emotions swirling inside me. "So, what does that mean? You're blaming your father for how you treated me?"

"It's not an excuse, but it's the truth. I let my family's issues dictate my choices. I thought I could handle it alone, but I couldn't. And when you needed me the most, I let you down."

I shook my head, fighting back the urge to feel pity. "You're trying to rewrite history, Aaron. I don't care about your family's drama. You made your choices, and I suffered because of them."

"I know," he said, stepping closer, desperation etched in his features. "But there's more. I can't leave this hanging. You need to know that my father has—"

Before he could finish, the sound of footsteps echoed from behind us, the heavy tread growing closer. I turned, my heart racing again, an uneasy feeling settling in my stomach. Two men in dark jackets approached, their expressions unreadable.

"Aaron," one of them called out, his voice laced with authority. "We need to talk. Now."

I felt the chill of dread wash over me as Aaron stiffened beside me, the tension in the air thickening like fog. The weight of his unfinished words hung heavy between us, and in that moment, I realized that whatever secrets he had kept buried might not stay hidden much longer. The shadows of the past were not fading; they were rising again, ready to ensnare us both.

Chapter 29: Crossing Boundaries

The air was thick with the rich aroma of coffee, a familiar warmth that once brought comfort but now clung to me like a heavy blanket. The diner, with its red vinyl booths and checkered linoleum floor, stood as a testament to countless mornings spent lost in thought or shared laughter. Each booth held memories, but this one felt heavy with anticipation. As I settled into a corner seat, my fingers traced the grooves of the table, the familiar scratches and dents telling stories of their own. I could almost hear the echoes of our past conversations swirling around me, intertwined with the sounds of clinking silverware and the sizzle of bacon on the griddle.

When Aaron entered, he looked different, almost unrecognizable. Gone was the boyish charm that used to ignite butterflies in my stomach; in its place was a man cloaked in an unsettling calmness. The familiar dark curls framed his face, but his posture was straight, his gaze steady. I couldn't help but notice the way he moved through the diner, not searching for approval, but rather striding with a newfound confidence. My heart fluttered with uncertainty, a blend of nostalgia and caution.

"Hey," he said, sliding into the booth opposite me. His voice was low, the timbre richer than I remembered. "Thanks for meeting me."

"Yeah, well, it's a diner, and I'm not one to turn down pancakes," I replied, forcing a lightness into my tone. I studied his face, searching for signs of the boy I once knew. "So, how's life treating you?"

"Pretty well, actually," he replied, his lips quirking into a smile that didn't quite reach his eyes. "I've been working on myself, you know? Therapy, support groups... I've even taken up painting. It's been eye-opening."

Painting? The thought was almost laughable, conjuring images of Aaron splattering color on canvas, perhaps channeling his inner

Van Gogh. I imagined him standing in front of an easel, brushes in hand, wrestling with his demons on a blank canvas. "Wow, that's... unexpected. You always said you couldn't draw a straight line."

He chuckled softly, and I felt a twinge of something—was it pity? "Yeah, well, sometimes we surprise ourselves. I just wanted to show you that I'm making changes, that I'm not the same person I was."

I nodded, feeling a storm brewing in my chest. "And what if the person you were is the reason we're sitting here? The person I wanted to forget." My words hung between us, heavy and sharp, slicing through the fragile air of reconciliation.

His gaze dropped to the table, a flicker of vulnerability crossing his features. "I know I hurt you, and I'm sorry. I don't expect you to forgive me right away. I just wanted you to know I'm trying. That you meant something to me—still do, in a way."

A rush of warmth filled my chest, a familiar ache, but I crushed it down. I had spent too long tethered to this man, too long waiting for him to change, to become someone worthy of the love I had poured into him. "I appreciate that, really. But my heart... it belongs to someone else now. I'm not the same person either, Aaron. I've found happiness in a different place."

His eyes narrowed, a flicker of hurt sparking in their depths. "With Max?" The name slipped off his tongue like an accusation, and for a brief moment, I felt guilty. But that guilt was quickly replaced by determination.

"Yeah, with Max," I affirmed, my voice steady. "He's everything I didn't know I needed—kind, patient, and willing to love me without the baggage. He sees me for who I am, not who I was."

Silence stretched between us, thick and tangible. Aaron shifted, and the tension was palpable. I could almost hear the gears turning in his mind as he processed my words. "You know I never wanted to hold you back," he said, almost defensively. "I just—"

"Just what?" I cut him off, the anger bubbling to the surface. "You just wanted to keep me in your orbit while you figured out your life? You had your chance, and you threw it away."

The waiter arrived, placing our orders on the table with a clatter. I offered a tight smile as he retreated, but my appetite vanished. The sight of pancakes and syrup, once inviting, felt like a mockery now.

"I'm not asking for a second chance," he said, his voice low. "I just thought maybe... we could have some sort of closure? You and I, together."

"Closure?" I echoed, the word tasting bitter on my tongue. "You think we can just wrap this up with a bow and walk away unscathed? You shattered my trust, Aaron. It's not something you can fix with a heartfelt conversation over pancakes."

He looked pained, and my heart softened, if only for a moment. "I know it's complicated. I just... I don't want to be the reason you're unhappy. If you're truly happy with Max, then I'll step back. But I needed you to know I'm trying to be better."

His sincerity was disarming, and I felt the remnants of our past tugging at my heartstrings. But I was done being a prisoner of nostalgia. My life had blossomed into something beautiful and new, and I had no intention of stepping back into the shadows of yesterday.

"Thank you for being honest," I replied, my voice firm. "But I need to take my life in a different direction now, one that doesn't include you. I wish you well, Aaron, but it's time for me to go."

As I stood, a weight lifted from my shoulders. The air outside felt fresher, as if the sun had finally broken through the clouds. I walked away with a sense of finality, knowing I had taken a significant step toward my future with Max, leaving behind the fragments of a past that no longer defined me.

Stepping outside the diner felt like emerging from a cocoon. The bright Brooklyn sun hit my face, and I took a deep breath, savoring the crisp air that brushed against my skin. With every step away from the past, I felt lighter, the burdens of yesterday slowly unfurling like the petals of a flower greeting the dawn. The streets buzzed with life; a cacophony of voices blended with the distant sounds of a saxophonist playing a soulful tune. I could feel the pulse of the city invigorating me, each heartbeat reminding me that I had chosen this path for myself.

I had texted Max earlier, hoping to surprise him. We had plans for later that evening—a quiet dinner at his favorite Italian restaurant, a cozy spot where the ambiance felt like home. With each stride, I thought of how I could share the news about my meeting with Aaron. I wanted to tell him everything, but a part of me hesitated. Would he feel insecure, wondering if I had really moved on? Yet, the more I replayed our last conversation, the more I realized there was nothing left to hold me back. I was ready to embrace the warmth and laughter that Max brought into my life, the way he made the world feel a little less complicated.

As I approached my apartment, I spotted Max lounging on the stoop, a small book in hand, his brow furrowed in concentration. The sight of him—a tangle of dark hair and those damnable dimples—made my heart race. The sun cast a halo around him, and I couldn't help but appreciate how he effortlessly filled the space with his vibrant energy.

"Hey, beautiful," he said, looking up and grinning as I approached. "You look like you just walked out of a rom-com." He gestured dramatically, mimicking a leading man ready to sweep me off my feet. "Do you need rescuing, or is it too late?"

I laughed, feeling my cheeks heat up. "Too late for rescuing, I think. I just wrapped up a little... business."

His expression shifted, curiosity igniting in his eyes. "Business? I hope it didn't involve a life-altering decision, like adopting a ferret."

"Oh, if only it were that simple." I sat down beside him, leaning into his shoulder, inhaling the familiar scent of his cologne mixed with the faint aroma of freshly brewed coffee. "I met with Aaron."

Max's playful demeanor vanished in an instant, replaced by an intensity that made my heart race. "And? How did that go?" His voice was steady, but I could see the tension in his jaw.

I took a deep breath, feeling the weight of my words settle between us. "It was... enlightening, I guess. He's changed, or at least claims to have. But I finally told him that I'm happy with you." The words felt liberating, each syllable an affirmation of the choices I had made.

"Good," he said, his lips forming a thin line. "You deserve to be happy. But I can't help but wonder... did he try to win you back?"

I nodded, feeling a swell of emotion. "He did. But it only reinforced my feelings for you. I realized that the past is just that—the past. I'm here, Max. With you."

His expression softened, and I could see the tension easing from his shoulders. "Okay. I just want to make sure you're not caught up in old feelings. I don't want to lose you."

"You won't," I assured him, the conviction in my voice surprising even myself. "I'm done looking back."

Just then, a car honked loudly, interrupting our moment. We turned to see an old friend, Lucy, barreling down the street in her beater car, the one she insisted was vintage but had clearly seen better days. She screeched to a halt beside us, her hair a chaotic halo around her head. "Get in, losers! We're going to the park!"

Max and I exchanged amused glances. "This isn't a movie," he quipped. "But why not?"

As we climbed into the car, I couldn't shake the giddiness building inside me. The wind rushed through the open windows, and Lucy blasted the radio, her laughter infectious. The drive felt like a whirlwind, pulling me away from the weight of my conversation with Aaron and thrusting me into the joy of spontaneous adventures.

When we arrived at the park, it was alive with the sounds of children laughing, dogs barking, and the rhythmic rustle of leaves dancing in the breeze. I caught sight of a group of friends gathered by a picnic blanket, the familiar faces lighting up with excitement as we approached. Max grabbed my hand, and I felt an electric connection, a silent promise that no matter what challenges lay ahead, we would face them together.

"Let's set up the food!" Lucy announced, already rummaging through her tote. As she pulled out sandwiches, chips, and a bottle of sparkling lemonade, I felt a sense of normalcy wash over me. Here, surrounded by friends and laughter, I could momentarily forget the heaviness of my past.

Max and I worked side by side, sharing easy banter as we arranged the picnic spread. "So, how are we defining this?" he asked, glancing at me with that familiar spark of mischief. "Is it a picnic date, a casual hangout, or just a well-deserved break from our responsibilities?"

"Let's call it an adventure," I replied, grinning. "A chance to celebrate the future."

He raised an eyebrow, his lips curling into a teasing smile. "An adventure, huh? I like the sound of that."

As we settled onto the blanket, I felt a wave of contentment wash over me. The sun dipped lower in the sky, casting a golden hue over everything, and for the first time in a long while, I felt genuinely at peace. I had shed the layers of my past, and the world stretched out before me, filled with endless possibilities. With Max beside me, I was ready to take on whatever came next, heart wide open and unafraid.

The laughter around me floated like the scent of fresh bread from the nearby bakery, warm and comforting. Lucy had orchestrated a veritable feast, complete with her infamous potato salad and a plethora of snacks that left no room for doubt about her culinary skills—or lack thereof. Max and I leaned into each other as our friends swapped stories, the atmosphere thick with camaraderie. The sun dipped lower in the sky, casting long shadows and bathing the park in a golden glow.

Max nudged me with his shoulder, breaking me from my reverie. "So, when do I get to taste that famous potato salad?" His tone was teasing, but I could hear the genuine curiosity beneath it. Lucy had a reputation for culinary experiments that sometimes veered dangerously into the realm of the unpalatable.

"Let's just say, I've had better," I replied, a smirk tugging at my lips. "But it's the thought that counts, right?"

"True, but if you want to keep my admiration, I'd advise against it," he shot back, his eyes sparkling with mischief. "Next time, we're going out for sushi."

I felt my heart swell at the playful banter, at the ease with which we interacted. It was a welcome change from the heaviness of my meeting earlier that day. With Max, I could be light, carefree, and yet, a part of me was still vigilant, still wary. But as we settled into our picnic, I promised myself that today was for celebrating, for living in the moment.

After a while, Lucy pulled out her phone and exclaimed, "Okay, enough eating! Let's take some pictures for Instagram!" She waved her phone around like it was a magic wand, demanding attention. My friends dutifully posed, their faces lighting up with exaggerated smiles, and I couldn't help but join in.

"Come on, Max! You need to show off those dimples!" I teased, nudging him with my elbow. He pretended to groan but leaned in closer, resting his chin on my shoulder. As Lucy snapped a few shots, I could feel the warmth radiating from him, the simple contact igniting a fire inside me that chased away the lingering shadows of my past.

But just as we settled back into our easy laughter, a shrill ringtone cut through the joy. Lucy fished her phone from her bag, and her face drained of color. "It's my dad," she whispered, panic etching itself into her features.

"Is everything okay?" Max asked, his expression shifting from playful to concerned in a heartbeat.

"I don't know," she muttered, stepping away from us as she answered. The jovial atmosphere around our picnic abruptly stilled, replaced by an undercurrent of worry. I exchanged a glance with Max, and in that moment, we both understood the shift. Something was wrong, and we couldn't shake the feeling that it was more than just Lucy's typical family drama.

She returned a few minutes later, her eyes wide, lips pressed into a thin line. "I have to go," she said, her voice barely above a whisper. "My brother's been in an accident. I don't know how serious it is, but... I need to be there."

Max and I jumped to our feet, instinctively moving closer. "Can we come with you?" I asked, my heart racing. "You shouldn't have to go through this alone."

"No, you guys stay here. I'll be okay," she insisted, but the tremor in her voice betrayed her. "I just need to make sure he's alright. I'll call you as soon as I know anything."

"Lucy, please," I urged, feeling the weight of her fear. "We're friends. We'll support you however you need us to."

Max nodded in agreement, his face a mask of determination. "Let us help. We can drive you."

She hesitated, glancing between us, and I could see the conflict in her eyes. Finally, she sighed, the fight leaving her. "Okay, fine. Just... hurry."

As we rushed to the car, adrenaline coursed through my veins. I grabbed the door handle, glancing back at Max. "This is serious, isn't it?"

He nodded, his face serious. "It is. Let's just focus on getting there."

Lucy was silent in the back seat, her hands clenched tightly in her lap. I glanced at her through the rearview mirror, wishing I could ease her fears, but the weight of her worry hung heavily in the air. The traffic felt like a torturous slow crawl, each stoplight stretching our anxiety further.

"Do you know what happened?" Max finally asked, his voice calm despite the tension.

"Not much," Lucy replied, her voice shaky. "Just that he was in a car accident on the highway. My parents are at the hospital already."

"Have you heard from them?" I probed gently, glancing back at her.

"Just a text saying they were on their way," she said, her tone flat. "I'm trying not to freak out."

"You're doing great," I said, though I felt the knot tightening in my stomach. How could anyone do "great" in a situation like this? I stole another glance at Max, who was gripping the steering wheel like it was the only thing anchoring him.

As we reached the hospital, the parking lot was a chaotic scene, families gathered outside, the atmosphere charged with a sense of urgency. We rushed inside, Lucy leading the way, her pace quickening as she navigated the stark white hallways.

The antiseptic smell of the hospital washed over us, mingling with the sound of distant beeping machines and hushed voices. We found Lucy's parents in the waiting area, their faces drawn with worry, and my heart sank at the sight.

"Mom! Dad!" Lucy cried, rushing into their embrace.

"Lucy, sweetheart, it's going to be okay," her mother soothed, but I could see the fear lurking in her eyes.

Max and I lingered back, sensing the need for privacy as Lucy's family surrounded her. I felt like an intruder in their moment of crisis, but I wanted to help, to be there for my friend.

"Do you think he'll be alright?" I whispered to Max, my voice trembling.

"I hope so," he replied, his eyes scanning the room, ever watchful. "Accidents can be tricky, but we have to stay positive."

Just then, a doctor emerged from a doorway, his face serious. My breath caught in my throat as I watched Lucy's parents turn to him, their expressions filled with a mix of hope and dread.

"Are you the family of Jake Adams?" the doctor asked, his tone professional yet warm.

I held my breath, feeling the tension in the air thickening. Lucy stepped forward, her voice steady despite the anxiety etched on her face. "Yes, that's my brother. How is he?"

The doctor hesitated for a moment, and I felt the world tilt beneath me. "He's stable, but he's in critical condition. We've done what we can, but we need to monitor him closely."

Lucy's face paled, and I felt my heart drop as she swayed slightly, the gravity of the situation crashing down around her.

"What does that mean?" she asked, her voice cracking. "Can I see him?"

"I'm afraid it's best to wait a little longer," the doctor replied, his expression softening. "We'll keep you updated."

I caught Max's eye, and we both understood the weight of those words. "We're here for you, Lucy," I whispered, stepping forward to wrap my arms around her.

As the doctor walked away, the atmosphere felt charged with uncertainty. I could sense that the day wasn't over yet, that life had more twists in store. But just as I was about to reassure Lucy again, my phone buzzed in my pocket.

Pulling it out, I saw an unknown number flashing on the screen. My heart raced as I answered, the words barely leaving my lips before the voice on the other end sent a shiver down my spine. "Is this [Your Name]? You need to come to the hospital. I have something important to tell you... about Aaron."

The world around me faded into a blur, and the implications of those words crashed over me like a wave.

Milton Keynes UK
Ingram Content Group UK Ltd.
UKHW032321221024
449917UK00001B/89